The Sisters Grimm

Also by Menna van Praag

The House at the End of Hope Street
The Dress Shop of Dreams
The Witches of Cambridge
The Lost Art of Letter Writing
The Patron Saint of Lost Souls
Men, Money and Chocolate

The Sisters Grimm

Menna van Praag

BANTAM PRESS

TRANSWORLD PUBLISHERS
61–63 Uxbridge Road, London W5 5SA
www.penguin.co.uk

Transworld is part of the Penguin Random House group of companies
whose addresses can be found at global.penguinrandomhouse.com

First published in Great Britain in 2020 by Bantam Press
an imprint of Transworld Publishers

A CIP catalogue record for this book
is available from the British Library.

ISBNs 9781787631663 (cased)
9781787631670 (tpb)

Typeset in 10.5/14.5 pt Berling LT Std by Jouve (UK), Milton Keynes
Printed and bound in Great Britain by Clays Ltd, Elcograf S.p.A.

Penguin Random House is committed to a sustainable
future for our business, our readers and our planet. This book
is made from Forest Stewardship Council® certified paper.

1 3 5 7 9 10 8 6 4 2

For my mother, my daughter, my sister and all the Sisters Grimm.

And for anyone who is ever awake at 3.33 a.m.

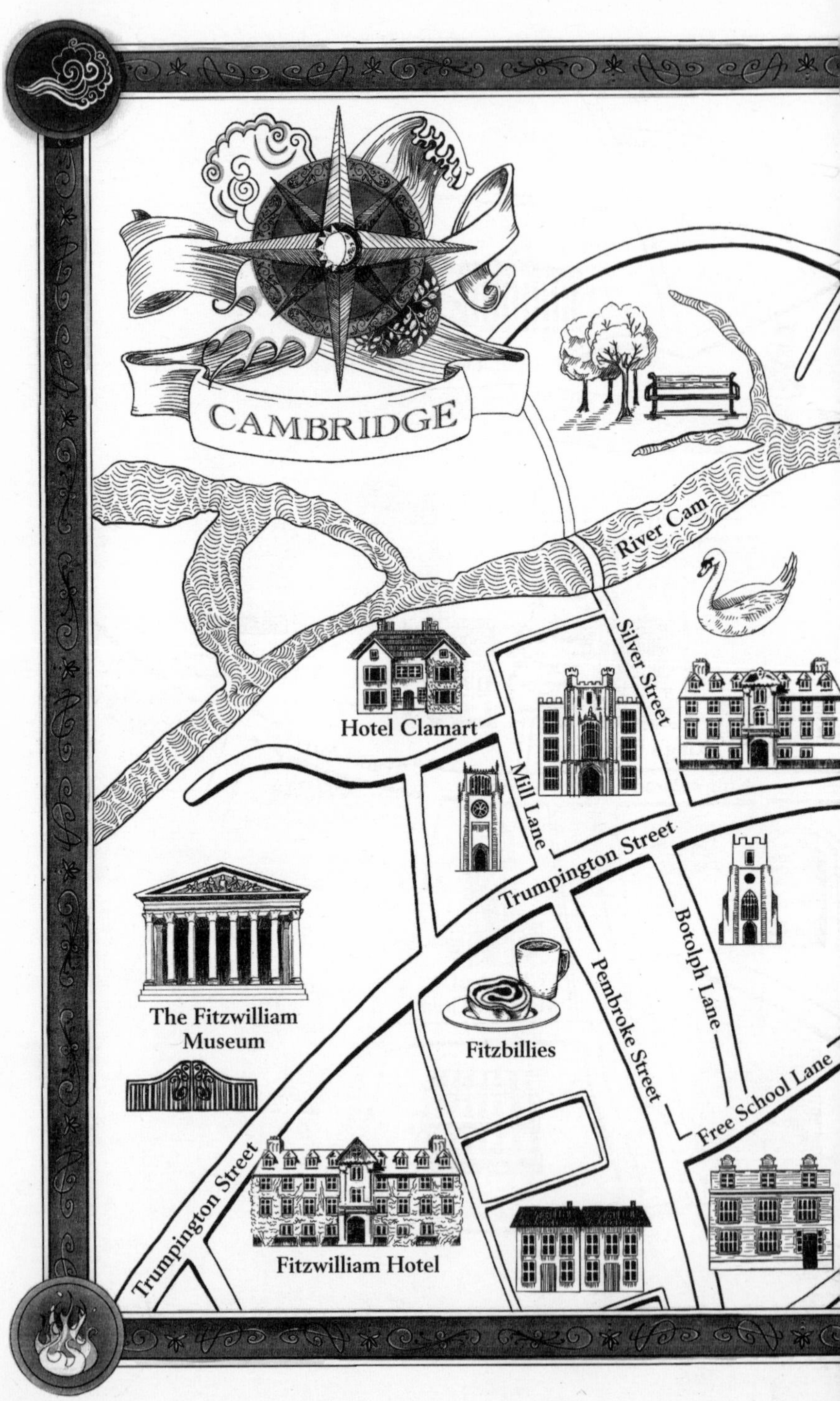
CAMBRIDGE
River Cam
Hotel Clamart
Silver Street
Mill Lane
Trumpington Street
The Fitzwilliam Museum
Botolph Lane
Pembroke Street
Fitzbillies
Free School Lane
Trumpington Street
Fitzwilliam Hotel

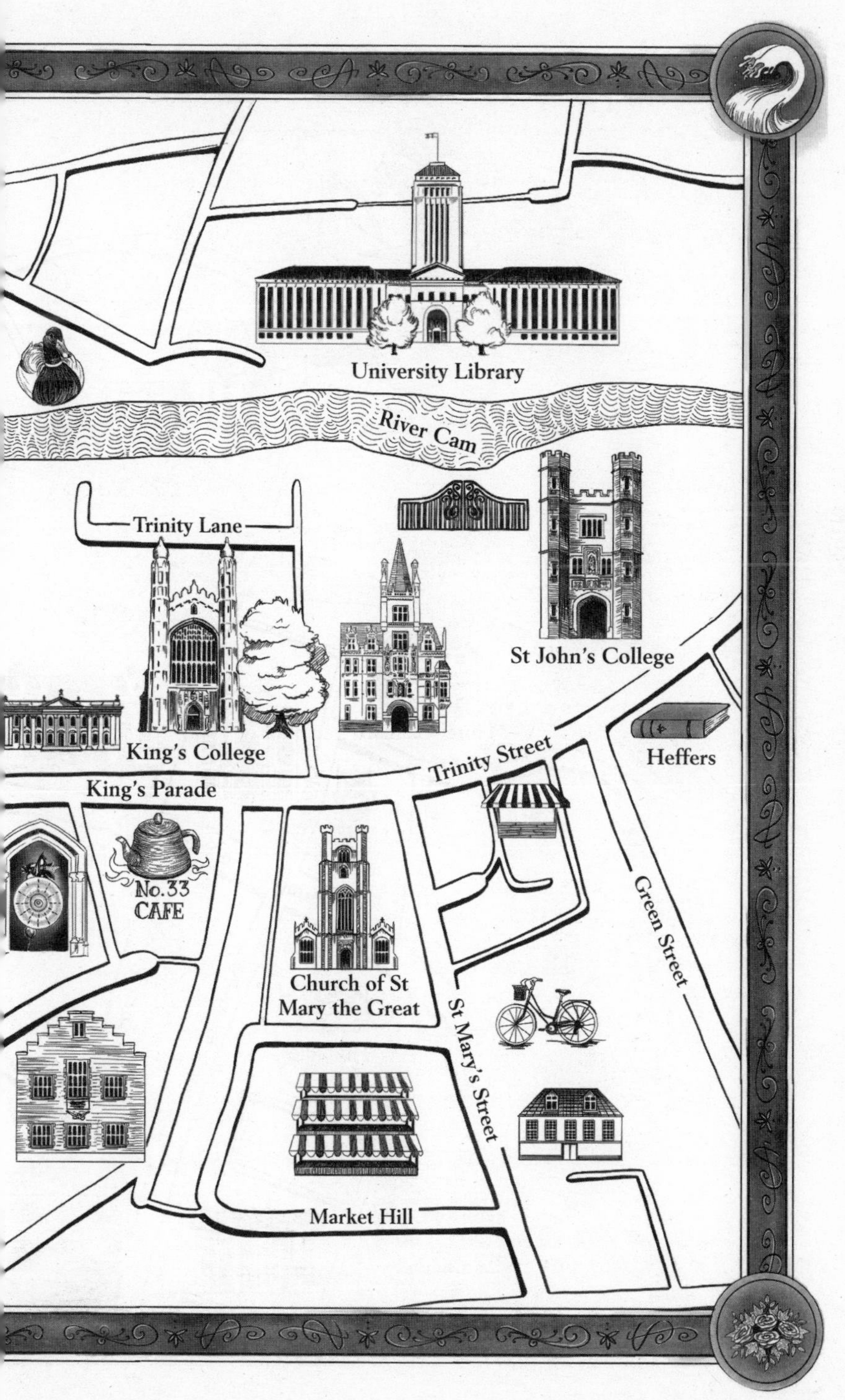
University Library
River Cam
Trinity Lane
St John's College
King's College
Heffers
Trinity Street
King's Parade
No.33
CAFE
Green Street
Church of St
Mary the Great
St Mary's Street
Market Hill

The dreamer awakes,
The shadow goes by,
This tale I will tell you,
This tale is a lie.
But listen to me,
Bright maiden, proud youth,
This tale is a lie;
What it tells is the truth.

Traditional folktale ending

Prologue

All souls are special. Son or daughter, Grimm or not, Life touches her spirit to every one of her creations. But the conception of a daughter is a particularly mystical event, requiring certain alchemical influences. For, to conceive a being who can bear and birth life herself needs a little something . . . extra.

Every daughter is born of an element, infused with its own particular powers. Some are born of earth: fertile as soil, strong as stone, steady as the ancient oak. Others of fire: explosive as gunpowder, seductive as light, fierce as an unbound flame. Others of water: calm as a lake, relentless as a wave, unfathomable as an ocean. The Sisters Grimm are daughters of air – at least they begin that way – born of dreams and prayer, faith and imagination, bright-white wishing and black-edged desire.

There are hundreds, possibly thousands, of Sisters Grimm on Earth and in Everwhere. You may well be one of them, though you might never know it. You think you're ordinary. You've never suspected that you're stronger than you seem, braver than you feel or greater than you imagine.

But I hope that by the time you finish this tale, you'll start listening to the whispers that speak of unknown things, the signs that point in unseen directions and the nudges that suggest unimagined possibilities. I hope too that you'll discover your own magnificence, your own magic.

COUNTDOWN

29th September – 33 days . . .

9.17 a.m. – Goldie

I've been a thief for as long as I can remember, a liar too. I might even be a murderer, though you'll have to make up your own mind about that.

'Goldie – get out here!'

I stuff the notebook into my apron pocket, along with the pen, smooth the bed sheets, wipe a last smudge from the gilded hallway mirror, blow a kiss and a line of poetry to the speckled pink orchid on the shelf beneath, before dashing out of room 13 and into the corridor.

Mr Garrick waits, his close-set eyes squinting, his head shining under the ceiling lights. He smooths his skull with greasy hands. If he could transplant the hairs from his hands to his head, he'd be on to something.

'Get down to the front desk, Goldie. Cassie's called in sick.'

'What?' I frown. 'But . . . No, that's not—'

'Now.' Garrick tweaks the knot in his tie – too tight around his fat neck which folds like a billowing sheet over his collar – then tries to snap his swollen fingers, but he's sweating too much and the sound is pathetic. I try not to show my disgust.

I follow Garrick into the lift, leeching to the wall. It does no good. Those greasy, greedy hands still slide over to paw at me, to trace the lines of territories he has no right to touch. When his fingertip brushes the swell of my breast, I'm empty of breath, a single taut muscle, contracting against the urge to urinate. I never could control it as a child, I usually can now. When the doors ping open, I fall out into the foyer.

Garrick takes his time, smoothing polyester waistcoat over swollen belly, adjusting polyester tie, before sauntering to the front desk.

I'm already there, waiting. If I didn't need this bloody job so much, to feed and clothe Teddy, I'd snap those fat fingers at the bone. I'd open my mouth to invite him in, then bite down until his blood dripped from my chin.

'Where's Cassie?' I ask.

'Sick.' Garrick lowers his voice, grinning a dirty grin. 'Women's problems.'

'Can't Liv fill in?' I protest. 'I'm not trained for the front desk.'

'I know.' Garrick sighs, expelling stale, smoky breath. 'But she's not answering her phone. Anyway, we're only expecting half a dozen guests today.' He smiles the dirty smile again. 'So you just have to stand behind the desk and look pretty. I'm sure even you can manage that.'

I stare at the empty space and say nothing.

'Hey, Goldie.'

I look up to see Jake, the porter, giving me a shy wave. We're sort of seeing each other. He's a little boring, but sweet and kind and doesn't ask for much. Which is fortunate, since I've little to offer.

Jake sidles up to the desk. 'What are you doing down here?'

He's quite handsome, but it won't last. I flinch whenever he tries to touch me. It's not his fault, but I can't seem to find the words to explain.

'Cassie's sick,' I say.

'Have you worked the front desk before?'

'Yeah,' I lie. Jake has only been working at the hotel for six weeks, so I can say what I like. I can pretend I'm brave, that I don't give a shit, that being shoved out onto the front desk doesn't feel like I've been strapped into stocks in the town square.

'I'd be nervous,' Jake says. 'I wouldn't know what to say.' He rests his right hand tentatively on the front desk. He wants to reach for me, but he won't.

'I don't know.' I pause. 'It's better than cleaning toilets, I suppose.'

'Jake – where the hell are you? Jake!'

Jake drops his hand. We turn towards the shouting.

'I'd better go,' he says, already halfway to the stairs. He doesn't look back to smile or wave – he can't. There's a great deal our boss can't tolerate, but waiting is what makes the veins in his bald head bulge the soonest.

Behind the desk, I glare at the phone, willing it to stay silent. I pick a few stray long hairs from the sleeve of my hotel-issue polyester shirt. I'm too dishevelled for this job. I curse Cassie. She should be here, the front desk princess. Beautiful Cassie, voluptuous as a vase of peonies. Beside her, I'm a daffodil. We used to clean rooms together but Cassie was always keen to get promoted. It's more money, more prestige. You don't have to wear a dowdy uniform and you earn your wage grinning at guests, instead of sticking your head in toilet bowls smelling (hopefully) of Harpic. Personally, the fewer people I see the better. Garrick is quite enough to swallow down every day.

Speaking of swallowing, it's a not-so-secret secret that Cassie did exactly that to get herself transferred up from the toilets to the front desk. Garrick's not managed to get those greedy hands very far with me – I've made sure we're never alone for long enough. So he can only grope, fondle and insinuate.

One day I'll take something heavy and bring it down hard on his bald head.

*

Standing behind the front desk, wearing the hotel crest and a rictus grin, I feel the press of my notebook in my pocket. I can't scribble out here, which is perhaps the worst thing about being put on the front desk. You see, I'm not simply a thief but a writer too. Possibly even a poet, but only by my own measure. I accommodate a constant chatter in my mind, a commentary on every mundane event of my life. I can't control it. But I write down anything worthwhile when I can. It soothes my mind a little.

Since I can't write, I think about Teddy. I wonder what he's learning, what new facts are now widening his eyes with excitement. Thinking about my brother always settles me. He's nearly ten and everything a child should be: innocent, joyful, kind. I'll make sure he stays that way. Whatever it takes. He's a good soul; I was a lost cause a long time ago.

After rent and bills, most of my wages go towards Teddy's school fees: £8,590 a year. And, since I earn £7.57 per hour for 63 hours a week, that's where the thieving comes in. I know he could go to a state school, but he's so happy at St Faith's. And, after everything, I want him happy for as long as possible. So, on occasion, I relieve our richer guests of their frivolous possessions. It's surprising what people don't miss when they have too much.

'Excuse me?'

I glance up to see a gentleman gazing down his Roman nose at me.

'S-sorry, s-sir, I didn't – how may I help you?'

He ignores my smile, my attempts to rewind inattentiveness.

'Charles Penry-Jones,' he says. 'We're staying ten nights. My wife requested a room overlooking the courtyard.'

I nod. I have no small talk to offer. I only pray the wife's request has been heeded. I've no finesse with irate guests. They twist me up with their condescension and contempt.

I tap the name into the computer and it comes up trumps, the wife's request and all. When I look up again, he has appeared at Penry-Jones's side.

He is tall and slender, but strong, like a silver birch tree, and almost as preternaturally pale – hair blond as sunlight cresting its topmost branches. The irises of his eyes are half a dozen shades of green: the lightest of newly seeded grass, of fresh shoots in spring, dark forest green, grey laurel green, bright pine green, shining myrtle green, creamy avocado green . . . He gives me a small, self-conscious smile. I stare back at him and then, all at once, feel something I've never felt before – suddenly and entirely alight.

'Where have you been, Leo?'

I smile to myself; I know his name. They must be father and son, though they aren't so similar. The father fits perfectly into this polished room, like a cultivated hot-house cactus, while the son seems slightly out of place.

'Where is your mother?'

'Getting something from the car. She's coming.'

His voice is soft and posh. His hands, hanging by his sides, are sturdy. His fingers long stems, so I imagine his touch tender and his hold strong. I feel ribbons of desire begin to unfurl inside me. I snip at their silky threads.

'She's sulking,' Penry-Jones says. 'She always clamours to come on these business trips, then complains when I conduct any business. At least you'll be here for a few days to take the heat off.'

'Your room keys,' I say, sliding them across the polished wood.

'I'd like a wake-up call at six thirty.' The father palms the keys. 'What time does the restaurant open for dinner?'

'S-seven o'clock,' I say. 'Would you like r-reservations?'

'That won't be necessary.' He looks to Leo. 'Let's go. Your mother can meet us in the bar.'

With that, the father strides off across the foyer. The son follows.

Turn back, I whisper. *Turn back*, I will him. *Turn back and look at me.*

When he reaches the lift, he does. As soon as our eyes meet, I glance down at the desk. When I glance up again, he's gone.

10.11 p.m. – Leo

What happens when a star falls to Earth? Leo can only imagine, since he never had the luxury. He was plucked, summoned, commanded from the heavens. Might he have retained his purity, his innocence, if he'd simply fallen? Perhaps it was the act of being untimely ripped that corrupted him. Rage and despair took root in his cold stone heart, and grew. Until he was capable of such things as stars would never do. Excepting the hundreds similarly plucked to do *his* bidding.

Leo recognizes other stars sometimes, though they are boys and men now, no longer spheres of burning gas. 'Star' is no longer fitting, once they've fallen. They no longer shine, no longer cast light, only darkness and death. 'Soldier' is more fitting. Because he didn't bring them down to twinkle. He brought them to kill, eradicate, exterminate. An army with a single mission: to extinguish that which has become illuminated.

As former illuminations themselves, these soldiers are uniquely gifted for the task. On Earth, they can spot a Grimm girl a mile off. In Everwhere, they can mark, track and (sometimes) kill her, without using any of their human senses. These star soldiers, or *lumen latros* as he prefers, pretentiously, to call them, need only wait until their own inner light flickers in recognition of its counterpart.

It was a long time before Leo discovered that the term 'soldier' was also misleading, implying the fight for a just cause against an unjust enemy. But the Grimm girls aren't his father's enemy but his greatest hope. And, in truth, his soldiers are cannon fodder, pitched against his daughters to test their strength, to give them a taste for blood and murder, to turn them towards the dark. Wilhelm Grimm doesn't want a war, he wants a battle. He wants his soldiers to lose and his daughters to win. He wants a massacre.

This sometimes enrages Leo so much that he feels the urge to desert this army and abandon its general. That he doesn't is both because he can't – his father punishes all deserters with death – and because he needs to kill in order to live; their imbibed illumination keeps him alight. Last, and not least, because he's still revenging the death of one he loved.

Leo sees other soldiers when he's out hunting, although it's rare, since they tend not to encroach on one another's territory. They hunt every month on the night of the moon's first quarter, stepping through gates at 3.33 a.m., from Earth and into Everwhere.

Everwhere is where they come, where they gather, where he finds them. The sisters visit whenever they wish, no matter the hour, no matter the day. While he can visit only on the set day, at the set hour. And they don't have to walk through gateways, though sometimes they like to – the ritual is a pleasing one – they need only fall asleep, close their eyes and slip into that place between light and dark, between the waking world and the world of dreams. Some, especially the young ones, don't even remember they've been, waking none the wiser. But most come intentionally, to meet their sisters, to practise their powers, readying themselves for the night when they will have to fight for their lives.

Leo can tell at a glance that Goldie doesn't remember Everwhere. She has forgotten herself, has no idea who she is, neither how skilled nor how strong. Which, if her ignorance holds, will tip the scales in his favour. Leo smiles. He can almost feel the light of her dissipating spirit surge in his veins – like a shock of electricity bringing him back to life.

11.11 p.m. – Goldie

The astonishing sight of that man – Leo – makes me wonder how I'd describe myself. We have the same hair, I think, though mine curls to my shoulders. It used to curl down my back but I cut it after Ma died. My skin isn't so pale and my eyes are blue not green. I'd like to say they're half a dozen shades of blue: delphiniums, larkspur, bluebells, cornflowers, hydrangeas, clematis . . . But I'd be lying, and I try not to lie to myself. The blue of my eyes is a light, watery, forget-me-not blue. Common, unremarkable.

It was only coincidence that he looked back at me. Though it certainly felt as if I commanded him. I know I'm being silly, yet I can't help wondering. Thoughts, questions, notions circle my mind, multiplying until my head aches.

For distraction, I mist the purple orchid on the mantelpiece, stroking its leaves, whispering Wordsworth into its petals, its stems now so heavy with buds that I search for pencils and twine to tie them up. Before I arrived the mortality rate for flowers was shocking. A dozen would die a month. But I've reversed that. I've always had green fingers. Afterwards, I stare at the computer. I polish the over-polished counter. I arrange and rearrange the drawers. I even wish for late guests to appear. But I can't stop thinking of that moment, the moment he turned upon reaching the lift. I'm so used to feeling always on edge – a crouched hare ever ready to dart to its burrow – I didn't know I could feel any different. But for that moment, I felt strong. As if I could command armies. As if I could topple nations. As if I had magic at my fingertips . . .

11.11 p.m. – Leo

To Leo's knowledge, he has never dreamed before. He doesn't need the restoration of REM sleep – indeed, doesn't need sleep, but sometimes takes pleasure in it – leaving his nights uninterrupted by the intrusion of needless, nonsensical images. So, when he drifts off then wakes tonight and the image of Goldie lingers, he's startled. Perhaps it's a subliminal warning against complacency, his subconscious cautioning him not to underestimate her as an opponent. He came to the hotel to watch her, but perhaps he should keep a closer eye, assess her strengths, determine her potential. Or perhaps he's developing an unnatural obsession. Admittedly, seeing her face again is far from disagreeable. Still, the question of why he is suddenly dreaming and whether Goldie might be the cause, keeps Leo alert till dawn.

30th September – 32 days . . .

6.33 p.m. – Bea

The first time Bea took off in a glider, she was terrified. Though she'd have sooner crashed than admit it. Indeed, it'd irked to admit it to herself. It wasn't the flying – once airborne she felt joy she'd never known – but the taking off that took some getting used to. The plunge of the roller-coaster in reverse: the slow stretch and pull of the ground catapult, the tightening, the almighty snap and fling.

The lift – oh, the lift! – was sublime. After the abrupt snap came the radiant soar. Rising into the air as if entirely weightless, the catapult forgotten, the plane forgotten, everything forgotten – all past experience erased by this single, spectacular moment of absolute presence. A moment that stretched until the glider began to quake and tilt, prompting the pilot to seize the joystick and seek an updraught.

It took half a dozen flights before Bea began to savour the catapult as much as the lift, the climax as much as the release. Now, as the giant elastic band pulls taut, Bea feels a coil of anticipation tighten inside her. She sits, in a state of both absolute stillness and ceaseless quivering, as if her entire body were on the brink of laughter. She has no understanding of the physical dynamics or meteorological phenomena that keep the glider in flight without an engine, and nor does she wish to. To define terms, to understand concepts, would weigh it down, would make concrete that which must remain celestial.

Bea glances out of the window at the diminishing figure of Dr Finch below, waving. She doesn't wave back. That their affair gives her unfettered access to the Cambridge University Royal Aeronautical Society's gliders is its main purpose. The sex is all right, but she feels nothing for him otherwise, excepting occasional disgust.

As she rises, Bea's breathing deepens and slows. A wisp of hair escapes her bun, intruding on the view. She pushes it back. When flying, Bea is sometimes seized by the urge to shave her head, to leave the scenery unsullied. It's an action that'd enrage her elegant *mamá* – reason enough to do it – and free herself. But, though she'd not admit this either, Bea's too vain. Looking in the mirror, she compares herself to what she loves. Sometimes, her skin and hair are the nut-brown colour of the female blackbird, her eyes the midnight black of the male. Though perhaps her hair is closer in colour to a crow's wing and certainly as fine – secretly she wishes it was a little fuller. Sometimes . . .

Be careful! Dr Finch's whine invades the sacred silence of the cockpit. Bea shuts him out of her mind. Forget shaving her head, now she'd like a lobotomy, if only to get a little peace.

Don't be so reckless.

Cállate. Bea presses finger and thumb to her temple. *Fuck off.*

Bea snatches at the joystick, dips the glider's nose, then pulls sharply back. The plane arcs up and, for one long Elysian moment all she can see is sky – around, above, within. She is free.

Bea screams an ecstatic scream. 'Wooooohoooooo!'

In the field below, her tutor will be cursing and shaking his fist at the heavens. Shutting him out, she gazes up at the clouds, made pink-bottomed by the setting sun, holding the suspension a second longer than she should, before allowing the plane to fall backwards, nose plummeting towards the ground in a full turn of the Catherine wheel, so all she sees is landscape – harvested fields and autumn trees. Until, at last, the inverted earth is scooped up and the plane righted and level again.

Bea gives another gleeful howl. 'Wooooooo!'

That's right, niña, you show him you're not some silly girl, you're a sister—

'*¡Vete a la mierda, Mamá!*' Bea hisses, as annoyed by the invasion of her mother's approval as she is by her teacher's rebuke. For nearly eighteen years her mother has encouraged her to act audaciously and, although Bea relishes nothing more than reckless behaviour, she's damned if she'll give her mother the satisfaction of knowing it.

Bea banks a sharp left, tipping the plane so suddenly and sharply that she slips across her seat, nearly cracking her forehead against the glare shield. She holds the joystick steady, pushing it as far as it'll go, so the glider tips and the sky slides. The ground rises to her right, then, all at once, the plane rolls sideways, tumbling, flipping, inverting the world so that earth is sky and sky is earth, suspending Bea like a bat in the cockpit, about to plummet headfirst 2,378 feet to the fields below, in a mash-up of body and bone and fuselage. But then she's rolling, following the circular arc of the left wing as it high-fives and low-fives and high-fives the air again.

'Woohooooo!'

As the glider balances, Bea's ecstatic shrieks above are seized by Finch's cursing cries below, both ascending to the heavens in a discordant harmony of exalted rage.

'Woooo – fucking – hoooo!'

'What the fucking hell were you playing at?'

'I knew you were seething,' Bea says, climbing out of the grounded glider. 'I could feel it. I could hear you howling obscenities at—'

'Of course I fucking was.' Dr Finch is beside Bea before her feet have touched soil. 'What the hell were you thinking? In fifteen years of flying I've never pulled a stunt like that – a backflip and a barrel roll, without a decent thermal lift. What the fucking hell—?'

'—was I thinking? Yeah, yeah. I know, I know.' Bea strides towards the stretch of lax elastic snaking across the grass. Now that she's grounded she only wants to be airborne again. 'Now, stop whining and give me a hand with the catapult.'

'What?' Dr Finch, rooted to the ground, stares at her. 'Are you fucking insane? You're not going back up there. It's nearly dark.'

'Nearly' – Bea lifts the elastic, finding the winch – 'but not quite.'

'Absolutely not.'

'Oh, come on,' Bea snaps. 'Don't be such a dick.'

'Society rules,' Dr Finch retorts. 'You'll get me kicked out. Dammit, you'll probably get me disciplined.'

Bea swears to herself. She wants to fly, wants to feel free again. It's all she's ever wanted – a legacy left by a peripatetic childhood ruled by strangers who sent her *mamá* to the dungeon of St Dymphna's while interning Bea in a dozen different foster homes, from which she tried to escape over and over again.

'You're such a bloody coward.'

'And you're bloody suicidal.'

So what if I am? Bea wants to say. Surely it's commendable not to cower from death, but leap into its jaws with a warrior's cry. Her maniacal, manic *mamá* at least taught her that. Bea opens her mouth, about to tell him so, then thinks better of it. 'Piss off.'

Dr Finch glares at her.

A taut silence stretches between them – the catapult

pulled too far, ready to snap. With one last, reluctant glance at the grounded glider, Bea drops the elastic to her feet. She eyes him instead: the thin, limp frame, weak-featured face, slightly anaemic pallor of the over-educated, affected scruffy hair and stubble growth to suggest that his mind is on more elevated subjects than personal grooming. *What a prick.* Bea wishes she had immediate access to a better option. Sadly, right now, she does not.

'So,' Bea says. 'If I can't fly, then I need the next best thing – is your wife expecting you home?'

Afterwards, Bea lies across the sofa in Dr Finch's office, while he scrambles about for his clothes – acting as if he can't quite imagine how this happened, as if that means he can later claim that it didn't actually happen at all. She scans the titles of his textbooks, searching for anything by her favourite philosopher.

She doesn't want to be here anymore. She wants to be in the air or, if she can't, then reading a book. An escape. An alternative world. She'd been wrong. The orgasm, especially as it'd been executed by the inattentive Dr Finch, was a pathetic echo of flight. She should have stayed in the air. She should have stolen the plane. Next time she will. Next time she won't come down.

1st October –
31 days . . .

5.31 a.m. – Liyana

The first dive is always the finest. The moment she slices the water and slides under. That is it. Her peak moment. A singular rush of joy floods her veins like a morphine shot as Liyana dives, arms like an arrow, moving so fast and free that she feels no longer solid but liquid.

'I hate being human,' Liyana often says. 'Imagine gliding through water all your life instead of stumbling through air.'

'You moan like a beached whale,' her aunt Nyasha often replies. 'Or that mermaid in that film you—'

'Madison,' Liyana interrupts. '*Splash*. Yeah, except the blonde hair and blue eyes, I wish I was.'

Liyana allows herself this joy once a month. She 'borrows' her aunt's membership, walking the half-mile to the Serpentine Spa on Upper Street, and swims for an hour. No more, no less. Then she leaves and doesn't return, no matter how much she wants to, until the next month and the next permitted trip. The enforced limitation is a regretful but necessary discipline to keep the inevitable aftermath of sorrow at bay.

'So why do you go, *vinye*?' Nya asks. 'If it makes you sad?'

'The same reason you chase men who make you miserable,' Liyana replies. 'Because if you didn't, you might as well be dead.'

Almost five years ago Liyana spent six hours a day in a swimming pool. Then swimming had anointed her only with joy. At ten she'd won enough trophies to fill an oak cabinet, at thirteen she was set for Olympic stardom. Then came the accident that beached Liyana for a year, casting her forever back into amateur waters. Now swimming brings joy and sorrow in equal measure. The first dive is still the finest, the final always the saddest. And then Liyana leaves, before the longing to stay becomes too overwhelming. It's already difficult enough to let go after only an hour. And in the following days the scent of chlorine clings to her skin no matter how she scrubs, twisting her guts and stinging her eyes. When at last it leaves, her skin – dark as the depths of the ocean, eyes black and bright as stones on a riverbed – is parched again. Until the next month.

Underwater, as her torpedoed-self slows, Liyana opens her eyes to the lengths of shimmering blue ceramic tiles, shaped into a sea serpent of two curling mosaic S's. She is poised to flip, to kick off from the tiles and push to the surface, when she sees a glimmering in the corner: a stone, bright white as a skull. It's as big as her fist and, as she glides towards it, Liyana thinks of Kumiko's face. Kumiko, her skin pale as bone within curtains of black hair like a waning moon in a midnight sky.

'If I'm the moon,' Kumiko had said, 'then you're the night sky, curling round me.'

Liyana laughed. 'All right then.'

'No, I'm not the moon.' Kumiko leaned forward. 'I'm the teeth in your dark, wet mouth.'

Kumiko touched her lips to Liyana's. Slowly, Liyana kissed her. 'You're trying to distract me.'

Kumiko smiled. 'Is it working?'

Kumiko's smile deepened. 'I'm trying – I want to draw you.'

'I want to fuck you.'

Liyana laughed again. 'You're not very ladylike, are you?'

Kumiko pulled back. 'By whose definition?'

'Well . . .' Liyana tapped her pen to her teeth. 'You'd certainly better not talk to my aunt like that.'

'That depends' – Kumiko's smile deepened – 'does she look like you?'

'Right,' Liyana said, setting down her pen. 'You're definitely not meeting her now.'

Kumiko rolled her eyes. 'Like I ever was.'

'You will,' Liyana said. 'I'm just . . .'

'Waiting for the right time,' Kumiko said. 'I know, I've heard your spiel enough times I could recite it back to you.'

'Please,' Liyana said. 'You've got to—'

'—give you time,' Kumiko finished. 'Yeah, yeah. Yada yada . . . You know what? *You* need to stop being so ladylike and grow some balls – or boobs, or whatever the fem equivalent is – and stop being such a fucking coward.'

Liyana surfaces still clutching the stone. Shaking the water from her hair, she looks up into the face of a man. Frowns and folds her arms over the poolside edge. He gazes down at her.

'I thought I'd have to call the lifeguard,' he says.

Liyana's frown deepens into a scowl.

'You can hold your breath for a really long time,' he clarifies. 'It looked like you might not come up.'

'Fifteen minutes, thirty-seven seconds,' Liyana says. She doesn't want to be talking with this man, and has no idea why *he* is talking to her, but the desire to speak about swimming is ever-present, the words escaping before she can stop them. 'I used to be able to hold it for tw— longer.'

'Used to?'

Liyana shrugs droplets from her shoulders. 'Out of

practice.' She glances back at the pool. She's wasting valuable water-time. 'I should—'

'How often do you come here?'

Liyana's frown returns. 'Did you just ask me if I come here often?'

He laughs. 'Yeah, I guess I did – sorry, I didn't mean to.' He pulls his hand over his hair. Liyana notices that he's quite attractive – tall, muscular, skin the colour of wet earth – exceedingly attractive, one might say, if one were that way inclined. 'I didn't mean it like that. I was only asking . . . this isn't my local gym. I wondered if it's worth the membership fee.'

Liyana rubs her thumb over the wet stone. It wants to return to the water. 'I suppose so, I don't know. I only come to swim.'

'How often?'

'Once a month.'

His eyebrows rise. 'Really? You don't – you look much fitter than that.'

Liyana shifts in the water, pulling her arms closer, covering the view to her breasts. 'I don't think—'

'Shit,' he says. 'I'm so sorry. That sentence should've stayed in my head. I didn't—'

'—mean it like that?' Liyana raises a single eyebrow.

'Yeah,' he says. 'I, um, I only meant to say that you, you look like an athlete.'

Liyana regards him. In addition to being handsome, he has a voice that, even when he's self-conscious and stumbling, sounds like a river smoothing rocks. Perhaps that's why she has let this conversation go on so long.

I was an athlete once. The words wait in Liyana's throat. But to let them out would incite questions she has no intention of answering.

'I've got to go,' she says instead. 'I've only got forty-seven minutes left.'

'That's – you're very . . . precise.'

He smiles again and Liyana is caught by it, reminded of something long ago. A moon breaking through clouds. A river catching its light.

2nd October – 30 days . . .

10.36 a.m. – Scarlet

Scarlet didn't want to go but her grandmother had insisted. Why she'd thought a day's apprenticeship with a Hatfield blacksmith was an appropriate eighteenth birthday present, Scarlet can't imagine. But, suspecting it's another pitiful example of how far and fast her grandmother's mind is declining – her birthday isn't till the end of the month. Even so, what could she do but go along with it?

The blacksmith, Owen Baker, is the sturdiest man Scarlet has ever seen, with a head as bald as her belly, a neck as thick as her thigh and hands almost as broad as hers are long. He could throw her over his shoulder and disappear into the forest in a flash. Not that she can see the forest. The forge is located in a courtyard, adjacent to a pig farm. Yet, when Scarlet thinks of blacksmiths, if she ever has since the age of eight, she thinks of fairy tales involving forests and vulnerable girls – or perhaps that's huntsmen?

'All right then, what is it you'll be wanting to make now, Miss Thorne?'

Scarlet looks up, momentarily blank. She'd been tuning out the blacksmith's introduction, with its potted history of the noble art of crafting rivets, but hadn't expected it to be over so soon.

'Sorry?' Scarlet starts twisting her hair into a bun – the thick dark red curls spring like flames from her head, framing her eyes, brown as the wood that feeds the fire. 'I didn't think I'd be . . .'

'Well, as I say' – the blacksmith rests both broad hands

on his anvil and leans forward – 'you'll be making whatever you want. A rivet, a nail, a sword . . .'

Scarlet stares at him, releasing her grip on her hair. 'A sword?'

'Oh yes.' The blacksmith grins, eyes suddenly bright as a three-year-old boy's. 'You want to be making a sword, Miss Thorne?'

Scarlet considers this curious proposal. 'No, not really.'

'Fair enough.' He straightens himself, the light in his eyes dimming. 'So, then what'll it be?'

Scarlet reaches for her hair again. 'But, I thought you'd tell me what to do.'

Owen Baker shakes his head. 'What's the fun in that now? No. It's up to you.'

Scarlet's thrown. She fingers her hair, chews her lip. Then, all at once, it comes to her. 'Okay, I know.' She grins, delighted by her inspiration. 'I want to make a gate.'

'A gate?'

'Yeah.' Scarlet warms to her theme. 'One of those fancy gates, with all the pretty swirls and curly bits. You know what I mean?'

'The finials and curlicues?' The blacksmith folds his arms. 'Well, I admire your ambition, Miss Thorne, I do. But I'm afraid that might be a tad much for a day's work. We've only got five hours.'

'Oh, right.' Scarlet glances at a hammer hanging on the stone wall. 'I see.'

'But we could make a part of a gate,' he suggests. 'How'd that be?'

Scarlet brightens. 'Great.'

'So, what d'you favour?' he says. 'A curly bit or a pointy bit?'

*

'Yes, that's right, use the corner when you're drawing down – good, that's good technique. Yes, that's it, bit slower now.' He nods. 'You're a dab hand with the hammer, Miss Thorne.'

Scarlet looks up, grinning, face flushed. 'Really? I've never—'

'No, don't stop now!' the blacksmith says. 'Don't let it cool. That's it, not the flat, the corners – you're wanting to push the metal along, like a rolling pin does to dough, or so the wife tells me.'

This comment misses its mark, so intent is Scarlet on the pull of her arm, the upswing of the hammer, the crack as it hits the burning metal bar, the shock of hammer on anvil if she misses her target.

'Right, bring it back to centre, that's it – remember the flat of the hammer now, start refining the shape. Lighter blows, or your point'll snap.'

Scarlet tumbles the bar, tapping out the slope – first one side, then the other – stretching the metal thinner and thinner towards the point. She hopes they'll have time to make another, to plunge more metal into the furnace, to see the flames leap and spit with delight to have a thing to burn. Scarlet wants to watch the fire till it's embers and ash. She wants to strike hammer to anvil, again and again, to feel the power of the blow as she brings it down, the glorious crack that shudders through her from tip to toe. Strangely, Scarlet finds she wants to immerse her hand in the flame, wants to feel the scorch on her skin. She believes, impossibly, that the fire will be kind to her. That it will lick her warm, that the warmth will spread and rise, till she's white hot at her core.

By rights Scarlet should be fearful of fire, should hate it, since it took her mother and her home. But she finds, perhaps because she has no memory of the event, that it's only when she thinks of fire that she feels scared. When she sees it, she's fascinated.

'Whatever are you doing with that frightful spike?' Her grandmother shrinks back in the chair, as if Scarlet had held the finial to her throat. 'Put it away.'

'I made it,' Scarlet says, hugging the spike protectively to her chest. 'With the blacksmith this morning.'

They sit now in the café's kitchen, eating buttered crumpets for dinner. A weekly treat.

Esme Thorne's brow furrows. 'The blacksmith?'

Scarlet bites into her crumpet, suppressing a flush of sorrow. 'You bought me an apprenticeship for my birthday, remember?'

Her grandmother's eyes cloud and Scarlet curses herself. Why did she use that bloody word? She should know better by now. But, too often, she forgets.

'But it's not your birthday.' All at once, her grandmother looks like a child: wide, anxious eyes, a smattering of freckles across her nose, bequeathed to three generations of Thorne women. 'Is it? I – I didn't forget your birthday, did I?'

'No, no, Grandma,' Scarlet says quickly. 'Of course you didn't. It's not till the end of the month.'

Her grandmother relaxes. 'I knew I couldn't forget my own Ruby's birthday.'

Scarlet puts down her crumpet. 'No, Grandma, I'm not Ruby,' she says, already regretting the words. 'I – I'm Scarlet.'

'I know,' Esme says, suddenly irritated. 'That's what I said.' She pulls back her long, grey hair – at seventy-eight she's only lately lost the last wisps of red – and tucks it behind her ears. 'I wish you'd stop correcting me, it's most obnoxious.'

Scarlet waits, poised to douse the flames of the fire she's just ignited. But then it seems to snuff out. Her grandmother licks melted butter from her thumb.

'When you were a little girl you wanted to be a blacksmith.'

'Really?' Scarlet says, relieved but unconvinced. For the past few years it's been trickier to distinguish fact from fiction in her grandmother's mind. Still, Scarlet plays along. 'Did I?'

Her grandmother nods. 'Oh, yes. I even bought you an anvil and hammer once – for your twelfth birthday, I think – a small set, but real enough.'

'That's amazing, Grandma.' Scarlet smiles, helpfully. 'I don't remember.'

'You don't? Gosh, I . . .' Esme falls silent, gazing down at her plate. 'You'd gone on a school trip – afterwards you begged and begged me to buy them for you.'

She still has no memory of the event, but somehow Scarlet feels that this time what her grandmother's saying is true. 'So, what happened?' she asks. 'Where are they?'

'I don't know.' Her grandmother looks thoughtful. 'I think . . . you didn't want them. You said it wasn't the same.'

Scarlet frowns. 'What wasn't?'

'I don't rightly know.' Her grandmother looks up from the plate, squinting as the memory slithers away. She reaches into the air grasping for it. 'I think, I think . . . you didn't want the tools. You wanted the fire.'

3rd October – 29 days . . .

1.03 a.m. – Leo

After settling his parents back at the hotel – he'll stay the coming weekend with them, at his mother's insistence; any longer would be unbearable – Leo returns to St John's. Tonight the moon is at the first quarter and the nearest gate into Everwhere is the one guarding the Master's garden. Tonight Leo must hunt, to sharpen his skills, and kill, to fuel his fading light. After observing Goldie for a few days, and continuing to dream about her at night, Leo knows that he must prepare diligently for the forthcoming fight to stand a chance of survival. For, even though she's forgotten herself, Goldie is still the most powerful Grimm girl he's ever seen. It'll be close combat, but at least he'll have the element of surprise on his side.

It's after three o'clock when Leo steps out of his room. Occasional blurts of sound punctuate his walk along the student-populated hallway – drunken laughter from one room, enthusiastic copulation from another. Leo hurries on. He's taking his degree at St John's since it's one of the few colleges with a gateway on the grounds, meaning Leo doesn't have to roam the streets of Cambridge on moonlit nights.

Only the most ancient and prestigious colleges contain such doorways: those whose bricks, towers, trees and soil have been steeped in thought for several centuries. Unfortunately, St John's is also one of the largest colleges and Leo's room is far from the Master's garden so he always risks being seen by an over-vigilant night porter.

Leo notices as he speeds along stone corridors and darts across forbidden lawns, that he's feeling out of sorts. Ordinarily, this is his favourite night of the month, but tonight he's not buoyed by his usual enthusiasm. Which is strange, since Leo is the best of them, the brightest star, his demon father's top recruit. He has the highest number of terminations of any soldier. And at only eighteen, depending on the world in which you're counting.

Leo has heard that it's possible, theoretically at least, for a soldier to travel to Everwhere on the coat-tails of a Grimm girl's dreams – thus not limiting his entrance to an exact date and time – but he won't manage this method himself, since it requires certain skills and deep intimacy with the girl in question. And Leo could never countenance loving a Grimm. Not truly. Not after what their kind has done to his.

Ten minutes later and a little breathless, Leo stands before the gate. He glances at his watch. At 3.33 a.m. he reaches up, pressing his palm lightly to the elaborate wrought-iron curls. The gate shimmers silver, as if brushed by moonlight. Leo pushes it open and steps through.

6.35 a.m. – Goldie

By now my thoughts of commanding armies and toppling nations have passed, replaced by the usual worries about providing for Teddy, avoiding Garrick, paying the rent . . . and I'm grateful. There was something slightly unsettling in feeling so powerful.

'G-G, come here.'

'What is it?' I shift from the kitchen to Teddy's bed – everything in our flat is only a few steps from everything else – to see what he wants. Although I already know, because we go through the same routine every morning. And, sure enough, I find Teddy naked, except for Batman underpants, beside a pile of discarded clothes.

He gives me a look of lament. 'What can I wear today?'

I survey the situation. 'Green trousers with red T-shirt and blue jumper?'

The look on Teddy's face tells me I'm a frump.

'What about your favourite jumper?' I point to the puff of soft blue cashmere acquired from the child of a Swiss banker (room 23) a month ago. It was one of half a dozen identical jumpers – I could have taken two, no problem. But thieving is all about limits; once you get greedy, you get caught.

'I've worn it nearly every day.' Teddy regards it. 'Yesterday, Caitlin said she'd lend me a tenner to buy a new one.'

'Little bit—' I bite my lip. Kids. Some are sweet, most need a good slap. I think of the French family staying in room 38, with a boy Teddy's age.

'I'll get you something new soon,' I promise. 'Don't worry.'

'You will?' Teddy barrels into me, arms flung wide. I hug him back. He's slight as a fresh-planted sapling, limbs so thin I worry they'll snap if I hug him too tight.

'Yes,' I say. Something so stupendous even that goblin child will have to admire it.

07.07 a.m. – Bea

'Get up, get up, get up.'

The elongated lump beneath Bea's bedcovers groans.

'Come on' – she finds his thigh with her heel and gives it a hefty kick – 'you lazy sod.'

A matted head of hair, along with a face she vaguely

remembers from last night, emerges from under the blankets and squints into the milky morning light. 'Have a heart.' He drops his head back to the pillow. 'It's barely dawn.'

'No it's not,' Bea snaps. She wishes, not for the first time, that she'd been able to sneak Little Cat into her college room since he gives comfort without reciprocal demands. 'Now fuck off, I've got a lecture.' This isn't true and they both know it. But, though Bea wants rid of him, she also has a standing date with the University Library. Every morning, as soon as it opens. To study Philosophy. She chose this subject in order to entertain and evaluate ideas which might, in another context, raise questions about her mental health. Since she still worries that the apple doesn't fall too far from the tree.

Her *mamá* is the first to remind her of this. Her falcon-featured *mamá*, whose nose is nearly as sharp as her tongue. 'This isn't your purpose, *niña*,' she says. 'You'll find that out soon enough.'

She speaks, every time, with such authority that Bea sometimes finds it hard to disregard her. Cleo García Pérez always sounds sincere telling invented tales she claims are true, of invented places she claims are real. As if she isn't either teasing or mad. When she's both. Which is why she spent Bea's childhood in and out of St Dymphna's Psychiatric Hospital, while Bea spent it in and out of foster homes. Cleo also spends an unusual amount of time extolling the virtues of vice, insisting Bea follow in her own murky footsteps. Unlike other mothers, Cleo approves of bad behaviour and admonishes good, praising her daughter for selfish acts, for anger and unkindness, while chastising slips of thoughtfulness or generosity. Her *mamá*, a chill wind of cruelty blowing through an otherwise calm world, a textbook example of how human beings can be so fucking foul to one another.

'Life is a fight for survival,' her *mamá* says. 'Good, by its nature, will lose this fight, leaving the rest to win. *¿Entiendes?* So you can't be good, if you want to survive.'

Fair enough, Bea thinks, though it's not an opinion she'll be sharing. It's always struck her as funny that, in all her ardent ramblings on the war between good and evil, her *mamá* has never tried to claim that these Sisters Grimm of which she speaks, of which she claims Bea is one, are fighting for good. For why be good when you can be great? Evil, she always says, is greatness. Evil means having the courage and ability to do what's needed in order to triumph: to rid the world of the weak.

'If you leave the future of humanity in the hands of the good,' Cleo says, 'they'll create a piteous race: people crippled by compassion, tolerance, empathy. People who accept what is instead of fighting for what's possible. Leave the *patetica* human race in their hands and we'll be wiped out – by the elements, the animals, any invading alien race . . .'

When her *mamá* talks like this, Bea has learned to nod along and say nothing. Arguing only means she won't shut up. Bea came to Cambridge to escape, to distance herself from Cleo's fascist opinions, to steep instead in gentle rumination, speculation, consideration. Socializing, except for the purposes of physical satisfaction, is not something that interests her.

Finally managing to extricate the interloper from her bed, Bea cycles (too fast) to the library, only slowing as she crosses Queen's Road to glance back across the river and inhale the beauty of King's College Chapel, its intricately carved spires reaching like immortal fingers towards the curve of the rising sun. Sometimes, Bea imagines that the spires are trying to pull the great weight of the college into the sky, to fly like a majestic migrating bird to warmer climes in winter – Paris, perhaps, to sit beside Notre-Dame, or Barcelona for the illustrious company of La Sagrada Familia.

Every day, Bea feels grateful to be here, among such beauty and inspiration. Grateful to sit in the University Library, to immerse herself in the opinions of Bertrand Russell who, predictably, proves far better company than the fumbling student she kicked out of her bed.

11.48 a.m. – Liyana

Liyana balances her sketchbook on her knees to draft the next panel of her graphic novel, the one she's been working on for nearly two years. With ink and pen she depicts BlackBird hurling LionEss from the top of the tallest oak tree in Elsewhere. BlackBird laughs as LionEss, flailing and unable to fly, plummets to the stones below. When Liyana has shaded in the last leaf of ivy, she starts to write the story of how BlackBird came to be.

BlackBird

> Once upon a time there was a girl born with ebony skin, jet-black hair and inky eyes. She was so dark that she could slip into any shadow unseen, so dark that she shone almost blue in the moonlight. She was also the most beautiful, enchanting and wisest girl in seven kingdoms. Far more beautiful than her pale stepsisters, all of whom had ashen skin, bleached hair and chalky eyes; all of whom were slightly dull and dim.
>
> The girl had one great delight in life. On nights when the moon was full, she could fly. She stood naked in their garden, her black skin brushed with a sheen of blue, waiting for her curls of jet hair to catch the wind and transform into magnificent wings. Then she would

soar above the lands and seas, her feathers glinting in the silver light, gliding on currents of pure joy.

Her sisters couldn't fly. They were as fixed to the ground as the cows who grazed the fields. But, rather than admit their jealousy, the sisters pretended that they simply didn't care to fly, that walking through the grasses was grander than swooping through the skies.

Her stepsisters were so jealous of Bee – as they named her, since they claimed she was nothing more than an insect – that they fashioned a plan to convince her that she was an ugly fool. Every day they told her so, inventing elaborate reasons and echoing each other's examples. At first, Bee, wise as she was, saw through their efforts. But, as the days and months passed, she began to waver and doubt herself. And, since there was only one of her and three of them, eventually she started to believe her stepsisters. Until Bee was convinced that she was indeed an ugly fool.

And so, feeling embarrassed, Bee flew only in secret now and then and found, when she did, that it didn't bring her the delight it once had. Months of unseen moons turned into years, until she no longer went out on moonlit nights at all. Until one day, Bee had forgotten that she could grow wings, had forgotten that she could fly, had forgotten the one thing that had brought her such joy.

Almost a lifetime had passed, when, walking in the woods, Bee met a stranger with skin, hair and eyes as dark as her own. After they'd exchanged the usual pleasantries about the weather, the price of cows and so forth, the old woman dropped her voice to a whisper.

'You've forgotten yourself,' the stranger said. 'So much so that you can't even remember your own name.'

Bee had to admit that this was true, since she could not recall, no matter how hard she tried, any name other than the one her stepsisters had given her.

'It's time to remember,' the old woman said. 'Before it's too late.'

'But how?' Bee asked. 'How can I?'

'Climb to the top of the tallest tree in this forest,' the stranger said. 'Then jump from the highest branch. As you fall, you will remember who you are.'

Bee regarded the woman with horror. 'You think it's worth giving my life to remember myself?'

The woman considered this for only a second. 'Yes,' she said. 'I do.'

For many months, Bee ignored the woman, thinking her mad. But, as months again turned into years, and she found herself growing heavier with sorrow, Bee finally decided that she had nothing to lose, for she no longer cared if she lived or died.

So she found an ancient oak in the forest, as high as three houses, and, branch by branch, climbed to the very top. There she sat, catching her breath and gazing down at the ground far, far below. Bee waited, until day turned to night, then she stood. She whispered her goodbyes to the living and said her greetings to the dead.

Then she leapt.

As Bee fell, soaring through the air so fast that it thundered in her ears, she remembered her name: BlackBird. And with it, herself.

Just as her body was about to hit the ground, as her skull was about to shatter on the stones, BlackBird threw back her head and laughed, her jet hair whipping out behind her, transforming into gigantic wings that lifted her into the winds, until she was soaring high above the trees – feathers glinting in the moonlight – once more gliding on currents of pure joy.

BlackBird never again forgot herself, her name or what she loved. And so, she spent the rest of her life

flying through the skies and never again coming back down to Earth.

Now, if you go into your own garden on a moonlit night, and if you listen very well, you will still be able to hear the echo of her laughter in the air.

Liyana bites the end of her pen. Then, recalling the time she stained her lips green, wipes her mouth. She selects a thicker pen, adding curls to BlackBird's afro, sketching in her wings. Liyana works slowly, in no rush to finish, since her comic-book world is an infinite improvement on reality: the good triumph, the bad perish, and if chaos is reaped along the way, in the end everything is always set right with the world. Justice prevails.

Liyana often finds herself stepping into the long black leather boots of her feminist superhero. She fights crime, saves lives, pines for her lover, honours her mother's memory. Truthfully, Liyana spends more time in Elsewhere than in London. She can be walking the streets, sitting on the Tube, bumping into pedestrians, when in fact she's alone and soaring through the air in a magical land.

'Ana, I need you!' her aunt shouts up the stairs.

Reluctantly, Liyana abandons BlackBird and LionEss (who bears an uncanny resemblance to both her aunt and Catwoman, an issue Liyana plans to resolve when the distant matter of publication arises) along with her drawings and pens and returns to Earth.

5.48 p.m. – Scarlet

'Scarlet!'

Catching sight of the finial she's placed proudly on a shelf balanced between a jar of sugar and a jar of salt, Scarlet stops sieving. She slaps the bag of flour onto the kitchen counter in a puff of white dust and hurries from the kitchen into the café.

'What is it, Grandma?' Scarlet asks, reaching the table.

Esme sits in her favourite spot beside the bay window, overlooking the intricate arches and turrets of King's College, contemplating the dimly lamp-lit rooms of the college where she met her husband. Before Alzheimer's took hold, Esme told great tales about her husband, though spoke rarely of her daughter. The only story she'd tell was the story of Scarlet's birth, how she was born feet first, on a river of screaming blood, in the moment between one day and the next. Whenever Scarlet asked for other, less gory, anecdotes about her mother, Esme fobbed her off with fripperies. And that was before; now Scarlet only gets information she can't trust at all.

Excepting the rare snapshot image, the main thing Scarlet remembers about Ruby is how she looked: the same red curls, the same brown eyes. Which is lucky since she doesn't have a photograph, everything destroyed in the house fire less than a decade ago, the fire that killed her mother.

'Look, Scarlet, isn't it beautiful?'

Scarlet follows the point of her grandma's curled finger to the orange sky breaking like cracked eggs above scalloped stone spires. Sometimes, when she's cleaning tables, Scarlet stops to gaze across the road at King's College, the latticed stained-glass windows of the chapel set into sculpted stone walls and topped with fluted pinnacles. A flag flickering atop the central tower like a flame. Scarlet feels comforted, though she can't quite say why, to imagine that stained glass being fired in a furnace nearly six centuries ago, created and crafted by expert hands over the course of two hundred years. The solidity of King's is reassuring, somehow, offering a pleasing permanence in this too-quickly changing world.

'Yes.' Scarlet smiles. 'It's like Bonfire Night. I've made cinnamon buns. Would you like one? A treat for dinner.' No matter that they'd eaten crumpets for dinner last night, her grandmother won't remember.

'Oh, yes.' Esme smiles like a delighted child. 'They're my favourite.'

'I know.' Scarlet touches her grandmother's shoulder before turning away. She hasn't made cinnamon buns, but still has a batch from yesterday. She'll heat them in the microwave, though Esme would have a fit if she knew it, believing microwaves to be the devil's work. She didn't speak to Scarlet for two days after she bought one, though her grandmother doesn't remember that anymore either.

The trick to reheating is not to overdo them, only warm the centres, then pop them under the grill, to get that slightly crisped, just-baked topping. And Grandma will never know. Although the heat of the plate might give Scarlet away. It's so hot that anyone else would drop it, but Scarlet can pull trays straight from the oven without flinching, something her grandmother has never been able to do. Not that Esme has baked in years.

In the kitchen, Scarlet fills the dishwasher – a concession to modernity even her grandmother couldn't resist – while the microwave whirs. When it pings, she sets the plate on the counter to cool a little and switches on the dishwasher. Nothing happens. No industrious sounds from behind the flip-up plastic door. Scarlet waits. She presses the button again.

'Shit.'

She kicks it. Still nothing. Last month the fridge – which, at £356, was cheaper to replace than to fix, despite an extra £125 to take it to the dump – now the fucking dishwasher. Which, at £2,575, must be fixed instead of replaced.

'Shit, shit, shit.'

Sliding the cinnamon buns under the grill, Scarlet glowers at the dishwasher, in the vain hope of intimidating it into working. When that fails, she gives it another swift kick, picks up the plate and stalks out of the kitchen.

Scarlet sets the buns on the table. For a moment, Esme seems not to notice, then pulls her gaze from the sunset to Scarlet.

'What, why' – a frown breaks across Esme's brow – 'what's this?'

'Cinnamon buns. A treat for dinner, reme—' Swallowing the word, Scarlet gives the plate a nudge. 'They're your favourite.'

Her grandmother frowns down at the buns. 'They are?'

'Try one, Grandma. You'll love it, I promise.'

Esme eyes the plate. Before Alzheimer's, she'd adored all baked goods. If it consisted of flour, sugar and butter, Esme gobbled it up, no question. Now she's suspicious of everything, like a child apprehensively eyeing a plate of broccoli. And it always breaks Scarlet's heart a little.

'Please, Grandma, just taste them.'

Esme considers the cinnamon buns for a moment longer, then nudges the plate away, folds her arms and returns her gaze to the sunset.

Over a decade ago

Everwhere

It is a place of falling leaves and hungry ivy, mist and fog, moonlight and ice, a place always shifting and always still. It never changes, though the mists rise and fall, the fog rolls in across the shores and sea. But the moonlight never ebbs, the ice never melts, the sun never shines. It's a nocturnal place, a place crafted from thoughts and dreams, hope and desire. It is lit by the silver of an unwavering moon, unfettered by clouds, illuminating everything but the shadows. It's an autumnal place, but with a winter chill and hue. Imagine a forest that reaches between now and forever, with ancient trunks stretching to the marbled sky and an infinite network of roots reaching out to the edge of eternity.

The entrance to this place is guarded by gates, perfectly ordinary if unusually ornate gates, that now and then – on that certain day, at that certain hour – transform into something extraordinary. And, if you've got a little Grimm blood in you, you might be able to see the shift.

Stepping through a gate, you'll first be met by trees. They'll greet you with white leaves falling like rain, dusting a crisp confetti across your path, which crunches under your feet as you begin to find your way. Step carefully over the slick stones, or you may slip. Reach out to steady yourself, palm pressed to the bleached moss that blankets every trunk and branch. Soon you'll hear the rush of water, a vein of the endless river that runs on and on, twisting through the trees, turning with the paths but never meeting the seas.

Over a decade ago

It's a while before you notice that everything around you is alive. You'll feel the hum of the earth beneath your feet, the breath of the trees in the rustle of their leaves, the murmur of the birds in flight. As your eyes adjust to the light you'll see the marks on rocks, crushed patches of leaves, slips in the mud.

Footprints.

Others have been here before and you're following in their footsteps. You wonder how many have preceded you, which paths they took, where they went and what they found. And so, you walk on . . .

As you walk be careful to avoid the shadows, steer clear of the creatures that lurk within. Don't listen to their voices, the persistent whispers that will linger in your mind. Instead, stick to the path, follow your heart and let it lead you to the others, as they will be led to you.

Goldie

I wanted to be different, special, exceptional. No doubt everyone felt the same, excepting the seven people on this planet happy exactly as they are. I wasn't. I'd wanted to be extraordinary ever since I was old enough to know I was not. I suppose that's why I liked sleeping so much, because in my dreams I was spectacular. I flew, breathed fire, became invisible. I moved objects with my mind, heard people's thoughts, transported myself from place to place in a blink.

I looked unusual. Not beautiful. At least, no one ever said so. I didn't care. I didn't care that I wasn't pretty like Juliet du Plessi, who sat at my reading table though she never bothered with the books. I didn't need pretty, I had my mind. My thoughts. I could always hide away in my own head. A bit like François, who always knew answers to questions even our teachers didn't know. I usually did too, though, unlike François, I never raised my hand.

In my dreams I sometimes used my magic powers for good, sometimes for evil. It didn't matter, since no one was ever hurt in dreams. Which was sometimes a relief, sometimes a shame. At night, I maimed my stepfather in elaborately inventive ways. Every morning, he remained disappointingly unbruised. Another reason why falling asleep was my favourite moment, waking up my worst.

Scarlet

It was a moment before Scarlet noticed she was being watched; her mother regarding her with a curious, sideways gaze. Scarlet glanced down to see that her fingertips were scorched, as if burnt by the sun. But it was a muted English day, warm enough to sit on the grass and string daisy chains, too cool to discard layers of clothing. Scarlet still wore a cotton vest under her dress, yet the petals of the daisy she held were singed.

'What did you do?'

Scarlet didn't meet her mother's eye. 'Nothing.'

'Then why . . . ?'

'It just happened,' Scarlet protested, sensing that her mother's anger, always quick to ignite, was starting to spark. 'I – I didn't do anything.'

Ruby Thorne's eyes narrowed. 'Just like you didn't flood the bathroom. Or burn my favourite, my only, silk shirt with the iron. Or swap the sugar for salt when I baked cinnamon buns yesterday.'

Scarlet opened her mouth to protest again, then closed it. What could she say? She had done those things. For, although she hadn't turned on the tap, brandished the iron or touched the sugar tin, Scarlet knew that she was still responsible. How, or why, she couldn't explain, but strange things happened around her. And, after seven years of such things, Scarlet had come to accept that this was the case.

'I'm sorry . . .' She fingered the daisy's petals. It upset her mother more when Scarlet claimed not to know how these things happened. It was better simply to confess and take the consequences. 'I, um . . .' She pulled at her hair, slowly twisting it into a bun at the nape of her neck. 'I was playing with a magnifying glass . . . Miss Dixon told us about burning things with—'

Her mother tut-tutted, shaking her head. 'What on earth are they teaching in schools nowadays? It's hardly appropriate education for eight-year-olds. I don't—'

'Seven, Mum,' Scarlet mumbled. 'I'm still seven.'

'Of course you are. Which makes it even worse, don't you think?'

Scarlet shook her head in turn, surprised again that her mother had accepted an illogical lie in place of an improbable truth. Here they were, sitting in the garden without a magnifying glass in sight, yet Ruby Thorne believed this explanation. And she'd believed far greater lies before.

Yet, despite her rational mother, Scarlet was a child who prayed for tornadoes to take her to Oz, who had upturned many a wardrobe seeking Narnia and spoiled several lawns digging holes to Wonderland. Ruby believed in none of these things and didn't like her daughter believing in them either. So, Scarlet had learned to keep quiet about her adventures and, indeed, about everything else.

Ruby stood, brushing from her skirt any insect or blade of grass impertinent enough to cling to the cotton. 'Let's go. Your grandma might need a hand with the afternoon tea rush,' she said. 'All those little old ladies clamouring for their teacakes . . .'

'What's "clamouring"?' Scarlet asked, pushing herself

up from the ground. But her mother was already striding across the lawn, halfway to the house. With a reluctant glance back at the charred daisy, Scarlet ran after her.

Liyana

'I've got something special to show you.'

Liyana looked up to see her mummy sitting on the sofa. On her lap she held a small carved wooden box, painted white. Liyana could tell, from the way Isisa clutched it, that this was a precious box.

'What?' Liyana abandoned her sketchbook – her incomplete scribblings of white trees shedding white leaves – on the coffee table. Her mummy pulled Liyana onto her lap.

'I'll show you,' she said. 'But you mustn't tell anyone.'

Liyana considered this. 'Not even *Nɔɖi?*'

'Auntie,' her mother corrected. 'And no. Especially not Auntie Nya.'

Liyana nodded. She didn't ask Isisa why. She never asked why. She didn't ask why they'd left Ghana one night and come to London and never left. She didn't ask about her father; not his name, his whereabouts or if he was alive or dead.

Upright and still, Liyana waited on her mother's lap. She sensed a secret on her mother's lips. And, since Isisa Chiweshe kept a lot of secrets but seldom, if ever, revealed any, this was quite a coup. Excitement twitched Liyana's fingertips.

'I've been wanting to show you these for a long time, *vinye,*' her mother said. 'But I had to wait until you were old enough.'

Liyana looked up. 'But I'm only seven.'

'Perhaps.'

Liyana frowned.

'Well yes, I suppose that's true,' Isisa conceded, 'if you're measuring in years. But you're already far more advanced than most – remember that.'

Liyana didn't know what to say to this, so she said nothing.

'Let's sit on the floor.' Setting Liyana aside, Isisa slid from the deep sofa, slipped off her snakeskin shoes and tucked herself under the coffee table. Liyana shuffled after her.

'Are we playing a game, *Dadá*?' Liyana asked, as her mother opened the box and, as if she were lifting a newborn babe from its cot, removed a pack of cards.

'Not quite,' Isisa said. She held the cards between her palms for several moments, then began to shuffle. Mumbling an inaudible secret beneath her breath, Isisa slowly drew three cards from the pack and placed them face down on the coffee table, alongside Liyana's drawing. 'And stop calling me that. In England, I'm "Mummy". Remember.'

'Is it snap?' Liyana said hopefully. Her mummy rarely allowed games, unless they had an educational angle.

'No.' Isisa discarded the suggestion with a flick of her wrist. 'These cards are special. If you ask them questions they'll give you answers.'

'About what?'

'About anything.'

'But, how?' Liyana asked. 'If they can't speak, how do they answer?'

'They don't speak like we do,' Isisa said. 'You just have to listen . . . a little differently.'

Liyana tried to make sense of this. But she couldn't; she had to ask. 'How?'

Her mummy leaned forward to turn over the first card. 'With your eyes instead of your ears.'

Liyana leaned forward too, peering at the picture on the card: a man and woman chained together by their ankles.

The woman was elaborately dressed in silk and fur. The man was naked, his skin green, his eyes red, his hair slicked into horns, his feet shaped into hooves. The woman turned away but he gazed at her, as if he wanted something from her that she didn't want to give. As Liyana stared at the card she started to cry.

'What's wrong, child? Why on earth are you crying?'

'No, I don't, I don't want to know,' Liyana mumbled. 'I didn't ask. I don't, I don't . . .'

'Don't want to know what?'

'He's dangerous, *Da*— Mummy,' Liyana said. 'He'll hurt you, he'll—'

'Don't be silly, Ana,' Isisa shushed. 'The Devil's not real, he's only a symbol.'

'What's a "symbol"?' Liyana asked.

Isisa frowned. 'You don't know that?'

'Of course I do,' Liyana said, though she didn't. 'I just, I . . .'

'Good.' Isisa gave her daughter a reassuring squeeze. 'And don't worry, The Devil doesn't mean what you think. Look . . .' She reached around Liyana to turn over the other two cards.

Still sniffling, Liyana eyed them from under her mother's arm.

The Six of Cups: a mermaid mummy with her merman son, who held up a vase of flowers and stars for his mother. This one cheered Liyana a little. But she found The Tower even more disturbing than The Devil. Upon it a grey wind blew, a tall stone tower crumbling beside a naked tree, a man and woman tumbling to their deaths from its windows.

Liyana felt her mummy tense. And, although Isisa said nothing, not then nor later, Liyana knew her fears were being confirmed. And, even when her mummy put the cards away and turned the subject to something else entirely, Liyana felt a disturbance that hung heavy in the air for days after.

Liyana snuck into her mummy's bedroom several times in the following week. She shuffled the pack as best she could, then picked three cards. But no matter how many times she shuffled or how many times she picked, the three cards were the same. Every time. Sometimes they appeared in a different order. But they always told the same story.

Bea

'I don't want to.'

'Oh go on,' her *mamá* said. 'Don't be such a scaredy cat.'

'I'm not,' Bea said. 'I just don't want to.'

With a sigh, Cleo picked up the rock and smashed it onto the snail. Bea flinched at the crack. Her *mamá* lifted the rock to reveal the squashed remnants – the splintered shell, the soft sticky body now oozing across the flagstone.

Bea wanted to say sorry to the snail, since it'd done nothing to deserve such cold-blooded treatment. It'd been sacrificed on the altar of practice, a lesson for greater callousness to come.

'Don't be so squeamish, *niña,*' Cleo said, pulling her long hair from her face. '*Ese es el punto.* We're not doing this for no reason. You need to toughen up. If you can't squash a snail how will you kill a stag, or hunt a man? How will you be ready for what's to come?'

Bea nodded. She knew what was to come – it was Cleo's favourite subject, one she could spin out for hours – and didn't want to talk about it. She wondered what her *abuela,* who liked only to cuddle and feed her, would think of how her granddaughter was spending Sunday afternoon, or what her friends at school would say. When Miss Evans asked the class how they'd spent their weekends, Bea doubted anyone would admit to the murder of molluscs. Why couldn't her *mamá* take her shopping at Selfridges, like Lucy Summer's *mamá*? Or for ballet lessons, like Nicky Challis's mamá did?

Bea couldn't trust her own *mamá* with either activity. Unleashed in department stores, Cleo was liable to be ejected for her exhibitions of public theatre involving randomly chosen couples she aimed to split up by pretending to be having an affair with one or other of the parties. Cleo had to be barred from ballet classes, lest she launch into a loud running commentary on the male gaze and female self-suppression. Bea had learned this to her cost when she'd begged for ballet lessons at age five and, finally consenting, her *mamá* had handed out copies to the other mothers of *How to Self-Hate Your Way to a Size Six*, an ironic self-help book she'd written and had published by a small feminist publisher.

'You think sympathy is a virtue,' her *mamá* said. 'It isn't. In a war, do you think the sympathetic will survive? Or do you think they'll be wiped out by the ruthless, the cold-blooded and the cut-throat. *¿Entiendes?* Animals suffer none of this – nature is "red in tooth and claw" – remember that.'

'*Sí, Mamá,*' Bea said, glancing down at the dead and unctuous snail. 'But why do I have to fight a war? Why can't I just live like other people and—'

Her *mamá*'s falcon-features sharpened and she fixed Bea with furious eyes. 'Because, thank the devil, you're *not* normal,' she said. 'You've been born with skills and strengths unparalleled in mere mortals. And how will you use those unique talents? Will you squander them? Or will you support your father's great mission to purify the human race?' Cleo handed Bea the rock. 'Come now, *niña*, enough stalling.'

Over a decade ago

Bea held the rock above the next victim making a too-slow bid for freedom across the stone-slabbed terrace. She watched it, studying the lengthening trail of slime the retreating snail left in its wake.

'*¡Por amor al . . . demonio!*' Cleo reached out to pinch her daughter's chin between forefinger and thumb. 'We'll stay here all day until you do it, so you may as well get it over with now.'

'Ow.' Bea squirmed. 'Stop, that hurts.'

Her *mamá* squeezed harder. 'I'm doing this for your own good. You don't want to be unprepared when it comes to The Choosing, trust me.'

Bea clenched her teeth, glaring at her *mamá*, thinking how deceptively beautiful she was – half Spanish, half Colombian – so no one would have guessed at the cruelty concealed within.

'I won't be there to protect you, *niña*.' Cleo let her daughter go. 'You'll have to fight for yourself.'

Bea said nothing.

'That's why you need to harden your heart now. If you can't kill a snail, then how are you going to kill a man?'

'I still don't understand why I must kill a man,' Bea said. 'What's the point? If we are Father's daughters and they're his soldiers, why does he make us fight each other? I don't—'

Cleo waved her hand, as if the inevitable slaughter of either daughters or soldiers was of no matter. 'Because he only wants the strongest to join his army, of course. It's a test – like a job interview. *¿Entiendes?*'

Bea nodded. Not because she did, but because she was sick of it all and wished she'd never have to hear anymore about it ever again. She wanted to be an adult, she wanted to make her own choices about her life. So, for all her *mamá*'s scaremongering, Bea looked forward to her eighteenth birthday like a prisoner looked forward to parole.

Leo

'What happens after we die?'

'I don't know,' his mother said. 'Some people think we go to heaven. Others believe in reincarnation, but most don't believe in anything at—'

'What's reincarnation?' Leo asked.

'It's the belief that we lead many lives. That, after we die, we're born again and again as another soul.' His mother smiled. 'In fact, when you were little, soon after you learned to talk, you used to tell me that you'd lived before.'

Leo sat up, wriggling out of his blankets. 'I did?'

'Oh no, young man,' his mother said, tucking him up again. 'I'm not falling for that old trick again. It's time for bed.'

'Please, Mummy,' Leo whined. 'Please tell me, just for five minutes. Please . . .'

His mother sighed. 'All right, but then it's lights out. Okay?'

Leo nodded. 'Promise.'

'Well, when you were about three years old, you used to tell me about your other life as a star.'

Leo frowned. 'A star?'

His mother nodded. 'You were very earnest about the whole thing and gave me plenty of details. You answered every question I asked. I was most impressed.'

'You didn't think I was mad?'

'No, I only thought you were an excellent storyteller. I thought one day you might grow up to be a writer.' His mother bent down to kiss his cheek. 'Sometimes I still do,' she said, dropping her voice to a whisper. 'But don't worry, I won't tell your father.'

4th October – 28 days . . .

2.58 a.m. – Leo

Leo has been a soldier since he fell to Earth. He was found, as an (apparently) human child, wailing and naked under an oak on Hampstead Heath, and taken into care. Being beautiful, bright and white, he was quickly adopted, by Charles Penry-Jones and his wife. So Leo has a double identity, as the privileged progeny of a millionaire businessman, and as a soldier. He plays both parts brilliantly because that is the expectation and he has never questioned it. As Penry-Jones Junior, he is studying Law at Cambridge, expected to graduate with a double First. As a star soldier he's fought and extinguished whichever Grimm girl was next in line. To date, he's never lost a fight.

For nearly six years, since he first entered Everwhere, he's lived these parallel lives and, in that time, he's not questioned the merits or morality of either. Yet he finds himself thinking on his latest target differently – not in the cold, calculating way he should. And, in all this thinking, Leo is starting to wonder whether he'd be fighting this battle, if he'd ever been given the choice.

Leo knows now why he thought he'd seen Goldie before. The familial resemblance is quite striking. Indeed, it's surprising that he hadn't realized it immediately. Goldie is more beautiful, though she doesn't seem to know it. And, naturally, far more powerful, though she doesn't know that either.

These ruminations on Goldie won't stop him from doing his duty when the time comes. He's been attracted to

Grimm girls before and it's never stopped him. Leo likes women well enough, though he's never loved one. Which is fortunate, given what he's required to do to so many of them. Admittedly, he's never felt so strongly drawn to one before, and he wonders why he's so drawn to her – more deeply each day. She's clearly extraordinarily gifted, even for a Grimm, though she doesn't know that either, not yet. But it's more than that. Leo is curious. He wants to *know* her. He wants to hear all her secrets, of which he's sure she has a good many. He wants to listen, he wants to talk. He wants to tell Goldie things he's never spoken aloud. Which is strange. He hasn't felt this way since he was a boy. And he's met a good many beautiful people in the intervening years, in this world and the other, for whom he's felt affection, even admiration, but no more than that. So why should she be any different?

7.32 a.m. – Goldie

I'm on the third floor, cleaning the hotel from top to bottom, reversing my usual habit. Garrick won't care, or even notice, since he's occupied with Cassie in his office.

I've been working at the Fitzwilliam Hotel for nine months and have developed a sort of sixth sense about its guests. I can tell, with a glance into their rooms, what their habits will be: when they'll be in or out, if they'll wake early or stay out late, whether they'll be tidy or filthy. The French family in room 38 are dawn risers, sightseers, stay-out-to-lunchers, six o'clock supperers, then straight to bed.

So, when I knock at their door I know no one will answer. I push my trolley inside and leave the door open behind me. The French family is neat and clean; most morning people are. It doesn't take long to change their sheets, replace their towels, dust, hoover and mop. A thick but delicate scent of honeysuckle hangs in the bathroom and, when I've finished scrubbing, I lift the heavy glass bottle and spray the scent onto my skin: wrists and neck. I pause to stroke the leaves of the white orchid beside the marble sink, murmuring a little poetry into its petals.

Then I get down to my real work. The child's clothes aren't hanging in the wardrobe but packed in careful piles in his suitcase. He doesn't own multiple versions of the same garment but everything he has – from socks to shirts – is of the highest quality. I pass reluctantly over a sumptuous linen jacket: navy blue, lined in silk with the crest of a shield and crown stitched in gold thread on the pocket. Teddy would worship the thing, but it's too risky to take it. Someone would kick up a fuss over the loss of something like that. I must be quick, so I select three pairs of silk socks and one striped cotton shirt. I slip them into my apron, take one last glance around the room, then drag my trolley across the carpet and close the door.

As I'm pushing my trolley along the corridor, I glance up at a clock on the wall: 11.11 a.m. I smile. It sounds silly, but whenever I see this time, morning or night, I feel it's a sign. Of what, I'm not sure. A reassurance, a reminder that there might be more to life. I'm not talking about magic. I don't believe in magic, but I do believe things aren't as clear-cut as most people think. It's 11.11 because that's the minute Teddy was born. Nearly ten years ago. On our living-room floor. His labour lasted less than two hours, his sudden appearance taking Ma by surprise. Later, in the hospital, he looked at me for the first time, his blue eyes – not watery blue like mine but bright, beautiful cornflower blue – unblinking.

When the clock ticks to 11.12 I go on. And, since I'm still not quite paying attention, I push my trolley straight into Leo.

'Oh, sh-shit, I'm sorry,' I say. 'Did I hurt you? I'm—'

He smiles at me as if this is the most amusing notion. 'No,' he says. 'I'm fine.'

'Great. Thank God for that. If you sued me, I – I'd be totally fucked.' I stare at him, slightly horrified. 'Sorry, I didn't mean to be so—'

'Don't worry,' he interrupts before I can make a total prat of myself. 'I won't sue you.'

'Thanks.'

I continue staring at him, though now I've run out of words. And there he is again, still looking slightly out of place, as if he belongs elsewhere. Today he reminds me not of a silver birch but a rare limber pine, uprooted from Utah and replanted in this genteel greenhouse of a hotel.

I gaze at him. He gazes at me. His gaze is odd, different – slow and intimate – as if he knows me all too well. As if he knows what I've been up to, as if he knows everything I've ever done. I hope not. His look unsettles but, strangely, doesn't scare me. It's intimate, yes, but not invasive. Like an offering at an altar. A gift given without asking anything in return.

Finally, I give him a curt nod, drop my eyes and shove my trolley on, its ancient wheels dragging through the thick carpet. It's probably my imagination but I feel his gaze stay on me as I walk away, as close and warm as if he were pressing his palm gently to my back.

08.31 a.m. – Scarlet

'Hello, Walt.'

'Hey, Scarlet.' Walt pauses at the counter. 'Shall I go straight through?'

'Great.' Scarlet nods. 'I've got a batch of brownies cooling in the kitchen – if you fancy a bite before you start?'

The electrician grins. 'That'd be fantastic, thanks.'

When Scarlet returns a few minutes later, with two brownies and a mug of builder's tea, Walt has pulled up a chair to her grandmother's table and is saying something to make Esme smile. Scarlet could kiss him for that, but baked goods, and the small fortune she's paying him – £90 call-out fee, £120 per hour labour, plus £365 for parts + VAT – to fix her dishwasher, will have to do. Naturally, the fucking thing had waited till it was two months out of warranty before breaking.

The bell above the door rings. Standing behind the counter, Scarlet glances up to greet the first customer of the day, but the words remain unsaid, hanging helplessly in her open mouth. She watches the man walk towards her – holding himself so straight and still that he seems to glide across the floorboards. His eyes are a startling blue, his hair pitch black, falling in curls over his ears. When he extends his hand, Scarlet thinks she hears Esme gasp. Or perhaps it's her.

'I take it you're the owner of this fine establishment?' His voice is deep, soft.

Scarlet manages a small nod. She'd thought Walt was all right, though not the type she'd look twice at in passing. For this man, women must stop in the street and stare. She takes his outstretched hand.

'I'm Eli,' he says. 'Ezekiel Wolfe. My friends call me Eli.'

'Scarlet,' she says, having momentarily misplaced her surname.

'A pleasure to meet you, Scarlet.'

He smiles that brilliant smile again and Scarlet feels she's being bewitched, drawn in. Like those suicidally tenacious moths that bump their bodies against bright lights until they die.

As Ezekiel Wolfe begins to extricate his hand from

hers, Scarlet glances down to see sparks at her fingertips. Real sparks, as from a lighter before it catches a flame. *Impossible.* She blinks and the sparks are gone.

'I'm making a courtesy call,' Eli says. 'My company is opening a new unit down the street.'

'Oh?' Scarlet says, distracted, thinking she must have imagined it.

He nods, hesitating for a second or two. 'It's a branch of Starbucks.'

Scarlet drops his hand.

8.57 a.m. – Liyana

When Liyana sinks into a bathtub of hot, perfumed water, she feels something approaching happiness. If only for an hour. It doesn't begin to touch the joy of the swimming pool, but then it doesn't evoke the same sorrow. The wet heat of the bath soaks up the loneliness that has permeated her skin since her mother died. By rights, she shouldn't feel so lonely, having a girlfriend, good friends, her Aunt Nya. And yet, when her mother died Liyana felt she lost a lot more than her only parent. It was as if Isisa Chiweshe, reluctant to let go, had snatched away an essential piece of her daughter and taken it with her into the afterlife; leaving Liyana eternally trying to find this missing piece. The mission being all the harder because she doesn't know what she's looking for.

Liyana slides under the water, watching bubbles of breath pop on the surface.

A knock on the door. A muffled voice. 'May I come in?'

Liyana wraps fingers around the cool porcelain and pulls herself reluctantly from the warm water. Droplets glisten on her hair, three inches of afro springing free into the air.

4th October – 28 days . . .

'Come in.'

The bathroom door creaks open and Aunt Nyasha shuffles across the heated marble floor, still in slippers and silk dressing gown, to perch on the edge of the loo. Her aunt who – with her large eyes, full lips and hair twisted into an intricate maze of cornrows, like an elaborate tattoo etched into her scalp – is undeniably radiant, is this morning dulled.

'What's up?' Liyana asks, impatient to submerge herself again.

Nyasha studies her slippered feet. 'There's something . . .'

'Yes?'

'Well, *vinye*' – Nyasha fiddles with the cap on Liyana's shampoo bottle – 'I'm in . . . well . . . a bit of a bind.'

Liyana suppresses a sigh, longing for silence and stillness again. 'Can't it wait till breakfast? I won't be long.'

Nyasha nods but doesn't move.

'All right then.' Liyana sinks down under the water, her knees and nipples still exposed to the chill air.

Her aunt knocks the bottle off the edge of the bath. It rolls behind the loo.

Liyana rises. 'Okay, what's going on?'

'I'm . . . financially, we're . . .'

'Oh, spit it out.'

Her aunt takes a deep breath. 'We're broke.'

Liyana frowns. 'An interesting perspective – I think most people would argue we're indecently rich.'

Nyasha gets down on her hands and knees, searching for the shampoo bottle.

'Nya?'

Her aunt looks up, bottle in hand.

'What exactly do you mean by broke?'

'It means we don't have any money.'

Liyana narrows her eyes. 'Yes, I know what it means. I just don't know why you're saying it.'

Nyasha sits back down on the loo, returning the bottle to the rim of the bath. 'I'm saying it because my accountant called, and it seems to be true.'

'What? No, that can't . . .' Liyana longs to submerge herself again, to hide beneath the still quiet of the water. 'But how does that mean . . . ? We can't be – this house alone must be worth a fortune.'

'Yes, it is.' Nyasha circles a slippered foot. 'Which is why I, um, remortgaged it a while ago.'

'You what? Why?'

'Well, it seems that we . . . Well, we've been . . . living a little beyond our means.'

'Oh?' Liyana is tempted to object to her aunt's use of the plural, but decides to let it go. 'Go on.'

Her aunt doesn't look up. 'We're, um, in a bit of debt.'

'How much?'

Her aunt, always so sculpted, so poised – a rock smoothed into shape by the ocean over a thousand years – looks as if she's suddenly crumbling. She mumbles.

'Nya?'

Finally, Nyasha meets Liyana's eye. 'Once we sell the house . . . After that, it'll be a hair under, um . . . six hundred and eighty-six thousand pounds, or thereabouts.'

Liyana sits up so fast that the bathroom floor is sluiced with bathwater. She looks at her aunt, unable to respond.

'I'm sorry, *vinye*.' Nyasha studies her feet again. 'I . . . I went a little off the rails when he who shall not be named left me for that . . . infant. I might have developed, well, it seems I sort of . . .'

'What? Spit it out!'

Nya coughs. 'Well, I suppose I channelled my feelings, suppressed my feelings with a bit of' – she tightens her dressing gown – 'a gambling habit.' A flush of shame colours her cheeks.

'No, *Nɔḍi*. Seriously?'

'I thought I could fix it, I didn't want to worry you. I tried, but I . . .' Her aunt's eyes fill. 'I never should have signed that pre-nup. It was monumentally naive of me. But I thought, I thought that this time . . .'

When Liyana was a child she'd felt fragile as cracked glass, ready to shatter at a touch. The stoical solidity of her aunt, who'd taken her under her wing, hadn't allowed it. Now Liyana's the adult and her aunt the child. She wants to reach out and wipe Nya's tears but she also wants to slap her. And then she realizes something else.

'But, but I'm starting at the Slade . . .' Liyana feels as if she's slipping under water. 'Term starts soon – less than three weeks. I, I . . .'

Studying at the Slade, arguably the best art school in England, has been all Liyana's wanted since she was fourteen, since that torn ligament ripped away her Olympic dream.

Nyasha gives a barely perceptible nod. 'I know, *vinye,* I know. It's okay, we'll postpone . . . I'll write to them, I'll explain. I'm sure they'll let you take a gap year, while we get the funding, you can start next October.'

Liyana stares at her aunt, incredulous. 'I don't want to wait another year. I'm ready, I've got so much to – I need to go now.'

'I know, I know,' her aunt says, stricken. 'But the fees, we can't possibly—'

'And what if it's not okay?' Liyana starts to shiver; the water suddenly icy. 'What if they won't defer my place? What then?'

'No, they will. Of course they will,' Nya says. 'It's all right. It's going to be all right, Ana. I've got an idea, I just—'

'What?' Liyana snaps. 'You're going to get a job?'

'Well . . .' her aunt nibbles the edge of her thumbnail.

'Yes, I'm certainly looking into that, but also I was thinking . . .'

'What?'

'Well . . . marriage.'

Liyana lets out a blurt of laughter, casting ripples across the water, warmer now. 'You're going to get married *again*?'

'*Nye me nya o*,' her aunt mumbles. '*Ao* . . .'

'English,' Liyana says. 'You know—'

'Well, no. Not exactly . . .' Nya loses the word in the folds of her dressing gown. 'I was, um, thinking perhaps it could be you.'

Liyana stares at her aunt. 'What?'

'Well . . .'

'Are you fucking serious?'

'Wait, let me—'

'I've got to get out.' Liyana stands, sending waves over the bath's rim, splashing her aunt's feet. 'The water's freezing.'

Pulling her towel from the radiator, Liyana strides towards the door. In her wake, silence swells in the room like a sudden flood.

6.32 p.m. – Bea

'Do you believe in free will?'

Bea looks up from *Logic and Knowledge* to see a student sitting across the table gazing at her. He is rotund, bearded and has hope in his eyes.

'No talking,' she mouths, then returns to her book.

The student coughs. Bea ignores him and focuses on Russell. He coughs again.

'What?' Bea hisses.

'Do you—?'

'No, I don't believe in free will,' Bea snaps, eliciting

pointed looks from several other students sitting along the same long table. 'Or, yes I do. Which one do you want to hear?'

'The first,' he says, giving a quick tug of his beard. 'I thought perhaps . . . if you believed in predeterminism you might . . .'

'Might what?'

He drops his voice to a whisper. 'Might go for a coffee with me after you've finished your date with Russell?'

Bea frowns at him, thrown. The frown shifts to a scowl once she realizes what he means. 'That is, without a doubt, the most pretentiously ridiculous pick-up line I've ever been subjected to,' she says. 'And no, I don't believe in fate. So, no.'

He looks crestfallen, then smiles. 'Well I do. So, I hope our paths will cross again.'

Bea returns the smile, the one in her lexicon reserved for lecherous creeps. 'Hold your breath on that hope,' she hisses. 'And we'll see what fate has in store for you then.'

Over a decade ago

Everwhere

You step out of a glade, where stones give way to a thick carpet of moss that sinks pleasantly under your feet. You go on and the moss springs back. You stop walking to glance up at the trees flanking this hidden space, so closely pressed together that their boughs entwine into a canopy of branches and leaves so dense that the sky is no longer visible. And yet, as you squint into the darkness, all at once it becomes brighter: the shadows retreat, the sounds fall silent, the air stills. Gradually, the fog rolls back and the mists lift. The veins of the leaves glimmer silver in the moonlight.

You notice you feel lighter too. You begin to realize that each of your senses is sharper. You see the imprint of the shadows as they flit away, you sniff the ebbing scent of bonfire smoke, burning peat and kindling, you hear the call of a bird in the distance and you know, without knowing how, that it's a raven. The beat of its wings disturbs the air as it takes flight. You reach out to touch the nearest tree and realize that your fingertips are tracing the grooves of the bark before they've even been pressed to the trunk. You taste the dew on your tongue, though you've not opened your mouth: wet earth and salt.

You feel clear. You find that you know answers to questions you've been wondering about for weeks, solutions to problems that have been plaguing you for months. You feel calm. Well-stoked anxieties crumble and dissolve to dust. You feel content. Violent wounds soften and fade, leaving no scars inside or out. You stand and breathe the moonlit air, slowly and steadily, until you no longer know what is breath and what is air. Until you no longer feel where you end and the forest begins.

Goldie

I always had vivid dreams and always remembered them when I woke. Sometimes they told me things, things that were going to happen. Sometimes, I went somewhere special. That night, the first time, I hadn't been able to sleep. I'd pressed my head under the pillow, trying not to hear Ma in the other room arguing. They argued about silly things. Usually money. Ma said he should earn more so we could get out of this flat, he said she should stop nagging and, if she cared so much about moving, ought to get a job herself. She'd say she couldn't, because of her panic attacks. They fought about babies. She wanted one, he didn't. Sometimes the fights ended in silence, sometimes in sex. I preferred the silence.

Before it happened, I peered out from under my pillow up at the clock, the luminous hands of the White Rabbit ticking across the numbers. It was very late, or very early – nearly half past three. I worried about falling asleep at my desk in school the next day, since Miss Drummond hated me to do that. She'd tell me I was 'wasting my potential'. I told her I was only seven. She told me I was 'nearly eight and ought to have higher aspirations'. I'd distract her by asking for definitions of her favourite words, like 'onomatopoeia'. That always worked. Miss Drummond loved the sound of her own voice; you needed only to ask her to explain or enunciate something and you were free and clear.

Anyway, that was the last I remember of being in bed or, rather, on the sofa where I slept. Then I was in a place full of trees and rocks and everything was muted white, a bit like Christmas but with leaves falling instead of snow. It was dark, except the moon was bright enough for me to see where I was walking and, strangely, though I'd never been to this place before, I knew where I was going. To meet my sisters. Which was stranger, since I didn't have any sisters. My stepfather was winning that fight.

I walked a path of stones scattered with white leaves, still falling all around me, I clambered over slippery rocks and fallen trees, their trunks wider than I was tall. Sometimes clouds covered the moon and the air was mist and I couldn't see so well. I hurt my knee and cut my hand but I didn't care. I felt the urge to fly, since I could often fly in my dreams.

For a while the path disappeared, leaving no signs of the direction to take, but I wasn't scared and didn't have any doubt about which way to go. I knew whether or not to cross a stream, I knew to take a left path or a right without thinking. It felt nice, to know. In my non-dream life I wasn't like this. I usually felt lost, considering choices for hours and even then, after finally deciding on something, I still wondered about it, worrying that I'd made the wrong choice. Here I didn't think, I simply followed wherever I took myself. Also, it was a relief to be alone, free from Ma and her fears for me.

Then I wasn't alone anymore. I slipped down over another rock, covered in moss, and fell into a clearing where the ground was entirely covered in ivy. It knitted itself a carpet of white-veined leaves and twisted up the trunks of four gigantic willow trees. Three girls were playing there, running and laughing and calling to each other. They stopped when they saw me. For a second I was scared again, as if I were back in the playground at school. Then the tallest one, with red hair that curled down her back, smiled and beckoned me. The other two – one with dark skin and a puff of dark dandelion hair, the other delicate as a bird with long brown hair – waved.

My sister, my sisters.

I stepped forward to meet them.

Scarlet

'What's your name?'

'Goldie.'

'I'm Scarlet,' she said. Of the three girls, she seemed to be the leader. 'This is Liyana—'

'Liyana Miriro Chiweshe,' the girl with the dandelion hair interjected, holding out her hand.

I stared at her hand, unsure of what to do, then took it. She shook for us both, then let me go.

'You can call me Ana,' she said, adding as an afterthought, 'if you like.'

I nodded. 'Okay.'

'—and Bea,' Scarlet said, nodding at the bird-girl, who doesn't offer her hand. 'We're playing "It". Want to join?'

I nodded again but didn't say that, although I knew the rules, I'd never played before. It wasn't a game that was possible without friends, unless you were good at conjuring imaginary ones, which I was. And good at not caring what other kids thought, which I wasn't.

'Okay,' Scarlet said. 'You can start. Count to ten to give us a chance – and the trees are safe, all right?'

I nodded a third time.

'Watch out for her.' Scarlet looked at Bea. 'She'll fool you into catching her – she always wants to be "It".'

'All right,' I said, as Bea laughed. But, if she wanted to be 'It', I'd happily let her. I'd rather stand under one of the willow trees and watch.

Scarlet gave the signal and my sisters flew off, shrieks of delight streaming like ribbons behind them. Liyana darted to the nearest tree and clung on while Scarlet raced around the edge.

'Run, run as fast as you can,' Bea sang, skipping around me in ever-decreasing circles. 'You can't catch me, I'm the gingerbread man!'

I stepped forward, reaching out to grab the edge of her sleeve before she pulled away, laughing.

'I'm "It",' Bea shouted. 'I am, I am!'

I turned and dashed towards a tree. Bea, clearly keen to hold on to her elevated position, let me go.

'Oh, Goldie,' Scarlet said, slowing down to a stop. 'What did I tell you? She'll never catch any of us now.'

Bea marched up and down, echoing her refrain. Despite her irritation, Scarlet smiled. 'You're so weird,' she said to her sister. 'I don't get you at all.'

Bea grinned. 'That's because I'm an enigma.'

'Stop showing off with your fancy words,' Scarlet said, her own tainted with both annoyance and affection. 'You don't even know what it means.'

Ignoring Scarlet, Bea looked at me. 'It's a shame,' she said, 'that you won't remember any of this in the morning.'

Liyana

Liyana sat at the end of her bed, the stolen cards in her lap. She'd been having strange dreams, the particulars of which she couldn't quite remember when she woke, though she tried hard, squeezing her eyes shut, struggling to catch sight of the evaporating images. But, though Liyana couldn't recall what she'd seen or heard, still the sense of the dream lingered, tapping at the edges of her thoughts, trying to catch her attention. She hoped the cards might help, might bring the images back, might turn them into a story. Though not like the story she'd seen before.

Liyana shuffled the cards. Again. And again. And once more for luck. As they sliced into each other, shifting from her right hand to her left, one snapped out of the pack and dropped to the floor.

Liyana slid down from the bed to pick it up. The Four of Cups. She stared at the picture: four women standing in a circle, each holding a star-engraved goblet aloft in a toast. An image tugged at the edges: moonlight on white leaves. Laughter. Girls calling her name.

Folding her legs, Liyana knelt on the bed and set the Four of Cups on the duvet in front of her. She picked another card. The Magician. A woman in a cloak held a shining wand that illuminated the sky. Birds flew beside her, an owl hovered above her, fairies and sprites danced at her feet.

Liyana set this card beside the first and picked a third. The Moon. A purple-haired wolf standing at a river's edge howled up at a fat yellow moon. Towering white trees flanked the river, their trunks encircled by a pair of two-headed snakes.

Liyana stared at the cards. All at once, the dream returned.

Bea

'Who wants to hear a story?'

We all looked up. I did, but I wouldn't say so. I knew who would.

'I do,' Liyana said.

Bea smiled. She looked to Scarlet and me. 'You'll want to listen to this too. You might learn something.'

Scarlet turned her attention from the leaves she was

setting alight – none of my sisters seemed alarmed by that, so I pretended I wasn't either – and looked at Bea.

'Are you all sitting comfortably?' Bea said, as if she were our ma and we her babes. 'Then I'll begin . . .'

Liyana clapped. Scarlet smiled. I did nothing.

'In the time before time,' Bea said, 'before the existence of Everwhere or Earth, there was nothing and nowhere, only the light and its shadow.' She waited, a self-satisfied pause. 'Then, at last, with the spark of life came the creation of humanity. Such was the explosive force of this creation that the light and its shadow were split apart and, once separated for long enough to forget it was ever whole, one half became the personification of good and the other half of evil.

'When this happened, the forces of good and evil fought a battle to see who'd win influence over humanity. But since both sides were always perfectly matched no victor ever emerged. Eventually, the powers that be invented the game of chess to decide the fate of humankind, since this method would be both less bloody and over far quicker. However, it didn't help, since every game still ended in a stalemate.

'Eventually it was decided, by an extremely lengthy and infinitely tedious board meeting, that the influence over humanity would be shared; the forces of good would influence their hearts, the forces of evil would influence their minds. Angels and demons were scattered throughout Earth and Everwhere to exert their influence by these means.

'So, humanity was left with a choice: to follow their hearts or their heads. But, once the agreement was made, it soon became clear that humans found it far easier to listen to their heads than their hearts, thus ensuring the demonic influence was far stronger than the angelic. It was widely believed, at least among the angels, that the demons had cheated. However, since they could never prove how, and since the terms of the deal, being sealed by both spirit and soul, were irreversible, there was nothing to be done.

'Thus, the whole of humanity was subjected to a terrible fate, fighting to feel the influence of good, to know fulfilment, contentment and joy, while all too often being drawn into fear, sorrow and despair. Being cursed with perpetual free will, humans struggled on, often being thrown back and forth between one and the other a dozen times a day. Many descended into madness.'

Another self-satisfied pause.

'Fortunately, those with pure Grimm blood running in their veins must only endure free will for the first eighteen years of their lives. Then they can choose between good and evil. Each comes with its own consequences, but both are blessed by the fact of only having to be chosen once.'

Bea grinned.

'So, know your head and know your heart, sisters. Remember what lies behind you, imagine what lies ahead of you, and make your choice carefully.'

Unable to hold my tongue, I fixed her with a sideways glance. 'How do you know all that?'

Bea shrugged, but I could tell she was pleased to have incited my curiosity. 'My *mamá* told me,' she said. 'She tells me everything.'

'Is it true?' Liyana asked.

Bea smiled. 'Every word.'

Leo

As a star Leo had never felt lonely, as a child he rarely felt anything else. He longed for companionship, but without siblings, with only a frequently distracted mother and a distant father, Leo relied solely on imaginary friends. Sometimes he imagined an impish boy he could make mischief with, a boy to replace the brother he'd never have. Sometimes he imagined a girl, one he pictured with blue eyes, blonde curls and a delirious disregard for authority, like a character in a book he'd once read about some bears. Leo himself couldn't afford to disregard authority, since Charles Penry-Jones was a man who must always be obeyed. Leo hoped that one day he'd have the courage to flout his father's rules, but he knew that'd be much easier and less terrifying with an ally at his side.

5th October – 27 days . . .

6.28 a.m. – Goldie

Teddy is delighted by his new acquisitions. He spins around the living-room carpet – stepping on the spot I never touch, because he doesn't know better – bubbling over with joy. If the French family is still there tomorrow I'll go back for the linen jacket. I shouldn't, since it's infinitely riskier stealing twice from the same person. But the desire to see Teddy grinning like this again outweighs my more rational sensibilities.

'Are you hungry, Ted? We've got herb-stuffed poussin, polenta and baby carrots for breakfast.'

Every day we eat whatever they're serving at the hotel, regardless. I was sort of seeing Kaz, the sous chef, for a few weeks when I started and whenever I finished a shift he'd give me two portions of something gourmet in plastic tubs. I broke it off when I realized I was flirting to get fed. But Kaz still gives me leftovers whenever he can.

Teddy stops spinning. 'Can I have breakfast in my new shirt?'

'If you're careful.' I step into the kitchen to decant the refrigerated plastic tubs onto plates. I stop a moment to stroke the leaves of my bonsai tree, which seems to give a little shiver of appreciation as I pass. Its trunk looks a little thicker than usual, like Ma's ankles when she was weighed down by Teddy, so I know it'll flower soon – filling our flat with a scent as strong and sweet as burnt caramel. We have a small wooden table pushed up against the wall alongside Teddy's bed (I still sleep on the sofa) where we eat. It's stupid, given our square footage situation, that we don't use our parents' room, but neither of us has set foot inside since Ma died.

'It's yummy, thanks.' Teddy scoops up a forkful of polenta, squinting at the aftertaste of soy sauce as he swallows. But he never complains, never asks for burgers and French fries, never says I don't spend enough time at home, that he has to look after himself too much. When I return in the evening, I find him finishing homework or housework, or sitting at the table, drawing. Or, if I'm on a late shift, already snoring.

I reward him as best I can. Whenever kids stay at the hotel they leave with fewer crayons and notebooks than they brought. I've created quite an eclectic collection during the past nine months. I usually take only as much as might be lost by natural means – down the backs of sofas, under restaurant tables, wedged between car seats – so neither kids nor parents notice anything amiss. Admittedly, last week I took an entire tin of oil pastels: all the colours of the rainbow and every hue in between. Teddy sleeps with them under his pillow. And he draws such exquisite pictures. The flat is wallpapered with Teddy's characters wearing flamboyant costumes of his own design.

'G-G . . . ?' He puts down his fork.

I sense a request coming. I swallow. 'Yes?'

'You know it's your birthday soon . . .'

'Yes?'

'There's a school trip to London that weekend.' He grins again, forgetting his fear over telling me. 'My class is going to the theatre to see the real Macbeth.'

'Oh?' We've been practising that play for weeks, especially Act One, Scene One, since Teddy is the Second Witch in the school production. I smile. '*When do we meet again? In rain—*'

'No, no, no.' Teddy shakes his head so vigorously his

mop of blond hair is flung from side to side. 'When *shall* we *three* meet again? In thunder, lightning or in rain?'

'Yeah, right,' I say. 'It was on the tip of my tongue.'

Teddy regards me, as if this is the biggest lie he's ever heard. Then he takes a deep breath, serious again. 'We're visiting Buckingham Palace too. And staying the night, in a hotel.'

'The night?' My smile falls. 'Is that absolutely—'

'But I won't go,' Teddy cuts me off. 'If you don't want. I can stay here and celebrate with you and—'

I swallow a forkful of polenta. It's sticky and sharp. 'No, I . . . of course you must go. I'll . . . I'll probably be working anyway.' He looks so pleased that I wish I didn't have to ask. 'So, um, how much will it cost?'

Teddy pokes at his carrots. 'Three hundred and forty-five pounds.'

I hold my breath.

He looks up again. 'I need to give it to Miss McNamara on Friday.'

'That's fine,' I say, quickly. 'Totally fine. No problem at all.'

'Thanks, G-G.' Teddy grins again, then stuffs three carrots into his mouth. 'You're the best.'

I nod, managing a smile.

Five days to find £345. Fuck.

10.28 a.m. – Liyana

Liyana had rejected her aunt's ludicrous idea, had dismissed it out of hand. But, though Nya hasn't mentioned it again, Liyana hasn't been able to focus on much else. The preoccupation fractures her thoughts – she's forgotten to call Kumiko, hasn't been able to draw. Although, now that her admission to art school hangs in the balance, does that matter anymore?

Liyana finds solace only in the bath. She dearly wants to return to the swimming pool but won't allow herself that. Twice in a single week is far too risky, the longing it'd invoke would be too great. It's already gnawing at her belly and bones.

Liyana sinks under the water, fully wrapped in her safety blanket. She'll soak until her skin is pruned and her senses numb. She cannot countenance what Nya asks. And yet, her aunt has done so much for her. She financed, albeit with her second husband's fortune, their fleeing from Ghana when Liyana was a baby. And paid for everything after that. The night her mother died, Liyana crept into her aunt's bed. They slept, or at least lay, together every night until Liyana was ready to move to her new bedroom in her new terraced home on Barnsbury Square, Islington.

Nya attended every swimming competition, every class, every school play, every concert. She dropped Liyana at school and picked her up. She comforted Liyana every time kids at school threw insults or dropped thinly veiled insinuations, or outright told her to go back to Africa, though they probably couldn't find Ghana on a map. She was there when Liyana lost her first tooth and, five years later, when she ripped that ligament in her left knee, dropping Liyana out of the Olympic race and into a depression for nearly a year. Aunt Nya sat by her bedside that summer, bringing food, brushing hair, reading fairy tales . . . She'd cast a lifebelt into the sea of despair and gradually pulled her niece back to shore. Nya bought Liyana her first comic book, encouraged her to start telling her own stories, to write and draw. Without Nya there would be no Slade in the first place. Given all this, and so much more, Liyana wonders if she can refuse her aunt this request. Or anything at all, no matter how unreasonable it might be.

*

Liyana wipes her hands on a towel and reaches for her phone. She'd emailed her Admissions Tutor at the Slade the same morning Nya revealed the devastating state of their finances. She's been waiting twenty-four hours and fifty-seven minutes for an answer. But, with every hour that passes, a towering wave of anguish rises up behind her. When she's out of the bath, she'll ask the Tarot again. It's not given her any reason to hope yet, but that won't stop her trying. Liyana hasn't yet asked the cards whether or not she should do what her aunt is asking. She's too afraid of the answer.

11.38 a.m. – Scarlet

This morning it's not only for financial reasons that Scarlet wishes the café were busier. When she's frothing milk, slicing cakes or extracting globules of baby food from the floorboards, Scarlet forgets Mr Wolfe. But this morning she has nothing more than a clutch of stingy students to entertain her, so Scarlet must find other sources of distraction. Today, Francisco, the cappuccino machine. Scarlet bought him, at some significant expense, on her sixteenth birthday after her grandmother had stapled a cheque for three thousand pounds into a glittery card. At the time, Scarlet was overjoyed. Now she sees it as a signpost on the road to Esme's decline, a slip of mind and pen.

Scarlet's halfway through cleaning when the door opens and Mr Wolfe, looking self-satisfied and smug, glides into the café. The knife Scarlet's using to dig out congealed coffee beans slips, scratching Francisco's fine stainless steel surface.

'Shit.' Scarlet rubs at the scratch, patting him. 'Sorry, Frannie.'

'Are you talking to your cappuccino machine?' Ezekiel asks, as he reaches her. 'Or did you forget my name?'

Scarlet ignores him.

Ezekiel pats the leather bag hanging from his shoulder. 'I call my briefcase Fred. He has a surname too, but I keep forgetting it.'

Scarlet lowers the knife she'd been brandishing like a sword. 'You're a strange man.'

'Thank you.'

'It wasn't a compliment.'

He smiles. 'Oh, but strange is far better than boring. It denotes a depth of character, a man of style and taste.'

'It does not.'

His smile deepens. 'Oh, but it does. If you don't think so, perhaps you ought to consult a dictionary. I'm quoting from the Oxford English. Inferior volumes may have misinformed you.'

Scarlet folds her arms. 'What do you want?'

'Is that how you greet all your illustrious customers?' He nods at the smattering of students, all hunched over laptops. 'Is that why you have so few?'

'Paying customers are treated with the utmost respect.' Scarlet sets down the knife. 'You, on the other hand, aren't here for a slice of cake. Am I right?'

'Yes, I suppose you are,' Ezekiel says, lifting his briefcase onto the counter. 'I've brought you an offer.'

Scarlet narrows her eyes. 'For what?'

'For your café.' Ezekiel clicks his briefcase open and extracts a thick folder. 'I've looked into your takings – you're struggling. We're offering to take over the lease and give you a rather generous signing bonus into the bargain.'

Scarlet feels heat rising in her hands, as if she was holding them too close to a fire. She clenches them into fists at her sides. She wants to snatch up the knife and scar his beautiful face. Arrogant prick.

'Are you willing to—?'

He's stopped short by a falling antique art deco lamp,

re-affixed to the ceiling by Walt only yesterday, that comes away with clumps of plaster, striking Ezekiel's head. He stumbles back as the lamp shatters on the floor in an explosion of colour. The smattering of students all glance up from their laptops, then, sensing themselves in no immediate danger, return to their screens.

'What the hell was that?' Ezekiel staggers to the counter, gripping the edge. He grabs a napkin and presses it to his forehead. 'Shit. It fucking hurts. Shit.'

Scarlet stares at him, speechless. A shard of glass has sliced Ezekiel's hairline. Blood runs down his face. He'll need stitches. *A scar on his beautiful face.* Scarlet's thoughts race. No, that's impossible. But then what the hell is happening? As Ezekiel continues to swear and moan, Scarlet feels her hands getting hotter.

She glances down to see sparks firing from her fingertips again.

6.38 p.m. – Bea

Bea stares at her hands splayed across the pages of Russell's *The Analysis of Mind,* trying to focus but thinking instead about her mother, about the line between madness and sanity, between fantasy and reality. Although Bea would extract her own toenails before admitting any weakness, she can't deny a morbid terror of madness, of inheriting maternal DNA. Beneath Bea's fingers, the letters blur into black lines and curls, words she knows so well shifting into hieroglyphics.

The ink on the page begins to pool under her palms, soaking into her hands, staining her skin. Bea watches as the ink seeps slowly into her veins, until they're running black instead of milky blue.

Bea lifts her left hand, bringing it to her face. *Surely not.*

She squeezes her eyes shut, then opens one eye and peers out. But her veins still pulse dark, her skin tattooed. Panic rises, hot and clammy. She's got to get out of here. She starts to stand but, as she's about to abandon her desk and flee to the nearest lavatory, fear gradually subsides into calm. And Bea begins to feel herself slipping seamlessly into this new ink-veined skin, until she's in a perfect alignment of body and soul. As if Judas had reached up from Hell to whisper in her ear: *Don't fear. This is who you are, who you've always been.*

Bea pushes her chair from the desk and stands. Only a scattering of students sit at their desks, all with heads bowed over their books. Not that she'd now care if they were staring at her, smirking and jeering.

Bea grins. How wonderful not to give a damn what strangers might think. How spectacularly liberating.

Bea steps up onto her chair, one booted foot then the other. She looks around. She's not high enough. So she steps onto her desk. Now Bea can survey her kingdom without impediment. She turns a slow circle to admire every bookcase, every book, every desk, every occupant. From here she can see as far as the librarian's desk, to the librarian bent over his computer, frowning at the screen.

How splendid it is to be so elevated, to see what others cannot, to feel like the lord of all you survey, in a unity of spirit and stature. Bea has always felt her small size an impairment, offering an inferior vantage point. She hates how often she must look up at people, how easily she gets shoved about in a crowd. Like a fucking child. Now she feels none of that. She is tall, powerful, deadly.

Bea wakes in a sweat. She shakes her head, looks to her hands: she's a wren again, not a raven. Bea blinks several times, pressing out the images, distancing herself from the dream. She's never fallen asleep over a book before. Bea thinks of her *mamá*. And, though she can hardly countenance it, the possibility that she too might be going mad stains her thoughts like the imaginary ink that stained her hands. This is Bea's greatest fear – to lose her mind – far greater than death.

Still shaking, Bea glances about for her chubby stalker, suddenly wanting the reassurance of his bearded face. But she's alone in the library now, not another student in sight.

11.45 p.m. – Leo

For every Grimm he's killed, Leo has a scar. For every girl, a crescent moon. For every mother, a star. Spread across his shoulder blades and along his spine is a constellation, a galaxy of scars. Most of the time he forgets, but lately he finds himself thinking about these marks more often. Because he's also thinking about her.

If, as he's started imagining, they were to find themselves in close and unveiled proximity, how would he explain these scars? And she would ask. Every woman he's been with has. Unless sufficient amounts of alcohol ensure that a good many things go unremarked upon. But Leo suspects Goldie isn't the type for drunken one-night stands. He can't be certain, but he'd be surprised. There seems a curious mixture of light and dark in her, a strange alchemical balance of innocence and experience.

Regarding the scars, he would lie, naturally. Since he cannot say: 'Oh, yes, they're stamped upon my skin on the battlefield, engraved by the last breath of my latest kill. *Who do I kill?* Why, your sisters, mothers, aunts, cousins . . . Some I hunt for sport, the ones who aren't pure-blooded, to keep me sharp, to ready myself for those I have to fight on the night they turn eighteen. *Will I kill you?* Why, yes, if I can. I'm afraid I'll have no choice, my dear.'

A conversation-stopper, if ever there was one.

By rights, he shouldn't be able to lie to her. By rights, she should be able to tell. Her powers are far above and beyond such simple psychic abilities. And yet, she has no idea. These powers remain untapped, untouched, potential.

And, even though she's the enemy, Leo still feels a twitch of sorrow at Goldie's ignorance. She's like a firework never lit, a flower that never blooms, a baby that's never born. He feels the desire to tell her, to teach her, to be the one to unlock her potential, the first to see the firework ignite, the flower bloom, the baby born. Despite himself, Leo wants to say: *'You're a Grimm unparalleled, the most powerful I've ever seen. You could be phenomenal, invincible, if only you knew.'*

Of course, he won't.

Such a thing would be stupid. Such a thing would be suicide.

11.59 p.m. – Goldie

I lie on the sofa, staring up at the cracked ceiling with its patches of damp, listening to Teddy's snores drifting across the room. Soon he's going to need more than I'll be able to provide. As he gets older the expenses will grow. Three hundred and forty-five quid will seem like nothing. How much longer will we be able to share a single room? Soon he'll want one of his own. He won't ask, but he'll need it all the same, especially when he starts doing teenage-boy-type things.

I'm going to need a bigger, better plan. A heist. A big score. I start to ponder banks, and then I wonder how much Garrick keeps in the hotel safe.

6th October – 26 days . . .

7.08 a.m. – Goldie

On my way to the staff room, I peek into the restaurant. There, eating a full English breakfast of the finest quality, is the French family. The mother pokes at the black pudding with distaste but the father and son gobble it up. This is their last morning, their bags will be packed upstairs. I can't explain how I know this. It's an air they have – an air of preparation, expectation – as if their minds have left ahead of their bodies and they're already halfway to France. Which means I must hustle.

Ten minutes later I'm on the third floor, pushing open the door to room 38. And, sure enough, it has that empty, vacated feel before I even step inside. Their bags are lined up in a neat row against the king-sized bed: one large, one medium, one small. I plug in the hoover and pull out the cord. I don't switch it on, because the noise would mask anyone returning to the room. Instead, I bite my feather duster between my teeth. Now, if I'm caught in the act of stealing I can pretend I'm in the act of cleaning. It's happened before and it's always worked.

I go for the rucksack next to the gilded mirror first, the sort of bag people keep with them while travelling, containing essentials such as passports, tickets, itineraries and cash. But here's the tricky part. If I move the bag into the bathroom, say, I get privacy to search it. But, if anyone returns to the room and finds me, I have no defence, no story. I'm caught red-handed. But, if I leave the bag where it is, then I'm in full view of the open door. And there's no plausible excuse there. However, it's quicker and I'll be able to hear anyone approaching from the corridor.

So, I search the rucksack in the room, heart thumping, eyes flitting to and from the bag to the open door. I find the cash: a clutch of fifties and twenties, quickly. Over £1,000. I hold it, taking a potentially fatal pause to soak in the fantasy, then pocket six fifty-pound notes. Guilt and relief entwine as I cross the room to the suitcases. As a rule, I limit myself to one note per person/room. But this time I couldn't help it, since I now only need another forty-five quid by Friday.

Relief soon eclipses guilt – it's funny how fast that fades, once the deed is done – as I reach the suitcases. Happily, these are away from the sightline of the door, though they're harder to open and if I'm caught rummaging through one of these, my fate will be the same. I set my feather duster down on the bed, seize the smallest suitcase, flip it onto the floor and pull at the zip. I yank too hard and it sticks.

I force myself to slow down – listening for the ping of the lift, for footsteps on the carpeted corridor – easing the zip along its path, watching the plastic teeth release as the mouth of the suitcase opens and the suppressed contents spring free.

I start rummaging, but can't immediately see the damn jacket. I lift piles of clothes, fingers skirting toys. Then I hear the unmistakable ping. I have about thirty seconds, depending on the speed of the lift's occupants, until I'm seen. I must close the suitcase. It's too late. I've no time. I've failed.

But I'm so close. My fingers sweep the suitcase again. Nothing. *Wait*. My thumb snags on a strip of silk. I tug. The linen jacket unfurls in a bloom of fabric on the floor, bringing with it several pairs of socks.

I feel a shift in the air. I stuff the jacket and the socks into my apron, while kneeling on the suitcase, zipping it shut.

'*Que faites-vous?*'

I stand, flattening the bulge in my apron, righting the suitcase. I don't know for certain what the French father is saying, but I can guess. I dip my head, assuming a deferential, innocent stance.

'I'm sorry, s-sir. Your s-suitcase fell while I was cleaning.' I pause, biting my tongue and the urge to continue. It takes guts to give short answers to tricky questions but lengthy explanations are a definite giveaway of guilt. I reclaim my feather duster.

'S-shall I leave the room while you pack?'

He hesitates, narrowed eyes flitting from me to his suitcase.

'*Non,*' he says, with a flick of his wrist. '*Nous partons maintenant.*'

I nod, resisting the sudden urge to curtsy. 'V-very good, s-sir.' I walk to the mirror and begin dusting it with great vigour, until the French family has departed, taking (nearly) all their possessions with them, until room 38 is silent and empty again.

Then I sit down on the bed and exhale.

During my negligible lunch break I hide the contraband in my staff locker, stuffing the three hundred quid into my bra. I'll have to take extra efforts to avoid grubby Garrick today, or at least keep him away from my left breast.

7.58 a.m. – Scarlet

Since the scalp-maiming incident with The Dastardly Mr Wolfe, as Scarlet has come, unaffectionately, to know him, she finds herself distracted. Both by the fact that he wants to rip her life apart, and by the fact that she may have the power to psychically cause harm. She'd, reluctantly, driven him to the hospital to be treated for the head wound she may or may not have inflicted, wishing she could have let him bleed to death on the floor instead. Except that it really wouldn't do to have a death on the premises – bad for business – and she'd be the one to scrub all the blood from her floorboards afterwards. So, she'd driven Wolfe to Addenbrooke's A&E, breaking the speed limit, skipping several red lights, then ejected the capitalist pig unceremoniously onto the pavement and sped off, vowing to banish all further thoughts of him. So far, she's failing rather spectacularly on that account.

8.08 a.m. – Bea

'What are you doing here?' Bea steps through the archway of Trinity College and onto the cobbled paving stones. The chubby bearded student whose name she doesn't know is sitting on the low stone wall enclosing the college's front gardens. 'Because this isn't fate, it's stalking.'

The student stands. 'No, no,' he says, looking mortified. 'Well yes, I see it might seem that way but – I was hoping you might help me with my homework. The, um, finer points of *Principia Mathematica* are eluding me.'

Bea hugs her books to her chest and scowls. 'Your homework? What are you, twelve?'

'You're funny.' He grins. 'That's why I like you.'

'You don't like me,' Bea says, contempt curling her top lip. 'You don't even know me.'

She starts walking.

'You're beautiful too – stunning.' He hurries after her. 'But that's by the by. Funny tops beauty every time.'

Bea stops walking. 'What do you want?'

'I told you—'

'No, not your cheesy pick-up lines,' Bea says. 'I mean, what do you hope to gain with this routine – you're hoping for a quick shag?'

At this, he looks both startled and slightly horrified. He pulls nervously at his beard. 'No, no . . . I didn't imagine, not in my wildest – well, perhaps in my wildest – but not in this world. No, I just wanted to know you.'

'Know me?' Bea narrows her eyes. 'So you can try to—?'

'No, no, no.' He holds up both hands, stepping back. 'No, not at all. I – there's something about you. I'm . . . drawn to you. But not, not in a creepy way. I only want to, um, spend a little time with you, if you'll let me. I want to know you, even a tiny bit better, that's all.'

Bea regards him as if she couldn't have imagined a more pathetic answer. She starts walking. 'Well, I don't want to know you,' she says, throwing the words behind her. 'So, please piss off.'

Only when she's sure he isn't following does Bea relax. Her shoulders drop and her view drifts up to the timbered Tudor buildings lining Trinity Street and the congregations of pigeons gathered on window ledges atop the elevated gargoyles and sculptures of eminent historical figures – every one of them, from their foppish stone hats to their stockinged stone feet, male.

For a moment, Bea imagines that she can hear the language of birds, that she need only listen closer to decipher their meaning: a bright twitter of delight, a low mournful caw, a twinkling flirtatious chirrup . . . But then tells herself to stop being so fanciful and hurries on.

4.31 p.m. – Liyana

'Married? She wants you to get married?' Kumiko slides to the edge of the bed. 'To a man? That's insane.'

'Well . . .' Liyana says, feeling defensive though she's thought the same thing herself many times. 'After all, arranged marriage is typical in lots of cultures, isn't it? In Ghana it's not uncommon, at least it used to—'

'That's not what I meant.' Kumiko kicks her heels against the wood. 'I wasn't questioning the institution in general, just specifically, in . . .' She regards Liyana. 'You did tell her about us, didn't you?'

Liyana, sitting on the floor, fiddles with the hem on Kumiko's rug, starting to plait the thin strands of black wool.

Kumiko narrows her eyes. 'You didn't.'

Liyana doesn't look up. 'Of course I did. And I told her I'd work night shifts in Tesco rather than seduce some gullible old duffer into bequeathing me half his kingdom.'

'And what did she say?'

'She said I wouldn't last a week. She said she'd do the seducing herself, if she could. But . . .'

Kumiko slides to the floor. 'But what?'

'Something about farts and tarts . . .' Liyana shrugs. 'I don't remember.'

'Yes, you do,' Kumiko says, shifting closer, extending a leg and wrapping it half around Liyana's back, so she's almost sitting in Liyana's lap.

Liyana sighs. 'She says a rich old fart doesn't want a pretty old tart, he wants . . .'

Kumiko raises an eyebrow so it disappears into a fringe of silky black hair. 'You.'

Liyana wraps her hands around Kumiko's ankles. 'I suppose. She was fairly drunk. Anyway, I told her I'd pick up the application to Tesco tomorrow.'

Kumiko laces her fingers in Liyana's. 'I'm afraid I have to agree with the senile old tart on that. You won't last a week.'

'Hey,' Liyana protests, removing her hands, folding her arms across her chest. 'What the—?'

'Oh, Ana, I love you, but you can't work at Tesco.'

'Why not?'

'Come on, have you ever done a day's hard graft in your life?'

'What? I trained to be an Olympic swimmer,' Liyana says. 'It doesn't get much harder than that, does it?'

'Yes, but that sort of thing is exhilarating, this would be utterly tedious.' Kumiko leans forward, stopping an inch from Liyana's mouth. 'I'm afraid you're only good for two things, my darling. The first is drawing, the second . . .'

'Yes?'

Kumiko fixes her eyes on Liyana's lips.

'You're such a tease.' Liyana closes the gap to kiss her. 'You—'

The phone in Liyana's pocket vibrates and pings. She scrambles to pull it out, capsizing them both and nearly knocking her head against the bed.

'Shit, shit.' Liyana types her password, opening her email.

There it is. The first and only unread message in her inbox. The answer. She can see the beginning of the first sentence but not how it ends. Liyana takes a deep breath, closes her eyes, whispers a prayer, then clicks on it.

From: Dr Martin Conway, admissions@ucl.co.uk
To: Liyana Miriro Chiweshe, liyanamc333@gmail.com

Dear Ms Chiweshe,
Thank you for your enquiry re the deferment of your place to study Fine Art at the Slade School of Art. We

> appreciate that your circumstances have suddenly and unexpectedly changed, but we regret to inform you that we are unable to—

Liyana closes her eyes. The ever-rising wave of anxiety finally crashes down.

11.59 p.m. – Leo

The fact that Leo is still dreaming continues to startle him. But, perhaps he's been dreaming every night of his life and simply hasn't remembered in the morning. Is that possible? Surely not, given that neither his body nor his mind is entirely human. But then, Leo thinks: '*There are more things in heaven and earth, Horatio . . .*' So, perhaps.

That he dreams of Goldie and always wakes the moment before they touch is a source of both frustration and relief. Frustration, naturally. Relief, because he knows what'd happen after the kiss and no longer wants to see that.

In his short lifetime Leo has murdered more women in Everwhere than he cares to remember. Some years more, some less, depending on the circumstances. In the months after Christopher's death he'd embarked on a killing spree. He prepared for every first-quarter moon as if training for the World Heavyweight Boxing Championship. Every morning he meditated for hours, honing the precision and strength of his senses. Every evening he ran for miles, pausing now and then to annihilate random obstacles in his path – kicking down bins, bashing in bikes, chasing cows across fields. Every night he stalked the streets, skin itching with the urgent need to torture and maim, to inflict as many elaborately violent deaths as his imagination and skill would allow.

That Leo could reach Everwhere only once every twenty-nine days or so (depending on the lunar cycle) was a source of distress that sharpened his grief into a white-hot rage that speared a great many Grimm girls' hearts. Leo trebled his usual kill count. He tore his way through the place of falling leaves, parting mists and fogs as he careened along stone paths, leaping over decaying trunks and turbulent rivers, in his furious determination to single-handedly transform Everwhere into a graveyard, greater than any on Earth. And so exact his revenge.

At the end of every night, no matter how many Leo had killed it was never enough. And, no matter how violent or vocal the deaths, the satisfaction of each quickly dissipated with the fog that rolled in to engulf the spirit of the dead girl. That the ever-increasing death toll didn't decrease Leo's grief in the slightest didn't serve to soften his zeal or quell his bloodlust. Indeed, it only fuelled his rage and drove him on, harder and faster, to kill ever more with every month that passed.

Over a decade ago

Goldie

I stared at my textbook; the numbers floated on the page and I tried to rein them in, put them in order. I didn't try hard. I couldn't make much sense of numbers at the best of times, unlike letters which have always made sense to me. I love to read. I taught myself. Ma, who read nothing but the local rag, gave me a copy of *The Guinness Book of World Records*, the only book in the flat, and let me teach myself. She didn't encourage reading beyond that, maybe thinking it might give me dangerous, adventurous ideas.

But I couldn't concentrate on fractions when I kept remembering that place, how it looked, how it felt. How *I* had felt. I'd been having the same dream for several nights. Every night I saw more, knew more. I started calling this other place Everwhere, since it was where I always wanted to be, instead of wherever I was. Frustratingly, I found that I couldn't control my dreams of Everwhere, I couldn't work out how I got there or how to get back. So, every night before I fell asleep I imagined every moonlit stone, every shifting shadow, every river, every tree. Inch by inch, breath by breath, I tried to conjure myself there by simple force of will. Sometimes it worked, sometimes it didn't.

I didn't always find my sisters in Everwhere, not every time I went. But that was all right since I sometimes preferred to be alone. I always felt their presence though: their touch on the falling leaves, their voices on the winds and the river currents. I felt them while I was awake too, while I ate my lunch at the edge of the cafeteria, while I walked home from school, while I watched TV before Ma got home to interrogate me about my day while making chips and egg for tea. Indeed, my dream sisters started to feel so real that when I talked to them out loud I heard their answers in my head.

Liyana

'Stop squirming, Ana.' Her mother held a spatula in one hand while leaning on her daughter's shoulders, pressing her down into the chair. 'I'm nearly finished.'

'It's burning, *Dadá*,' Liyana protested. 'Please stop, it hurts.'

Isisa bent to her daughter's ear. 'Mummy,' she hissed. 'Call me *Mummy*. How many times do I tell you?'

Liyana said nothing, not daring to challenge her mummy, who was fluid and gentle only until pushed, when she had all the force of a gathering wave. Instead Liyana scowled into the bathroom mirror, at the bottle beside the sink. *Dr Miracle's No-Lye Relaxer.* No lie? It was nothing but lies, like her Judas mummy who claimed it would only take a minute and she wouldn't feel a thing. It'd already taken thirty minutes and was burning her scalp as if Isisa had poured a bottle of acid over her head.

'Have you done your letters today?' her mummy asked.

'Yes,' Liyana said, thinking that since she was being burned alive by lies, she'd be stupid to tell the truth.

'Good.' Isisa spread the thick white gloop onto the nape of Liyana's neck. 'I bought a new bedtime book – you shouldn't waste time anymore with those silly stories your teacher gives you, they're too easy.'

Liyana closed her eyes and locked her jaw. She hated story time, while she read aloud and her mummy watched, pouncing on every stumbled word.

'Here you must work harder than everyone else, Ana,' she said. 'In Ghana you were somebody: daughter of Isisa Sibusisiwe Londiwe Chiweshe, granddaughter of the late Zwelethu Sibusiso Londisizwe Chiweshe. Here you are nobody. Less than the poorest, filthiest white woman living on the streets.'

Liyana opened her eyes. A protest rose in her throat; she swallowed it down. There were enough battles with her mummy, she'd pick the ones she stood some chance of winning.

'To stand out, you must fight,' Isisa continued, spreading the gloop around Liyana's ears. 'No one will give you a favour, every chance you will snatch from someone else's hand, okay?'

When Liyana realized her mother was looking at her, waiting for a response, she nodded.

'You must train harder, study closer, speak smart and strong,' Isisa said, brandishing the gloopy spatula aloft. 'You must struggle every day to prove you are better than the best of them. Then you might stand out, then you might survive.'

Liyana wanted to say that although she certainly wanted to survive she didn't particularly want to stand out. Quite the opposite.

Instead, she nodded, biting down the pain of her burning hot scalp and wondering at the contradiction of striving to stand out while also sweating to fit in.

Scarlet

When she had a little girl of her own, Scarlet vowed, she would spoil her rotten, would give her everything she asked for and plenty more she didn't. She wasn't entirely certain how to go about getting a daughter. But if her mother, who didn't seem to want one, had managed to get one then it couldn't be too difficult. And once Scarlet had worked out the particulars, she would ensure that her own child felt exceedingly and excessively loved.

Scarlet's own daughter would grow up under a blanket of devotion, she'd be almost smothered, she'd never have to cling to tiny maternal scraps, ripped cloths of almost-affection. Scarlet didn't know why her mother didn't feel for her what mothers were supposed to feel, but she knew she would be different. Scarlet would dote on her daughter, would nurse her, stroke her soft tufts of red hair, her plump cheeks, her tight-curled fists. Scarlet would adore her daughter right from the start, before she'd done anything to earn it, when all Red (as she'd be called) could do was cry.

Scarlet often thought about how it might feel to be loved for no special reason at all. Without trying to twist yourself into agreeable knots, without having to give what you might not want to give, safe in the knowledge that you were loved for just being your own simple self. With her own daughter, Scarlet determined to prove that unconditional love was possible, to prove that it was her mother and not her who was flawed.

Bea

'Careful!' Liyana called up to the soles of Bea's disappearing shoes. 'Don't climb too high.'

'Don't listen to her,' Scarlet shouted. 'Go as high as you can!'

Bea paused to look down from the branch. When she met Scarlet's gaze, she grinned, stood straighter, lengthening her spine, reaching towards the canopy. 'I'm going all the way up!'

Why not, she thought. It wasn't too far. And this place was different, after all. It wasn't like Earth, where a fall from a tree this high would have killed her. The physical laws here were all askew – how else to explain the perpetually falling leaves? Gravity was more forgiving in Everwhere.

When Bea reached the highest branch, she found a firmer footing and readied herself to leap. Then, as she wiggled her toes to the edge, Bea looked down to find her sisters' eyes, to make sure they were fixed on her.

'If you fall, I'll catch you.' Liyana stood at the base of the tree, hands pressed to the trunk. 'But please don't fall.'

'I'm not going to fall,' Bea cried. 'I'm going to fly!'

Leo

'Pssst!'

Leo, stiff and straight in his dormitory bed, twisted in his blankets to turn halfway towards the bed beside his. He saw a hand reaching out across the darkness. He waited.

'Pssst.'

'What?' Leo hissed.

The boy in the next bed waggled his hand, as if expecting Leo to take it.

'Marsden, Christopher,' he whispered. 'You can call me Chris if you like.'

Leo looked down at the hand but didn't shake it. 'Penry-Jones, Leo.'

'Good to meet you,' Christopher said. He retracted his hand and sat up. Leo did the same. 'You're new, aren't you?'

'Yeah.'

'Why so late?'

'What do you mean?' Leo said, hugging his knees.

'Well, most boys start here before they're six, don't they? I did.'

'Yeah, well, my mother wanted me at home,' Leo said. 'My father allowed it for a while, but when I turned eight, he insisted.'

Christopher slipped down under his blankets again and pressed his head into the pillow. 'You're lucky.' He smiled. 'I bet your mother's missing you like mad. Mine hasn't even noticed I'm gone.'

Leo smiled back. 'If you've been here three years then I bet she has.'

Christopher gave a slight snort, as if he couldn't even begin to tell Leo how wrong he was. 'Do you miss your mother?'

'I, um . . .' Leo was reluctant to confess just how much he did.

'You can come in here with me,' Christopher whispered. 'If you like.'

And Leo knew that, although several metres of floor and several inches of bedding separated them, Christopher still felt the frantic pulse of his loneliness unsettling the air. Leo cast a quick eye over the twelve other dormitory beds, at the boys cocooned in sleep and tight sheets. And, before he could chicken out, Leo gave a quick tug to his sheets and set his feet onto the cold stone floor.

A few minutes later Christopher was asleep, curled towards Leo, his soft snores tickling Leo's ear. Until dawn, Leo watched his new friend sleep. And not until the morning sun began to light the dormitory did Leo sneak back into his own bed.

7th October – 25 days . . .

7.11 a.m. – Goldie

I have a confession. I'm sort of stalking Leo. I'm not tapping his phone or following him home – though I happen to know he's studying Law at St John's, and for some reason (probably an overprotective mother – I recognize the signs) he spends some nights at the hotel with his parents. Admittedly, I clean his family's suite more thoroughly than is strictly necessary, lingering over certain things such as his shampoo and shirts. I know it's not part of my job description to tend to his wardrobe, or sniff his toiletries, but I like to go above and beyond in my duties.

Last night, while dusting the interior of Leo's bedside table, I discovered his diary. I didn't read it. I may be a thief and a liar, but I still have certain moral standards. I haven't even opened it. And I won't. No matter how tempted I am. *Cross My Heart and Hope to Die.*

After the curious experience of commanding Leo, nothing out of the ordinary has happened. Life has been boring and benign, which, though I don't exactly revel in it, is certainly preferable to strange and unexpected. I go to work, clean lavatories, daydream about Leo, hoover floors, polish mirrors, dust carriage clocks. I go home, feed Teddy, help with his homework, clean the flat, go to bed. After nearly a week of that, I've almost forgotten the experience altogether. Which is why I'm shocked when it happens again.

I'm hoovering the first-floor corridors when I glance up to see Mr Penry-Jones striding towards me. For a second I'm still, since there's every chance his son might be striding along behind him. He isn't. But, before I can continue hoovering, Mr Penry-Jones steps past me, treading on the hoover cord without a word of excuse me, or anything else to acknowledge my existence, and continues on his merry way.

Dickhead, I think. *I hope you fall and twist your bloody ankle.*

A second later, he trips over the twisting cord and is thrown forward, splayed out on the plush purple carpet like a starfish. I nearly laugh but am stopped by shock. A coincidence, surely?

'Don't stand there gawping, idiotic girl,' he snaps, half-lifting his head. 'Call the doctor. I think I've twisted my bloody ankle.'

That has me gawping a good few seconds longer but I pull myself together and go. As I'm hurrying down the hallway, I feel another surge of strength. All at once I'm taller, stronger, faster. *I can command armies*, I think. *I can topple nations, I have magic at my fingertips* . . . I feel as if my head were brushing the ceiling and my feet have lifted from the floor. I'm seized by a strange sensation of slipping my fingers into wet earth, touching elongated roots. I'm coaxing them, controlling them, pulling a fully formed tree fresh from the ground. Then, all at once, the roots are rebelling, wrapping round my wrists, tugging me underground. A rush of panic snatches hold of me – I start to shrink back and sink down so, by the time I reach the stairs, I'm small and insignificant again. What the hell was that? I think, as I hurry to get help.

7.48 a.m. – Goldie

Garrick dismisses me as soon as he reaches Mr Penry-Jones, still prostrate on the carpet and whining like a little girl, clutching at his ankle. I leave the letch clucking and fawning over the toff like a neurotic ma. I wait till I'm safe behind the door to room 17 before I burst out laughing, stifling the sound in my apron.

I go slower after that, though, distracted by my thoughts. I don't know. It's strange. As a kid, all I wanted was to be strong. Stronger than the adults around me. But, now that I might be, I find it oddly unnerving.

I save Leo's room for last, the way I used to save sweets as a kid. I've not taken anything but I've done worse, since a violation of privacy is a far greater sin than theft. Okay, so I lied. Not only have I been through Leo's personal things, but I've now read his personal thoughts, and some of them are quite surprising.

I'm still sitting on the single bed, when he walks into the room. Mercifully, I've just returned the diary to its drawer. I leap up.

'What are you doing?'

I stare at him open-mouthed but say nothing.

He eyes me curiously. 'Are you – stealing?'

I frown, before noticing a black leather wallet on the bed, next to the imprint I'd left on the quilt. 'Oh, no, I—' Then, I reconsider. It's better he thinks me a thief (I am, after all) than a snoop. So, I hang my head.

Leo crosses the room in three strides. He's in front of me before I can take my next breath, his mouth now closer to mine than a man's has ever been since—

'You're not . . .' He reaches out towards my cheek and I flinch. But, as I feel the heat of his hand, the pulse of his fingers, I find I'm not scared. I meet his eyes, half a dozen shades of green and, I now notice, a splash of yellow at the centre. Sunlight on leaves. There's curiosity in his eyes, tenderness too.

'Leo! What the hell's going on?' Mr Penry-Jones stands

in the doorway leaning on a gilded walking stick, his left foot elevated, his face flushed with fury.

Leo drops his hand and steps away.

'Do you want to explain yourself?' Mr Penry-Jones hobbles into the room, taking in the scene: his son, me, the wallet. 'Leo?'

I look to Leo who's staring at his father.

'Leo.' His voice drops. 'Were you engaging in something untoward with this—?'

'No, sir. Of course not.'

'Well then, what in hell were you doing?'

'I was only asking her—'

I step forward. 'H-he caught me,' I say. 'I – I was . . . t-trying to take your . . . wallet.'

11.59 a.m. – Goldie

Leo denies it. He tells his father it isn't true. Heated words (father's loud, son's soft) are exchanged. While I stand next to the bed, looking from one to the other and then at my feet. I don't know why I did it, why I said it. It was a stupid, stupid impulse. I know only that I felt a sudden desire to protect him from his father's shaming. After they've been arguing for a while, the elder Penry-Jones hobbles to the telephone and picks it up.

'I'd like to speak with the manager, please. Yes, I'll wait.'

My spirits sink through the floor down to Garrick's office. I knew this was coming and I'm already regretting my foolish chivalry. But it's too late to deny it now.

When Garrick doesn't even try to grope me in the lift, I realize the full severity of my situation. I enter his office first, he closes the door behind us. At the click of the lock, my spirits sink down to the basement. As Garrick eases his bulk into the cheap faux-leather chair behind his desk, the fabric squeaks and he coughs to cover it. He crosses his thick legs.

'Oh, Goldie. What a disappointment you've proved to be.' He sighs theatrically, as if he's a high court judge sentencing a serial killer. I suppress the urge to roll my eyes.

'Well then . . .' He sits back, steepling his fingers and pressing them to his lips – the ridiculous pose he's affected to ponder my fate. 'How . . . are we going to handle this?'

I stay silent. I won't deny the charges or beg for leniency. I feel the quicksand rising and know any such tactics will only hasten my descent. Garrick lowers his hands, uncrosses his legs. He leans forward, his bald spot shining with sweaty excitement. It pulses off him in sticky waves.

'Now, under ordinary circumstances I'd have to dismiss you, effective immediately. And call the police. However,' he pauses for further dramatic effect, 'there are . . . alternative options to consider.'

He pushes the chair back and stands; the faux leather squeaks as it releases him. He steps around the desk. Watching him, I bite my upper lip. All the blood blanches from it.

'What do you think to that?'

I say nothing, eyeing the locked door.

'That's okay, you don't need to speak.' He grins. 'I mean, I like a potty mouth as much as the next man, but I don't need you to rev me up. I'm all revved up already.' He takes another step towards me. 'You stand against the wall like a good little girl. I'll do all the work.'

He steps closer. I stumble back. He reaches out to steady me. I flinch but, since his office is almost as small as the lift, I'm now backed up against the wall. I start to hyperventilate. Garrick pushes on me with all his weight so I'm pinned to the wall.

'Would you like to do the honours?' He nods down at his groin. 'Or shall I?'

I try to speak, but I'm struggling to breathe.

'Cat got your tongue?' He brings his face so close that I can see the pores of his sweaty skin and smell his stale, smoky breath. For one horrific moment, I think he's going to kiss me. Instead he slips a fat finger into my mouth. My eyes go wide, unblinking.

'You like that?' He grins again. 'Suck it up, sweetheart – a small preview of coming attractions.'

Then, somehow, I do what I've never been able to do before. Instead of freezing, I fight. It's an impulse, I don't think strategy, I just bite. I bite down so hard on his finger that his skin breaks and blood fills my mouth.

Garrick shrieks and leaps back, grasping his bloodied finger, hopping and twitching and squealing like a pig being slaughtered.

'You – you little fucking bitch!' he screams. 'What the fuck do you—?'

A cascade of curses gush forth, words so crude, so colourful, that for a second I'm pinned to the spot in shock. Then I turn and run.

12.34 p.m. – Liyana

Other than her Tarot cards, when Liyana feels lost it is blackbirds she looks for. They are her own personal angels, messengers from a benevolent universe, if such a thing exists, to reassure and remind her, to tell her when she's on the right track. At the sight of a blackbird Liyana feels that, ultimately, all is right with the world, no matter how hopeless it might seem at the time.

It's blackbirds because, though she'd never admit this to another living soul, Liyana believes that, in some esoteric and inexplicable way, they embody her mother's spirit. Perhaps because Isisa used to sing a song about blackbirds so often it became a soundtrack to Liyana's dreams. Sometimes, she would wake with the lyrics still on her lips. Sadly, she can't remember any of the words anymore, no matter how hard she tries.

Liyana hasn't picked up a feather or seen a blackbird in weeks. The angels have deserted her. So Liyana returns to the Tarot. She asks about money, about marriage, about the chance of miracles. She deals The Tower, the Three of Swords, the Five of Cups. She asks the same questions over and over, dealing again and again for the chance of different cards. She shuffles and reshuffles, deals and re-deals, in the desperate hope of a single reassuring sign. She gets none.

2.59 p.m. – Scarlet

Scarlet leans against her beloved cappuccino machine, half-heartedly polishing Francisco's flank with a dishcloth, trying not to think about Ezekiel Wolfe and his plans to erect another monument to global capitalism on the site of her grandmother's little café. Scarlet feels a fool. Still, she'll be damned if she'll let Mr Wolfe get his claws on the café. It's still beloved, after all. The old stalwarts still come. Cambridge is a city of tradition, ritual, memory. Sadly, though, this loyalty doesn't increase with the same eager ferocity as the rent.

Glancing at her blurred reflection in the shining stainless steel, Scarlet allows herself to wonder what she might do if she weren't doing this. She hasn't thought about doing anything else, not for years. Why would she? She's qualified for nothing – where will ten GCSEs get you nowadays? Even if they are all As. Which, given that she was helping her grandmother out in the café every day after school, is quite impressive. But what employer would think so? She'd need to continue studying, or take a training course. Either of which would require time and money, neither of which she has in plentiful supply.

While Esme still worked in the café, before the disease had been diagnosed, Scarlet had been set to go on to sixth form, with the vague notion of pursuing a career in Chemistry. The idea of sitting in a lab and blowing things up – which is how she liked to imagine she'd spend her time – seemed like a perfect career. She didn't particularly mind that it had never come to fruition, since it'd only been an idea in the absence of any others. And she still found the kitchen a satisfying alternative to a laboratory. Admittedly, the bubbling alchemy of baking soda with water was tame in comparison to, say, the explosive satisfaction of red phosphorus with potassium chlorate, but it remained rather magical nevertheless.

Scarlet had noticed the signs only slowly. At first, Esme started forgetting the names of simple things: a plate, the fridge, cinnamon buns. Then she started losing things and finding them again in inappropriate places: her car keys in the freezer, a pint of milk in the bathroom cabinet, a teaspoon in the till among the five-pound notes. Still, Scarlet didn't say anything to her grandmother. She didn't want her fears confirmed, she hoped that the symptoms would disappear – like a spider in the bath that, if left long enough, will eventually fall foul of the plughole.

Finally, neither Scarlet nor Esme could ignore it any longer. So, Esme went to the doctor and the worst was confirmed. And Scarlet surrendered to the fact that baking cakes was as exciting as her science experiments were ever going to get.

10.58 p.m. – Bea

In addition to her unnervingly empowering experience in the library – slipping seamlessly into her ink-veined skin in a perfect alignment of body and soul – Bea has started noticing things. Things that make her wonder, with all evidence to the contrary, if her *mamá*'s tales might be true. Or, at the very least, born of a tiny kernel of truth. Rationally, it's impossible. Yet Bea is now being forced to expand the boundaries of what she believes possible.

Lately, Bea has found that she knows what people are going to say before they say it. Not word for word, but the general gist. She thinks of people just before seeing them. And, last week, she predicted almost every question on her moral philosophy paper, a phenomenon that might have been put down to studious diligence except that she'd dreamed of them the night before. Such experiences are still a far cry from the dark premonitions her *mamá* claims, but they're inexplicable nevertheless.

As a result, Bea, much to her own dismay, has found herself seeking out certain gates, studying them for anomalies, signs that they might not be exactly as they appear. She's stopped short of trying to walk through one at 3.33 a.m., though she isn't sure whether this is because she draws the line at endorsing her *mamá*'s fantastical notions about fantastical worlds, or because the moon won't be in the right phase again until November 1st. Still, if she happens to find herself with nothing better to do that night, she might give it a try.

'When you were a child you could do all that in your sleep,' her *mamá* says, when she calls, which she does more often than Bea would like.

'So you keep saying,' Bea says. 'I wish you'd stop, you're making me feel inadequate.'

'*Por qué?* It should be the opposite. Just wait and see.'

'I've no memory of these things, and no evidence of them now, so . . .' Bea shrugs. 'I'm only left with the gap between who you say I am and who I feel myself to be.'

'Stop shrugging,' her *mamá* says. 'It's bad for your posture.'

'Stop nagging,' Bea says. 'And I'm not.'

'Lie to anyone you like but not to me,' Cleo says. 'You only demean yourself. Besides, it's fucking annoying. *¡Por amor al . . . demonio!*'

'You're fucking annoying,' Bea says, wanting to hang up. 'And I don't know why you persist in telling me these ridiculous stories – anyone would think you're raring to return to St Dymphna's. I'd have thought you'd had enough of that place.'

Her *mamá* is silent.

'You'll be back there if someone overhears you,' Bea says, unable to resist twisting the knife. 'They'll think you've flipped.'

'That's because most people have zero imagination and even less intelligence,' her *mamá* says. 'If you walked them through a gate, if you held their hand till dawn, they'd still claim it'd all been a dream. *¿Entiendes?* If they saw a spike of blue light in their black-and-white worlds, it'd blow their tiny mortal minds. If they saw anything extraordinary, they'd rationalize it into dust.'

Bea rolls her eyes.

'*¡Deja!*' Cleo snaps. 'Stop disrespecting me.'

'I'm not,' Bea says, annoyed at her *mamá*'s uncanny ability to know exactly how she's reacting, even when they're talking on the phone.

'You know, I much preferred you when you were younger.'

'So you keep telling me.'

'Well, I did. And I'll say it again. I can't wait till you turn eighteen and I finally get my daughter back.'

Bea starts to roll her eyes again, then stops.

11.11 p.m. – Leo

Leo likes to walk the streets of Cambridge at night, especially when the colleges are bursting at the seams with students, their thoughts seeping through the ancient stones, tumbling from every open window and door, drifting through the air like bonfire smoke. He breathes in their desires, their disappointments, their despair.

Unlike London, here the streets are usually empty late at night, save for a few lone wanderers, and a few too many huddled down to sleep in shop fronts.

Light spills onto the pavements, illuminating the residents within. Leo wonders who they are, these people whose thoughts he can hear but whose names he doesn't know. Behind one window, he senses a Grimm girl, one with strengths and skills still dormant, with no idea yet of who she is or what's to come.

Most of all, he thinks of Goldie, wondering what happened to her afterwards at the hands of her boss. He'll find out tomorrow. He hopes she didn't take any shit from the jumped-up little toad, he hopes she gave as good as she got, hopes she bit off his tiny dick. He smiles when he thinks of her reading his diary. Fortunately he hadn't written anything incriminating, or he'd have lost his all-important upper hand: the element of surprise.

Over a decade ago

Everwhere

As you step outside the gates you notice the shift. It's so subtle that, at first, you hardly perceive it. But, as you begin to leave Everwhere behind, as the scent of bonfires no longer lingers on your skin, as your eyes adjust to the sharper light – feet quickening on concrete instead of moss, ears twitching at the close honk of a car horn and the distant bark of a dog, you notice that you feel a little duller, a little denser – a little sadder. Your head feels heavy, as if you haven't been sleeping well. Something niggles at you, as if you'd recently received bad news but can't quite recall what it was.

As you walk deeper into the world you've always known, this place where the bricks and mortar are so familiar, the shift feels ever stronger, more acute. The contentment you had felt, the calm, the clarity, is evaporating. The touch of sadness presses on your chest until it seems to pierce your core. Steadily, you feel as if your spirit, every memory of laughter, every capacity for joy, is being sucked out of you, just as clouds leach light from the sky.

You want to turn back, want to run to the place you've left but you know you cannot. There's no going back, not until the next first-quarter moon, not until the gates open again. And so you walk on. Until you no longer notice the dull ache of disappointment and sorrow, for now it's as much a part of you as the blood flowing in your veins. And, after a while, you forget how you once felt. And, finally, you forget that you were ever there at all.

Goldie

'You know I only want to keep you safe, don't you, pet?'

I nodded. I wanted to tell Ma to stop calling me that. I wanted to ask: '*Safe from what?*' But I sensed it'd unleash a hysterical flood of fear I didn't want to deal with. Whenever Ma was in this sort of mood it was easier to agree with everything and wait. So I tuned out, took a deep breath and dived under the waters, while currents of anxiety swirled above as Ma chattered on.

I wished I could tell Ma I'd be fine, there was nothing to worry about because I could take care of myself. I wanted to tell Ma about my sisters, about what I could do in Everwhere. But I knew she'd dismiss me as a silly girl having fantastical dreams or, worse, subject me to a regurgitated lecture on the infinite perils of life. So, I held my breath and kept quiet.

'Why don't I tell you a story?' Ma asked, reaching out to twine a finger through my hair. She had blonde hair like mine but with a fine fuzz of close-cut curls that gave her a halo effect, a saintly look that sometimes belied her behaviour. 'A new one.'

I flinched. I didn't often like her stories, but I never knew how to say so. Ma told stories to scare me into staying safe, into never doing anything audacious. She didn't want me to have adventures, to fall – or fly – over the edges of expectation. One day I would – not under Ma's custodial eye, but when I was old enough I knew I'd leave. Leave home and go to London, or even farther. Perhaps I wouldn't even come back.

Maybe I'd return one day, when I'd been away long enough to miss Ma. But only when I'd seen as much of the world as it was possible to see. Nothing Ma said would change that; no matter how many sad stories she told, it wouldn't stop me from running away as soon as I could. I'd already learned that when apron strings were tied too tight, it only made the captive child fight all the harder to flee.

But Ma was a good storyteller, there was no denying that. As a baby, I was wrapped in words as snugly as I was swaddled. But they were silly stories of girls whose only desire was to wed, lonely girls who longed for husbands and homes, for expanding families to whom they could dedicate their lives. Boring stories. I tried not to roll my eyes at their beginnings and I never cared to know how they'd end. But, even though the tales were so dry their dust stuck in my throat, the way Ma told them was still enchanting, which meant I couldn't help but listen to the words weave together, wrapping strands of sentences through my fingers and hair.

'Tell me the story of my birth instead,' I said.

'Oh, pet.' Ma laughed, pulling me into her lap. It was always a bit strange sitting in my mother's lap since she was so small, almost as small as a child. As if she'd decided at thirteen that she couldn't spare the effort to grow any taller. It wouldn't be long before I was as tall as Ma. 'I've told you that one a hundred times.'

'I don't care, I love it.'

'No, tonight I have a different story,' Ma insisted.

'Okay,' I said, thinking that maybe this time it'd be different.

Ma smiled, hugging me tight. 'All right then, pet. This one's called *Rapunzel*.'

'I know this one,' I said.

'No,' Ma said. 'Not this version you don't.'

I shrugged, pulling away slightly, so there was still an inch of air between us.

'Once upon a time there lived a queen who longed for a child,' Ma began. 'Unfortunately, though she tried every trick and spell to conceive, the queen remained barren.

'One day a dark fairy came to the kingdom promising he could give the queen what she most desired. After casting his spell the fairy issued a warning, that the queen must not try to possess that which could not be possessed. "Love that is craved too deeply," he advised, "love that is born of bright-white wishing and black-edged desire, will bring more sorrow than joy."

'Within a year, the queen gave birth to a beautiful baby girl whom she named Rapunzel. And, happily, the queen found that the fairy had been quite wrong, for Rapunzel only brought her greater joy with every day that passed. She'd never loved another soul so completely, nor been so deeply loved in return.

'By the time the princess turned thirteen, the queen had forgotten the fairy's warning. However, now that she was older Rapunzel frequently left her mother's side and began to love others. She had many friends and was courted by princes from every kingdom. Soon, the queen became scared.

'"Do you still love me?" she asked every night. "Do you still love me as I love you?"

'"I do," Rapunzel always replied, for she did.

'But the queen didn't believe her daughter and, one day, locked her up in a tower so Rapunzel could see no one else. Every night, the queen repeated her plea. Finally, Rapunzel stopped saying that she loved her mother in return, for now she found that she didn't as she had done before. She begged her mother to free her, for she longed to see the world. But the queen could not let her daughter go.

'One night, the dark fairy visited the queen, reminding her of his warning. "If you do not let her go," he said, "she will soon grow to hate you."

'"I don't care," the queen said, "so long as she stays."

'"Then you no longer love her," the fairy said.

'The queen was devastated. After all, had any mother ever loved her daughter more? She kept a vigil outside the tower, ensuring that the dark fairy never returned. Yet, every day the queen saw that Rapunzel's sorrow only grew and every night she heard her daughter weep louder than the night before. Until, one day, the queen was suddenly filled with regret and released Rapunzel.

'Delighted to finally be free, Rapunzel fled to the edges of the Earth. Leaving the queen to mourn the love she'd lost and pray every night that her daughter would one day return. As the years passed and the queen grew pale and thin with grief, still she never lost hope that her daughter would come back. At the other end of the world, Rapunzel felt the pull of her mother's longing and fled farther still.

'One winter's eve, when the queen was at last on her deathbed, she sent word to bring her daughter home. Rapunzel, shocked by the news and suddenly sorry for all that she'd done, took the fastest ship bound for the kingdom and prayed that she would reach her mother in time.

'Sadly, Rapunzel arrived too late, for the queen had died a few hours before. Filled with regret, and blaming herself for her mother's death, Rapunzel never again left the castle. Every night she locked herself in the tower and wept for the love she'd lost and would never find again.'

Ma fell silent then, probably expecting me to speak. I said nothing. I tried not to cry. I tried my hardest. But I couldn't help it. I stiffened, squeezing my eyes shut as tears fell down my cheeks. I supposed I shouldn't have been surprised. But I hated myself for crying, for not having the gumption to brush the fallen sentences from my shoulders, the way I shrugged off Ma's too-tight hugs. But I couldn't. I was still only seven, after all, and the stupid story seeped into my stupid soft heart despite my every effort to keep it out. And the stupid story wasn't even true. In the mouth of a lesser teller it would have sounded silly and stale, but not in Ma's mouth. In her mouth it only sounded true. Ma told me that story over and again until I had every word memorized. And so, the apron strings tied themselves ever more tightly around my wrists.

Scarlet

The timer on the oven sang – Scarlet's favourite sound. She dashed across the kitchen floor and pressed her nose to the glass.

'Grandma,' she called. 'They're ready!'

'Then take them out,' her grandmother called back across the kitchen. 'Don't let them burn.'

She was the only one who permitted Scarlet such responsibilities. Scarlet's mother wouldn't let her close to the oven, let alone allow her to remove piping hot cakes from within.

Glancing about, Scarlet grabbed for a dishcloth with one hand and tugged at the oven door with the other. In truth, she didn't need the cloth, since her hands never seemed to feel the heat, but she suspected that her grandmother (who always used two dishcloths – one for each side) might think it strange if she pulled out the tray with bare fingers.

Scarlet loved the rush of warmth at opening the oven door. Sometimes she had to suppress a longing to climb in and join the cinnamon buns within. But she'd read *Hansel and Gretel* and wouldn't do anything so stupid. Scarlet heard her grandmother's sigh of pleasure as the scent of sugar and spice wafted across the kitchen to where she was mixing the crumpet batter.

'Heavenly,' her grandmother said. 'You know, your grandfather used to bake those for me every Sunday morning while we danced in the kitchen to Bessie Smith. And sometimes . . .'

'Sometimes what?' Scarlet asked, as she set each bun on the cooling rack.

'Oh, nothing.' Esme smiled. 'I should wait till you're older before I tell you such things.'

'I'm nearly eight, Grandma.' Scarlet set her hands on her hips. 'I think that's quite old enough.'

Esme laughed, dipped her finger into the bowl and licked at the peak of crumpet batter slowly. In certain ways her grandmother did Scarlet the honour of treating her like an adult, in others it was as if she were still a baby. When and how was unpredictable.

'Come and taste this.'

Scarlet scurried over, mouth already open. Her grandmother bent to offer up a spoonful of the batter. Scarlet tasted it thoughtfully.

'Needs a pinch more salt,' she said, echoing a phrase she'd heard her grandmother say many times before.

Her grandmother added a pinch of salt to the bowl. 'Yes, I thought so too.'

Scarlet watched, thinking the things she would never admit out loud: how she wished Esme was her mother instead of Ruby, how she wanted to live in the flat above the café and eat cinnamon buns for breakfast every day, how she never wanted to go home. Scarlet's other secret wish was for siblings but, sadly, she was sure that was yet another wish that would never come to pass.

Bea

Bea didn't often levitate on Earth, though she sometimes hovered a few inches above the ground for fun, to remind herself of her own power. In Everwhere she could fly for hours and, on occasion, did. She swooped through the falling leaves, looking down on lakes and trees, until she was nothing more than a rush of air, instead of a girl who everyone thought they knew. Usually, though, Bea preferred to stay with her sisters – not that she'd tell them that.

It was a weakness, this love for her sisters, as her *mamá* often reminded her. She mustn't get too attached, given the likelihood that they would meet the same fate as Bea's aunts. Or, if they went dark, Bea would need to watch herself.

'Especially Goldie,' her *mamá* warned. 'She sits high in your father's regard. Should he pit you against each other, you want to be sure of—'

'*¿Pero, por qué?*' Bea frowned. 'Why would he do that?'

Cleo gave her daughter a look then, both knowing and incredulous, that clearly said Wilhelm Grimm was capable of anything.

'When did you last see *a papito*?'

Her *mamá*'s smile was like a flower blooming. 'I see him often enough.'

'When will I meet him?'

'Your father comes and goes as he pleases,' Cleo said. 'But it's when you meet him on your eighteenth birthday that matters most of all. *¿Entiendes?*'

When her *mamá* revealed her own coming-of-age story she omitted certain moments, particularly the murderous and incestuous parts, but Bea was made to understand that she needed to keep her distance. Bea knew that her sisters would probably have preferred her to leave altogether, let them enjoy Everwhere without her. She didn't blame them. She said cruel things, though she couldn't seem to help it, the words slipped out before she could stop them.

Sometimes, Bea thought it'd be better for everyone if she passed the rest of her days gliding above the trees, soaring up into the moonlight within touching distance of the stars, never speaking to or seeing another soul. It'd probably be safer that way; in her absence she'd be far more loved. And she could be with her father, feel his breath on the winds, his whisper on the air. Just the two of them up there. She could do it. She'd have to stop now and then to eat, it wouldn't matter what. She'd become a forager, eating whatever she could find: mushrooms, berries, acorns – was moss edible? It seemed like it might be. Bea had never cared much for food anyway, had always been skinny as a sparrow, despite her *abuela*'s best efforts to fatten her up. Lately, though, Bea had been purposely eschewing food, skipping lunch at school, pushing her dinner around her plate until her *mamá* finally gave up trying to force her. Because, Bea reasoned, the thinner she was the higher she'd be able to fly. If only she had hollow bones like birds she might be able to fly right up to the moon.

Goldie

Sometimes I caught my stepfather watching me. Always from the corner of his eye or the edge of a room, but I felt it as surely as if he were shining a spotlight on me. I'd shrink when I felt his stare, like a tree losing its leaves. Sometimes I was sure I felt his thoughts, long tendrils of longing that tugged at my skirt like a toddler trying to get my attention.

He was a child, my stepfather, a sicky, icky baby with an elongated body, thin and stringy as a weed. He was always seeking the nearest chair to flop into, limbs folded, too lazy to stand. Fingers insidious as ivy, clinging to whatever didn't want him. He'd sit on the sofa gobbling oversized bags of sweets, scattering sugar all over his clothes, leaving fallen sweets for me to roll over in bed, like a tacky version of 'The Princess and the Pea'.

He'd been like that ever since Ma brought him home. I tried to tell her, but she wouldn't listen. She wanted him too much, God knows why, insisting that he was a good one, unlike my unspeakable father, and ignored all the warning signs to the contrary. Including the fact that he was a filthy excuse for a human being. Sometimes I'd look at him and think that, if Ma thought him an improvement, then my father must have been the devil.

My stepfather grew worse after he'd lost the baby-fight with Ma, from the moment she started waddling around the flat smiling to herself. I'd never seen her so happy. I wondered if she'd been that happy while pregnant with me. I doubted it, since this baby was the product of so-called love, while I was the product of bright-white wishing and black-edged desire, according to Bea. I asked Ma if that was true but she didn't confirm or deny. Instead, an odd look passed across her face, as if she was struggling to recall anything about my conception at all, before she asked what I wanted for tea.

As Ma's pregnancy advanced she began retreating into herself, which was a relief. But then my stepfather stepped into that space, which wasn't. At dinner he started asking about my day (something Ma now forgot to do), leaning across our tiny table so I could smell the beer on his breath. I started locking the bathroom door when I showered, wrapping myself tight in my duvet when I went to bed. I started wishing I had my own room. I agreed with Ma that we should move. The flat was too small for three, let alone four. But my stepfather insisted that we couldn't afford the rent increase, not with the baby coming. Strangely, Ma didn't seem to care anymore, so didn't press him. Probably to minimize his moaning about all the new things she was buying for the baby. So, she got fatter and further away, and he got thinner and closer, while the walls of our tiny flat felt like they were closing in on us all.

Leo

Lately Leo was seized by sudden, inexplicable rages. He'd recently smashed six windows in the refectory with a cricket bat, only escaping expulsion when his father bestowed a substantial donation on the Headmaster's discretionary fund. Then Leo ripped the pocket off Robin Walker's blazer and earned five days' lunchtime detention. While Leo sat at his desk, facing the wall, writing, *I will control my temper*, over and over again, he wondered why he'd done it and couldn't explain it even to himself. Despite the detentions, he then repeatedly thumped a random boy in the playground, only escaping punishment because the boy had been too scared to report him.

Then, one afternoon, Leo came across a book in the school library by Robert Louis Stevenson: *The Strange Case of Dr Jekyll and Mr Hyde*. Apparently, it was a first edition, and the librarian refused to let Leo remove it from its glass case. But Leo needed to read it. And not any edition, that very one. He couldn't explain the why of that either. So, reasoning that the ditzy old duffer librarian wouldn't notice, Leo stole the book and replaced it with another. It took three nights under his bedclothes with a torch (also stolen, to add insult to injury, from Robin Walker) to read the book cover to cover.

When he'd finished, Leo had his answer. He was dangerous. A madman with two sides – one (relatively) good and one (increasingly) bad. He wondered if that bastard Walker had poisoned him with something concocted in the Chemistry lab. He wondered if there was an antidote. Then

Leo realized, somewhat to his surprise, that even if there was he wouldn't take it. He didn't want to suppress his rages because, although the external consequences could be unfortunate, the internal effects were rather glorious. When he was overcome with rage, when pure fury was pumping in his veins, Leo felt more exalted, more invincible, more himself than he ever had before.

8th October – 24 days . . .

9.59 a.m. – Goldie

I need a job fast, one that doesn't require references and pays in cash. Frustratingly, my search must be geographically confined, meaning a mile exclusion radius around the Fitzwilliam Hotel. Although Garrick rarely strays more than a few hundred metres from his office, preferring to send his minions on external errands, I've known him to go to the corner shop for cigarettes when he's sick of the place and wants out. Personally, I'd like to go back and trim his other fingers. But I need to stay safe, if only for Teddy's sake.

I dropped Ted at school, then went straight into town to start searching. When I reach King's Parade I've already been summarily rejected from two cafés and three restaurants. I'm beginning to feel so desperate by this point I even include shops in my search, but I'm told 'no' by four before I've barely opened my mouth. I see the sign for the No. 33 Café, something of a Cambridge institution, I believe, though I've never been inside. Still, it looks nice enough from the outside, with one big bay window overlooking King's College. Sitting at a table, staring out onto the street, is an old lady, perhaps in her seventies or eighties, with a mass of white hair and a wistful smile. I catch her eye and she grins at me. I take it as a sign.

'Good morning,' I say, pushing open the door. But now the old lady doesn't look at me, doesn't take her eyes off the window. Other than her, the café is empty and, as I approach the unmanned counter, I start having second thoughts. No customers means no need for extra staff and

I've had my fill of rejections today. I'm about to turn back when a young woman with an enormous amount of curly red hair hurries out of the kitchen, wiping her hands on her apron. There's something familiar about her, though I can't put my finger on what. Perhaps I've seen her around town, though I'm sure I'd have remembered that red hair.

'Sorry,' she says, a little breathless. 'What can I get you? Tea? Coffee? Cake?'

'No, um, I,' I stumble. 'I didn't – I just wondered i-if you might need any s-staff?'

She laughs. 'Do we look like we need staff?'

'N-no,' I admit. 'Th-thank you.' I turn to go.

'Wait.'

I stop.

She regards me. 'Have we met before?'

'I don't think so.'

She gives me a thoughtful look, the way Teddy will look at me sometimes, as if he's searching for secrets. Then she glances at the old lady sitting by the window, a glance so private, so intimate and so filled with sorrow, that I feel embarrassed to witness it. I begin to back away. 'Th-thank you anyway. And, um . . . g-good luck.'

The beautiful girl doesn't say anything. She's still gazing at the old woman, so lost in thought now that she doesn't even see me leave.

11.15 a.m. – Scarlet

When Scarlet looks again the girl is gone. Although she is and she isn't. Because it's as if she has left an imprint of herself on the air. Scarlet can still see the curling hair, like her own, except golden instead of auburn. She can still hear her nervous chatter, can still feel the sense of slightly off-kilter strength. For a moment, Scarlet's struck by the notion that they could be friends. Then thinks that befriending her might be a bit like biting into a fresh doughnut while not being entirely certain what you're going to find at its centre.

'Scarlet!'

The soundwave of her grandmother's panic knocks Scarlet out of her thoughts. She moves so fast she hits her hip against the counter as she runs across the café.

'What is it?' Scarlet reaches her grandma. 'What's wrong?'

Esme points at the window, where a large brown moth is bumping against the glass. 'Get it away, Scarlet, get it away from me . . .'

'It's okay,' Scarlet says, relieved as she reaches out to the window. 'It's only a moth – I'll catch it.' She scoops up the flapping insect between her palms and opens the door with her foot. Its frantic wings flutter in her cupped hands.

'Bugger off, you bloody little troublemaker.' Scarlet leans out of the door, into the fresh, chill air, and opens her hands. But the moth has gone. And in place of frantic wings is only a pinch of ashes that sprinkles the pavement like icing sugar on a bun.

11.59 a.m. – Liyana

'So, you're a . . . lesbian?'

Liyana looks up to see Aunt Nya folding and unfolding her long legs. Her aunt, at fifty-two, is still an exceedingly beautiful woman. Surely, Liyana thinks, she could find herself another husband if she set her mind to it.

'I suppose so,' Liyana says, though that isn't how she necessarily labels herself. Not as a lover of women, but a lover of Kumiko. Liyana can't separate knowing Kumiko from loving her. For, the moment they met, it was nothing and it was everything. The way she looked: small and slight, porcelain skin, midnight hair, dark almond eyes that seemed to take up half her face. The way she dressed: black silk, white cotton, red lipstick. The way she spoke: slow and soft, so you had to lean in to listen. The way she moved: seeming not to walk but glide through life like a river fish. The way she was: confident, certain, unlike any other teenager Liyana knew. And, perhaps most of all, it was the way Kumiko made Liyana feel about herself: as if she was exactly as she should be.

Nyasha folds her legs again. She picks up her teacup. 'Oh.'

'Oh?' Liyana looks up from her milky coffee. For days, weeks, months, she's been anticipating her aunt's reaction to this news, expecting rejection, vilification, tears and screams. What she hadn't expected was no reaction at all. 'Is that all you have to say?'

'And what should I say, Ana?'

Liyana considers. 'I don't know. I thought you'd say . . . something.'

Aunt Nya sips her tea. 'Do you have a girlfriend?'

'Yes,' Liyana says. 'Her name's Kumiko.'

'Okay.' Nya nods. 'And how long have you . . . had Kumiko for?'

'Nine and a half months.'

'Well, well.' Her aunt raises an elegant eyebrow. 'You certainly kept that quiet.'

With her index finger, Liyana circles the rim of her coffee cup. 'I wanted to tell you sooner – I wasn't sure how you'd react.'

Aunt Nya crosses her legs again. 'And how am I doing?'

'Well, I thought you might be a little more . . . surprised.'

'I was a lesbian once, you know,' her aunt says. 'At a

party with a girl called Sefryn. Very pretty she was, like a pixie. That was . . . over thirty years ago – can you believe it?'

'This isn't one night at a party, *Nɔḍi*,' Liyana says. 'I love her.'

'And does she love you?'

Liyana glances at the still pool of coffee in her cup. She nods.

'Then you're a lucky girl, *vinye*.' Nya sits back in her chair and sets down her cup. 'So, I've been thinking that I'll get a job, one that'll pay enough for—'

'Sorry, what?' Liyana sits forward. 'I must be mistaken, but I thought you said you'd get a job.'

'You're not wrong,' her aunt says. 'That's exactly what I'm going to do.'

Liyana stifles a smile.

Nya frowns. 'And what's so funny about that?'

'I'm sorry, but—' Liyana shakes her head. 'You can barely stack the dishwasher. What are you qualified for?' Liyana won't say that she's already applied for several jobs, including Tesco, and is waiting to hear back.

'That's hardly fair,' Nya protests. 'I have several highly desirable skills—'

'True, but you're not allowed to charge for them.'

Her aunt scowls, then sighs. 'I could've made an excellent living, though, twenty years ago. Possibly ten.'

Liyana smiles. 'The African Julia Roberts.'

'Oh, I think I can do better than Richard Gere.' Nyasha pulls herself up, chest forward, shoulders back. 'I'd rather be Violetta in *La traviata*.'

'What, and die of TB? I think Julia had the happier ending.'

Her aunt shrugs. 'Depends on your perspective, I suppose. God, I remember the first time you saw that opera, you cried so loud when she died we had to leave.'

Liyana reaches for the memory but can't find it. 'I don't—'

'We hid in the ladies' loos,' Nya continues. 'A bosomy cleaner eventually kicked us out.'

'Oh,' Liyana says, half to herself. The coffee in her cup begins to boil. 'Yeah, you . . . you promised I'd never have to be a courtesan, that you'd always . . .'

'You slept in my bed for a week.'

'I did?' Liyana says. The bubbling coffee stills. 'I'd forgotten.'

Aunt Nya sips her tea and sits back in her chair. 'I hadn't.'

For a few moments neither speaks, then Liyana sighs softly into the silence. 'Okay, perhaps we can compromise.'

Her aunt brightens. 'We can?'

'I'm not making any promises,' Liyana says. 'But I'll talk to Kumiko again . . . And, if you can find a man who'll agree to a platonic marriage then—'

'What?' Her aunt's smile drops. 'No, that's ridiculous. No man will agree to that, unless he's gay.'

'Then find a gay one,' Liyana says. 'Or one who'll agree to an open marriage, but without any of the . . .'

'No,' Nya objects. 'That'll never—'

'Those are my terms,' Liyana says. 'And they're not up for negotiation.'

4.37 p.m. – Goldie

I've read stories about people realizing unknown skills when put under extreme pressure, like mothers lifting trucks off babies. Well, poverty has realized in me a hitherto untapped aptitude for pickpocketing. I discovered this earlier, quite by accident.

I was trawling the shops, restaurants, cafés for potential serving positions, navigating crowds of tourists and clusters of students. Then, somewhere along King's Parade I saw it: a fat purse sticking out of a Chanel handbag. My first impulse was to alert the owner to the precarious position of their purse. My second impulse was to relieve them of that purse. I followed the second impulse.

I'll limit myself to one theft a day, and take only purses and wallets of clear pedigree. If they're carrying less than thirty quid, I'll let them keep it. Anything above that, I'll take half. I'll leave anything important – credit cards, driving licences, passports. It's hit-and-run theft, but I'll bruise instead of maim. Except when I find a toff with a Coutts card. They're fair game.

8.58 p.m. – Bea

'You might want to pick that up.' Bea nods at the buzzing phone on his desk. 'It's your wife.'

Dr Finch gropes for his glasses. 'It can't be, she's at the cinema seeing—'

'I don't care.' Bea stands up on the sofa. 'And it is.'

Slipping his glasses onto his nose, he squints at the screen. 'How the hell did you know that?'

Bea shrugs. 'Perhaps she can smell a guilty conscience.' She reaches for her dress, slipping it over her shoulders.

'Wouldn't surprise me.' Dr Finch drops the phone back onto his desk. 'I've often thought she was a witch.'

'Piss off,' Bea snaps, unsure why his use of the word annoys her so much. 'That's your wife you're talking about, the woman who gave birth to your kids – you have kids, right? – and I bet you're no domestic angel. You leave the toilet seat up, never make dinner or do the school run and' – Bea searches for another fact she doesn't know how she knows – 'download particularly filthy porn to your son's computer.'

Her Logic and Language lecturer casts her an incredulous look, then busies himself with rearranging cushions on his sofa, saying nothing to confirm Bea's CliffsNotes on his character. She doesn't care, she knows she's right.

'You're hardly in a position to cast moral disapprobation.' He sits up. 'You weren't showing much concern for my wife's welfare twenty minutes ago.'

Bea gets up, picks her bag off the floor. 'Well, I'm not married to her, Prince Charming, you are.'

She doesn't hear what he says in response, something about daddy issues, since she's already slamming the door shut behind her. The sex, such as it was, hadn't been worth leaving the library for. She'd suspected as much when he'd invited her, and it irks Bea that she hadn't followed her instincts.

11.58 p.m. – Leo

Tomorrow Leo will bump into her. He's waited long enough to ensure it'll appear coincidental. He feels Goldie's power increasing every day, every hour that brings her closer to her eighteenth birthday. Now he knows that, if he's to stand a chance of victory, he must maximize his tactical advantages. He still has the element of surprise and knows how he might enhance it. It'd be easy enough to seduce her, exceedingly pleasant too, and would leave her far more vulnerable at the moment of attack. Admittedly, Leo won't feel proud of such an unsporting ambush. But, if it's his only chance of survival, then he'll have to take it.

9th October – 23 days . . .

1.57 a.m. – Scarlet

It takes Scarlet hours of intense rationalization to recover from the moth-exterminating episode. In the end, she settles on the explanation of spontaneous combustion. Quite how this could have occurred, Scarlet isn't certain, but it's sort of scientific and means that she isn't delusional, bewitched or dangerous, which is surely all that matters.

Scarlet wishes she could talk to her grandmother, share her worries, ask advice. Most of the time Scarlet is okay, strong and self-sufficient. An almost adult who looks, generally, as if she's got her act together. But sometimes she feels like an eight-year-old whose mother has just died, scared and alone, wanting to be held. Especially late at night when all she can hear is the tick-tock of the grandfather clock in the stillness and it feels like an eternity until morning.

Which is how she feels tonight. She wishes it were raining. Thunderstorms are best. When one can luxuriate in the comfort of being safely tucked up instead of out getting soaked. Sadly, the night is still, the sky clear. The moon is nearing full, a shard of light falling into the room.

Scarlet feels a tug towards the window, as if a lover were coaxing her out of bed. Without thinking why, she slips out from under the duvet and steps across the carpet. Looking up at the moon, Scarlet thinks of the café, wondering if she's doing the right thing struggling so hard to hold on. Perhaps she should stop fighting to save a sinking ship, especially when her grandmother's drowning. Perhaps she should take the lifeboat being offered by Mr Wolfe – though she's not seen hide nor hair of him since dropping him off at the hospital – sell up and take care of Esme properly. Scarlet could find a nice nursing home, get a job in a café (anywhere but Starbucks) and let someone else worry about the bills while she collects an hourly wage and a free lunch.

For a moment, the light of the moon seems to brighten. Scarlet's shoulders drop, her breathing slows and she feels a sense of calm she's not felt in a long while. Scarlet watches the sky until clouds drift over the moon and, all at once, she imagines the clouds slipping out of the sky and falling to Earth. Then they aren't clouds but leaves, perpetually falling from a nocturnal sky.

6.46 a.m. – Goldie

'I don't want you to get another job,' Teddy says, uncomplainingly munching a piece of burnt toast. He doesn't mind the endless toast and tins of beans, since it means I'm home for breakfast every morning and dinner every night. 'I want you to stay home.'

I smile. 'I want that too. And, if I suddenly found a few thousand quid, that's what I'd do. But sadly—' I'm about to say: 'money doesn't grow on trees', but it's something my stepfather used to say, so I don't.

Yet again, I lament that I hadn't been able to hit the safe before fleeing the hotel. Teddy interrupts my thoughts.

'What kind of job will you get?'

'I don't know,' I say. 'Nothing fancy, I'm not qualified for much.'

Teddy peers over his singed toast, fixing me with his blue eyes. 'I don't care,' he says. 'I think you can do anything in the whole wide world.'

I give him a rueful smile, leaning across the table to stroke his hair, the curls soft as moss, and say nothing.

9th October – 23 days . . .

6.45 a.m. – Liyana

'Good morning.'

Liyana looks up, startled to see her aunt – rarely awake before sunrise – walking into the kitchen. She's annoyed since she'd wanted to be alone, filling out more application forms for exploitative minimum-wage jobs. She's still not heard back from Tesco.

'Morning, *Nɔɖi*.'

Her aunt pulls out a chair as if it weighs ten tonnes, then flops onto it with a deep and sorrowful sigh. 'Coffee,' she says. 'I need coffee.'

'You don't drink coffee,' Liyana says. 'You drink weird types of trendy tea.'

'It's dawn, I need caffeine.' Nyasha rests her head on the table. 'Please. Help a frail old lady.'

When Liyana sets down the mug, she hears soft snores emanating from beneath an intricate maze of cornrows. Liyana gives her aunt a poke in the ribs.

Nya squeals and sits upright with a snap, looking confused. 'What did you do that for?'

'I just made you an excellent cup of coffee. I wasn't going to let it go to waste.'

'What are you talking about? I was wide awake.' Nya takes a tentative sip of the scalding coffee. '*Vinye*, I think I've found The One.'

'Which one?'

'Well, the first one,' Nya says. 'He's over-privileged, flexible in his sexuality and looking for a wife. At least' – she sets down her cup – 'his mother's looking for his wife. Anyway, he's perfect.'

'Wait.' Liyana sits forward, heart quickening. She needs to stall, needs more time to prepare. 'Where did you find him?'

'His mother is my cousin's sister-in-law. She arranged my first marriage.'

'Who did?' Liyana asks, confused.

'My cousin. Pay attention, Ana, he'll be here any minute.'

Liyana sits up. 'What? No, wait, I'm not—'

She's interrupted by the ring of the doorbell, which instantly propels Nya from her chair. 'I'll get it!'

As the door opens, Liyana wonders if she has time to run. When she hears her aunt's voice rise into honeyed sweetness, Liyana knows her time is up.

Nya returns to the kitchen like a lion tamer leading her prize lion. And she's holding a man. A man Liyana recognizes but can't quite place.

'It's so good of you to come for breakfast,' she's saying. 'I know you're very busy.'

'That's fine,' he smiles. 'I'm not due into the office till nine.'

Nya nods as if he's just said something profoundly wise. Then she drops her gaze to her niece, looking a little surprised, as if she'd forgotten that Liyana was there at all.

'Ana, allow me to introduce Mazmo Owethu Muzenda-Kasteni.' Nya's hand rests on Mazmo's shoulder. 'Mazmo, I'd like you to meet my niece, Liyana Miriro Chiweshe.'

Liyana considers him. 'But we've met before.'

'You have?' Nya looks delighted. 'Where and when? Do you know each other well?'

'Not yet,' Mazmo says. 'We met about a week ago. At the gym on Upper Street—'

'The Serpentine Spa.' Aunt Nya shoots a self-satisfied look at Liyana, since it was her membership that occasioned this auspicious initial meeting. 'I'm there three times a week – I'm surprised I've never had the pleasure of bumping into you myself.'

'It's not my usual gym,' Mazmo says. 'But I had a meeting in Islington that day, so – serendipity.'

Gazing at Mazmo, Nya snaps out of her reverie. 'Where are my manners? What can I get you, Mazmo – tea, coffee, warm lemon water?'

Mazmo slides into the chair beside Liyana. 'Do you have kombucha?'

'I've run out.' Nya's momentarily mortified. 'But I can nip out to—'

'No, no, it's fine.' Mazmo waves his hand. 'How about matcha green?'

'Absolutely. Ana, what would you—?'

'Nothing for me.' Liyana glowers at her aunt, who's busying herself with teacups, then casts a sideways glance at Mazmo. Admittedly, he isn't a bald septuagenarian with a paunch and halitosis. He is, as her aunt promised, both young and attractive. Exceedingly attractive, excessively attractive. And that voice. She'd forgotten the velvet of his voice, a river smoothing rocks.

'So . . .' Mazmo's saying. 'I hear you enjoy dancing.'

'Do I?' Liyana casts another scorching glance at her aunt, who's fiddling with the water filter.

'If you want to go, I'm good friends with the chap who owns the M25.'

Liyana frowns. 'The motorway?'

He laughs and Liyana looks at him, caught off guard by the sound of the river again. Liyana feels her aunt's glow emanating from the espresso machine. A moment later, she hands Mazmo his tea as if it were an offering of frankincense and myrrh. She lingers at the table. 'Oat milk? Almond?'

'No, thanks.' Mazmo pats his washboard stomach. 'I'm paleo.'

'Of course,' Nya says, as if this were the only sensible dietary choice. 'Well then, I'll leave you two to get better acquainted . . .'

Mazmo half-stands. 'You won't stay?'

'No,' Nya says, the word weighted with reluctance and longing. 'No, I should go.'

'No, stay.' Liyana grabs her aunt's hand and squeezes tight. 'You really should stay, *Nɔḍi*. You know how I met Mazmo, now I want to hear how—'

With a swift tug, Nya extricates herself from Liyana's grip. 'I'll let him tell you that funny little story. I'll be back in a few hours.'

As her aunt wafts out of the kitchen on an air of regret, Liyana turns with equal reluctance to Mazmo. How embarrassing to meet him again under such circumstances. And how, she wonders, does one charm a man without the promise of sexual favours? She thinks of what her aunt said about his sexuality – is he gay and wanting an heir to satisfy his mother? That she cannot do. Or does he simply want a wife, to draw a veil over his pansexual practices? *That* she might be able to do – Kumiko permitting. Still, how to raise the delicate matter of finances? Liyana thinks of her heroine. BlackBird would simply threaten bodily harm if premarital funds weren't immediately forthcoming, but Liyana will need to be slightly more subtle than that.

'So . . .' Mazmo says.

'So . . .' Liyana echoes.

He smiles again. And again she's caught by it, reminded of that something long ago. The moon breaking through clouds. The river catching its light.

11.03 a.m. – Nyasha

Nyasha will never forget her first time. The first time she tasted champagne. The first time she saw diamonds. The first time she heard opera. And each of these things had happened on the same night. Fittingly, it had been the first husband who introduced her to them all. For this reason alone, she's always held him in fond regard. That he was an inconsiderate lover and serial philanderer meant she'd never liked him much, though she'd loved him once.

Under the watchful eye and instruction of her cousin Akosua, Nyasha had been courting Kwesi Xoese Mayat for three weeks when she was told that tonight she must finally agree to marry him. Timing, according to Akosua, was everything. One must make a suitor wait a suitable period: long enough to garner respect, but not long enough to engender frustration. And so, Nyasha was prepared. She didn't particularly want to marry Kwesi, but Akosua had assured her that love had little to do with relationships, it was all about family.

'If you like him and he will take care of you,' her cousin said, 'that is enough.'

That he liked her was clear. That night he drove her from Ayitepa to Accra, for a night at the National Theatre to see *La traviata*. Afterwards they dined at La Chaumière, a formidably chic and forbiddingly pricey restaurant. Nyasha had been so spellbound by the opera that she passed the dinner in a daze. A shame since she'd barely tasted the exquisitely expensive food. She was so spellbound that, when Kwesi slid a long black leather box across the table, Nyasha didn't notice until he emitted a self-conscious cough.

'Sorry,' she said. 'What?' – then looking down – '*Ao?* Is it for me?'

'Of course.' Kwesi smiled, as if he were a judge bestowing a medal. 'Open it.'

She did, and *La traviata* was eclipsed by three long strings of sparkling diamonds and fat pearls that glittered and glistened in the candlelight.

Kwesi laughed. 'Well, aren't you going to try it on?'

Slowly Nyasha reached out, lifting the necklace as if it might be spun of moonlight and cloud, between forefingers and thumbs.

Kwesi took a swig of his champagne. 'It won't bite.'

Nyasha nodded, not looking up as she hung the necklace, fumbling with the clasp until, finally, it fastened. As the cool jewels touched her warm skin she held her breath.

'C-can I . . . keep it?'

Kwesi laughed again. It was a laugh of easy wealth, of silk, cashmere and Scotch, the laugh of a man who'd never had to strive for anything. 'Of course, I just gave it to you.'

'*Nyó ta*. Yes, I . . .' Nyasha dropped her fingers from the pearls. '*Akpe* . . . And, is it – or do I . . . will I give it back to you, if . . . ?'

His smile deepened, plumping out his satisfied cheeks. 'You mean, if we break up?'

Nyasha turned her eyes to the table, settling her gaze on the silver cutlery, resisting the urge to clutch the necklace again.

'I certainly hope that won't happen.' Kwesi Xoese slid his hand across the thick linen tablecloth, taking hers. 'But yes, if you divorce me it's still yours.'

She lifted her eyes to meet his. That was it. A marriage proposal that was an assumption instead of a question. She hadn't even been given the chance to say 'yes'.

'You might divorce me,' Nyasha said instead.

'O*h, ao!*' Kwesi lifted her hand to his mouth, kissing her knuckles. 'I can't ever imagine such a thing.'

Nyasha gave him a shy little smile, reaching up with her other hand to rest her fingers back on the strings of diamonds and pearls. *Hers*. No matter what. It was then Nyasha experienced another first. The first time she felt safe.

11.11 a.m. – Goldie

'Wait!'

I'm nursing my sixth rejection of the day when I see

him. On Trinity Street, amid the bustling tourists and students. Fortunately, I'm not caught in the act of lifting a fat wallet from a fancy bag. Still, I've no desire to relive the shame of our last encounter, so I turn to avoid him.

'Goldie, wait.'

I stop. When he reaches me, I can't meet his eye.

'Are you all right?' he says. 'I've been worrying about you since . . .'

'I'm fine.' I feign an effortless shrug. 'No harm, no foul.'

'But . . . your manager, he didn't call the police?'

'Probably,' I say. 'I didn't stay around to find out.'

'Oh.'

I wait for him to ask exactly how I escaped, but he doesn't. Instead, he reaches out, as if he's going to touch my shoulder, then drops his hand.

'So, you've found another job?'

'No, that's what I'm doing right now – looking for another job – but it doesn't seem like anyone's hiring.' I glance at the pavement. 'I guess I picked the wrong time to steal your wallet then bite off my boss's finger.'

'You bit off your boss's finger?' Leo's incredulous.

Hardly surprising, I suppose, that Garrick kept that detail to himself.

I shrug again, as if it's of no matter, as if I'm biting off fingers all the time. 'I exaggerate,' I admit. 'But only slightly.'

Leo smiles. 'And how did you get hold of his finger in the first place?'

'A long and unseemly story. Let's just say, I'm not pining for my old job back.' I glance again at the hand that almost touched my shoulder. I still can't meet his eye. 'Though I wish it wasn't so bloody impossible to find a new one.'

'Oh,' Leo says. 'But that's all right, I can get you a job.'

'Really?' I look up, instantly caught by those green eyes

and unable to look away. I should be speaking, should be enquiring as to the details, relaying my qualifications, but I can't form a coherent sentence or thought.

Leo smiles.

I smile back. He steps towards me. I hold my breath.

He reaches out. I lean forwards.

Then I stumble back again, bumped by an errant tourist with a selfie-stick. I tip, then right myself, catching his eye again. 'So, um, this job sounds great. What does it involve exactly?'

'Well' – Leo casts a glance at the oblivious tourist – 'my father owns a chain of hotels, he's here opening a new one—'

'Your father?' I say, feeling the great canyon of wealth and class between us deepen. 'I hardly think he would hire me to—'

Leo laughs. 'Oh, don't worry about that. He won't remember you – he doesn't pay any attention to the staff. Anyway, he doesn't do the hiring, I do.'

'You do?' I can't keep the note of surprise from my voice, though I stop short of revealing that I know plenty of other things about him, such as can only be gleaned from reading a person's private diary.

'I'm only helping him out, I'm studying here, so . . .' Leo trails off, perhaps not wanting to further highlight the gulf in our circumstances. 'Anyway, he's just acquired the Hotel Clamart, the one on—'

'I know it,' I say. 'It's . . . fancy.'

'Well, if you want a job there, it's yours.'

'Really?' I ask, trying not to sound quite as desperate as I am. 'That'd be a— But you already know, I'm not . . .'

'Oh, I don't think we'll have a problem with that.' Leo smiles, as if we're sharing a particularly pleasing secret. 'So long as you're discreet.'

I look at him, but he shrugs.

'Minimum wage is scandalous, especially as reparation for cleaning toilets. Our guests are richer than they deserve. I don't see that a little . . . redistribution of wealth is going to hurt anyone.'

I grin. 'You must be the most understanding boss I've ever had.'

'Does that mean you'll take the job?' He smiles and, all at once, I want to kiss him. 'I felt so guilty for getting you fired, and now—'

'It wasn't your fault. If I hadn't been . . .' I glance at the strangers milling around us, though no one's listening. '. . . stealing from you in the first place, then . . .'

Leo's smile deepens. 'Oh, we both know you weren't doing anything of the sort.'

'No, I—'

'You were reading my diary.'

Now I wish I'd run. 'Oh, God, I – I'm s-sorry,' I say, unable to deny it. 'I never should have, it's . . . unforgivable. It's . . . After I saw you, I felt . . . And I couldn't, I just couldn't . . .'

'Nothing is unforgivable,' Leo says, lifting his hand to settle lightly on my shoulder. 'Especially not something as small as that.'

'Really?'

'Really.'

He looks at me with such tenderness then that all I can think is: I'm going to be working in his hotel. I will see him every day. I can hardly believe my luck.

4.34 p.m. – Leo

Leo knew what had happened at the hotel. He knew about the finger, the firing and the fact that the greasy manager had tried to set the police on Goldie. But, since Garrick had been unwilling to divulge the circumstances of how exactly his finger had found its way into her mouth in the first place, that particular investigation had died a quick death.

Now Leo wonders if he can finagle a few more management shifts from his father at the hotel. It shouldn't be a problem, since his father is such a great believer in hard work, in 'getting one's hands dirty'. A pretense since naturally his father never expects him to go anywhere near a begrimed lavatory.

God, how he'd wanted to hold her, to kiss her . . . He wonders how Goldie would react if she knew a day hasn't passed when he hasn't thought about her. He'd felt how much she wanted to touch him too, how much effort she'd exerted to hold back. Seducing her will be far easier even than he'd imagined. Though he'll have to be careful not to unbalance this strange alchemy of desire and death that he sustains within himself. For, regardless of how lustful he feels towards his opponent, in twenty-three days they must fight to the death. And, no matter how Leo might feel for Goldie, he would still rather live than die.

6.40 p.m. – Bea

Bea has been feeling uneasy, as if she's being watched, as if she's being stalked by something or someone who half wants to be seen. Now and then she turns to catch sight of him, to give shape to the shadow flickering at the edges of her eye-line. But, whenever she looks, the shadow has gone.

Several times, it feels as if this shifting is happening from within, as if something is creeping up inside her by stealth. Bea tells herself she's probably caught the flu, that she'd benefit from taking a break from the library and spending a few days in bed. Though nothing short of the bubonic plague will keep Bea from her desk. It's a testament to how bad she feels that lately she hasn't been able to even countenance going up in a glider. So, she settles into the fuzzy-headed unease, an ache she will wait out.

When staring at pages of dense philosophical text begins to hurt her eyes, Bea rests her head on her book, the paper cool on her skin; she feels a sudden need for the comfort of company. Since the death of her *abuela* three years ago, Bea has no one whose company brings cheer. Her *mamá*'s certainly doesn't.

She closes her eyes, clothing herself with a blanket of longing. A few minutes later, she sees him: a man standing in front of her. A man with golden eyes, white hair and a face wrinkled as a dried plum.

'Beauty,' he says. 'What a pleasure to see you again, my love.'

Her father. There is no one else he can be, since she feels a sudden, reluctant affinity with him that she's only ever felt before with her *mamá*. And he says her name as if he was the one who gave it to her.

'You can do anything you wish, Bea,' he says, as if replying to a question. 'You are bound by nothing. Not the laws of gravity, nor the properties of the physical world. Only the limits of your own imagination.'

When Bea doesn't respond, he holds out his left hand, palm up, as if making an offering. Then he raises his arm. Bea watches as, all at once, an entire library shelf is stripped clean of books that lift into the air as one, cover-to-cover, spine-to-spine. They hover there for a moment then begin to separate, displaying a concertina of pages. Bea stares open-mouthed as the pages become feathers and the feathers become wings, and the spines of the books shift and fatten into the bodies of birds.

Her father nods: an instruction. Bea pushes back her chair, climbs onto it and stands on the table as she'd done before. Then she outstretches her left arm, opens her hand, palm up, and begins curling and uncurling her fingers.

'That's right, good girl.'

Bea imagines herself tapping on invisible keys, as if she'd learned to play the piano long ago and is trying to recall her favourite sonata. But the book-birds don't move. They hover in the air, waiting. Bea's about to drop her hand when her father gives an almost imperceptible shake of his head. So her fingers continue searching for something, until she strikes the first note of the sonata and, all at once, the book-birds begin to transform.

The leather-bound volumes stretch and shift into eagles that soar to the library ceiling, circling in long elegant loops, stirring the stale air with the beat of their wings. Slight, yellowed paperbacks become flittering, twittering canaries; dense textbooks grow into magpies, ravens or jays, according to subject. Oversized manuscripts assume the shape of swans that glide so effortlessly past every other bird they might be entirely alone. Every first edition floats elegantly to the wooden floor, as white pages elongate into emerald-sapphire feathers to adorn peacocks that strut proudly along the library aisles.

Bea gawps, awestruck, at her creations. She is Hera, Isis, Gaia. She is all the goddesses of birth, of life, of all that she surveys. She feels her father's smile of pride, the sudden warmth of the sun on her cheek. And, in that moment, she will do anything to keep that smile, to evoke it again.

'Yes,' he says. 'And now what?'

Without asking, she knows what he wants. So, under his gaze, Bea shifts and transforms until she is Kali, Nephthys, Athena. The goddesses of death and war.

With a single snap of forefinger and thumb, Bea brings the eagles swooping down from the ceiling, screeching through the air, their talons ripping through feathers, their beaks snapping through bone in a riot of colour and blood. Until at last the library is a silent battlefield with the victors feasting on the dead and the feathers of the slain still floating to the floorboards like the perpetually falling leaves of Everwhere.

Bea catches her father's eye and mirrors his smile. She has fulfilled his wish and made him proud. She is his protégée, his legacy. She will execute his every desire.

Her father nods. 'Yes, you are my love. And I know you will.'

Then he's gone. Before he has a chance to tell her what his desires are. Still, the echo of his voice remains, along with the shimmer of his smile. But it's not this that freezes Bea when she opens her eyes, not the shock nor the stain of blood. It's her growing sense that the massacre wasn't a dream but a memory.

Over a decade ago

Goldie

I wanted to grow up quickly, to leave home and find my own way in the world. Maybe other children felt secure in the clutches of their parents, tethered to the ground, rooted in the soil. But I didn't, I longed to drift through life like an unplanted seed, a lucky puff of dandelion or milkweed, no one watching, no one telling me what to do.

In Everwhere it was different. There I could be a floating seed in a place full of floating seeds and falling leaves. There we could go where we wished, before being brought together on currents of water and air. We didn't need a meeting place or a map. We were drawn to one another, like spawning salmon or migrating birds. As soon as I stepped into Everwhere something inside me switched on – a radar that resonated with my sisters. The feeling I had there of belonging, of connecting, was not a feeling I'd ever known before. But the first time I felt it, I knew what it was. And every night I followed this beacon until I found them.

Most of the time we'd stick together, but sometimes we'd split up. One night I sat with Bea in the glade while Scarlet and Ana searched for a river and a midnight swim. I'd conjured up an elaborate excuse not to go; Bea simply said she couldn't be bothered.

'This place is real, you know. You're not dreaming.'

'How do you know?'

'*Mamá* told me,' Bea said. 'She's a Grimm too, so she knows.'

I frowned. 'What's a Grimm?'

Bea laughed. Her full name, and I don't know how I knew, since I'd never asked, was 'Beauty'. Personally, I'd be mortified to have such a name, but she didn't seem to mind.

'Don't you know?' Bea asked, still laughing. 'How don't you know that?'

I shrugged, trying to pretend it didn't matter to me either way.

But Bea, seeing straight through me, gave a self-satisfied grin. 'I can't believe you don't know what you are,' she said. 'You're a Grimm. So am I, my *mamá* too.' Her smile shifted then into something else: a little nice, a little nasty – as if she loved and hated me both. 'Your *mamá* isn't, or she'd have told you. So you're not pure Grimm like me.'

I tried to shrug again, but I couldn't. 'Okay,' I persisted, wishing I didn't have to ask again. 'But, what's a Grimm?'

Liyana

'I have news.'

Liyana looked up at her mummy, excited by the promise in her voice.

Isisa smiled. 'Auntie Nya's coming to stay for a few days.'

Liyana's excitement evaporated. 'Boring,' she said, returning to her drawing.

'Don't say that, Ana. You love your auntie.'

Liyana picked a red crayon out of her box. 'She's only coming to visit because she's lonely, because she's getting divorced again. She never visits otherwise.'

'That's not . . . Well, anyway we'll cheer her up. She'll be happy to see you. You can help heal her broken heart. That's what family is for, Ana.'

Liyana bit down the sudden anger that swelled in her like a gathering wave. She didn't want to be responsible for healing anyone's heart – the burden of her mummy's expectations was enough, without adding her aunt's hopes on top.

'*Nɔḍi* doesn't have a broken heart.' Liyana reached for an orange crayon to capture Scarlet's hair and the fire sparking in her hands. 'She loves money, not husbands.'

'Hush,' her mummy said. 'And you shouldn't be so contemptuous of money, only people who have it do that. Aunt Nya's money is the reason we're here.'

Liyana wanted to say that she didn't think that was such a great thing. She wanted to ask the meaning of 'contemptuous' but didn't, in case her mummy scolded her for not already knowing.

Biting the end of her orange crayon, Liyana also wanted to ask why her mummy had never had even one husband, skirting a sneaky side street into the question of her own father. But timing was everything with her mummy and now was not the right time. Perhaps when she was drunk with Aunt Nya.

'Maybe you could find a husband, *Da*— Mummy, then you might be—'

'Hush!' Isisa's simmering anger suddenly boiled over. 'Don't talk nonsense, *vinye*.'

'But, maybe he'd be better than Daddy,' Liyana persisted. 'Maybe—'

Mummy stopped, as if she'd just been slapped. She narrowed her eyes. Silence shifted the air like static before a storm.

Liyana fixed her eyes on her drawing, trying to think of something to say to make everything better again. 'I, um . . . Do you like my picture?' Liyana held it up, hiding her face behind the page.

Her mummy glanced at it. 'Colour inside the lines, Ana,' she said. 'You're not a baby anymore.'

Over a decade ago

Scarlet

Scarlet stared into the flames. She stood as close as she could to the fire, closer than anyone else, her gloveless hands clutching the protection rail, glowing in the firelight. She wished Bonfire Night was celebrated every day, instead of once a year. She wished her mother would light fires in their fireplace at home, she wished she was allowed to do it alone. Sometimes Scarlet found herself gazing into the empty grate, conjuring imaginary flames. Sometimes she did this so well she could feel their heat on her cheeks.

For a moment Scarlet pulled her gaze from the bonfire to her mother standing behind her. There she was, gazing intently into the fire. But, strangely, Scarlet also felt as if she weren't there, as if she'd wandered off to find toffee apples, perhaps. The chance to watch her mother like this, unseen, to stare as long as she wanted, was rare. So she did. And, as she did, Scarlet wished she could tether Ruby to the ground, to stop her taking flight.

Finally, Scarlet took a step back and reached up to slip her bare hand into her mother's gloved one. When their fingers touched, Ruby flinched. She glanced down, frowning as if she'd thought she was alone, as if she'd forgotten her daughter was there, as if she'd forgotten she had a daughter at all.

Bea

'You flew again?' Liyana asked. 'Higher than the first time?'

Bea nodded. 'Above the trees, into the clouds.'

'Are you sure?' Liyana asked. 'You didn't imagine it?'

Bea scowled at the impertinent question, not dignifying it with an answer.

'But how?' Liyana persisted. 'How did you do it?'

Bea shrugged. 'Flying here is simple. You just have to want it enough, *et voilà*.' All at once she's hovering above the ground, grinning down at us.

'You're so lucky.' Liyana sighed, gazing up at her elevated sister. 'Can you teach me?'

'I told you,' Bea said. 'This place is created from thoughts, from . . . bright-white wishing, from black-edged desire. All you have to do is want to fly, and you will.'

Liyana's frown deepened, as did Bea's smile.

'We're here to discover how powerful we are,' she said, rising higher. 'And, once we're able to do anything we want – in this world and the other – then we get to choose.'

Liyana tipped her head back to stare up at Bea, though she could now only see the soles of her shoes.

'Choose what?' Scarlet said, stepping forward into the clearing, her own feet bare on the moss.

Bea's laughter tumbled down, as if she'd just emptied a bucket of water onto their heads. She rose higher still and, when she spoke again, they strained to hear, only catching occasional words they couldn't string into comprehensible sentences.

Though she delighted in teasing her sisters, Bea looked forward to seeing them. Every morning and afternoon she ticked each dreary daylight hour off on her fingertips, and never fought bedtime. Sometimes she'd even fall asleep before seven, in order to visit Everwhere all the sooner. But, in addition to seeing her sisters, Bea loved Everwhere because here she felt her father more vividly than anywhere else. Here was the only place she didn't miss him, for his imprint was on every falling leaf, every drop of rain, every gust of wind. Sometimes Bea felt him watching her. Sometimes she whispered to him, sometimes he whispered back.

Sometimes, Bea guiltily wished that she didn't have sisters, that she was the only daughter for her absent father to love.

Leo

'Leave him alone!'

'Oh yeah? And what are you going to do about it, Penury-Holmes?'

Instead of answering, Leo strode up to the captain of the rugby team, who was pinning Christopher up against the school gates, and kicked him hard in the shin.

'You little shit!' Henry Sykes shouted, dropping his grip on Christopher to clutch his leg. 'You're dead for this! You're fucking dead!'

Leo seized Christopher's hand and pulled him up, while expletives from Sykes's undiminished rant scorched the air.

'You're insane, Sykes,' Christopher said, rubbing his neck. 'I heard you once bit the head off a rat.'

Now Leo reapproached Sykes, grinning. He wasn't scared, he realized, not remotely. And the feeling, the complete absence of fear, was electrifying. He didn't care what happened next, didn't give a fuck. The thrill of fearlessness pulsed though him and, by the time he reached Sykes, Leo's eyes were wide with it.

'Never. Touch. My. Friend. Again,' Leo said. 'All right?'

Behind him, Christopher clapped. 'You're fucked now, Rugby Boy!'

Sykes was silent now. And the two boys flanking him shrank back against the gates. Leo waited. And, as he waited, he realized something else. Not only was he not afraid of being hurt, but he wanted Sykes to hit him, because then

Leo could strike back, could slam him into the gates and thump him till he bled.

But Sykes nodded, mumbling in the direction of his cohorts and the three boys slunk away. Watching them go, Leo felt the electric thrill of violence begin to ebb, replaced by the dull ache of disappointment.

10th October – 22 days . . .

8.34 a.m. – Scarlet

'So, what'll you do?' Walt asks. He's returned, following a six-day absence while waiting on a replacement float switch for the dishwasher and leaving a disgruntled Scarlet to wash everything by hand. She feels grateful, for once, that the café hasn't been too busy.

'I haven't a clue.'

They sit atop the kitchen counter, cradling cinnamon buns and coffee. Behind them the finial Scarlet hammered into being seems to glow, as if it's still in the furnace, so Scarlet imagines she can feel its heat pressing against her back.

'I won't sell the café, and certainly not to *him*.'

'You know . . .' Walt swallows the last of his cinnamon bun. 'As well as being a dab hand with a wrench, I also moonlight as a hit man. I don't mean to be immodest but, in certain circles, my expertise is quite renowned.'

Scarlet can't help a smile. 'Oh yes?'

Walt nods. 'You'll have to take my word for it, though. My clientele aren't the sort to offer references.'

'I imagine not.'

'As luck would have it,' he says, 'I specialize in the assassination of corporate capitalist pigs.'

'That is convenient.' Scarlet sips her coffee. 'So, do you only murder or will you maim too?'

Walt considers this. 'A simple no-frills assassination will cost you five grand. I charge extra for torture and dismembering. Now, the deluxe package – that includes the gouging of eyeballs, removal of toenails, strangulation of the victim with his own intestinal tract – will set you back an even ten.'

'Do you take direct debit?'

'Cash only, I'm afraid,' Walt says. 'As you might imagine, the Inland Revenue tends to take a dim view of my line of work.'

Scarlet sets down her coffee cup. 'They might take a dimmer view of your tax evasion.'

'True,' Walt concedes. 'Can I trust you to be discreet?'

'Well, I do prefer my intestines on the inside, so yes I think you can.' Scarlet inches closer, giving Walt a grateful nudge. 'Thank you.'

'For what?'

'For letting me forget about it all,' Scarlet says – failing grandmothers, financial struggles and combustible moths – 'for a few minutes.'

8.11 p.m. – Liyana

Liyana stares at the ceiling, trying not to think about all the things making her miserable: imminent penury, her failure so far to procure employment. Instead she thinks of Kumiko, Mazmo, the Slade . . . which is no better. Liyana sighs, her eyes filling. She blinks the tears away. One rebels and rolls down her cheek.

Liyana sits up. It's no use, she needs comfort. She contemplates her options. First, her girlfriend. But she's already walking on thin ice with Kumiko and doesn't want to crack it. Second, her aunt. A reflex thought, since when it comes to physical affection (of the platonic sort) Nya is, unless the circumstances are exceptional, about as cuddly as a shark. She tries, but she's been built too brittle. Third, the fridge. But given the way Liyana's feeling right now, she'll gobble up everything before moving on to the cupboards. Which leaves option four: her mother. Unfortunately, Isisa Chiweshe hadn't been a great source of comfort in life and nor is she in death. So, Liyana reaches under her bed for the box. It contains twelve things, including a copy of *The Water-Babies* that Mummy used to read as a special treat when they weren't trudging through Dickens. And her Tarot cards.

Liyana shuffles the cards until her panic begins to subside. She selects four and sets them on the bed, their pictures bright against the white sheets. The Page of Wands: a boy standing straight and proud, holding a white feather. *New perspectives, not afraid of challenges or risk.* The Five of Pentacles: two girls huddled together in the snow, three birds watching protectively, the coins scattered at their feet. *Despair, loss, hardship, poverty, survival.* The Moon: an arched purple wolf howls at the sky. *Prophetic dreams, illusions, the unconscious mind.* The King of Wands sits on his throne with a snake at his side, surveying his kingdom. *Self-assertion, leadership, confidence.*

Liyana stares at the cards. Something is different. As she looks down at them, elements in the pictures begin to shift and connect, forming patterns until they're giving her a clear instruction. Liyana frowns, confused. The echo of her mother's voice is sharp in her head: 'Don't claim to know anything, Ana, until you're absolutely certain.' Self-doubt seeps in. But still, the message is clear. The cards are telling her to find her sisters.

Which is strange, since she doesn't have any sisters.

8.59 p.m. – Bea

'You're starting to believe me.'

'Of course I'm not,' Bea says, already wishing she hadn't called.

'You are. I can feel it.'

'I'm not.'

Her *mamá*'s laugh is a warning. 'A little hint, my dear. When it comes to lying, don't underestimate your *mamá*.'

Bea is silent. She thinks about last night, how vivid the dream had been, how shocking the emotions. But what shocks most of all is her growing sense that it hadn't taken place in a library, or in Cambridge or, indeed, in this world at all. The books had once been white leaves, the library a grove of willow trees, and the place the subject of her *mamá*'s tales: Everwhere. But while Bea might be used to playing with philosophical notions of truth and reality, she's drawn her line in the sand far behind the fantastical. 'Well, so what if I am?'

'Well, thank the devil for that.' Her *mamá* lets out a theatrical sigh. 'Now you can stop being such a bloody shadow of yourself and start embracing who you really are.'

'Which, as far as you're concerned, is an evil bitch,' Bea says. 'Right?'

'You say that as if it's a bad thing.'

'I think you'll find that is the general consensus.'

'*¡Mierda!*' Cleo snaps. 'Fuck the general consensus – *pura mierda*. The general consensus is made by millions of passive conformists, thus the general consensus is invariably bullshit.'

Bea pictures herself cocking a pistol and marching ten paces. 'Maybe I'm not who you think I am.'

'*Y veremos*.' There's that smile in her mother's voice. 'We'll see.'

Bea grits her teeth. 'Look, I've got to go. My Moral Philosophy essay is due on Monday—'

'I already told you' – now she knows the smile is gone – 'don't lie to me.'

'I'll call you on Sunday night,' Bea says and hangs up.

10th October – 22 days . . .

10.27 p.m. – Goldie

Working at the Hotel Clamart is a dream compared with the Fitz. Due to both the absence of Garrick and the presence of Leo. The shitty toilets are the same, the sticky sheets, the filthy bathroom floors . . . but being able to clean – and pilfer from – the rooms and walk the corridors without watching out for grabby hands and with the expectation of seeing Leo, is a joy indeed.

And the place is a gold mine. Leo was right about that. If the Fitz's guests were rich, these are super-rich. It's quite something to see. And the Americans leave incredible tips. This morning a family of four left me a twenty-pound note on the dressing table. I felt a little guilty, since it wasn't the only thing I'd taken from them during their stay. Still, I don't suppose they'll ever notice.

But, by far the best thing about the job is that I will see Leo every day. The best and the worst. Because the temptation is torture. I wish he'd touch me. This morning I tried commanding him, as I had the first time we met, to no avail. I think I was too nervous. I could say something. But I won't. If he turned me down I'd be so mortified I'd have to quit and I can't afford to do that.

11.59 p.m. – Leo

After Christopher died, Leo decided to never again entwine himself with another, boy or girl, mortal or immortal. He's been safer on his own, stronger. And, if he's had to forgo love to escape grief, it's a bargain he's been happy to make.

Until now, until Goldie, Leo has never been tempted, never even been curious. With her it's different, and he can't say why. Now he's curious. Now he wants to know. And, although he knows a great deal about her that she doesn't, he also suspects she has secrets he can't see. And he wants to know everything. Not by sleight of hand or silver tongue, but for her to tell him, willing and free.

He wants to pretend, to play make-believe. He wants to hold her, to feel the pulse of her heart under his palm. He wants to imagine that, if he held her tight against his chest, she would feel his heart beating too.

Leo never thought it would be possible for longing to co-exist with loathing, at least not like this. It seems impossible that he can want someone so much while also knowing that, when the time comes, he will have to kill her.

11th October – 21 days . . .

3.33 a.m.

Wilhelm Grimm watches his four favourite daughters. He watches and he waits. Over centuries he's developed the patience of a saint, so to speak, since he's anything but. However, when it comes to humans, demons need to be as patient as angels. He doesn't have much longer to wait now: a strike of lightning, a flicker of starlight. In three weeks they'll turn eighteen.

He doesn't yet know how the night of the Choosing will go. It'll be a particular shame if he must kill them, as he has so many of his other daughters before – he can't afford, after all, to have such powerful forces working against him. But, Wilhelm has high hopes for these four, especially Bea. And, if he can win over Goldie, that'll be a coup indeed. She's the most powerful Grimm girl he's seen in four hundred years, not that she has any inkling of that just yet. Her potential for darkness delights him. It's surprisingly great, given that her mother was such a wimp. Although the stepfather had helped to twist her spirit and stoke her rage. Now all she needs is a nudge in the right direction.

Just imagine the devastation she could wreak, the agony, the misery . . . Unleashed on the world, she could do in a week what a dozen other diligent sisters could only do in a decade. If Goldie goes dark, Wilhelm knows, she will be unstoppable.

3.33 a.m. – Goldie

When I wake, the feeling that I've been with Leo, that I'm holding his hand, is so strong I can feel the warmth on my skin. But he's not beside me. I'm alone. My sheets are cold. Except where I've lain, where they are wet with sweat.

In the dark I think about the first time I saw him. I start to wonder if I could call Leo to me, if I could summon him with my thoughts as I did the first time we met. If I could override his reticence. Is it possible I have the power to do that?

3.33 a.m. – Leo

For now, Leo waits. Seducing Goldie will have its strategic advantages, certainly. But he's still not certain that he can be trusted not to compromise himself in the process. He's already thinking about her far too often. He already feels more than he should feel.

It isn't easy. When they speak, exchanging pleasantries on the weather or breakfast, Leo wants to stop her. When they pass in the corridor, Leo wants to seize hold of her. Instead, he watches her walk away and waits until the next time, when he does the same thing all over again.

6.58 a.m. – Scarlet

It had taken Scarlet no time to discover that nursing homes, even crappy ones, cost a fortune. She's looking at anything between five hundred (dire) and two thousand (plush) pounds a week. A week! Which means Scarlet will not only have to sell the café for an extremely tidy sum but also find something far more lucrative than waitressing to finance the shortfall. But there's no point in worrying about all that right now. First things first. She has, much to her regret, called Ezekiel Wolfe.

They've arranged to meet tomorrow, on neutral territory. Walt – who's still working on the damn dishwasher – has kindly agreed to sit with Esme while Scarlet's gone, in exchange for a tray of cinnamon buns. She'd offered him a batch of brownies too, to sweeten the deal, but he looked offended and said he didn't need to be bribed to do something he'd happily do for free. Scarlet had wished, in that moment, that she could hire him to look after Esme full-time. She couldn't afford £120 an hour but perhaps she could pay him in cakes.

9.09 a.m. – Bea

He is sitting on the rain-soaked library steps when Bea sees him again. She slows her stride, stopping at the step below him. 'You really can't take a hint, can you?' Bea says. 'And I didn't think I was that subtle.'

'You weren't,' he says. 'You made your feelings quite clear.'

'That's what I thought,' Bea says, twirling her umbrella. 'Then why are you here? I presume you're not sitting here just to soak up the rain?'

He hesitates.

'Come on, I haven't got all day.'

'I . . . I thought it might be weighing on your conscience – your slightly callous dismissal,' he says. 'So, I thought I'd give you the chance to be a bit politer this time.'

Bea eyes him as an owl might a mouse. 'You're serious?'

He shrugs.

Bea kicks at the stone step. 'All right then, I'll be civil when I tell you to piss off this time. So, what's your name?'

He tugs at his beard. 'Valállat.'

Bea narrows her eyes. 'Did you make that up?' she asks, annoyed at being unable to pronounce it. 'I've never heard it before.'

'It's Vali.'

'That's not what you just said.'

He shrugs again, pulling his jumper down from riding up over his belly. 'It's Hungarian. I'm adapting it for' – he's unable to resist glancing at Bea's mouth when he says this – 'the English tongue.'

'Watch it,' Bea warns.

'Sorry, sorry, I . . . Anyway, you can call me Vali, or Val, whatever you want.'

'Why shouldn't I call you – the other thing?' Bea asks. 'I'm perfectly capable of learning to pronounce your real name.'

'I know, but I'd rather you didn't.'

'Why not?'

Vali hesitates, wiping rainwater from his brow. 'It's not really a proper name.'

'What is it then?' Bea says, curiosity momentarily trumping cruelty.

Vali fixes his eyes on his feet. 'It, it means . . . "Beast".'

Bea frowns. 'Why the hell would your *mamá* call you that?'

Vali shrugs. 'Apparently that's how I looked when I was born, like a little beast – all red and wrinkled and covered in hair.'

'Hair?'

'I had tufts on my ears, supposedly, and on my back. Not much, I think, but enough to set my mother's mind. Her opinion didn't improve over the years, either—' He looks suddenly startled. 'Oh, but you should know that I don't anymore. My back is now entirely hair-free.'

Bea glares at him. 'Why the hell should I care how hirsute you are?'

'Yes, of course. Not at all. Apologies for the digression,' Vali says. 'Anyway, now you know my name you can tell me to piss off again.'

'Right.' Bea looks down at him. He looks up at her. She bites the inside of her lip. 'All right then . . . Perhaps that can wait. Get up, you're soaked.'

Frowning, Vali stands.

Bea holds out her umbrella.

Vali grins.

'Stop grinning.'

Vali doesn't.

'Stop it.' Bea rolls her eyes. 'You look like a fat hamster.'

12.34 p.m. – Liyana

Liyana stands in the long lunch queue at Ottolenghi, her aunt's favourite Islington café. In the time before their financial crash, Nyasha liked to say that Ottolenghi's fare could be bettered only by Blé Sucré in Paris or Panificio Bonci in Rome. Now, by rights, Liyana shouldn't be here at all. But when all is lost, and the swimming pool is out of bounds, some small solace can be sought in Ottolenghi's lemon brûlée tarts.

The lunch line inches forward while Liyana's thoughts settle gloomily on the Slade. She's decided to reapply for the next academic year, determined to spend the time between now and then working and saving to meet that part of the £18,900 first-year fees and expenses not covered by loans. Loans she'll spend the rest of her life paying back, but so be it. It's only a shame that her passions and talents aren't inclined towards a more financially stable subject, like Economics or Law. Even Media Studies would be a safer bet than Fine Art.

Liyana sighs, turning her thoughts to less upsetting matters, musing on a problematic plot point in BlackBird's latest escapade. Might she strip the leaves from the trees and stitch them together to—

'I'm going to kill Cassie when I see her.'

Surprised by the acidity of the statement, Liyana glances at the customer behind her. 'I'm sorry, what?'

A polished white woman, all linen and gold, regards Liyana with silent suspicion. Embarrassed, Liyana quickly turns back to her place in the queue.

'Oh, Grandma, what are we going to do?'

Confused, Liyana glances over her shoulder again. But the suspicious woman is still silent and none of the chatter undulating along the lunch line is being directed at Liyana. However, those two sentences were, she's sure. She heard them as clearly as if someone had spoken into her ear.

The line shifts forward. An emaciated blonde woman relays her intricate order to the patient blonde girl behind the counter. Why is it that everyone – customers and staff – in these places is always so fucking pale? Liyana waits, alert until it's her turn.

'Can I help you?'

Liyana fumbles for her list.

'Now you look like a constipated hamster.'

Liyana frowns. 'Surely not. Sorry, what did you just say?'

The blonde girl frowns. 'What?'

Liyana feels a surge of frustration. 'Why are you insulting me? What have I done to you?'

The girl looks alarmed. 'I didn't insult you, I only asked what you wanted.'

'But, I heard you—'

It's then, seeing the utterly perplexed look on the girl's face that Liyana realizes that no one is speaking to her. At least, not in Ottolenghi. She's hearing the voices in her head.

Over a decade ago

Goldie

I knew I shouldn't have said it almost as soon as the words left my mouth. But Mrs Chadha was looking at me, wanting more.

'You think Reyansh shouldn't go on his trip?'

I glanced back at the lengthening queue of customers – a fat woman behind me was expelling impatient sighs – suddenly no longer at all sure what I'd meant. It was just a silly dream, I should have kept my mouth shut.

'N-no . . .' I shook my head. I couldn't tell Mrs Chadha to cancel her husband's holiday, not because of something I'd dreamed. And yet, I couldn't shake the image of him: face underwater, dead eyes staring up at me. 'I d-don't know,' I stalled. 'M-maybe. Or maybe he could go another time. I, I . . .'

Mrs Chadha leaned forward, her large breasts flattening on the counter. 'What did you see? Tell me what you saw.'

I opened my mouth again, trying to form the image into words. 'I, I . . .'

'Goldie!'

I turned to see Ma pushing through the queue, eliciting further huffs and snorts from the irate customers. When she reached the counter, her eyes flitted from the pint of milk and pound coin to Mrs Chadha.

'I'm sorry.' Ma took my hand. 'Has Goldie been bothering you?'

'Oh no,' Mrs Chadha said, shaking her head. 'No, I was only asking . . .'

I coughed and, mercifully, Mrs Chadha caught my pleading eyes and stopped.

'Good.' Ma returned to me. 'You've been gone half an hour. I thought you'd been run over or abducted or . . .'

She grabbed the pint of milk, forgot her change, and dragged me out of the shop.

We hurried along the pavement together. Usually, you might mistake Ma for me, since she was so short and slight, but not with her being heavily pregnant.

'S-sorry, Ma.' I squinted in the sunshine. 'I – I didn't realize I'd been—'

'Then you should think, Goldie, instead of . . .' With a sigh she stopped walking, then hefted up her belly to half-kneel, half-squat on the pavement so we were eye to eye. 'I just worry about you. You're different, you've got to be careful what you . . .'

I waited for Ma to finish, to tell me how I was different, what I had to be careful of and why she worried about me so much. But instead she heaved herself back up, abandoning her sentence to take my hand again and usher me home.

Scarlet

Something was bothering Scarlet, a stone in her shoe she couldn't quite shake out. Images flickered at the edges of her sight – sounds, smells, the sense of something teasing but never fully revealing itself. Sometimes she thought she saw someone she knew, girls her own age, each with curling hair of a different colour: blonde, brown, black. But, when she caught sight of their faces, Scarlet realized they were strangers.

'Today's the day,' Esme called, as soon as Scarlet stepped into the café, the bell above the door tinkling. 'You're late.'

Scarlet glanced at her watch as she hurried across the creaky wooden floor towards the kitchen. She was early.

'I am not,' she said, appearing at the door. Ella Fitzgerald filled the kitchen – *My Baby Just Cares for Me* – lifting into the air with the scent of cinnamon. 'You said six o'clock.'

'Well, it's always best to arrive five or ten minutes earlier than the required time,' Esme said. 'It demonstrates a pleasing keenness.'

Scarlet rolled her eyes. 'I'm not your staff, Grandma. That's why I'm here at six o'clock. Those lazy bums wouldn't be here now if you paid them double. And I'm here for free.'

'True enough.' Esme laughed. 'Now, where's your mother?'

Scarlet swallowed. 'She told me to tell you she's tired, she'll come later.'

Her grandmother frowned. 'She let you come alone?'

Scarlet shrugged and Esme muttered under her breath.

'You've already started?' Scarlet frowned at the mixing bowl. 'How many have you made?'

Esme kept her head down. 'Five trays.'

'Five? But that's . . .'

'Sixty,' her grandmother finished. 'I know, I'm—'

Scarlet let out a small shriek. 'You promised you'd wait for me, you—'

'I know, my dear, I'm sorry.' Esme looked ashamed. 'Excitement overcame me and I couldn't wait.'

Scarlet narrowed her eyes. 'I'm the kid at Christmas, not you.'

Esme laughed. 'Yes, you're quite right. Then let's get on. No time to waste.'

Three hours later they were stacking one hundred and sixty-eight choux buns (Scarlet having gobbled several during the baking process for necessary quality control checks) filled with cinnamon-nutmeg crème pâtissière into a croquembouche tower bound by caramel threads. Every bun was iced silver or gold, dusted with icing sugar and sprinkled with glitter.

Esme had dipped each bun in hot caramel, placing it with precision on the rising spire of sugar and spice. When the last bun was set atop the rest, Scarlet fixed gingerbread stars, crystallized snowdrops and tiny chocolate owls to their tower. Finally, Esme pierced the syrupy steeple with six long sparklers to light on Christmas Eve.

They stepped back to critique their creation.

'It's definitely taller than last year.' Scarlet folded her arms. 'More stars too. I think it's . . .' she searched her vocabulary for a suitable adjective and, failing to find one fitting, borrowed from her grandma's '. . . really rather splendid.'

'I agree.' Esme smiled. 'I do think we've outdone ourselves this year.'

Already, a large crowd had gathered outside the café's bay window, gazing up at the sugar sculpture with wide eyes and wet tongues. A few tested the door, hoping to warm their fingers on mugs of tea and fill their bellies with slices of cake, before they saw the sign, 'Closed on Mondays', and turned away.

'Mum should be here.'

Esme pulled her granddaughter into a hug. 'I'm sure she'll be here soon. She won't miss this.'

Scarlet nodded, allowing the lies to lift into the air and settle among the gingerbread stars.

Liyana

Everyone in the playground was laughing and pointing at her. At least, that was how it seemed to Liyana. Even her so-called friends were joining in. Why had she said it? What was she thinking? Christine Bradley had never kept a secret in her life, despite being Liyana's best friend. She'd told Olivia Greene, who'd told Rosie Bailey, who told the entire school. So now everyone thought that Liyana was delusional, claiming that she could fly. She wanted to disappear, she wanted to die. She wanted to unravel time, go back and keep her mouth shut. It was such a monumentally stupid thing to do since she couldn't fly, not here. Here, she couldn't do anything at all.

If only Liyana could take them to Everwhere then she'd show them. But she didn't even know how she got there herself. And, if Bea was to be believed, most people weren't able to get there anyway. Liyana had no idea why this might be so, but since Bea seemed to know everything else about Everwhere, there seemed no reason she wouldn't be right about that too.

Either way, Liyana was in intractable amounts of trouble. This story of humiliation would enter school lore. And the memory of a school was long. She would become The Girl Who Thought She Could Fly. She would never be allowed to forget. And the story would be passed down through the classes like the legend of The Boy Who Drowned Himself in the School Swimming Pool from twenty years ago.

Then, as Liyana was descending into absolute despair, a miracle occurred. Someone started shouting from the top of the climbing frame and everyone turned to look. A boy, about Liyana's age, stood astride the metal bars proclaiming in insistent tones that he too could fly. A snigger rippled through the crowd.

'I can,' he shouted. 'Watch and see!'

The laughter ceased and the children held a collective breath, waiting, breath and hope suspended, to see if the boy would come good on his promise. Liyana watched with them, deeply grateful for the distraction and wondering how on earth he'd extricate himself gracefully from the situation.

Instead, he did the unthinkable. He jumped.

Liyana watched as the boy seemed to fall through the air in slow motion before hitting the tarmac with a thud. Nobody moved. Not the boy, not a single child in the crowd. Until, like a magician performing a trick, he stood and bowed. For a single, stretched second, the air was still. In the next, the crowd erupted in an arm-waving, whistle-whooping cacophony of cheers and applause.

Liyana exhaled. She was safe. No one would remember her ridiculous claim now, they'd only remember the boy who said he could fly, then leapt from the climbing frame to prove it. She could fade into the background again.

Liyana waited until the crowd dispersed to the four corners of the playground, then stepped forward to the boy.

'How did you do that?'

He smiled. 'I've been practising for years.'

'Thank you. I think you just saved my life.'

Curiously, the following day no one was talking about The Boy Who Flew From the Climbing Frame. Instead, the school buzzed with an incident that had occurred at the same time. While class 4B were doing laps of the school swimming pool the water had begun to boil like a kettle. Mercifully, no one died, though most of the class were being treated for second- and third-degree burns at St Thomas' Hospital. One girl was in intensive care, though it was thought that she'd live. And Liyana, as shocked as everyone else, had no idea that the incident had anything to do with her at all.

Over a decade ago

Bea

I sat astride an enormous rotting tree trunk with Bea. The bark was so soft it peeled off in great strips; chunks fell off inside the hollow when I kicked it, like kicking a horse to gallop. At least, that's what Bea said since, naturally, she'd ridden a horse. She'd done everything.

A white leaf settled atop my head. I brushed it off. 'She told you about this place? Really?'

Bea shrugged. '*Mamá* tells me everything.'

I stared at her, jealous but unwilling to admit it.

'No one else believes her. But I do.'

I was silent.

'Your *mamá* probably doesn't know anything. If she's not a Grimm too, then she won't have a clue.' Bea sighed, as if her familial brilliance was a burden. 'Most people have zero imagination and even less intelligence, that's what *Mamá* says.'

'Oh.' I felt an urge to defend Ma, but didn't know how.

'It's rare.' Bea kicked the trunk so clumps of bark broke free, echoing in the cavity of the tree. 'Having a *mamá* and daughter who are both pure Grimm.'

'Why?'

'You don't know?' But I suspected, from the flicker of frustration on her face, that she didn't either. 'Most *mamás* have some Grimm blood in them,' she said, as if that answered my question. 'If they've only got a little they can come here but they'll think it was just a dream, like you did in the beginning. If they've got a lot, then they can walk through one of the gates, but that's rare.' She gave a knowing nod. 'Most of them don't know about the gates.'

I teased off a soft strip of bark, bending it into an arc. I didn't want to ask, especially since Bea was goading me with this information, bait to distract from her prior ignorance. But it didn't take long for curiosity to trump pride.

'What gates?' I asked.

Bea raised an eyebrow in mock surprise. 'Oh, you don't know about the gates either?' She sighed, as if burdened by the weight of my ignorance and her knowledge. 'Seems like you're as clueless as your *mamá*.'

I snapped my bridge of bark.

'The gates are the only other way of coming here.' She folded her arms. It's how non-Grimms can enter Everwhere.'

I'd imagined having a sister would be a source of comfort, not competition. It made me worry about the baby in Ma's belly, the sibling lying in wait.

Bea grinned again, ridiculously beautiful, even when she was being mean. 'That's how the soldiers get here,' she said. 'But only on nights of the first-quarter moon.'

I dug a fingernail into the tree trunk, etching out a furrow. 'Soldiers?' I said, without looking up.

Bea laughed. 'You don't know about them either? Shit, you don't know anything, do you?'

I looked up, startled by her use of that word. I'd heard my parents use it, and worse, but never someone my own age. Bea looked at me, the edges of her beautiful mouth twitching with withheld information, waiting for me to admit to my ignorance, to publicly acknowledge her superiority.

'No,' I said, as carelessly as if I'd just brushed a fallen leaf from my knee. 'I don't.'

Bea sat up a little straighter. 'Then aren't you lucky that I do.'

Over a decade ago

Leo

Every month, when the moon reached its first quarter, Leo left his bed in the early morning hours to walk through the school gardens. He waited until everyone on the grounds had fallen asleep before he snuck out. Leo couldn't remember when the urge for these walks had caught hold of him, nor did he know what he was looking for, but he was certainly looking for something.

He walked across forbidden lawns, pressing bare toes into wet grass; he sauntered along stone corridors, his soft steps carrying no echo. He sat under the shadow of the school chapel, gazing up at the clock tower that spiked into a great bronze cross, and wondered at the significance of the time tonight. And, with every second that ticked by, Leo felt the tug of the moon pulling him on.

No matter the route he took, Leo always ended in the same place in front of the school gates. The gates were tall and wide, the height of five boys standing on each other's shoulders, the width of ten holding each other's outstretched arms. The gates were four hundred and seventeen years old, forged when the first foundations were dug, welded when the first bricks were laid. The gates were fierce – thick pickets with sharp finials piercing the air like pitchforks – a stern deterrent to any aspiring escapees. The gates were ornate – posts engraved with Latin script and wrapped with long tendrils of delicate iron ivy that crept across the pickets and wound between elaborate curlicues. The gate was hand-wrought by King James I's own blacksmith, or so school legend claimed.

Leo gazed at the gates for hours, studying the veins of each leaf, drawing his fingers along every curl with such care that an ignorant onlooker might have thought he had been the one who'd burned his own skin in the fires of the gates' creation.

Whenever the moon slipped from behind clouds and cast the iron with a silver sheen, Leo was overcome with the sudden desire to push at the gates and step through, as if they weren't locked and the way wasn't barred. But, strange though this desire was, it wasn't nearly so strange as the accompanying thought: the certain belief that if he did so, he wouldn't step through onto gravel and concrete but into another world altogether.

12th October – 20 days . . .

6.33 a.m. – Leo

He knows where to find her. She's like a beacon to him now. He doesn't even need to think. All he does is close his eyes and he sees her. The fading light in him flickers, spluttering, quickening, as he hurries towards the ever brightening light of her.

Outside room 13, Leo hesitates. If he goes to her now he'll say things and do things that should be left unsaid and undone. Things that will lead only to greater pain and misery over what is already coming. He clenches his fists and tells himself to turn back. It's too risky, too hard to navigate, too difficult to balance on that line between lust and love.

When Leo finally steps through the door, Goldie looks up. She doesn't seem surprised, as if she knew he was coming, as if she'd expected him, as if she's been waiting. When he reaches her, when he cups her cheeks in his hands, she tips her head up to meet him, opens her mouth and lets him in.

6.33 a.m. – Goldie

I'm stealing two pairs of silk socks from the family in room 13 when I look up and see him standing in the doorway, watching me, smiling as if I'm doing something incredibly wonderful, instead of slightly immoral. He steps towards me and I stop, still holding the socks.

I smile.

Even now, I can't quite believe it worked. I summoned him, I commanded him. Just as I'd done the first time. Through sheer force of will I've conjured him to my side. *Stop.* I thought. *Walk up the stairs, turn left. Open the door to room 13. Come in and kiss me.*

I've spent so long imagining this moment that now it feels entirely natural, normal, not at all new. I know every inch of him, I fit into his embrace, I anticipate what he'll say next. And yet, there's a feeling about being with Leo now that I've never felt before. Not in all my life, not with anyone else. It takes a few hours for me to realize what it is. Right. It feels right. Nothing about my life has ever felt right before. I've always struggled to make things fit, to patch holes, ignore cracks, press mismatched puzzle pieces into place. But with Leo I don't have to be what I don't want to be, or do what I don't want to do. I don't need to do anything different, anything special. I don't have to do anything at all. Just breathe. Just be. And that is enough.

3.03 p.m. – Scarlet

Scarlet meets Ezekiel Wolfe in Fitzbillies, one of the few cafés in Cambridge that isn't a Starbucks or similar chain. Ezekiel is already sitting when Scarlet arrives, though she's ten minutes early. She wants to buy a slice of Bakewell tart, but feels it might undermine her professionalism, so orders a black coffee.

He looks up when she reaches his table. 'You came.'

She looks down at him.

'Won't you sit?' he asks.

Scarlet sits, annoyed that it's now at his invitation. She sets her coffee cup on the table and eyes his half-devoured crumpets and jam.

Ezekiel leans forward. 'I wanted to apologize for—'

'Ruining my life?' Scarlet snatches up the sugar pot, tipping a good amount of it into her coffee. 'Destroying my livelihood?'

'That's a bit harsh, don't you think?'

'No, I don't. If your bloody Starbucks didn't spring up on every corner, if they gave independent cafés a fighting chance . . .' Scarlet stirs the sugar into her coffee, trying to calm herself. 'You go from café to café shutting them down, not giving a shit about the owners who've invested their whole lives – everything they own, all their time, all their hopes into . . .'

Ezekiel waits to see if she's going to finish her sentence, then pushes the crumpets aside. 'You don't have to sell, no one's forcing you.' He meets her eye. 'But if you're thinking about it, even a little, I recommend you do it sooner rather than later. I've looked at your accounts and my company's offering you more than the market value. That figure will drop, the longer you wait to make a decision.'

He sits back and Scarlet takes a deep breath, then blurts out, 'Have you ever had something you wanted, something you cared so deeply about that – that . . . you feel incomplete without it, like a piece of you is missing?'

'No,' Ezekiel says. 'I can't say that I have. It must be quite something.'

'Not if you lose it.'

He hesitates, as if contemplating the wisdom of what he might be able to say. 'But the café isn't your something, is it? It's your grandmother's.'

Scarlet is silent. Under the table her left knee starts to shake. Her fingers twitch. She glares at the sugar bowl, then Ezekiel's untouched coffee cup.

'You're not drinking,' Scarlet says, still not meeting his eye.

'It's too hot. I think the barista wanted to burn my tongue.'

'She probably had her reasons.'

Ezekiel grins, licking his spoon. 'You've been telling tales about me?'

'It's a small city.' Scarlet shrugs. 'I can't help it if word gets round.'

Her fingers twitch again and suddenly Scarlet feels as if she has a secret, hidden like a chocolate in her pocket. She's looking at his cup when it unbalances, tipping its scalding sweetness over Ezekiel's hand.

He snatches his hand away. 'Damn.'

Scarlet rights the cup, plucking wads of tissues to dam the expanding lake of coffee. 'Sorry, I don't know, I didn't mean—'

He's already standing. 'You're a liability,' he says, half-smiling despite the pain. 'At this rate, I'll be hospitalized again before sundown.'

'Quick, run it under cold water.'

Ezekiel disappears and Scarlet stuffs the sodden tissues into the empty coffee cup. Surely the cup hadn't tipped of its own accord? She'd brushed against the saucer and knocked it over. That's the only sensible explanation. And Scarlet is a stickler for sense. Bread won't rise without yeast and cups don't fall unless they're pushed. Likewise, she explained the incinerated moth and the sparks (static) and the light fixture falling onto Ezekiel Wolfe's head (faulty wiring). But what Scarlet can't deny is the surge of power she felt just before the cup tipped. As if her veins were copper wires humming with electric currents.

'Oh, don't worry about me, I'm fine.'

Scarlet looks up. She'd entirely forgotten about Ezekiel, who's now standing beside the table holding out his hand: a splash of scorching red flared across his pale skin.

'I'm sorry,' Scarlet says. 'It was an accident.'

'I certainly hope so,' Ezekiel says. 'But given the

number of accidents that keep happening around you, I'm starting to worry for my safety.'

'I – I didn't mean to.'

He smiles. 'Are you sure? You probably hate me enough to . . .'

Scarlet frowns. She certainly thought she hated him. But now that she hears the words out loud, and from his own mouth, she's no longer sure. 'I don't hate you.'

Ezekiel nods towards the door. 'Look, do you fancy a walk? I think I need to stay away from hot beverages for a little while. We can talk about everything but with a view.'

Scarlet half-shrugs, half-nods. 'I suppose so.'

'Well, try to contain your enthusiasm.' Ezekiel laughs. 'Or I might get the wrong idea.'

The wrong idea? Scarlet thinks of how she felt the first time she saw him, of how she's been feeling ever since, though she's tried to deny it to herself. *Run*. She should run. No good can come of this. Only very ill-advised, hideously complicated things. Instead, she stands and follows Ezekiel Wolfe outside. In the street, he stops too quickly so she bumps into him, stumbling as he turns to steady her. The same smile twitches his lips.

'You're looking at me,' he says, 'like I'm that slice of Bakewell tart.'

Scarlet frowns. 'I . . . ?'

'You wanted it,' he says. 'When you first walked in.'

Scarlet wants to say something but can only look at him, can only will him to walk away, can only try to channel her burgeoning powers into the banishment of this man from her immediate vicinity and life. But Ezekiel doesn't move. Instead he leans down to press his mouth to her ear.

'I know what you're thinking,' he whispers. 'And I want you too.'

Run.

Instead, she kisses him.

3.31 p.m. – Liyana

Liyana sits on the train, tapping her knees, waiting for the eleventh stop on the Northern Line, counting each station as the train judders alongside the platform then trundles out again. She's trying not to dwell on the voice she heard in Ottolenghi, trying not to think: *schizophrenia*. She's on her way home, though it won't be home for much longer, not unless she can convince Kumiko, not unless she can negotiate with Mazmo, who turned out to be far nicer than she'd feared. She could, possibly, countenance being married to him. So long as it was an open – a very, *very* open – marriage.

When the train pulls into Kennington station, Liyana stands. It's not her stop, she still has three to go. So, when the doors slide open, why does she walk out onto the platform? Among the churning throng of commuters, Liyana is still, wondering what to do next. She's never been to Kennington before, doesn't know anyone who lives here, doesn't know her way around. The neighbourhood might not be a friendly one – too many white faces tended to mean too many small minds – she should probably get back on the train.

Then Liyana sees, behind the yellow line, a feather. She bends and picks it up. A blackbird feather. Brushing it across her cheek, she smiles. Perhaps she is going mad but, right now, Liyana doesn't care. She has, at last, been given a sign.

Still clutching the feather, Liyana steps onto the escalator, standing until it spills her out in front of the ticket machines. Then she walks outside and waits on the pavement for another sign. When none presents itself, Liyana turns left and walks on.

Ten minutes and four left turns later, Liyana finds herself standing at the foot of a church: Great Saint Mary's. In a birch tree beside the church a blackbird is perched on the lowest branch. Liyana smiles and starts to climb the stone steps.

She pushes open the heavy wooden door and walks up the aisle. About to slide into a pew, Liyana spots the confessional. Then it dawns on her. She's here to confess, to tell the events of the past few weeks to someone who doesn't know her, can't see her and isn't allowed to judge her.

So, when a few minutes later a diminutive woman shuffles out of the confessional, Liyana steps in. She sits in silence for a while, before realizing that the priest is waiting for her to speak.

'Confess me, Father – I mean, forgive me, Father, for I have, um, sinned,' Liyana says. 'Well, I wouldn't really call it sinning, but I . . .'

'How long has it been since your last confession?'

Liyana wonders what a reasonable length of time would be. 'Er, two . . . weeks.'

'Go on.'

'Okay, right, well, there's a lot going on at home. My aunt's bankrupted us and now she wants me to get married for money to save us – which is what she's always done – but my girlfriend isn't keen and I certainly wasn't at first, but now I think it could solve a lot of problems, but—'

The priest coughs. 'That certainly is a lot to unpack,' he says. 'Shall we start from the beginning? Remind me—'

'Oh, and I've also started, at least it's only happened once, well, three times in one day. But, yes, I'm also hearing voices.'

Liyana braces herself for censure, laughter, instant dismissal.

'And you say this is the first time you've heard voices?'

Liyana nods. 'Yes.'

'Are you currently taking medication for any . . . ?'

'No, no, I . . .'

'And what are the voices saying?'

'Well, um,' Liyana says, reluctant to get into specifics. 'It's a bit like overhearing only half of someone else's conversation.'

The priest is silent for several minutes. Twisting her hands in her lap, Liyana waits for the verdict.

'Well,' he says, at last. 'So long as they aren't telling you to kill kittens or push old ladies from their bicycles, I wouldn't worry too much. You might want to tell your doctor, see what he says. But, you know, you aren't in bad company. Joan of Arc heard voices, Francis of Assisi too.' He pauses. *'But why can't I stop thinking about Ezekiel Wolfe in bed eating cinnamon buns?'*

'I'm sorry? Who's E-zekiel Wolfe?' Liyana asks, wondering if he's an obscure Catholic saint: the patron saint of baking, perhaps.

'I'm sorry?'

'E-ze-kiel Wolfe?' Liyana repeats, thinking maybe she'd pronounced it incorrectly. 'You were wondering what he looked like, um . . . naked.'

'Excuse me?' The priest sounds amused. 'I certainly don't think I was. And, given the Church's intractable position on homosexuality, if I were I'd most certainly be keeping any such thoughts to myself.'

'Oh, no,' Liyana backtracks. 'No, of course not, I didn't mean to—'

'Might I suggest,' the priest interrupts, 'that you seek support of a less spiritual and more . . . corporeal' – he coughs again – 'psychiatric – nature.'

When Liyana steps outside again, the blackbird is

singing. She's stopped to look up into the birch tree when she hears the voice again: *It's time to find your sisters.*

4.57 p.m. – Bea

'You're lovely.'

Bea thinks of the massacre of birds, of the ink pulsing through her veins, of the smashing of defenceless snails. 'I'm not.'

'You are.'

Bea eyes Vali over the rim of the coffee she has allowed him, after persistent requests, to buy her. 'If you think that, then I don't think you should be studying here, because you're clearly an idiot.'

'On the contrary.' Vali adds three sugars to his tea. 'I see you – *you* – not all that smoke-and-mirrors bullshit you throw at everyone—'

'"Bullshit"?' Bea arches an eyebrow. 'It didn't take too long for you to get cocky, did it?'

'You're hardly a paragon of politeness.' Vali takes a tentative sip of tea. Tutting, he adds two more spoonfuls of sugar. 'But all right, let me rephrase. Your id, or your superego, if you prefer' – he takes another sip of tea and nods – 'are fighting hard to present—'

'Oh, Christ, you're a psychology student.' Bea gulps down her coffee as if it were gin and she dearly needed to get drunk. 'I should – you got me here under false pretences. You said you were studying philosophy.'

'I didn't, I never said that.' Vali reaches for the plate of scones that sits between them. He takes a bite of one, brushing the crumbs from his beard. 'You assumed and I— anyway I am studying philosophy, just not officially.'

Bea regards him. 'What's that supposed to mean?'

'Scones should be served warm, don't you think? And

with butter that'll melt and drip down your chin.' Vali sighs, then gives a slight shrug. 'Oh well. Anyway, the point is, I sit in on philosophy lectures for fun and read up on various topics whenever I can.'

'Jesus, you're even more pathetic than I thought.' Bea swigs down the dregs of her coffee. 'Who reads *Principia Mathematica* for fun? You don't dabble in that stuff, you have to . . .' She flicks her fingers, as if flicking away cigarette smoke, but is unable to keep the note of admiration from her voice. 'You're ridiculous.'

'Studying philosophy is as good a way to pass the time as any,' Vali says, finishing off the scone and reaching for another. 'Far better than drinking till you pass out, or playing video games till four a.m.'

Bea twists a raisin from a scone. 'Some people find those things fun.'

'Do you?'

'No.'

'Then perhaps I'm compensating for . . .' Vali shrugs again. 'I don't know. Maybe if my mother hadn't thought me so fucking ugly then maybe I wouldn't study so hard.'

Bea chews on the raisin. 'You're not *so* fucking ugly.'

Vali tugs at his beard. 'Thanks.'

Bea shrugs. They sit in silence.

'Don't get the wrong idea,' she says. 'I still wouldn't shag you.'

13th October – 19 days . . .

3.33 a.m. – Goldie

'It's strange,' I say, running my finger along his face, following the shape of his eyebrows, nose, lips.

'What's strange?'

'All I want to do is touch you.'

Leo smiles. 'Ditto.'

'Yeah, I know, you're insatiable,' I say, resting on his cheek. 'I'd think you hadn't been with a woman in a hundred years.'

'I haven't been with you,' he says. 'Which is much the same thing.'

I laugh. 'I bet you're with a different woman every night of the week.'

A look passes across Leo's face that I don't recognize and I realize, despite how I feel, how little I really know him. I can tell how Teddy is feeling, often what he's thinking, by the look in his eyes or the tone of his voice. By this standard, Leo is still a stranger to me.

'Did I offend you?' I ask.

He smiles. 'In suggesting I'm something of a slut?'

'I don't think I used that particular word, did I?' I say. 'A slight insinuation, perhaps. But then you're a man, aren't you, so—'

'—we wouldn't have been able to do everything we've just done if I wasn't—'

I pinch his nose and he laughs. 'I meant, as a man, the more women you sleep with the more of a stud you are, as opposed to—'

'If I'd known you felt that way about promiscuity,' Leo says, 'I'd have put more effort into it before I met you.'

'Shut up.' I give him a playful nudge. 'You know what I mean.' But I'm touched by his use of 'before'. I can't talk about love yet – I know it's far too soon. Still, I can't help wondering if there's a chance he feels even remotely for me as I do for him.

'But why is it strange?' Leo says.

'What?'

'That you want to touch me. I'd have thought that was the natural thing' – he gives me a coy smile – 'in the circumstances.'

'Yeah, I guess so.' I shrug, not ready to tell him yet. 'I don't know.'

'You say that a lot.'

'Do I?'

Leo nods. 'Yeah.'

'Oh, sorry.'

'Don't be sorry,' he says. 'It's nothing to be sorry for.'

3.33 a.m. – Scarlet

Scarlet hurls *Rebecca* across the room. It hits the wall with a satisfying thud. Then she feels guilty. It's her favourite book and had been her mother's too. Although that copy, the one she'd first read as a little girl, had burned in the fire.

Scarlet hurries out of bed to recover the novel, gives the cover an apologetic stroke and hops back into bed. She sighs. She wants to be unconscious. Awake leaves her vulnerable to thoughts she shouldn't be thinking. Thoughts about failing cafés and ill-advised kisses. Scarlet opens *Rebecca* again. She blinks at the page, trying to get a foothold in a sentence. But it's no good. She shuts it again and switches off her bedside lamp.

In the darkness, Scarlet's thoughts return inevitably to Ezekiel Wolfe, to his hand so close to her thigh, to their fingers nearly touching, to that kiss. She starts to stroke her hand across her chest, imagining it to be his, her touch as light and soft as the cotton sheets. Shivering slightly, Scarlet slides her hand along her ribs, gathering her T-shirt so it settles in folds over her belly. Scarlet closes her eyes and licks her finger and strokes it across her skin as the street lamp outside her window begins to flicker.

Ezekiel slides his hand up her thigh. Scarlet twists her body in the sheets. He pulls her into his lap. Scarlet holds her breath. Downstairs, in the café, the kettle's plug blows its fuse. He begins to unbutton her, to place single kisses along her throat, to her breasts, her ribs . . .

As Scarlet begins to shudder, the kitchen lights begin to flicker and flicker. Until, at last, Scarlet lets out a long low moan of delight, and the streetlamp outside shatters, scattering glass and sparks into the night.

3.33 a.m. – Esme

It is in the early morning hours that Esme thinks of her daughter. She wakes from the same dream she's had every night for the past ten years, ever since the last time she saw Ruby.

In the dream, Esme's on a carousel, not fashioned from psychedelic painted metal but stitched from spiders' webs and spinning so fast that Esme grips the muzzle of the sculpted horse on which she sits. It's surprisingly solid, given that, along with every other animal, it's crafted from silken threads. As the carousel spins, Esme begins to find her balance, adapting to the dizzying speed.

The moon is bright and the spider-webs glimmer as they catch the light. Esme realizes that the carousel is suspended in mid-air, tethered to the clouds, always spinning but always still. It's then that she sees her little girl sitting astride a gossamer unicorn, red hair streaming out as they turn, one chubby hand ungripping the unicorn's horn as Ruby waves.

'No!' Esme screams. 'Don't let go!'

Esme slides down from her horse and runs, reaching towards her daughter, slipping, stumbling, shouting – it's then that *he* appears. Every night the same. A tall man with white hair, golden eyes and a face so lined with wrinkles he might be ten thousand years old. One moment he's standing alone, the next he's beside Ruby, his hands at her waist.

'No!' Esme screams. 'Don't touch her!'

But he lifts Ruby from the unicorn. Her legs kick out as she starts to cry.

As Esme stumbles forward the cobwebs soften, her feet sinking into sticky threads. She's pulling against them when the spiders appear, long thin legs uncurling towards her ankles. The carousel spins, faster and faster, as Esme cries for her daughter. Ruby's captor leaps into the air, rising into the clouds like a balloon, glancing back with a final, triumphant grin.

Esme wakes at 3.33 a.m. Every night the same. As if she's been switched on, lit up, alarmed. There's no return to sleep, not yet, not for a long while. Years ago, she fought it. Now she surrenders. Now she waits. She watches the ceiling as doors creak ajar and corridors of memory open.

Sometimes Esme sees her daughter as a baby, with wide brown eyes, wispy red curls and tiny pink toes. Sometimes as a teenager, with braces, acne and self-doubt. Sometimes she's pregnant, or playing with her baby, or teaching Ruby to ride a bike. Over the past decade, Esme must have recalled every moment, every day, month, year of Ruby's life. The only way Esme never sees her daughter is old.

4.37 a.m. – Goldie

When I finally get back to the flat, Teddy is still asleep, just as I'd left him. I know I shouldn't have left him, technically, but it felt safe. He rarely wakes before six. Seven, if I'm lucky. Anything after eight is, perhaps, a biannual miracle. Instead of slumping on the sofa, I curl up beside him. He's so small, so thin, all bones. After being with Leo, lying next to Teddy is almost like being alone. He's still only half of a human, almost a pet. I can't find comfort in my little brother's arms. And yet, I know he loves me more than anything else in the world. Even more than his new blue blazer, that, I now notice, he's wearing with his pyjamas.

4. 37 p.m. – Bea

'I've been thinking about what you said yesterday,' Bea says.

Vali grins. 'You've been thinking about me?'

'I didn't say that. That's not what I said.'

Vali's grin only deepens. 'Then what were you thinking about?'

They stroll along Trinity Street, side by side. Vali has brought coffee and croissants. Bea has let him.

'All your psychologizing. All that shit you were saying about my ego and other people's expectations,' Bea says. '*Mamá* tells me I'm – it always comes back to the mother, doesn't it? – that's what all you fucking shrinks think, isn't it?'

Vali rips into his croissant. 'Well, Bowlby and Freud certainly did skew things in that direction. But don't forget the father – only fair he should shoulder half the blame.'

'I never had one.' Bea bites the lip of her coffee cup. 'So does that make it solely *Mamá*'s fault, or half mine?'

'Your father still had an effect' – Vali chews – 'after all, absence is as affecting as presence, don't you think?'

Bea shrugs. 'I don't remember missing him.'

Vali gulps his coffee. 'So you say. But I think this tough act – as if you don't need nothing or no one – is all pretence.'

'Piss off.'

'Psychologically speaking, those with the stoniest exteriors have the softest interiors,' Vali says through another mouthful of croissant. 'And vice versa. No one realizes, of course, because everyone takes everyone else at face value – but it's the violent ones who, deep down, are the most vulnerable. Though they'll probably never know it themselves. Or, if they do' – he gives her a pointed look – 'they'd rather kill or die than admit it.'

Bea scowls at him. 'Oh, I'm sorry, I didn't realize I was paying for the privilege of this little drink with you.'

'You're not,' Vali says. 'I am.'

'Then stop fucking psychologizing me.'

Vali grins again. 'Did I hit a nerve?'

Bea ignores him. At the corner of Trinity Lane, Vali doesn't turn but keeps walking.

'Hey.' Bea stops. 'Where are you going?'

He shrugs. 'What's the rush? Let's take the scenic route.'

Bea frowns, but follows him.

'You know, the reverse is true too,' Vali says, swallowing the last of his croissant. 'It's the nice ones you should watch out for. It's the simpering, smiling ones who secretly want to slap everyone—'

'So I should watch out for you then.' Bea sips her coffee.

Vali laughs. 'Touché.'

'Well, you're wrong,' Bea says. 'I'm stone inside and out. I never missed my father. And, frankly, I wish my *mamá* would fuck off too. I'll tell you who I miss: my cat.'

'You don't mean that.'

'I do,' Bea says. 'I love that cat.'

As they pass King's College Chapel, sunlight through the stained-glass windows scatters cubes of coloured light on the pavement like brightly wrapped sweets at their feet.

'You know what I mean.'

'Yeah,' Bea says. 'And you've never met *Mamá*.'

Vali brightens. 'I'd like to. If—'

Bea drops her paper cup in a dustbin. 'No chance. Never. Not happening.'

'Okay, no need to sugar-coat it.' Vali pats his stomach. 'I've got enough padding to absorb the blows.'

'Don't do that.'

'What?'

'You're not very perceptive for a shrink, are you?' Bea nibbles at her croissant. 'All that self-deprecating bullshit. Just cos your *mamá* treated you like crap, doesn't mean you need to do it too.'

Vali tugs his beard, smiling. 'I didn't know you cared.'

'I don't,' Bea says. 'It's just annoying. Anyway, if you're going to sort out other people's shit, you'd better sort out your own first, don't you think?'

'I never claimed to be doing anything of the sort,' Vali says. 'My focus is more theoretical than practical. Are you going to eat that?'

Bea hands Vali her nibbled croissant. 'What use is that to anyone?'

'Thanks.' Vali takes it. 'Says the philosopher.'

'Touché to you too, you little prick.' Bea smiles. 'And your *mamá* was wrong. Being fat isn't so bad.' She stops walking to eye him up and down. 'You're soft and cuddly, like a baby owl.'

'I thought you were the owl,' Vali says. 'And I'm the mouse.'

'Yeah,' Bea says. 'That was before I knew you. Anyway, if you're an owl, then I'm an eagle.'

Above them, the golden weather vanes of Corpus Christi College spin unseen in the wind. Catching a reflected glint of light on the pavement, Bea glances up, thinking she'll drop in on Dr Finch later and finagle him into giving her access to the glider again.

11.59 p.m. – Liyana

Liyana can't stop thinking about the damn voice and its cryptic messages. She'd been shocked and scared to hear it again. But, as experience became memory, fear began to fade and frustration had seeped in. She's been searching for clues, for a possible code. But she's never liked crossword puzzles, and only has four sentences to work with: *I'm going to kill Cassie when I see her. Oh, Grandma, what are we going to do? Now you look like a constipated hamster. It's time to find your sisters.*

Liyana doesn't want to kill anyone. She doesn't have a grandmother, at least not living. And she's certainly never called anyone a constipated hamster. Her insults, learned at her aunt's knee, are in her mother tongue. But strangest of all is the instruction, since Liyana doesn't have any sisters. Also, why should she be trying to find these fictitious sisters, when what she really needs to find is a job?

Liyana sits up in bed shading the contours of BlackBird's breasts underneath her leather jacket. As she curls the halo of BlackBird's hair, Liyana pauses. She touches her hand to her own hair and thinks of her mummy, of the bottle of thick white gloop that burned her skin. An echo of pain flushes Liyana's scalp. She rubs at the sting and the memory pinballs to sitting in her mummy's arms, snuggling into her approval, asking to be told the story of her birth.

13th October – 19 days . . .

You were born with the rain. As I birthed you the rain rushed from the gutters and drains, flooding the streets. You were born on the bridge from one day to the next – your head emerging a moment before midnight, your limbs a moment after. You didn't cry. You hardly ever cried. You were a good baby, so soft, so quiet.

I was the first to hold you, the first to whisper secrets into the tiny shells of your ears. We chatted in a language without words, cementing a connection that rose from the roots of life itself. When you blinked up at me I saw your soul in your watery eyes and I knew your name. You were a daughter of the rain, so I called you Liyana. A good, strong Zulu name, in honour of your maternal great-grandfather, meaning 'it is raining'. And I knew that whenever I called your name I would be calling the rain. This would be my gift to you. You were birthed in a flood and you, like every plant and animal in our magnificent country, would thrive in the rain. Then Aunt Nya added your middle name. Miriro: she who was wished for.

Liyana stares at her drawing and realizes, all of a sudden, that she needs to stop. To stop being so soft and quiet. To stop being this sicker, subtler shade of her own spirit. To stop being so white, this pale ghost of herself. To stop being so cowardly. To stop being so full of fucking self-doubt.

Liyana needs to throw off her mother's expectations. Enough of fading into the background, of trying so hard to be accepted, to fit into their adopted homeland with fake straight hair and soft voices. Why hadn't her mother let her be who she truly was? Why had her mother fought so hard to shave off Liyana's edges, to shape her into something suitable, to whittle her essence away? What good had it done but to leave Liyana full of fear? Fear of being different, fear of standing out, fear of being judged.

But Liyana will not succumb to this fear. She's tried so hard to be accepted and approved of, to be well spoken and well behaved, to be that which she is not. But no longer. She has tried and she has failed. Her true self has been fighting to be felt, struggling to be seen. Now it will rise.

The priest was wrong. Liyana isn't losing her grip on reality. She doesn't know what the hell is going on, but she knows it's nothing to fear. The voices are telling her something. And, instead of being scared over the state of her sanity, Liyana will listen. She will consult her cards. Instead of cowering in the corner, she will leap into the fray. Instead of hiding from the enormity of the unknown, she'll face it, will try to make sense of it. She'll stop hiding, will stop avoiding her girlfriend and confront the situation. She'll return Mazmo's calls. She'll apply for every single job she can find. And, even though she believes she has no sisters, Liyana will start looking for them.

A decade ago

Everwhere

You've been waiting for the next first-quarter moon, counting the days, the hours, the minutes. The first time you went was an accident. This time you've planned everything, down to the last second. You don't know if there are any other entrances, so you go to the same place, the same gate you found yourself in front of before. At 3.33 a.m. What were you doing there? Can you remember? Could you explain yourself, if called upon? You probably wouldn't care to. Alone on the streets of London in the early morning hours, wandering aimlessly, until you found yourself standing in front of a rather charming church on Tavistock Place, Bloomsbury. Not your usual neighbourhood. What brought you here last time? An overflow of sadness or an overflow of joy? Either way, you stood there for a while. An hour passed, maybe two. The church clock chimed and you glanced up.

That was when you felt it. A shift in the air. You looked around, wondering if someone was watching you. You saw nothing in the shadows but noticed the wrought-iron gate, a one-time entrance to the graveyard long since locked and barred. You gazed at it, for some reason caught and held – by the intricate workings in the metal, perhaps? – for several seconds. Just as, stepping forward, you reached up to touch the black petals of a metal rose, the moon came out from behind the clouds to cast a silver shimmer over the iron and the moment you pressed your fingertips to the gate it swung open. As if it had been waiting for you.

Tonight, you arrive early. You can't quite recall the exact time the gate opened before. You don't know if it was important or not – how precise do you need to be? – but you're not taking any chances. Although the experience of Everwhere has faded, it's still been at the back of your mind, humming at the edges of every day, every hour since you left. A few times, maybe more, you've taken long circuitous walks home from work, simply to look at the gate, though you never tried to push it open, never even touched it. If anyone had asked, you'd have told them you were there for the chocolate pecan biscuits sold in the café across the street. You even told yourself the same thing at first, though you don't especially like chocolate.

Tonight, the streets are empty, thanks to the lateness of the hour and the chill in the air. You hug your coat close, wish you'd worn a jumper and, almost, wish the café were open so you could have a cup of burning hot coffee and even a biscuit or two. You stick your bare fingers under your armpits and press them tight against your chest. You pace back and forth, marking time with each misty puff of air.

When the hour strikes, your heart quickens. Three o'clock. You continue pacing. You hope no one is watching, no curious insomniacs behind twitching curtains or homeless people searching for a warm spot on a winter night. When at last the half-hour strikes, you feel that shift in the air again and release a long puff of breath you didn't realize you'd been holding. Recently, you'd been having doubts, worried you might have imagined the whole thing. Perhaps you'd been drunk or dreaming.

But now you know you weren't wrong.

Your fingertips twitch with recognition. It's the same. The moon. The air. The gate. It's about to happen again. And, sure enough, at precisely 3.33 a.m. (you check your watch) the clouds part and moonlight illuminates the gate. You reach up to touch the same black rose, you push the gate open and step through.

Goldie

The thing I missed most of all was a garden. More than a real father, since by Ma's account I wasn't missing much there anyway. And if my stepfather was anything to go by . . . Anyway, I decided that a garden was better than a father, in a great many ways. A living, breathing thing that brought comfort but never hugged you too tight or interrogated you about your day. Instead it waited, steadfast and dependable, for you to come on your own terms. So, when I sat under a tree or in a patch of daisies, I felt alone and in company all at once.

I believed that gardens had their own gods, protective spirits imbuing each place with its own particular feeling. It was the same with inside places too, just different. When I was six Ma took me, on a rare foray into culture, to hear the carols in King's College Chapel on Christmas Eve. It was the most spectacular place I'd ever been, and when I looked up at the soaring stained-glass windows reaching fifty feet to the delicate carved stone ceiling, I started to cry. But still, being in a garden has always felt more spiritual than being in a house, no matter how beautiful the house.

As soon as I stepped into any garden I felt calmer. I felt connected to it all, as if the soles of my feet were the earth, the branches of the trees my fingertips. I imagined that if I stood still long enough roots would grow from my toes and plant me in the soil. I felt strong, as immovable and immortal as an ancient oak.

I'd felt this way since I was a little girl. The earliest

memory I had was of staring up into a jigsaw puzzle of leaves, pieces of white sky visible between the green. Perhaps that was why I felt so drawn to Everwhere, it being a place where nature seemed to have taken over entirely, not a brick in sight. I'd have loved to live in a place like that. I didn't know how I'd survive, but I thought I'd be fine.

In our tiny flat I had only one thing of my own I truly loved: a bonsai, a miniature juniper tree. I found it abandoned on the street, branches bare, roots dry, spirit broken. It took months of care but I brought it back to life, leafy and happy again. It sat on the coffee table, so it was the last thing I saw every night before I fell asleep. I loved that we shared the same air while I slept, that I inhaled Juniper's oxygen and Juniper my carbon dioxide – out and in, in and out, in a perfect balance of breath.

One day my stepfather started moving Juniper, taking her from the table and leaving her in random spots for me to retrieve. I didn't understand why, probably just another way he enjoyed tormenting me. Too often I found her in the bathroom or next to his side of the bed. I always moved her back without comment, refusing to play his silly games, whatever they were. My only fear was that one day I'd come home from school to find her missing, flushed down the toilet, or blitzed in the blender. I wouldn't have put it past him. He had a history of similarly stupid things.

Before Juniper, I'd had a teddy bear called Teddy. I don't know when Ma gave him to me, he was simply always there. And then, one day, he wasn't. I never found him. Ma maintained I must have lost him, dropped him in a park, left him on a bus, but I hadn't. I'd never been careless. My stepfather took him. I could never prove it but I knew that, whatever had happened to Teddy, he was responsible.

I wished I could protect Juniper. I wished I had somewhere else to keep her safe, but I didn't. There were no hiding places in the flat. I could only wait as my stepfather circled us, day by day, closing in.

Scarlet

Scarlet bit her lip and narrowed her eyes, scrutinizing the sparkling sugar tower for imperfections. Over the week the magnificent croquembouche creation had held well, dropping only a few gingerbread stars – quickly snaffled up by The No. 33 Café's more observant patrons. The lies her grandmother had told about her mother – *I'm sure she'll be here soon. She won't miss this* – had endured too, proving as sturdy as the rest of the creation, despite being fashioned from hot air instead of sugar. Indeed, they seemed to have solidified over time, taking shape as the days passed, becoming crisper, harder with each instance Ruby Thorne let her down, becoming such a part of the structure they might have been sprinkled with glitter too.

That evening Scarlet and Esme planned to put up the tree Ruby had promised to come to the café to meet them, after she'd 'run a few errands'. It wouldn't take too long, she'd be so quick they wouldn't even notice she'd been gone. But an hour had already passed and still there was no sign of her.

'Perhaps we should just make a start,' Esme suggested.

The battered cardboard box, containing tissue-wrapped silver baubles and glass angels and the fairy, sat at her feet like a patient dog.

Scarlet shook her head. 'She promised this time.'

'She's probably been stalled by the throngs of Christmas shoppers,' Esme agreed. 'I expect she's on her way.'

Scarlet nodded while Esme pulled out a chair. They watched the window in silence as the sky darkened and the shoppers dwindled.

Finally, Scarlet slid over to the box and started plucking at a strip of crisp Sellotape, new layers taped over old. Absently, she teased at a raised edge of Sellotape, digging her fingernail into the soft cardboard, prising it open. Esme watched her granddaughter, sniffing as if she might have a cold coming on, pinching the bridge of her nose.

'Oh!'

Scarlet snapped her head up to check that her grandma was okay. Then, seeing her staring at the window, turned to see her mother at the door. Springing to her feet, Scarlet ran to meet her.

'You made it,' Esme said, relaxing back into her chair.

'You made it!' Scarlet squealed.

'Of course,' Ruby said, fire in her voice and ice in her eyes. 'Why wouldn't I?'

She didn't look happy, but she was there, and that was enough for Scarlet. The crystallized lies atop the croquembouche tower finally shattered, decorating the pastry with yet more glittering shards.

'We waited for you, Mum,' Scarlet said. 'We didn't do anything without you.' She gave her mother's skirted legs a quick, insistent squeeze.

'Let me put down these bags,' Ruby said, stepping towards the nearest table and setting them down, though she didn't pick up her daughter afterwards.

'Ah!' Her gaze alighted on the box. 'Ah! The box of delights.'

She swooped down to the floor, skirt billowing like a parachute, before opening the cardboard flaps with one swift rip of the freshest strip of Sellotape. She lifted out fistfuls of tissue paper, deftly unwrapping and setting each ornament among the silken folds of her skirt. Looking on, Scarlet wished she could elongate time and store up every moment, rations of memory to nibble at night.

A decade ago

'You should set the fairy on top of the tree this year,' Ruby said, passing her daughter the tiny doll of china and lace.

'Really?' Scarlet took the doll as if it were a newborn kitten. 'I can?'

'Oh yes,' Esme echoed. 'You've waited long enough. Your mother was eight, I think, the first time she was given the job.'

Scarlet grinned. She'd been waiting forever for this opportunity. The fairy had been in the family since her grandmother was a little girl, and setting it atop the tree every Christmas was a much-coveted task.

For the next hour, the three generations of Thorne women decorated the tree. Scarlet hung the silver baubles, thinking of the Everwhere moon whenever a silvery shadow was cast across the back of her hand. She wondered if she'd meet her sisters tonight. Recently, Bea had taught Scarlet how to will herself there, setting the intention before she fell asleep, instead of simply hoping her dreams would take her along for the ride.

Esme twisted twinkling lights through the piney branches, while Ruby carefully placed all the trinkets collected over the years: a tiny Victorian rocking horse, a clutch of hand-painted Russian dolls, a dozen miniature stars, a coterie of carved woodland animals: a deer, an owl, a fox, a hare. When every ball, trinket and bell had been set in its place, Esme lifted the fairy from her bed of tissue paper.

'It's time,' Esme said, placing the fairy in her granddaughter's open hands.

Scarlet held the doll, who gazed glassy-eyed up at the tree as if anticipating her ascent. 'How will I do it?'

'Stand on the table,' Ruby instructed. 'You'll be able to reach from there.'

Scarlet hesitated.

'It's okay, sweetheart,' Esme said. 'You can do it.'

'Of course you can,' her mother said. 'Don't be such a scaredy cat.'

'Here' – her grandma stepped over to Scarlet – 'I'll give you a hand.'

When Scarlet was standing on the table, she stretched up and set the fairy in the crook of a high branch.

'Not there, the very top,' Ruby said. 'Come on, you're not going to fall.'

Scarlet rose onto the tips of her toes. 'Hold me.'

'I've got you.'

Scarlet reached again, elongating her body until her fingertips grazed the top of the tree, then wiggled the tiny china doll astride the highest branch.

'There you go.' Her mother clapped. 'I told you—'

As the fairy fell, three pairs of eyes followed her swift descent. The crack of china on the wooden floor was like the snap of a whip.

'Scarlet!' Ruby's anger spat like logs on a fire.

Esme scooped Scarlet off the table. 'Hush, Rube, it wasn't her fault.'

Scarlet's mother was already picking up fragments of the china face: the painted red lips, the black-lashed blue eyes, the curve of a nose – each feature parted from the other, scattered across the floorboards.

Scarlet stared at the broken doll, tears sliding down her cheeks.

'Scarlet, you're so careless,' her mother snapped. 'No one's dropped her in over a century and the first time you touch—'

'Calm down, Rube, it wasn't her fault. It could have been any of us.'

'But it wasn't, was it? It was her.'

Scarlet stared at her mother, who stared back, until the flare of fury slowly cooled into a chip of ice in her eye that spread until it had frozen her face into contempt. Scarlet turned to the tree, reaching out to hold a branch, taking one of the twinkling lights between finger and thumb.

Later, Esme insisted a blown fuse had started the fire. Ruby said nothing. Scarlet never forgot how each light exploded, popping one by one in a shower of sparks, before the whole tree went up in flames.

Bea

Unlike her sisters, Bea liked to listen to the shadows, to the unseen creatures that whispered unknown things. She often didn't understand exactly what they were saying but she knew how to channel the dark. She was her *mamá*'s daughter after all. And, she hoped, her father's.

Cleo, also a beauty, fell in love with a beast. Though this beast wasn't a handsome prince under a spell. He was handsome, certainly, but he was also demonic, in the truest sense of the word. Bea's mother loved him before she realized it, and she loved him after. Indeed, she loves him still. They met in Everwhere the night Cleo turned eighteen and Wilhelm Grimm was, well, he'd existed so long by then he'd long lost count. It was love at first sight.

It was also the night of her Choosing, the night she'd pick dark or light, life or death. And since Cleo was in love the choice was quite clear. Her sisters, however, didn't choose likewise. Perhaps their father's charisma had worn thin once he'd picked his favourite. So, they eschewed his offer and died for their cause. Cleo watched them die. Indeed, she was the one who killed them. Usually, her father would have done it but that night, in an act of generosity, he allowed his daughter the honour. Cleo took the gift and returned it in full force. And, although she was new to murder, Cleo discovered she had a knack for it.

Bea was conceived that night, on a blanket of crushed roses wet with her aunts' blood.

The shadows will try to trick you, niña, Cleo told Bea, *they'll try to catch you unawares. If they do, they can floor you.* ¿Entiendes? *But if you're prepared you can trick them in turn, harness their power and use it to soar as far and high as you wish.*

So, Bea lingered in the shadows, waiting for the whispers. She closed her eyes and steeled herself. In the silence Bea mumbled an incantation, imagining her ribs stretching and thickening across her chest, enclosing her heart until the bone was solid enough to withstand any bullet, yet supple enough to swallow any strike. Bea strengthened herself until she could filter the whispers – spit out their intent and soak up their power – until she found that she was indeed able to do anything, both in that world and this.

When Bea returned home to her *mamá,* she recounted stories of what she'd done, then always asked for a story in return.

'Tell me,' Bea said, though she'd heard it a thousand times before; though she could speak every word in her sleep, still she asked. 'Tell me *my* story.'

'Strictly speaking it should be your sister's story,' Cleo said, as she always did. 'Since this Beauty is a water spirit, like Liyana. But I believe one day she'll write you a story – though she'll think it's her own until she'll realize it's not – so everything will even out.'

'I don't care,' Bea said. 'I love this one the most and so it belongs to me.'

'*¡Bien!*' Cleo laughed. 'As you wish. Close your eyes, *niña,* and I'll begin.'

Bea smiled and did as she was told.

A decade ago

'There was once a baby girl born so uncommonly beautiful that her *mamá* named her Beauty,' Cleo began.

Beauty and the Beast

'As Beauty grew, it became clear that her temperament matched her name for she was as kind and true as she was beautiful. As she grew, her sweetness and loveliness only grew too. Long before she came of age, every prince wanted her for his wife. At sixteen, Beauty was keen to marry for, though she was loved by everyone, still she felt consumed by a sense of longing, though she didn't know for what.

'"True love is what you want," her *mamá* said. "For, while it is pleasing to be loved by a great many people, true happiness lies in being loved completely by only one."

'Being a dutiful daughter, Beauty heeded her *mamá*'s words and married the prince who seemed to love her more than any other. She knew she would come to love him in turn because it would surely be easy to love someone who adored you so completely. Fortunately, Beauty found that, in this at least, she was right. She delighted in being a wife, mother and queen.

'She helped her newly crowned husband rule his people with a firm and fair hand and their kingdom prospered. Their children grew, married, and had children of their own. However, as the years passed, Beauty again began to feel the longing for something she couldn't quite place. And she noticed that strangers no longer gazed upon her open-mouthed or spoke of her radiance in reverent tones.

'So Beauty had every mirror in the castle covered with thick velvet cloths and forbade the servants to polish any window or silver plate too well, so she'd never again have to catch sight of her reflection.

'The following year, on her seventieth birthday, a wizard arrived uninvited to the palace celebrations, demanding to meet the queen. At first, Beauty was scared since the wizard had a fearsome reputation, being known throughout the kingdom as The Beast. But she found, once they began talking, that she rather liked him.

'"I have a gift for you, my queen," he said. "An invitation."

'"Yes?" Beauty asked, no longer fearful but intrigued.

'"I invite you," the wizard said, "to pretend, for a year, that you are me."

'The queen frowned. "What sort of a gift is that?" she said. "I think I'd prefer Everlasting Happiness or Eternal Youth, please. Since I suspect you're in a position to afford me both those things."

'"Oh, but Your Majesty, the gift I'm offering is far better than either," the wizard promised. "Trust me."

'The queen did not believe him for an instant but found, curiously, that she did indeed trust him, though she couldn't say why. So, she accepted the wizard's invitation and began to act as he did. With a few minor modifications.

'Beauty stopped saying "yes" when she wanted to say "no", stopped smiling at someone when she wanted to slap them, stopped staying silent when she needed to shout. She stood on parapets and screamed into the wind, so loud and long that the villagers began fearing dragons. Sometimes the strength of her voice brought the rain from the clouds and with it the ravens, whose high cries dropped into the chorus of her screaming song. Beauty shot arrows into the air and set off cannons. She swam naked in the rivers on moonless nights, bringing waves crashing down on the spies she caught, drowning a man who dared to thrust himself upon her.

Beauty ran along stone passageways wielding an enormous sword, terrifying the servants and even the king, who leapt out of the way once he saw his wife wasn't going to do the same.

'In short, Beauty began, for the first time in her life, to please herself and act as she wished. And she found, much to her surprise, that the wizard had been right, his gift was far better than the Everlasting Happiness and Eternal Youth she'd asked for.

'One evening the queen was striding through the banquet hall, on her way to a parapet, when she saw a mirror draped in thick velvet cloth. Having entirely forgotten her decree, and no longer fearing her own reflection, she tore off the cloth. Upon seeing herself again, the bright light in her eyes and the deep lines on her face, Beauty realized that the wizard's gift hadn't simply been better than the gifts she'd asked for but had indeed given her those things too.

'From that day, and for the rest of her life, the queen never again felt a longing for something she couldn't quite place. Or, indeed, for anything else at all.'

Liyana

Liyana had lied to her mummy. And now she was scared, both of the lie and of being alone on the streets of London in the middle of the night, and excited too. She'd never done anything so reckless before, so dangerous. Not even close. She'd never lied to her mother before. Still, Liyana had to find out if what Bea said about the gates was true. She'd been waiting nearly a full month for the next first-quarter moon, and now it was here.

A few months ago, Liyana would never, not in a hundred thousand years, have dreamed of doing something so wild. She'd have been too scared of disobeying her mother and, frankly, too scared of death or dismemberment or whatever dreadful consequences might result from actions of such stupidity. But since finding Everwhere, since discovering that she hadn't been dreaming, Liyana had felt different: gifted, special, brave.

Bea had told her the timing, the precise moment she must open a gate into Everwhere, but hadn't told Liyana the precise, or even general, locations of any of these gates. It'd be a test, she'd said, of Liyana's skills. At first, Liyana thought her sister had been mocking her.

But Bea hadn't made this declaration in her usual derisive tones. It was as if she really did want to teach Liyana how to reach her full potential. And not in the way her mother did, by trying to make Liyana less of herself. Bea wanted Liyana to be more herself, not less. And for that, Liyana was deeply grateful. So grateful that it had made Bea her new favourite sister, shifting Goldie off the top spot. The positions of Bea and Scarlet had shifted on an almost nightly basis. But quiet, thoughtful Goldie had always been Liyana's favourite. Until now.

Being unused to the business of trusting her instincts, Liyana had assumed that the night would be an exercise in fruitless courage. She'd readied herself against the anticipated barrage of rapists and murderers, arming herself with various alarms and defences. But the streets of Islington were quiet during the early hours of that Wednesday morning, not a person of ominous intent in sight.

As she walked, Liyana was surprised to discover that, despite not knowing where she was going, she seemed to know where she was heading. Although she didn't know her destination, she nevertheless knew the way. So she walked on, turning left or right when she reached the end of a road, as her inclination took her. Liyana stopped before she saw it. She was standing in front of a walled garden she'd never noticed before. The gate was locked and roped with ivy so thick that it couldn't have been opened in decades.

Surely, Liyana thought, this couldn't be the right one. And yet, at the same time she knew that it was. She stared at the lock, so mottled with rust, so intricately entwined with vines that it must be impossible to open, even if she had the key, which she did not.

Liyana glanced at her watch. She had, according to Bea's instructions, only five minutes until the essential moment. But what was she supposed to do next? Liyana squinted at the problem, shifting from foot to foot to shake up her brain cells.

One minute to go.

Liyana grasped a rusty iron curlicue and rattled the gate. She was rewarded with several satisfying clangs. But that was all. She tried again, shaking it so hard this time that every limb of her little body shook with it. And then Liyana found that she didn't have to do anything at all. At precisely 3.33 a.m., the moon slid out from under a cloud, shining its soft light to illuminate the metal. And, despite the rust and leafy ropes, the gate swung open with only a slight creak. Liyana hesitated a second, before stepping through.

On the other side of the gate, Bea was waiting.

'Well done,' she said, with the smallest of smug smiles. 'You passed the test.'

14th October – 18 days . . .

9.45 a.m. – Goldie

'What is it?'

'Well, it *is* a silk scarf,' Leo says. 'But I suppose you can use it for whatever purpose you see fit.'

We're standing in an empty corridor on the third floor. I'm meant to be cleaning room sixteen, but I've been interrupted by Leo.

'I know that.' I smile. 'I meant, what's it for? I mean – I'm not making much sense, am I?'

'Not a lot, no.'

'I meant – why are you giving it to me?'

Now Leo smiles. 'Can't I give you a present for no reason at all?'

'I don't know . . .' I shrug. 'I'm not used to it.'

'Well,' he says, 'I've been thinking that you're always acquiring things for your little brother. But you never seem to acquire much for yourself.'

'You say that like I'm a generous shopper,' I say, 'rather than a gifted thief.'

'"Gifted", eh? I like that you know your own skills. Nothing worse than false modesty.'

I shrug again. 'I take credit where I can. It's not like I've got much else going for me. I don't—'

'Oh no, I'm afraid I'll have to stop you there and respectfully disagree,' Leo says, leaning down to kiss me. 'You've got a hell of a lot going for you.'

I duck away from him. 'I won't have anything going for

me if someone catches us kissing and reports it to management, Mr Penry-Jones.'

But Leo leans in closer to whisper in my ear. 'Then I'm lucky no one caught me stealing that scarf from room twenty-seven.'

I narrow my eyes at him. 'You didn't.'

'You're not the only one with skills.'

'What? No, you can't do that, you're the manager, you're crazy—'

He lands the quickest of kisses on my cheek as I stuff the scarf into my apron pocket. 'About you.'

I roll my eyes. 'Now you're crazy and cheesy.'

Leo shrugs. I meet his gaze and hold it.

'You didn't steal this from room twenty-seven, did you?' I say. 'You bought it.'

Leo laughs and kisses me again. This time, I let him.

2.59 p.m. – Scarlet

The kiss. Scarlet hasn't been able to think about much else since. Which is something of a blessed relief, eclipsing, as it does, the events preceding the kiss and the implications thereof. However, that was two days ago and she's not seen him since. Scarlet's clearing a table recently deserted by overconfident, over-loud Cambridge students – the sort under the illusion that they're both the only people in the café and the most important – when he walks in.

Relief and joy spark at her fingertips. 'You.'

'What, you thought I'd kiss and run?' Eli smiles, walking up to her. 'What sort of cad do you think I am?'

'Oh, I know exactly what kind of cad you are.' Scarlet sets the plates back on the table. She's flirting. A monumentally foolish thing to do. But she can't seem to help it.

Eli laughs. 'You're a feisty one, aren't you?'

Scarlet shrugs. 'It's the hair. But I imagine you already know that.'

'Actually . . .' Eli reaches out to touch her cheek. 'I've never had the pleasure of knowing a redhead intimately before.'

As his fingers brush her skin, Scarlet feels a sudden and disturbing desire to have him scoop her up and lay her down upon the nearest table.

'Hey, Scarlet, which wood did you want—?'

She turns. Eli steps back and Walt, standing in the kitchen doorway, eyes them both with a suspicious frown.

'Am I interrupting?'

'Oh, no.' Scarlet straightens herself. 'No, Mr Wolfe and I were just, um . . . He's brought—'

'Some papers for Miss Thorne to sign,' Eli finishes.

'Okay, well, that's . . . none of my business,' Walt says. 'I only came to ask if you wanted pine or oak for the replacement shelves.'

'I, um . . .' Scarlet tries and fails to summon any interest in the subject. 'Whatever you think's best.'

'All right then,' Walt says, turning to walk back into the kitchen.

'Shouldn't you be supervising him?' Eli says. 'He might suddenly decide to paint the shelves bright orange or lime green.'

'He's not a painter,' Scarlet says, absently. 'He's not even a carpenter. He's just doing me a favour. He's . . . nice.'

Eli's smile deepens. 'Unlike me?'

'Absolutely.' If Walt was fire, Scarlet thinks, he'd be a spluttering candle. Ezekiel Wolfe is an inferno. 'Did you bring the papers?'

'Of course. I'd brought them to Fitzbillies, but then you callously abandoned me after that rather spectacular kiss. So now I keep them with me at all times.' Eli taps his jacket pocket. 'To catch you whenever you're ready to see sense.'

'Mocking the target – is this some sort of reverse psychology strategy?' Scarlet asks. 'Or are you actually trying to talk yourself out of a sale?'

'Neither, I'm just having a little fun.' Eli pulls out a chair to sit at the cluttered table. 'Okay, let's start again.'

Scarlet waits before sitting and taking the papers from him. For several studious minutes, she scans them, attempting to look as if she knows what she's doing.

'You only need to read one,' he says. 'They're duplicates.'

'I know that,' Scarlet snaps. 'Now, shush.'

Eli sits back in his chair, looking like a mischievous child. His large eyes seem even bigger, his lips moist, his smile wide, his two rows of perfectly straight, white teeth . . . Scarlet pulls her eyes from his face and forces herself to focus on the page.

When she's finally finished, she looks up. 'All right.' She folds her arms. 'How about adding another five thousand to your offer?'

'I'm afraid I'm not authorized to do that,' Eli says. 'I'd have to go back to my bosses and run it past them.'

Scarlet regards him. 'Oh, I'm sure you've been given a little wiggle room.'

'You're a sly one, aren't you?' Eli gives her a coy smile, then plucks a fountain pen from his pocket, adjusts the figure – in purple ink, on both documents – and signs the alterations.

Scarlet takes a deep breath. 'The pen.'

'Don't you want to get your solicitor to look those over first?'

'Give me the pen.'

Their fingers touch, igniting a single spark.

'What was that?'

'Static,' Scarlet says, focusing on the papers. Then she stops, pen poised, and looks up. 'Ten thousand.'

'Sorry?'

'I think you've been authorized to increase the offer by ten thousand.'

Eli says nothing.

'Am I right?'

Still he says nothing. But she can tell, from the surprise in his eyes, that she is.

'Excellent,' she says. 'Do that, and we've definitely got a deal.'

She slides the papers and pen back across the table. He takes them.

'You drive a hard bargain, Miss Thorne,' Eli says, grinning a wolfish grin.

7.45 p.m. – Goldie

'What's wrong?'

'Nothing.'

We're standing behind the restaurant bar in the hotel. He's crouched beside the fridges, doing the stock count. I'm standing on a stool, half-heartedly dusting the bottles of Bollinger lining the glass shelves above.

'It's not,' I say.

Leo stops counting and looks up. 'Have you ever wanted something you couldn't have?'

'I don't know.' I shrug. A million things, I suppose. But, right now, when I feel I've got everything I could possibly want, it's hard to pinpoint anything. 'Anyway, I'm a thief extraordinaire,' I say, in a stage-whisper. 'Whatever I want, I take.'

Leo laughs, but it's not his usual laugh. It's heavier, weighed down by his thoughts, whatever they are.

'Even you aren't that good a thief,' he says. 'No one is.'

We fall into silence.

'I was thinking about what you said the other day,' I say.

He waits.

'About me saying "I don't know" a lot.'

Leo nods.

'Well, I feel like, I . . . maybe I used to know. When I was a little kid.' I search for words, trying to find my meaning. Leo waits. 'Before things happened that I didn't know could happen. Things that . . .' I trail off.

'The reason you flinched when I first touched you?'

I nod, once.

He doesn't ask anything more, only reaches for my hand and holds it gently between his palms.

11.47 p.m. – Liyana

She's done it. Liyana has been brave, has faced life head on. She's filled out fifteen more job applications, stopped stalling Kumiko with texts and finally called to arrange a meeting tomorrow. She's also seeing Mazmo on Saturday night. So, twelve hours to prepare a winning argument for her girlfriend and four days to prepare an unconventional marriage proposal for her potential husband. Now she sits cross-legged on her bed, shuffling the Tarot cards and, before she's even had a chance to lay them out, one falls from the pack between her folded legs.

The Three of Cups. *Team spirit, unity, friendship, unconditional love.*

Liyana picks it up, studying the picture of three women in a forest, each holding a goblet aloft. Small woodland creatures surround them, looking on and applauding. She's seen this card many times, but has never drawn it.

Liyana sets the Three of Cups on the duvet, then pulls more cards from the pack: the Three of Pentacles, The Devil, Nine of Wands. An army. Warriors, like her own BlackBird. An opponent. A battle.

Liyana spends another hour studying the cards, trying to decipher the story, hoping deeper layers of meaning will float to the surface, if only she waits long enough. But, this time, they don't.

11.57 p.m. – Bea

Bea falls asleep as soon as she returns to her room, dropping her bag, collapsing into bed without removing her shoes. She meant to lie down only a moment, but tumbles down the rabbit hole the second she closes her eyes.

Bea watches as objects begin to shift: a carriage clock on her desk lifting into the air then settling on her bedside table. It ousts an art deco lamp so it falls, halting and hovering an inch above the floorboards before alighting, in a dignified manner, upon the edge of a bookshelf.

Then all chaos breaks loose. As if they only needed a nudge, every object in Bea's bedroom hurls itself into the air, gathering speed into a sweeping tornado that tears through the air, ripping up the carpet, wrenching anything still stationary into its vortex, including the bed and Bea upon it.

Bea wakes screaming, sitting up so fast that she nearly falls back. But no objects are flying above her head; no storm is wreaking havoc upon her room. All is hushed and still. Bea stops screaming and falls silent. She's drawing a deep breath, reaching for calm, when she sees the peacock feather resting in the palm of her left hand. It's as inert as everything else, as if it's been patiently waiting to be seen.

Bea stares at it. Perhaps, by some giant leap of imagination, she could explain its presence. Perhaps she'd left her door ajar, perhaps a trickster friend or malicious ex-boyfriend is trying to spook her. It's highly unlikely, but possible. What happens next, is not.

The feather begins to transform in her hand. The nib begins to darken, as if dipped in ink. The quill draws it up, spreading the ink to each barb until the whole feather is black.

First a book, now a feather.

And the feeling that she's being watched.

15th October – 17 days . . .

3.33 a.m. – Leo

I know what you're thinking.

Leo stiffens. Goldie is lying beside him in bed and, though she can't hear the voice that has just invaded his head, still it feels too close. He tries to quiet his mind, so his father can't read his thoughts.

Wilhelm's laughter cracks along Leo's synapses. *I believe that's what they call locking the stable door after the horse has bolted. I'm in your mind now, I can see it all.*

Leo is silent.

You're falling in love with her.

No, Leo thinks. I—

You know I can't allow it.

Leo is silent. I know.

Wilhelm waits.

If you won't fight her, then I'm afraid you're of no use to me. It pains me, but—

Leo feels as if every muscle in his body has turned to stone. He feels Goldie shift beside him, waking up. No, I – I will. I'll fight her.

I'm not entirely sure I believe you. His words are soft, slow, marking time. *Perhaps I should extinguish you now, find another to replace you.*

No! A scream crouches in Leo's chest. Please, don't. I, I'll . . .

Oh, calm down. Wilhelm's sigh blows a chill breath through Leo's body. *I'm a foolish old man and you're my favourite son, so I'll give you a second chance.*

Leo waits.

You have until the night of her Choosing. He pauses. *I admit, I'm quite certain she'll win anyway. Still, she must be subjected to the challenge, just like everyone else* – his laughter cracks again through Leo's mind – *after all, what would a gladiator be without a lion?*

Leo imagines himself impaled on Goldie's sword. He blinks the image away.

If you won't put up a fight, I'll find another who will.

3.36 a.m. – Goldie

'I love falling asleep with you.'

Leo turns his head to kiss my cheek but kisses my ear instead. 'Me too.'

'I don't think you ever sleep,' I say. 'Whenever I wake, your eyes are always open.'

'I'm keeping guard,' he says.

'That's kind of you, but I think Teddy and I can take care of ourselves,' I say with a smile. 'We don't talk to strangers, we're pretty shirty with murderers and, after a close-call terrorism incident last summer, we now operate a strict invite-only policy to our cocktail parties. So, I think we're safe.'

'I'm glad to hear it. But how do you know you can trust me?' Leo smiles, although there's something in the tone of his voice that suggests he's not entirely joking. 'I might be a terrorist too.'

'No,' I say. 'I put all my lovers through a rigorous screening system.'

Leo's smile deepens. 'Oh?'

I nod. 'You've been subjected to background checks, DNA tests—'

'—scrutiny of personal diaries.'

'Oh, God,' I mumble, burying my face in his chest. 'I was hoping you'd forgotten that most embarrassing moment of my life.'

'Never,' Leo says. 'I'll still be reminding you of that when . . .'

I wait for him to finish the sentence, what I hoped would be a promise about our future. But he doesn't.

3.39 a.m. – Goldie

I'm having the same dream every night. At first, everything is white: I'm staring into a lightbulb, a field of snow, a Tupperware sky. Shadows start to take shape. I'm standing in a garden, though still everything is white: the grass, the plants, the birds, the butterflies . . . A white cat stalks through white grass, picking his paws through daisies and dandelions, before disappearing into a clutch of cow parsley. Albino blackbirds trill from white willow trees, their song floating on a breeze that carries white bumblebees to and from white roses.

Hundreds, thousands of roses, sprinkled through the garden, as voluptuous as peonies, on every stalk and stem. As I stand, wondering if I too am pure white, I see that the garden is getting larger, expanding in every direction and expanding still, until all I can see are millions of roses, their scent so strong and sweet that I can taste their nectar on my tongue.

There's something special about these roses, though I don't know what. But the longer I stand among them, the surer I become. I'm connected to them somehow. And, as I stand there, I start to wonder if I too am a rose.

4.34 p.m. – Liyana

'I still think it'll implode.'

'Maybe not,' Liyana says, holding out her hand to catch the falling rain. Her hands are free since Kumiko, arms folded across her chest as she walks, has silently rebuffed Liyana's overtures at hand-holding.

They'd sat inside Ottolenghi for three hours – making two lemon brûlée tarts last longer than anyone thought possible – analysing the potential problems of the proposal from every possible angle. Finally, Liyana persuaded Kumiko that they needed fresh air.

'I think it might work.'

'Is that what your aunt says?' Kumiko says, for the thirtieth time that afternoon, and more bitterly every time.

'Let's just see what *he* says.' Liyana follows Kumiko across Shillingford Street. 'You never know, we might be able to work it out in a way to suit everyone.'

'Then you're more naive than your aunt,' Kumiko says. 'What if he's not content simply to sleep around. What if he wants kids?'

'Then he'll have to have them with someone else.'

'He's rich. He'll want a legitimate heir,' Kumiko says. 'He'll want family photos and ridiculous Christmas cards with his fat squalling babies dressed as cherubs. He'll want—'

'We don't know what he'll want until I ask him,' Liyana says, for the twentieth time, though it feels like the fiftieth.

'And who will I be in this cosy scenario?' Kumiko snorts. 'The nanny?'

'Oh, don't be so melodramatic.' Liyana won't admit it to Kumiko, but the idea of not having to work night shifts at Tesco – she's been invited for an interview next Saturday – to fund three years at the Slade, the thought of graduating with no debt, makes her quite giddy. 'It won't be that bad. It won't need to change anything at all.'

'If you think that,' Kumiko snaps, 'then you're the naivest idiot in all of London.'

'Trust me,' Liyana says, desperate to step off the exhausting merry-go-round of an unwinnable argument. 'All that matters is he agrees to a platonic arrangement. I won't sleep with him. I won't even kiss him, I promise.'

'I should bloody well hope not.'

Liyana sighs, thinking of BlackBird and how differently the conversation might be going if she had her heroine's gumption. What happened to no longer being a pale ghost of herself, to being brave, to being bold? What happened to being fearless? Except that Liyana can't pretend she's not terrified of losing Kumiko. 'It might not be so bad. It's . . . suggesting the possibility of something, that's all.'

'Yeah, keep telling yourself that,' Kumiko says. 'You just wait, you'll see.'

'But we don't have to worry about all that yet, do we?' Liyana says. 'It's still early days. He hasn't even agreed to anything yet.' She hasn't told Kumiko about her trip to the priest. Nor the voice or its directive to find her sisters. She wants to, but her girlfriend is hardly in a receptive mood.

Kumiko shakes her head. 'You're playing with fire, Ana.'

'I can handle it.'

'So you keep saying.'

4.58 p.m. – Bea

Bea sits in the University Library opposite Vali, who has his nose pressed up against *Tractatus Logico-Philosophicus* while Bea studies Russell's *Principles of Social Reconstruction*.

'Jesus!' Bea slaps her hand down hard on the table, then looks slightly embarrassed. 'Sorry,' she hisses, not directing this at Vali so much as the library itself. 'Sorry.'

Fortunately, it's empty except for the two of them, although the librarian does throw an admonishing glare in her direction.

'What did you do that for?' Vali hisses back.

Bea, glancing at the librarian, leans across the table. 'Bertrand Russell is a fucking genius,' she says, in a high whisper. 'I tell you, if he was alive today, I'd— Have you ever had sex with someone just because they're so fucking clever it blows your fucking mind?'

Vali gives Bea his own, softer, admonishing glare. 'Hardly suitable discourse under present conditions, do you think?'

'Why? Who am I going to offend?' Bea hisses. 'You're the only one here.'

Vali shrugs. 'Respect the sanctity of the church, perhaps.'

'What are you talking about?' Bea frowns. 'We're not in church.'

Vali nods at the vast bookshelves surrounding them in every direction, raising his eyebrows as if to suggest the books are parishioners huddled in their pews.

'Right,' Bea concedes, giving a nominal nod at the books. 'Sorry. But, why are you suddenly so puritanical? What's wrong with a bit of fucking now and then?'

She eyes Vali – who's now staring at *Tractatus Logico-Philosophicus* with renewed purpose – scrutinizing him like she's trying to fathom a particularly problematic philosophical theorem.

'Oh, Christ.' Bea sighs. 'I get it. You're a virgin.'

Vali remains glued to the page.

'You are,' Bea persists. 'Aren't you?'

Vali looks up, fixing her with a valiant stare that quickly, under her eagle eye, crumbles into a conceding shrug.

'Oh, Val, we're going to have to do something about that.'

Vali attempts a smile but manages only a mournful gaze. Bea frowns, as fresh recognition dawns. She can read the truth on his chubby, hairy face as easily as she can read the truth in *Principles of Social Reconstruction*. Bertrand Russell is a fucking genius and Vali has never even been kissed.

'Really?' Bea says. 'Nothing, never? Not a blow job, not a peck on the lips?'

Vali closes Wittgenstein, failing at a nonchalant shrug.

Bea sighs. 'Jesus, Val, just when I think you couldn't be any more pitiful, you go and outdo yourself yet again.'

6.26 p.m. – Scarlet

Walking into the café, having nipped to M&S for a fish pie – it's about time she fed her grandmother some nutrients – Scarlet stops. She hears music coming from the kitchen. And laughter. Hurrying across the creaking floorboards, she pauses at the open door.

In the kitchen Esme is dancing, waltzing across the linoleum floor with Walt. He whispers in her ear and she giggles. On the radio Bessie Smith is singing *Backwater Blues*. Scarlet knows every word to this song and every other Smith ever sang. She was raised on Bessie Smith, Ella Fitzgerald, Nina Simone . . . Now, seeing her grandmother happy, carefree, herself again, gives Scarlet more joy than she could have imagined possible.

'Hey, Boss,' Walt says, as Scarlet steps into the kitchen. 'You never told me your grandma was so swift on her toes.'

'Oh, yes, she's a mover,' Scarlet says, wondering why

he's still here, since the recalcitrant dishwasher has, for a small fortune, finally been resurrected and all shelves now installed. 'Taught me everything I know.'

'Is that right?' Walt says, giving Esme a quick dip that makes her giggle. 'Then will you give me the next dance?'

'Oh, no.' Scarlet shakes her head. 'No, she's the dancer, not me.'

Walt grins, reaching out his hand. 'We'll have no false modesty here,' he says. 'Come on.'

With a shrug, and only because Esme's still smiling, Scarlet concedes, letting him pull her onto the dance floor. Nina Simone snatches up the next song and the accelerating notes of *Sinnerman* fill the kitchen.

'We can't dance to this,' Scarlet protests. 'It's too fast.'

'Pish,' Walt says. 'Don't be so defeatist. Anyway, you've got cause to celebrate.'

'I have?'

Drawing Scarlet to his chest Walt starts to twirl her across the kitchen floor. 'I've left your invoice on top of the till,' he says. 'I've just come from fixing the air con at Pembroke and—'

Scarlet slows, pulling back. 'How's that cause for celebration?'

Walt smiles. 'Because I only charged you for parts, no labour. A hundred and forty-five pounds total.'

'No, but I . . .' Scarlet stops. 'You can't do that.'

'I can and I did.' Walt shifts his feet. 'So come on, let's dance.'

'But,' Scarlet says, still dragging hers. 'But, how?'

Walt shrugs. 'It's my company, I can do what I like. Now, shut up and dance!'

Scarlet squeals as he twirls her, around and around and around. Her grandmother claps. *If I could be any happier right now,* Scarlet thinks, *I can't imagine how.* As Simone starts to sing *'Go to the devil, the Lord said . . .'* Walt reaches out for Esme and brings Scarlet into her grandmother's arms. Throwing him a grateful smile, Scarlet starts to slowly waltz across the kitchen with her grandmother.

'Rube used to do that sometimes,' Esme whispers.

Scarlet frowns. 'What?'

'That,' Esme says, nodding at the sparks firing from Scarlet's fingertips.

'Oh, sh—' Scarlet glances to Walt.

Mercifully, the electrician isn't watching but sneaking a cinnamon bun from an open tin on the counter. Mercifully too, Esme doesn't seem remotely surprised or troubled by the phenomenon.

'Did she – this happened to her too?' Scarlet whispers. 'Are you sure?'

'What?' Esme asks.

'This,' Scarlet says, nodding at her hands. But the sparks have gone and her fingers are cool. And no matter how hard she tries, Scarlet cannot will them to spark again.

11.48 p.m. – Leo

Leo still plans how he'll kill Goldie, even though, paradoxically, he now feels he can't bear to hurt her. Lately, he finds himself increasingly thinking of the night he killed Goldie's mother. He can't tell Goldie, since it'll cause her such pain and it's the one thing that'll ensure she'll never love him in return.

He'd done nothing unusual. Most mothers meet the same fate, since they're defenceless when they come unwittingly to Everwhere on the coat-tails of their daughters' dreams. Just as Goldie's mother had done – her body remaining on Earth, her auric form in Everwhere – though teenage Goldie could, of course, no longer join her. So, once their spirit is extinguished in one world, their body simply dies in another. The soldiers kill them for sport, for practice. Or because their light is low and a mother's death will buy them another month of life.

However, since these kills were so unsporting, Leo had never taken any particular pleasure in extinguishing those flames. And he disagreed with his demonic father's belief that the sainted mothers posed any great influential threat for the good – didn't most daughters rebel against their mothers anyway? So their deaths tended to weigh on him, as the deaths of their daughters never had. Although he couldn't have known that he'd have cause to regret one death so much.

There'd been nothing remarkable about that night. Nothing special, nothing different, nothing strange. He'd been given his target. He'd heard her name, closed his eyes and seen her.

Leo was fourteen. The nearest gate was in the grounds of the British Museum, fifteen minutes' walk from home. He knew the way by heart, every street, every stone step. He followed streetlamps, golden breadcrumbs in the moonlight, his path curling past darkened windows and silent doors. The gateway stood behind the museum, a small side entrance on Bloomsbury Street. It was locked, and looked as if it had been for the best part of two hundred years. It'd been Leo's birthday three months earlier and his father had bought him a Patek Philippe watch at, as Charles Penry-Jones was always at pains to point out, great expense. Its intricate and delicate platinum cogs glinted in the silvery light. Leo kept his eyes fixed to its hands as they ticked towards the half-hour. At 3.33 a.m., the silver light illuminated the ancient rusty gate and Leo pushed it open and walked through.

He stepped not onto the clipped lawn of the museum's grounds but into a place of falling leaves and rapacious ivy, of mist and fog, of moonlight and ice; a place always shifting but always still.

It didn't take Leo long to find her. Even as a child, his senses were stronger than any other soldier's, including those who'd been around for centuries. He did it without question or hesitation. It was effortless. When Leo had placed his hand over her heart, when he'd taken the light from her, when her final breath had etched the seventh star onto his skin, he'd never given it a second thought.

16th October –
16 days . . .

3.33 a.m. – Liyana

Liyana wakes, hair sticky with sweat, T-shirt clinging to her chest. Her heart is beating so fast that the tips of her fingers throb with the pulse and her lungs hurt as if she's burst to the surface, taking her first breath after holding it underwater for far too long.

She has just seen her sister.

11.11 a.m. – Goldie

'I've always loved gardens,' I say. We're walking through the Botanical Gardens, over the rock gardens, towards the lake.

'Me too,' Leo says.

'Some of the trees are over five hundred years old.'

'Magnificent,' Leo says. 'You know, Pliny the Younger wrote that gardens feel so spiritual because the trees used to be the temples of the gods and neither the trees nor the gods have forgotten this.'

'Who's Pliny?' With anyone else I wouldn't ask, I'd let the conversation continue, pretending by omission that I knew. I never feel embarrassed or ashamed by my ignorance with Leo.

'A clever Roman chap who wrote a lot of stuff,' Leo says. 'When can I meet your brother?'

'What?'

'You heard.'

I'm silent. 'I – I don't know.'

'You're protecting him from me?'

I shrug, unwilling to admit it. We reach the edge of the lake. Five flattened raised rocks, half submerged in the water, lie between us and the other bank.

'Why?' Leo asks.

'Not only from you,' I say. 'From us.'

'I don't understand.'

I shrug again. 'Well, if we . . . I mean, I don't want him to meet you and love you and . . .'

'And what?' Leo asks. 'And then I leave and he never sees me again?'

I'm silent.

'Oh, Goldie,' Leo says, cupping my chin in his hands. 'Of everything, of all the awful things that could possibly happen, I promise you, I swear, it won't be that.'

I smile. Then frown. 'What awful things?'

This time it's Leo who's silent.

2.34 p.m. – Bea

'I like that you think I'm nice. Or that you think I've got the potential to be nice,' Bea says. 'You're the first person who's ever—'

'Thought so?'

Bea nods.

'Then it sounds like your mother's as much of a bitch as mine,' Vali says.

'Yeah,' Bea says. 'Except that mine's proud of it.'

'She sounds like a challenging parent.'

Bea smiles. 'I'm not telling you some sob story about my childhood, if that's what you're hoping for. You can look for your kicks elsewhere.'

'Oh, go on,' Vali says, tugging at his beard. 'Just a short one.'

'Piss off.'

Vali grins. 'I'll tell you mine, if you tell me yours.'

'No thanks.'

Vali meets Bea's eye. 'You're impenetrable.'

'Too right. I'm not having you fishing around in my psyche. It'd give you nightmares.'

'You underestimate me.'

'You could get three PhDs in behavioural psychology, moral philosophy and theoretical politics.' Bea glances away. 'And you still wouldn't be qualified to delve into my mind.'

Vali smooths his jumper over his stomach. 'Don't you ever tire of being mean?'

'You love it,' Bea says. 'I remind you of your *mamá*. And all men fall in love with their *mamá*, don't they? That's primary-school psychology. If I was any nicer, you wouldn't love me anymore.'

Vali smiles, stroking his beard between forefinger and thumb. 'Who said I was in love with you?'

'You're mad about me.'

'Well, I'd certainly be mad if I was.'

'You're certifiable.'

'Maybe. But I don't think I'm the only one.'

Bea smiles, catching his eye. This time she doesn't look away.

8.07 p.m. – Scarlet

Scarlet puts down the book she's been hiding behind – retreating into the words, the world of Middle Earth, when she can't stand the silences any longer. 'What's wrong, Grandma? You don't like the chicken?'

Scarlet made an effort today to prepare a decent meal, but her grandmother hasn't touched her food. Now she holds a glass of water and is frowning at it, as if she not only cannot recall picking it up but cannot understand why she would've done so in the first place.

'Grandma?'

Esme blinks at her granddaughter.

'Is everything okay?' Scarlet asks, suddenly paranoid that her grandmother somehow knows that she's selling the café. She's dearly hoping that, when she finally confesses, the loss won't mean anything to Esme anymore.

'Would you like something else?'

'Your mother was conceived in this café,' Esme says, almost to herself. 'Did you know that?'

Scarlet brightens. 'Really?'

'Behind the counter, after we closed one night.' Esme gazes at the counter, as if seeing something Scarlet can't. 'Harry brought me cinnamon buns afterwards.'

'You've never told me that.'

'One day you'll teach your daughter how to make them. And perhaps your husband will bring you cinnamon buns afterwards too.'

'But I don't have a daughter, Grandma. I don't want children.'

'Don't be ridiculous,' her grandmother says with a smile. 'When you were a little girl you told me: you'll have a daughter and you'll call her Red. Remember?'

She tries to remember, to sniff out the trail of breadcrumbs that might lead her back to this unknown. A memory tugs at the edges of Scarlet's mind: pretending to have a baby girl, stroking her soft tufts of red hair, plump cheeks, tight-curled fists . . .

'If you have two daughters, perhaps you can call one of them Ruby.'

This mention of her mother ignites a guttering flame in Scarlet's heart. She snuffs out the flame. 'I'm not a little girl anymore, Grandma.'

Esme leans forward to cup Scarlet's chin in her palm and look her granddaughter straight in the eye.

'Oh, Scarlet,' she says. 'Sometimes you say the silliest things.'

And all at once Scarlet knows that no matter how much it makes sense, she cannot sell the café.

11.59 p.m. – Goldie

'I don't know how you function,' I say.

'What do you mean?'

'You never seem to sleep.'

He shrugs. 'I sleep more than I used to.'

I press my face into his chest. 'Sometimes I wonder if you're entirely human.'

'I'm not.'

I smile. 'Neither am I.'

Leo kisses my forehead. 'I know, it's one of the things I love about you most of all.'

For a moment, I'm not sure I heard right. But then I'm sure I did, and I sit up so fast I almost fall back and hit my head on the headboard.

Leo smiles. 'What?'

'I thought – did you just say what I think you said?'

Leo laughs, as if the declaration is as much of a surprise to him as it is to me. 'Yes,' he says, still smiling. 'I believe I did.'

A little less than a decade ago

Everwhere

This time it feels different. This time you're scared.

You hesitate. You consider turning back. But you've waited so long that curiosity overcomes fear. Just enough to push you on, from one world and into another.

You walk the stone path, tentative at first, then faster as you start to forget the fear. What is there to fear, after all? Everything is exactly as you remember it: the misty bonfire air, the stillness, the shadows, the trees casting down a confetti of bright white leaves at your feet.

As you go deeper into the woods, falling leaves settling on your shoulders, the kinks of crooked branches at your fingertips, you find you're no longer cold, no longer concerned about whatever it is you might have been worried about before. You hope to find that glade again, you hope to feel as you felt, you hope to hold on to that feeling longer this time.

You hear a noise behind you – the crack of a twig? the call of a bird? the scuff of a shoe on stone? – but when you turn there's nothing to see. Your eyes have adjusted to the moonlight now and you watch the shadows as you pass, as you walk deeper and deeper into this place.

When you hear another sound, you stop. Leaves rustling. Someone *is* following you. You wait. And wait. But no one comes.

There it is again.

You hold your breath. But it's not rustling, it's whispering. Soft voices, low. You listen. The voices are not human.

How do you know this? You're not sure, but it's as clear to you as your own name. Your name. The voices are saying your name. It's a hook in your mouth, pulling you on. You stumble forward, towards the voices, towards the shadows. You're a fish snagged on a line being slowly reeled in. Then the hook begins to twist. It tears into your cheek as the words darken, taunting you, mocking, saying things you never wanted to hear aloud, never wanted to believe to be true. Fear and despair surge in you, coursing through your blood, clogging your heart. You clutch your chest as it starts to constrict. You gulp, but the air is mustard gas. Your breath comes in gasps, until it doesn't come at all. And you are falling through the mists and fog to the ground.

Goldie

My baby brother was born yesterday. My stepfather took me to the hospital with him that same afternoon, but I wasn't excited. Truth be told, I didn't even want to go. I would've made an excuse, if I'd been able to think of one.

When Ma offered to let me hold him, I shook my head. I'd never seen her so happy, so calm, so content and I didn't want to ruin it, I wanted to make it last as long as I possibly could. Only when she pressed, I relented. She placed him so carefully, so gently, into my arms.

'Watch his head,' my ma and stepfather said, in unison.

'Yes,' I said. 'I know.' Though I didn't.

I peered down at him. He didn't look up or open his eyes. He had a puff of dandelion hair so light I thought it might blow away if I sneezed. I held my breath.

'He's sleeping,' Ma said. 'He sleeps a lot.'

'How long will they keep you in?' my stepfather asked, already with an edge to his voice.

'Five days at least,' she said.

My heart sank.

'Shit,' my stepfather said.

'Shush,' Ma said, since she never liked him swearing around me.

They started to bicker and I tuned them out, nudging the baby in the hopes that he'd cry and provide a distraction. And then he opened his eyes. He didn't look at me, he stared unblinking into the space between us, at something I couldn't see. His eyes were tiny and round and bright, bright blue. And I discovered that I'd been wrong. I didn't love my juniper tree more than anything else in the world. I loved my brother.

Liyana

Liyana was eight years old when she discovered she was a pluviophile. She learned the word during Art class, while drawing a picture of her favourite sort of day: tucked into the sofa under a woollen blanket while the rain poured down outside, soaking the windows.

'That's your favourite day?' Mr Nash asked.

Liyana gave a half-shrug, half-nod.

'You don't prefer the sunshine?' He cast a hand towards her classmates, all of whom had drawn pictures featuring a bright yellow sun, regardless of subject.

'No,' Liyana mumbled, anxious at incurring his disapproval but reluctant to lie. 'I prefer the rain.'

She wanted to tell him that her name, in Zulu, meant 'it's raining', but didn't want to bring attention to the fact that she wasn't called Stella or Susie or Sarah, that she – her name, her colour, her origins – was different from the majority of her classmates.

Liyana was surprised when Mr Nash smiled and winked.

'Then you're a pluviophile,' he said. 'We've got to stick together, there aren't too many of us about.'

Leaning over her, he wrote in his tiny, neat teacher-script at the top of her page:

pluviophile: (n.) a lover of rain, someone who finds joy and peace of mind during rainy days.

Liyana read the words, then returned to her drawing, feigning to have lost interest. She didn't tell him that she also liked to take long walks in the rain without a coat, until her clothes were soaked and her skin slick. This, she imagined, was not something normal people did. She didn't tell him that on returning home she didn't dry herself off, didn't take a hot bath. Instead, she sat in the kitchen and dripped onto the tile floor, enjoying the evaporation of every drop. She also didn't mention that she'd taught herself to hold her breath underwater for twenty-four minutes and thirty-one seconds, beating the current world record holder by two minutes and nine seconds.

Liyana had found that such things prompted people to ask questions, to start probing into emotions that ought to remain untouched. Liyana liked Mr Nash well enough and, upon discovering that they were both pluviophiles, wanted to tell him her secrets since it was possible that he might share these traits and feats too – making them more similar than different. However, he was an adult and, worse still, a teacher. And adults, Liyana knew, were not to be trusted with secrets.

She'd learned that from Bea, the importance of concealing certain information from parents and other authorities. Sometimes, it seemed, it was worse to tell the truth than to lie. Especially when it came to Everwhere.

'They won't understand,' Bea said. 'And they won't believe you, then you'll just get into trouble. If they've never been, if they can't get here, if they've got no Grimm blood at all, then they'll think you're mad and send you to a shrink.'

Liyana, who didn't have Mr Nash to explain this last word, shuddered at the thought of being shrunk like Alice upon drinking the 'drink me' bottle. She'd never be able to soak up the rain after that, since she might drown in a single drop.

'They sent my *mamá* to the loony bin,' Bea had said, darkly. 'For three months, until she told them what they wanted to hear, what they already believed was true.'

Bea's mother, it seemed, was the only exception to the rule of untrustworthy adults. Liyana's mother, however, being a mere mortal, a boring human from blood to bones, had to remain unenlightened. Liyana didn't want to lie, but she didn't want to be locked in a bin either. The choice then, when it came, proved a fairly easy one to make.

Bea

Bea had no such compunction about lying to her own *mamá* nor, indeed, any fears of being locked in a bin. She knew she would escape easily enough. She would succeed where her *mamá* had failed. While Cleo foolishly allowed herself to be contained by institutions like the dreaded St Dymphna's, Bea would simply flee to Everwhere and fly away.

Lately, Bea had been spending much of her time watching birds take flight. She wanted to freeze-frame them, to study every movement, every moment, every feather. She was most attracted to ravens. Blackbirds too, but ravens more. She loved ravens for their size, their stature, the high battle cry of their call. Bea wanted to announce herself thus: swoop into rooms, arms splayed, chest forward, trumpeting her name with a throaty howl. Instead of stepping in softly with a shy smile.

Lately, Bea was finding herself angry. Why was it that in one place she could be so strong – could soar into the skies and scream up into the heavens – while in the other she was expected (by everyone but her *mamá*) to be sweet and small, to look pretty and act likewise?

Bea didn't give a damn for prettiness now. She used to wear dresses with bows and frills, used to let her *abuela*, aunts, foster-mothers lace her long brown hair into plaits and tie them with ribbons. No longer. Now she wanted to shred every ribbon unfortunate enough to curl across her path, wanted to rip holes in every sequinned dress, wear only black and pretend to be a raven. Lately, Bea had found herself wondering if it was possible to go to Everwhere one night and never return to Earth.

Scarlet

'You know what burns well?' Bea said to Scarlet, looking pointedly at the falling leaves.

Scarlet frowned. 'What?'

Bea smiled. 'You've got no secrets from me.'

'I don't know what you mean.'

Bea reached up to catch a falling leaf between finger and thumb. She twirled it slowly, this way and that. 'Oh, I think you do.'

'What's she talking about?' Liyana asked.

Scarlet was silent but Bea's smile widened.

'Our sister likes to burn things,' she said. 'Don't you, Sis?'

Scarlet gave a slight shrug, as if this particular piece of information was of no importance at all, as if Bea might have remarked on the colour of her hair.

'It's too wet here,' Liyana said. 'A fire wouldn't catch light.'

Bea slipped from the rock she was sitting on. 'Oh, I

don't think a little thing like water could stop our Scarlet, do you?'

Liyana seemed slightly perturbed by this comment, though she also seemed to not entirely understand why.

'Scarlet could set this whole place alight,' Bea said. 'If she wanted to.'

I glanced at Scarlet to see a flicker of a smile – of gratitude and pride – and felt proud of her too.

'But, why?' Liyana protested. 'Why would she want to do that?'

Bea laughed. 'Oh, keep your knickers on. Not even our Scarlet is so supreme. Anyway, no one can destroy this place. Not even *him*.'

I glanced at each of my sisters in turn, wondering which one of them would be first to ask her who.

Leo

On nights when the sky was clear, when the clouds drifted to the edges of the Earth and the moon was bright, Leo curled onto the cold stone ledge of his dormitory window and gazed, unblinking, at the stars. As Christopher's snores shifted the air, Leo reached up to press his palm to the glass, as if trying to reach into the sky and set himself among the stars. On these nights Leo felt drawn to them more strongly than anything he'd ever felt before. He couldn't understand it, though he tried. But stranger than his attraction to the night sky was his sense that this attraction was reciprocated, that the stars longed for him as deeply as he longed for the stars.

17th October – 15 days . . .

3.33 a.m. – Goldie

A week into my dreams something starts to change. The scenery is still the same: the white willow trees, the white birds, the thousands of white roses . . . And though I can't see him, I know Leo is there too.

Tonight, I feel more deeply connected to this place than before. As if the veins of the roses flow with my blood, as if the birds are lifted by my breath, as if the life of this place is powered by my heartbeat. I feel that if I flex my fingers the branches of the trees will shift in response, if I step through the grass the roses will pull up their roots and follow me, if I draw figures of eight in the air the birds' flight will follow the pattern of my hands . . .

The feeling rises until my fingers start to fidget at my sides. Then, all at once, I have that power surging through me again, as if I've been struck by lightning and am conducting ten thousand volts of electricity. *I can command armies. I can topple nations. I can . . .*

I pick a willow tree and focus on the cascading leaves of a single hanging branch. I stretch out my hand, fingers long and flat. Imagining that my longest finger is the branch, I twitch it.

I watch and wait. But the branch doesn't shift. The breeze has fallen and now even the leaves are still. I draw up a deep breath and try again.

Nothing.

Perhaps I'm not feeling anything at all. Perhaps it's only imagination, wishful thinking. I stand, barefoot in the grass, wondering. Perhaps I've been too ambitious. A tree is too sturdy, too unyielding. I should start with something smaller. I glance about. A rose.

Scanning the bushes, I pick one of the hundreds within reach, a small white barely opened bud, curled petals beginning to unfurl. I focus, fixing my eyes, my breath, my body on that single flower until everything else in the garden is a blur, until I see only that rose. Then I reach out, stretching my palm flat, elongating my wrist and, ever so slightly, lift my longest finger into the air.

I watch. I wait.

Nothing.

I lower my finger and, after a few minutes, I try again. And again. And again.

7.35 a.m. – Bea

When Bea steps through the gates of Trinity College, Vali is waiting for her on the wall. He stands when he sees her, holding two takeaway coffees and a brown paper bag. 'They only had chocolate croissants today.'

'Thanks.' Bea takes the cup and the bag, then hands him an envelope. 'A gift.'

'What is it?' Vali sets down his cup on the wall, having already eaten his croissant.

'That's the point of opening it, so you can find out.'

Vali presses the envelope between his palms. 'I'm cherishing the moment. I can't remember the last time anyone gave me a gift.'

'You're breaking my heart.' Bea sighs. 'Just open the fucking thing, will you?'

'All right, all right – thank you.' Vali rips it open, pulling out a glimmering black card, embossed with silver lettering. 'I don't understand.'

'It's a voucher,' Bea says. 'For a night at the Hotel Clamart.'

'Yes, I see that. But . . . why?'

'Because I'm not having sex with you in college,' Bea says. 'God knows it's embarrassing enough without having it witnessed by the entire student body.'

Vali stares at her.

'I know, I know,' Bea says. 'You can thank me later.'

She starts walking, but Vali remains planted to the pavement.

'Come on.' Bea sighs again. 'So, all right, maybe you and your expectations were right after all. Maybe you thinking I'm a nice person is starting to turn me into one, maybe I'm not as much of an evil bitch as *Mamá* claims.'

'I, I . . .' Vali tries to reply but finds himself unable to form words.

11.01 a.m. – Liyana

'But I didn't think you had a sister,' Kumiko says.

'Neither did I.'

'Then how did you find her?'

'I, um, well . . .' Liyana stalls, fingering the edge of her toast. How should she put it? Can she admit that she dreamed of this unknown sister? Saw her face, heard her voice. Or will Kumiko think she's truly unhinged? No, Liyana needs to channel BlackBird again and say it – to stop being this pale ghost of herself, to be brave and bold, without fear of the consequences.

'Was she illegitimate? Did your father have an affair? Did she contact you?'

'Yeah,' Liyana says. Melted butter drips onto her thumb. She licks it off. 'That's right. Exactly that.'

'What's right?' Kumiko says. 'Everything I just said?'

'No, I mean – I meant . . . Yes, she found me. I'm not sure about the rest. Not yet.'

'But didn't she tell you?' Kumiko takes a bite of her own buttered toast. 'Surely you asked.'

'Well, no . . . I . . . It was all very quick and, um . . . emotional.'

'Yeah, I suppose it would be.' Kumiko frowns. 'But, a sister. Seventeen – nearly eighteen – years of thinking you've got no siblings, then . . . Shit.'

'Exactly,' Liyana says, now wishing she hadn't mentioned anything in the first place. Although, happily, the unexpectedly dramatic news has taken the attention off the matter of arranged marriages. But Liyana can't think about that now. She simply wants to find her sister. And Liyana has no idea who she is, only what she looks like: white, blonde hair, blue eyes. She was polishing a mirror and wearing a uniform, with a logo. *F.H.* Not much to go on. Still, it's a start.

9.14 p.m. – Scarlet

Why Scarlet goes to see Eli that night, she can't explain. Rationally, she thought it best to deal with the confrontation quickly. It's only when she's knocking on the door of his hotel room that she realizes this might have been a mistake. She should have arranged to meet on neutral ground. At a café, a library, a church. Anywhere but in a bedroom.

'Why, Miss Thorne,' Eli says, as he opens the door. 'What a great surprise, and an even greater pleasure. Do come in.'

Scarlet doesn't. 'Are you alone?' she asks, trying to maintain a modicum of formality. 'I'd like – I need to discuss the contract.'

'Please, come in.' Somehow he manages to look innocent

and guilty, surprised and smug, all at once. 'Don't be shy.' He opens the door, stepping aside.

The room is smaller than Scarlet imagined, having imagined it more often than perhaps she should have. It's tiny. She's almost forced to sit on the bed to avoid standing too close to him, but thinks better of it.

'May I get you a drink?' Eli gestures towards the mini-bar. 'Water? Wine? Whisky?'

Scarlet shakes her head. No alcohol. Absolutely not.

'Water is fine, thank you,' she says, then remembers she's here to renege on their deal. 'Actually, I'm not thirsty.'

Eli shrugs. 'Suit yourself.' He opens the mini-bar and removes a half-empty bottle of red wine. 'Let me know if you change your mind.'

'I won't.'

'Well, all right then.' Eli pours himself a deep glass, then sits at the edge of the bed, lounging back. He catches Scarlet's eye and grins a wicked grin. She studies the mediocre painting on the wall above his head – two horses frolicking in a meadow – fixing it with far more attention than it deserves.

'So,' Eli says. 'What brings you to my bedroom at this time of night?'

Scarlet assumes an affronted scowl. 'I didn't come to your *bed*room. I came to your hotel room, because I didn't know where else to find you.'

'Suit yourself.' Eli Wolfe gives a nonchalant shrug. 'So, how may I service you?' He coughs. 'Sorry, that's to say: how may I be of service?'

'Stop it.'

'Stop what?'

'You know what.' Scarlet focuses on the painting. 'Anyway, you're not going to like what I have to say.'

Eli sits up, sporting a mock-serious expression. 'Oh?'

'Well . . .'

'Out with it. Don't be a tease.'

Scarlet shifts from foot to foot. 'Okay, so I know this is bad practice and all that, but . . .'

Eli rubs the wine glass between his palms. 'Oh, get on with it, would you? I'll be asleep before you've finished. Not my preferred choice of activity on a Friday night.'

'All right.' Scarlet steadies herself. 'I'm afraid I . . . I'm going to have to withdraw my, um, agreement to our . . . agreement.'

'Ah.' He sips his wine. 'So you've come to tell me you want to welch on our deal?'

'I, um, yes, I am. And I know—'

'Well, I am sorry to hear that.'

Scarlet frowns. 'You don't look sorry.'

He shrugs. 'What can I say? I enjoy our negotiations.'

'Oh no,' Scarlet says. 'This isn't part of that, this isn't me trying to get more money, or anything—'

'Good. Because you won't get it.'

'Well, that's fine, because I don't want it.'

Eli looks sceptical. 'In my experience everyone wants more money if they can possibly get it.'

'Well, I don't.'

He shrugs again. 'Suit yourself. So, what do you want?'

'Nothing,' Scarlet says. 'I just came to tell you about . . . the deal. I decided last night and I didn't want to wait. It didn't seem fair.'

'It's not fair.' He pats the duvet. 'So why don't you come and make it up to me . . .'

'I most certainly will not,' Scarlet says, trying to sound like she means it. 'I don't know what kind of girl you think I am, but—'

Eli smiles. 'Oh, I know exactly what kind of girl you are.'

'You do not.'

Eli stands and steps forward. 'Oh, but I do.'

Scarlet steps back. He comes closer and Scarlet stops. When they are only inches apart Eli reaches out, as if he's trying to pet a wild deer, and gently takes hold of her hand. Scarlet doesn't have to look to know that sparks are firing between their fingertips. When they kiss this time, every light in the hotel blows its fuse.

9.33 p.m. – Goldie

'What the hell was that?'

Leo sits up in the darkness. 'I haven't a clue.' He slides off the bed we're currently occupying in room 49. 'But I need to investigate. The new night porter is bloody useless.'

It must be a power outage, I think, as Leo leaves, banging the door behind him. But just before it happened I felt a shift in the air – like the way the light changes before a thunderstorm.

It's slightly unnerving. I feel again that surge of power in my veins, as if I'm pulsing with electricity instead of blood. I think of Leo to steady myself. Never in my life did I imagine it possible to feel this way with another human being: so reckless and so safe all at once. I thought, after my stepfather, I'd never feel safe with a man again. Not that, never that. And yet, here we are. I smile to myself. A small miracle.

11.59 p.m. – Leo

Leo watches Goldie sleep, watches the rise and fall of her chest, listens to her breath. Now and then, he strokes the tips of his fingers along her cheek.

Of all the despicable things Leo has ever done this must be the worst. It's not the killing that bothers him as much as the method. The way he killed before had a sense of symmetry, a certain cleanness, a guiltless inevitability. He's followed the dictates of nature or the rules of war. This is how he's killed every Grimm girl to date.

But with Goldie it's no longer simply the kill, it's deceit and betrayal too. And not only of her but them both. Every day he's increasingly torn. When Leo's with her he's sure he won't be able to do it. But when they're apart he feels the soldier in him strengthening – his nervous system, his predatory instincts, overriding his heart.

The human heart, Leo thinks, is a strange thing. It should fight for its own survival, but it doesn't, not always anyway. He's seen enough examples of selfless heroics on Earth, even strangers sacrificing their lives to save others. Of animals, Leo isn't sure. But in stars, in soldiers, the survival instinct is so strong it overrides everything else, even love.

18th October – 14 days . . .

9.06 a.m. – Goldie

'I never thought I'd have this,' I say.

'What do you mean?'

I burrow my face in his bare chest. 'This.' He cups my head in his hand, wrapping blonde curls around his fingers.

'I'm glad.'

I try to shape my feelings into words. 'I suppose I always felt like . . . like I'd never be loved, not simply for myself . . .'

Leo nods.

'Just for me, without doing things I don't . . . Thank you.'

'For what?'

I shrug. 'Everything.'

We lie together for one long perfect hour, silence settling between us like dawn light. Eventually, I sit up to touch the tiny scar of a crescent moon on his shoulder blade.

'What are these?'

I've been waiting to ask this question since the first time I caught sight of the scars. I told myself to wait until Leo told me himself. But I find myself too impatient, too curious. I draw my fingertip along his spine and across his back, tracing the spaces between the scars, a map of roads and rivers always encircling, never touching.

'You don't have to tell me,' I say.

'I will.' He takes a deep breath. 'I just don't know how.'

'Whatever it is, I won't mind.'

He falls silent. I want to stroke his scars, to show I'm

not scared even though I am, a little. I want to reassure him it won't repulse me, whatever his confession.

'I promise,' I say. 'It doesn't matter.'

I feel a sudden rush of heat under my fingertips and snatch my hand away.

'Don't say stupid things.' Leo shrinks back, pulling into himself, though he doesn't pull away from me.

It's the first time I've felt his fire, and for the first time I wonder if perhaps he burned the scars into his own skin. He might have been a member of a sadistic cult. I realize, again, how little I know about Leo. Which suddenly seems dangerous, given how deeply I feel for him. When he doesn't speak, I place a tentative hand on his back.

'You don't have to tell me,' I repeat. 'It doesn't matter.'

'It does,' Leo says. 'More than you know.'

'I shouldn't have asked. Forget it.'

We're silent. I wait, deciding not to speak again until he does. Perhaps a minute passes, perhaps an hour.

'I'll tell you one day,' he says. 'I will, it's just . . .'

I wait.

'When I do, when I tell you – all this . . .' Still, he won't look at me. 'I want at least a little time with you when . . . I want you to remember me with . . . I don't want you to hate me.'

'Remember you? Hate you?' I reach for him. 'Why are you saying that, when I love—'

'When I tell you' – he drops his eyes and his voice – 'you won't want to see me again.'

I laugh. 'That's not possible – nothing you say could . . .' I try to lift his chin, try to catch his eye. 'Hey, if I told you some of the things I'd done, then I doubt you'd like me very much either.'

Leo looks up at me. 'I know everything about you.'

'No, you don't. You know hardly anything about me.'

I laugh again, hoping to lift his mood, to make him smile. 'It's not as if we've spent much time talking.'

Leo falls silent again and so do I.

What can I say to make it better? What can I say to take it back? I wish I'd waited, I wish I'd shut up, I wish I'd not said anything at all.

9.06 a.m. – Leo

He's a selfish coward. He should warn Goldie what's coming. When he's with her he imagines he might. But he knows that if he did he'd lose her. And how can he tell Goldie that in fourteen nights, at the next first-quarter moon, one of them will die? Already his fingers twitch with anticipation. Every time they're together, Leo suppresses the urge. When he strokes her neck, his fingers throb with the desire to take the life, the light, from her.

The temptation is so great that his whole body is pained by the restraint. When Goldie lies beneath him, when Leo kisses her skin, he sees the light that pulses with the beat of her heart. Sometimes the light is golden: sunset on a lake. Sometimes it's silver: moonlight on fresh snow. And it calls to him; as if it's his for the taking, as if she's an animal he has the right to slaughter. It takes everything Leo has to hold back, all his willpower not to extinguish her light, not to steal her life.

He can't help it. It's his nature; it's what he's been doing for centuries. At least, that's how it feels. Almost as soon as their mouths touch, his hand rests over her heart. Even as they kiss, even as he's filled with the joy of it, he's imagining drawing the life from her, pulling the spirit from her body, the last breath from her lips. He's still kissing Goldie, still holding her, as the fog thickens and the mists envelop them, entwining with her essence so she dissolves into the air, until Leo's left with only the echo of her barely glimmering in the moonlight. Then she's gone and he's torn between sorrow and joy.

Leo can't help the joy since, when the last breath of a Grimm girl etches the scar on his skin, when her light enters him, Leo is filled with a vital surge of life, as if being suddenly powered by the sun. It's what he needs to live. But the sorrow is there, as it's never been before. And Leo wonders whether, when the time comes, it will be what stops him, what allows her to win.

7.17 p.m. – Scarlet

'Scarlet!'

Scarlet runs into the kitchen from the café to find her grandmother poking a fork into the toaster. Scarlet skids across the linoleum floor to snatch it from Esme's shaking hands.

'Grandma, what the hell are you doing? You could electrocute yourself,' Scarlet snaps. A sudden memory rises, of her grandmother saying exactly that on catching a ten-year-old Scarlet extracting a teacake with a knife from the very same toaster.

'What do you want? I'll make it. Were you making toast?' Scarlet depresses the metal handle but it springs back. 'Fuck, it must've blown a fuse. Everything in this bloody place is falling—'

'Language, Scarlet.'

Scarlet stops, turning to grin at her grandmother, thrilled by the unexpected reprimand. Today might be a good day. Or, at the very least, in this moment she has her grandmother back. 'Sorry, Grandma. But anyway it's dinner time, why don't I make you something proper to eat?'

Esme shakes her head, like a stubborn child.

'All right then.' Scarlet fishes into the toaster to retrieve the two slices of still untoasted bread. 'We can use the grill.'

But, as she steps over to the oven, Scarlet has a better idea.

'Hey, Grandma, want to see something special?'

Her grandmother frowns.

'Remember the sparks from my fingertips?' Scarlet holds her breath. 'When we were dancing to Bessie Smith? I burned your hands a bit – still sorry about that, by the way – and you said—'

Esme's eyes light with recognition and she smiles. 'Like Ruby.'

'Exactly. But that's not all I can do. Check this out.'

She sets the two pieces of bread on the counter, then holds her hands an inch above them. 'This is how I've started heating your cinnamon buns. I thought you'd prefer it to the microwave.'

Her grandmother is transfixed by the slices of bread, like a child waiting for a magic trick. At first, nothing happens, and then the air between the bread and Scarlet's hands starts to shimmer, like heatwaves coming off tarmac on a hot day. Then the edges of the bread begin to singe and, slowly, to toast. Esme claps.

'Pretty cool, huh?' Scarlet grins, flipping the bread over.

The thrill of seeing her grandmother so delighted, of being the cause of that delight, sends fresh sparks down Scarlet's fingers that, all at once, burn the toast. A bitter charred scent singes the air. For a second, Esme looks shocked. Then she laughs, as if she's never seen anything so funny in all her life.

Scarlet watches her grandmother, smiling. There are moments, brief transient moments, of unexpected joy in this frightful disease. Moments when her grandmother is returned to herself as a child, when she's serene, when she's full of wonder and awe. Moments to be cherished. Moments too quickly gone.

Still laughing, her grandmother looks up to the ceiling and falls silent.

'What's that?' She frowns. 'It's a m–m . . .' The word slips away, then she catches hold of its tail, 'mistake.'

'Where?' Scarlet follows her grandmother's gaze. 'Oh.'

Snaking diagonally across the ceiling is a long, large crack.

'Shit.' Scarlet exhales.

This time, Esme says nothing.

8.25 p.m. – Liyana

'What are you thinking about?'

Liyana looks at Mazmo across the table. 'Oh, sorry, I was just . . . It's nothing.'

'Are you all right?'

'I'm fine.' A hundred thorough Internet searches have still not brought Liyana any closer to identifying her sister and her frustration and impatience builds by the minute. She tries to focus on the date. Aunt Nya is so hopeful that this one might prove fruitful, if they're able to finagle the finer details of sexual freedoms and financial obligations, that Liyana feels she should at least give it her best shot. And, though she's still reluctant to admit it, the promise of three years' full funding for the Slade is a not insignificant bonus. 'Sorry, I . . .' Besides, the fact that he'll be picking up the bill for this ridiculously overpriced dinner means she should give Mazmo a modicum of attention. 'I'm fine.'

'What do you think of the soufflé?' Mazmo says, sticking his fork into the fluff of gooey chocolate on his plate. 'Is it not the best bloody soufflé you've ever eaten?'

He flashes her that smile again, the one that tugs the

silver threads of a memory, of a moon breaking through clouds, casting its light on dark water. She returns his smile. 'It bloody well should be, at this price.'

Mazmo laughs. 'Well, this is Le Gavroche, darling. What do you expect?'

'A bit more for twenty quid. After all, it's only chocolate and air with – what? – a bit of burnt milk foam and salted caramel crumb on the side.'

'*Just* chocolate and air? What sacrilege!' Mazmo cups his hands protectively over his plate. 'Don't let the soufflé hear you say that.'

Liyana smiles. She hasn't told Kumiko about meeting Mazmo tonight and is feeling guilty about it. And, though she won't admit she feels any attraction, she can't deny that he is a particularly spectacular specimen of manhood.

'You're funny,' she says. 'And sweet.'

'Oh, please.' Mazmo rolls his eyes. 'Not *that* word. It's the death knell of dating. And I'll have you know, I'm extremely sour and incredibly masculine' – he winks – 'despite my pansexual tendencies. Otherwise, I'm an entirely blokeish bloke. I've a nasty habit of queue-jumping, swearing at slow drivers, never talking about my feelings. On occasion, I've even been known to snatch lollipops off toddlers.'

Liyana laughs. 'You have not.'

'Well, perhaps not in actuality,' Mazmo admits. 'But I've certainly considered it several times.'

Liyana takes a bite of soufflé. 'Why is it that men, even pansexual men, it seems, so hate to be called sweet? It's a compliment.'

Mazmo picks a stray salted caramel crumb from the tablecloth, setting it on the tip of his tongue. 'Perhaps because it's like being compared to a squirrel, when I'd prefer to be thought of as a . . . lion, or a bear. Or' – he lights upon an even more attractive image – 'a silverback gorilla.'

Liyana regards him over her wine glass. 'Is that your favourite fantasy?'

'Why not?'

'Well, all right then. You're a strong, dark, silverback gorilla. Is that better?' Sipping the sweet dessert wine, Liyana realizes that she's flirting and should stop. She should probably stop drinking too. She's had – how much? – too much if she can't remember. Then Liyana has a thought that makes her feel guiltier still, the thought that perhaps being married to Mazmo Owethu Muzenda-Kasteni, with all its affiliated benefits, might not be quite so frightful after all.

'Yes,' he says. That smile again. The sliver of an unwavering moon in a midnight sky. 'That's much better.'

11.39 p.m. – Liyana

Later that night Liyana, still slightly drunk and over-stuffed, sits on her bed shuffling her Tarot cards. Every time she glances down, The Devil has come to the front. She slices him back into the deck, again and again. But, when Liyana deals out five cards onto her duvet, he's the first to appear. Followed by the Four of Wands: a fairy picks a rose from her flowered garden, the turrets of her castle rise up into the sky. *Prosperity, celebration, romance.* The Four of Swords: a female warrior emerges from a dark wood into the sunshine, seeking out a cave in which to rest and recuperate. *Retreat, solitude, preparation for conflict.* The Empress: clothed in a grass-green dress, the empress dances with all of nature at her feet and a crown of stars on her head. *Sexuality, pleasure, abundance.* And The Star: an *en pointe* ballerina floats on a lily leaf on a lake, a frog leaps towards her and a bird flies into her open hand. *Healing, strength, trust.*

At first, the pictures make no sense. Then, gradually,

they seem to rearrange themselves into a story. For a split second, Liyana feels her mother sitting on the bed beside her, reading the tale the cards are telling. A tale of four sisters, their childhood adventures, their family secrets, their hidden strengths, their unclaimed powers, their far-off father watching it all . . .

'What does it mean, *Dadá*?'

Still the desire for reassurance, for approval, lingers. But her mother is no longer there.

Echoes of expensive champagne tug at her eyelids and Liyana lays down her head, curling up around the cards still spread across the duvet. Just before she tumbles into sleep, Liyana thinks she spots something on the carpet: a tiny black fluff of a feather. But when she cranes her neck to be sure, it's only a smudge on her sightline. Liyana thinks of BlackBird, but the last thought she has before closing her eyes is of her sisters.

11.59 p.m. – Bea

'That wasn't bad. That was, surprisingly, all right.'

'All right?' Vali virtually squeals, before letting out a long, deep sigh. 'It was absolutely fucking phenomenal.'

'I wouldn't go that far.' Bea lies back on the bed beside him. 'But it was quite good. Especially for your first time.'

'Thanks, but I think that was mostly down to you. You give excellent direction.'

Bea nods, as if this is self-evident. She props herself up on her elbow. 'You know, you're quite large.'

Vali grins. 'Really? Well, I'm glad you were sat—'

Bea rolls her eyes. 'I wasn't talking about your penis.'

'Oh.' Vali's euphoria collapses into dejection. 'Yeah, I—'

'I'm talking about' – Bea gestures at him – 'the whole of you. You're large.'

'You mean fat.'

'No, I say what I mean. I don't fuck about with euphemisms. Yes, you're fat and I say you're fat. But you're large too. Sturdy. Strong. I hadn't noticed that before.'

Vali brightens.

'Yeah,' Bea continues, as if she's debating a particular philosophical theory. 'It feels good, being held by you.' She pauses, while Vali looks as happy as he might if she'd just proposed marriage. 'So, want to try again?'

Vali sits up, as if propelled from an ejector seat. 'What? Is that on the cards? Really? I thought this was a one-time thing.'

'Why not?' Bea shrugs, as if she doesn't care one way or the other. 'We've got the room for the night – might as well make the most of it.'

A little less than a decade ago

Everwhere

When you awaken, you're looking into the face of a man with golden eyes, white hair and skin so creased with wrinkles he might be ten thousand years old. You wonder if you've died and this is the Devil, for he fixes you with a look such as you've never seen before and wish never to see again, though you find you're unable to look away. It's a look of such undiluted malice that you start to shiver, as if you were suddenly freezing cold.

When you're able to turn away, the relief is palpable. You want to run but you're frozen. You tell your legs to move but they seem detached, separate, as if owned by someone else altogether.

When you look at him again you realize that in fact he wasn't looking at you in any particular way, this is simply the carving of his features. When he smiles a spasm shoots up your spine, a red-hot scarring, a rage of pain. His smile drops and the pain subsides. You realize that he's assessing you, deciding, weighing up unspecified options. Do his eyes glow a little brighter, or are you imagining it? It seems he is pleased, though you don't know why. Perhaps he sees something in you: promise, potential, possibility . . .

He steps back, lifting his chin: a nudge, an instruction, an offer. Slowly, you pull yourself up from the ground. Your legs are so weak that you stumble. Then, finding a footing, you stagger forward as he watches you, falling once, twice. You drag yourself up again, then start to topple but find balance. Then, with every ounce of everything you have, you run.

This time, he lets you go.

Goldie

He told me it was my fault. My fault for being pretty. My fault for being there. As if he'd simply been walking along and – oops – slipped on a banana skin and fallen into my bed. It started after Teddy was born. Ma slept with him in their bed and my stepfather complained he couldn't sleep with 'that bloody thing squawking all the time'. His affection for his son always diminished at night. During the day he doted on Teddy almost as much as Ma did, rocking and cooing and all that. But when Teddy kept him awake, he wasn't so keen. Still, at some point, I suppose he decided to make the most of those interruptions.

The first night he lay beside me. The second, his hand rested atop my nightdress. The third, it found its way underneath. By the end of the month there was no part of me he hadn't found.

Liyana

Liyana lay belly-up, floating. She could float for hours, capsizing herself now and then, rolling over like a seal, skin slick with water. And, although Liyana wasn't swimming in the sea but resting on her bed, buoyed only by three hot-water bottles, her sense of the ocean was so strong she could taste the salt on her tongue. When at last Liyana closed her eyes, it was on the lapping waves of this sea that she was borne from her dreams and into Everwhere.

Tonight, she followed her sisters on the stone paths, winding alongside rivers and trees, cutting through clearings of ivy and moss. Bea led the line of four sisters, as always. Though, every so often, Scarlet managed to sneak out in front. Liyana was always last in line. Which meant that, when she suddenly stopped, no one noticed.

'Wait!' Liyana called out. We turned to see her pointing to a still, dark snake of water under a bank of willow trees. 'Let's go swimming.'

'But we don't have our costumes,' I said.

'It doesn't matter.' Liyana threw the words over her shoulder as she tugged at the sleeve of her nightgown, pulling it over her head.

'Great idea,' Scarlet said, unbuttoning her shirt as she darted across moss and stone. 'I'll race you.'

I looked to Bea, hoping she wouldn't want to join in. Behind my back, I crossed my fingers. Bea regarded the river, then, with a shrug, crossed her legs and sat in a patch of moss. 'Go ahead. I don't want to get wet, it's too cold.'

Bea affected a shiver, though it wasn't even chilly. I wanted to hug her, my sudden, unexpected ally. Instead, afraid she might slap me if I tried, I sat down beside her.

'Me neither,' I said, as Scarlet slid down the mossy bank to join Ana.

Together, we watched them.

'It's okay.' Bea leaned over to me, speaking in an amplified whisper. 'There's a girl in my class who can't swim either. You shouldn't be ashamed.'

I stiffened, all feelings of affection draining away, praying my other sisters hadn't heard.

'What are you talking about?' Scarlet dropped into the water. 'Goldie never said she couldn't swim.' She looked back at me. 'You can, can't you?'

I nodded. 'Of course. I just . . . don't like it.'

'Go on then,' Bea said. 'Show us.'

'Stop it.' Scarlet sank into the water until her hair pooled around her head. 'She doesn't have to prove it.'

I pressed a finger into the soil. I felt Bea's self-satisfied smile. 'I'm right, aren't I?'

I dug my finger deeper into the dirt, feeling slightly soothed by the damp earth, but only for a moment.

'Leave her alone.' Scarlet, stretching her arms, brought her hands together into an arrow pointing at the treetops, then dived under the water.

I watched the silvery ripple of her body gliding away, thinking a silent thank you, suddenly loving Scarlet as much as I now hated Bea.

'I'll teach you, if you like,' Bea said. 'You just have to admit—'

'Stop it!'

We both turned in the direction of the river. I thought Scarlet must have surfaced, but it was Liyana shouting. I looked at her, pulled suddenly from the water, standing tall, dark skin glistening almost blue, black dandelion hair heavy with droplets.

'Stop!' She slapped her palms down onto the surface with such force that we were splashed on the bank. 'Stop fighting!'

'Oh, Sis, you're so sensitive.' Bea grinned. 'This isn't fighting, this isn't even close.'

Liyana mumbled something I couldn't hear but, as she spoke, the water started to ripple. The wave gathered so fast that we didn't even see it coming, didn't have a chance to shift before Bea was struck with a great sheet of water and soaked through.

Scarlet surfaced, as if sensing something exciting had happened above her. We all stared at Bea. I glanced at Liyana, who seemed as shocked as the rest of us. I wanted to kiss her. The sister I'd always thought of as the baby, the one who needed protecting, was now protecting me. We waited for Bea to scream, to lift the largest stone within reach and hurl it into the river. But she didn't move. Then she started to laugh.

'My, my, Sis. Well, aren't you a surprise?' Bea regarded Liyana as she might a thrillingly volatile science experiment. 'You're much more interesting than I thought.'

Bea

Bea ran faster than she'd ever run before, hurtling through the fog, her feet darting across moss and stone and logs so swiftly they seemed never to touch the ground. She grinned into the wind, hair whipping back, heart pounding, lungs stinging.

On she ran and on.

As seconds flicked by, minutes gulped down, Bea picked up such speed that soon she was no longer simply taking great steps over the stones, she was leaping over fallen tree trunks, legs stretched out straight in the perfect parallel line of a prima ballerina. And then, in another leap, she lifted into the air. Higher and higher, above the rivers and rocks, up through the falling leaves, up beyond the thinnest branches of the tallest trees, soaring out into the moonlight.

At last she was flying, she was free.

Leo

'All right, all right, I'll give you a clue if you stop nagging,' Christopher said. 'Hell, you're worse than my mother.'

Leo smiled, sitting back in his chair. 'Go on then, spill it.'

But Christopher shook his head. 'Not here.' He stood. 'Come with me.'

Ten minutes later they'd abandoned the school library for the school gates.

'Why here?' Leo asked. 'Do you know a secret tunnel? Are we making a break for freedom?'

Christopher laughed. 'Not exactly. At least, not yet and not in the way you think.'

'What do you mean?'

'You come here sometimes, don't you?' Christopher reached up to rub his thumb across an iron ivy leaf. 'On a night when the first quarter-moon is showing in the sky. You don't know why, but you do. Don't you?'

Leo frowned. 'How do you know that?'

'Because I do the same thing.'

'No, you don't.' Leo's frown deepened. 'I've never seen you.'

'That's because you've always left before I arrive. I come at half past three in the morning. Three thirty-three, to be exact.'

'Why?'

Christopher dropped his hand to gaze through the gate's thick iron pickets. 'Because, when you go through these gates then, you step into another world.'

Leo laughed. 'Stop messing about.'

'It's true.'

'You're having me on.'

'You know it. If you think about it, you know I'm telling the truth.'

'Shut up.'

Christopher didn't reply, didn't deny anything or defend himself. And in the silence, Leo was forced to do as his friend suggested. He thought. He thought about all the strange and unexplained things: his desire for the stars, his nocturnal walks, his midnight vigils at this gate, his notion that perhaps something unearthly lay beyond it . . .

'Go on then,' he said at last.

'It's Everwhere,' Christopher said. 'It's where a war is being fought between good and evil. You and me, we're both soldiers in that war.'

Again, Leo's brow furrowed. 'We're not soldiers, we're kids.'

'Only on Earth. Up there' – he nodded at the sky – 'we were stars, once. And in there' – he nodded beyond the gate – 'we're soldiers.'

'What? But, I . . . If that's true, and it makes no sense at all, then which side are we fighting for? Good or evil?'

Christopher laughed. 'What do you think? Good, of course. But I bet, if you asked the other side, they'd say the same thing. Anyway, you don't need to think about that yet. First you need to learn how to protect yourself, how to fight, how to kill. Then you can get to the rest of it.'

Leo thought of his uncontrollable rages, of Jekyll and Hyde, and wondered if this was the reason why. 'But . . . how? How can I do that?'

'I can teach you a few things,' Christopher said. 'But the first time you go to Everwhere, the night you turn thirteen—'

'Why thirteen?' Leo interrupted. 'Why do we have to wait so long? Why can't we go now?'

'Because that's when we become men,' Christopher said, as if this was a self-evident fact. 'And that's when the Grimm girls can't get into Everwhere anymore.' He grinned. 'They lose their power when we gain ours. Which just shows how much better we are.'

Though he still didn't really understand, Leo grinned back to show that he did.

'That's when you'll meet our father. And he'll—'

'Father?' Leo interrupted again. 'Our father?'

'Yeah. I mean, not physically, but in every other way that matters. He's our leader, our captain, he . . .'

But Leo had stopped listening. He'd been right all along. Charles Penry-Jones wasn't his real father. He was adopted. And Christopher, this boy he loved as much as himself, was his brother.

19th October – 13 days . . .

3.03 a.m. – Leo

Leo didn't discover his fate until he was thirteen and stepped through a Grimm gate for the first time. By then he knew the full truth of who he and Christopher were: *lumen latros*, fallen stars, soldiers.

The cascading leaves, the mists and fog, the moonlight had mesmerized Leo, captivating him so that he'd almost fallen foul of the same fate as his dearest friend. Except, it turned out he had a sixth sense that Christopher didn't, at least not that night. The friends had temporarily lost sight of each other and only reunited when the Grimm girl – perhaps twenty, though she seemed so old to him then – was wrapping her hands around Christopher's neck.

Leo reached him as he fell. But he was already dust and ash before Leo had a chance to touch him, to hold him tight.

That night, Leo acquired the first scar on his back. A tiny crescent moon at the tip of his left shoulder blade. She wasn't the one he wanted to kill, but he knew she would have to do. And as the Grimm girl's final breath etched itself onto his skin, as the mists engulfed her spirit and the ground soaked up her soul, Leo's spirits had soared and his chest swelled with pride.

And in the echo of the girl's death, in the shifting air, in the momentary opening of heaven and hell, Leo had felt his friend: the sound of his laugh on the winds, his smile illuminated in the moonlight, his touch carried by the fog.

Then he was gone, and Leo left once more bereft. This wound ripped open a pain that burned inside Leo, stoked and stirred as he grew, fuelling a desire to avenge his friend, to kill as many Grimm girls as he could, in the hopes that one day he would stop the heart of the one responsible for his sorrow.

3.33 a.m. – Goldie

I'm back among the white roses. But tonight I am a rose. I am everything. My hair is the tumbling white leaves of the willow trees, my fingers the stems of the flowers, my breath the birdsong, my tears the daisies, my heart the cat stalking through the grass, my spirit the breeze that blows through it all . . .

Today I don't simply believe I can move everything in the garden, I *know* it. As easily as I breathe, as effortlessly as I lift my hand. There's no question, no trying, no striving.

I can.

For a few minutes, I focus. And, sure enough, this time I don't have to hope and pray, try and fail.

Now, with a single twitch of my fingers I pluck a dozen daisies from the lawn. They lift and hover patiently in the air, waiting on my command. I press forefinger to thumb and the daisies gather into a suspended circle. I snap my fingers, and they slowly thread themselves together until they form a floral crown. I smile as the ring of daisies alights on my head.

'It suits you.'

Ma stands before me on the grass, dressed all in white. For a moment I think she's a ghost – I used to think the same after Teddy was born, the aftermath of birth giving her an ethereal appearance, as if she wasn't quite certain whether she belonged in this world or the next. Which is perhaps why she died inexplicably young.

'Th-thank you.'

'You loved making daisy chains when you were a little girl,' Ma says. 'You'd do it for hours. We'd sit in the park with Teddy and you'd have bracelets, necklaces, five daisy crowns on your head before teatime.'

I look at her. 'I don't remember that.'

'I do.' Ma smiles. 'I remember everything.'

3.53 a.m. – Goldie

I open my eyes. I feel the warmth of Leo at my back. I've twisted away from him in my sleep. I turn to him.

'See, I was right. You never sleep.'

'I was watching you.'

'I just dreamed about my ma. I can't remember when I last did that.'

I think I see a startled look flash across Leo's face, a brief narrowing of his green eyes. But it happens so fast and is gone so quickly that I wonder if I might have imagined it.

'What was she doing?' Leo asks. 'What did she say?'

'She told me I loved to make daisy chains.'

He drags long fingers through messy hair. 'Nothing else?'

'Ma was a woman of few words,' I say.

Leo hesitates. 'How do you think she would feel about . . . ?'

'What?'

Leo says the word so softly I can't hear.

'Sorry?'

It seems to pain him. 'Me.'

'You?' I say, relieved. 'She'd love you.'

8.36 a.m. – Scarlet

Scarlet glances up from the bag of flour she's sieving to see Walt walking into the kitchen. She's experimenting with breadmaking. If the café can't survive solely as a café, she thinks, it might fare better as a bakery.

'There's a queue of eager, expectant customers out there.' Walt nods in the direction of the counter.

'Really?' Scarlet brightens, wiping her floury hands on her apron.

'Yeah,' he says. 'Do you like the shelves?'

'I love them. Great colour,' she says, heading towards the counter. Though, if he'd asked what colour they were, she couldn't have said. She can't even recall if he painted them or not.

When the small flurry of customers is settled with caffeine and cakes, Scarlet hurries back into the kitchen to continue examination of the sourdough book and finds Walt standing vigil beside it.

'How's the dishwasher?'

'Excellent.' Scarlet flips over the page. 'Thank you.'

He kicks his toe into the floor. 'So . . .'

'So . . . ?'

'So, I was wondering . . . since I've fixed the dishwasher, put up a few shelves, changed the washers on the sink – I've pretty much exhausted all my excuses . . .'

Scarlet glances up from her open book, wondering if he's angling for more work.

'I was, well, hoping that perhaps you might like to . . . go out sometime' – Walt takes a quick breath – 'for a drink, food, whatever.'

Scarlet looks at him. 'Oh.'

'It doesn't matter, if. . .' Walt offers a self-deprecating smile. 'I thought perhaps . . . No harm in asking, is there? Except for the hefty dent to my ego.'

'No, sorry,' Scarlet says. 'I didn't mean to sound so . . .'

'Nonplussed?' Walt offers. 'Taken aback? Slightly terrified?'

Scarlet laughs. 'Did I? Sorry. No, I was just surprised.'

'Well, that shows how crap I am at reading signs,' Walt says. 'I thought perhaps I sensed a . . . frisson, or something.' He pushes himself away from the counter. He's halfway across the kitchen when he stops and turns. 'Is this because – have you got . . . are you already going out with that ridiculously handsome bloke?'

'What ridiculously handsome bloke?' Scarlet asks. She knows exactly who he means, though she's barely thought of Ezekiel Wolfe since that night, when she'd done everything she'd wanted to do with him – and more; and since he's a deplorable specimen of humanity, she hopes never to see him again.

'The one I offered to assassinate,' Walt says. 'The offer still stands, by the way. Especially if you're dating him.'

'Don't be— What makes you think we're dating?'

'I may be rubbish at reading signs,' Walt says. 'But a blind man could sense the frisson between the two of you.'

Scarlet smiles. 'You rather like that word, don't you?'

'I memorize French words to make myself sound sophisticated.' He nods down at the builder's belt slung round his waist. 'In case anyone assumes I'm thick cos I ain't got a degree or nothing.'

'Me neither.'

'You might have two PhDs by the time you're my age.'

Scarlet laughs. 'Hardly. How old are you anyway?'

'Twenty-eight.'

'Oh,' Scarlet says, genuinely surprised. 'I thought you were younger.'

Walt smiles. 'Wise of mind, fair of face.'

'Yeah, well, you're certainly not hideous.'

Walt glances at his boots. '"Certainly not hideous"? Gosh, that's a helluva compliment.'

Scarlet laughs again. 'Sorry, I didn't mean it like that.'

She casts a curious eye over Walt. He, unlike Ezekiel Wolfe, clearly *is* an exceedingly good specimen of humanity. And, although she's not especially attracted to him, she believes that goodness ought to be rewarded. After all, when sexual desire fades one is left with the essence of the man. 'Okay, look. So, we're practically on a date right now already, don't you think? It's not such a leap to make it official.'

'So, you're not . . . with the . . .'

'No,' Scarlet says. 'Ridiculously handsome blokes aren't my type.'

Walt smiles. 'Thank goodness for that.'

10.37 a.m. – Liyana

At last, Liyana has a lead. Which is excellent news, since the interview she's just had at Tesco's was a humiliating washout. She has, it transpired, very little common sense or, indeed, any sense at all. Still, they'd obviously been desperate for bodies since she'd been offered a trial shift on Wednesday. But, although Liyana hates to admit it, Kumiko had been right: stocking shelves will make her miserable. She'd known it as soon as she'd walked along the aisles. A fake marriage to Mazmo would be an infinitely preferable way to support her through art school, and keep her aunt in Givenchy.

More importantly, Liyana has found the logo that matches her sister's uniform. The green crest embroidered with the letters FH in gold. Now, she sits at her laptop continuing her search. Miraculously, it doesn't take long to find the place. Even more miraculously, the Fitzwilliam Hotel is in Cambridge. Liyana only has to take a train, which she will do first thing tomorrow. But what will she say when she meets this girl? This blonde-haired, blue-eyed girl who couldn't look any more unlike her. This girl who's as pale as she is dark, as poor as she was once rich. The girl doesn't look like a raving racist – but how, in the absence of any visible white supremacist tattoos, does one tell? And even if the girl's perfectly lovely, how the hell will Liyana convince her that they're sisters?

If Liyana mentions the dream her mirror-sister will surely think her certifiable. She might call the police, or a psychiatric centre. So, Liyana must tread carefully, must take the softly, softly approach. She'll start with a little innocuous chat and move on from there . . .

Liyana shuts her laptop to consult the Tarot for answers. She shuffles, then plucks out five cards and lays them out on her desk, their pictures and stories weaving together to tell their unique tale. The Two of Wands: a flamboyant drummer with twirling moustaches and wings sprouting from his hat, marches beside two white peacocks who brandish his wands in their beaks. The Seven of Cups: a glamorous woman with curling feathers in her hair walks among the mists, dreamily contemplating the floating cups on offer. The Fool: a purple-haired girl, wearing a ruff and dressed like a dashing page, saunters unknowingly towards the edge of a cliff while bright birds decorate the sky above her head. The Five of Wands: four winged, sharp-toothed, long-beaked creatures with snaking tails clash their wands like swords in battle. A fifth, filigreed wand rises up between them. The Wheel of Fortune: the zodiac wheel spins among the stars, flanked by a mermaid, an eagle, a bull and a cat. Two entwined snakes rise up from the ground beneath, while sprites and dragonflies dance among the flowers.

Liyana sees herself in the tale, her journey embodied in the Two of Wands: being bold, seizing the day, walking to the beat of her own drum. But also The Fool: optimistic, impulsive, inexperienced. The Seven of Cups isn't a good omen, suggesting that she's caught in illusions. But the worst is the Five of Wands, promising discord, conflict and struggle. Yet the Wheel of Fortune, with its chance of good luck, gives cause to renew Liyana's flagging hopes.

11.35 a.m. – Bea

Bea wakes tangled in hotel sheets that would be crisp and fresh, but for the sweat that soaked into them last night. Bea winces slightly as snapshots of details return. The things he did. The things *she* did. Oh, God. Bea hadn't known she was capable of such things, emotionally or physically. She certainly hadn't expected Vali to be. Worst of all: she'd do it again in a heartbeat. She doesn't know what it is about this chubby, bearded bloke, but he makes her want to do wickedly delightful things.

Bea turns to him, still sleeping. She wants to reach down and kiss him, tenderly, on the cheek, but holds back.

'Wake up, Romeo.'

Vali doesn't stir, though Bea imagines she hears a soft snore.

'All right then, you lazy bum, I shall avail myself of the posh facilities. I'm afraid I'll use up all the soap, in a vain attempt to cleanse body and soul.'

Bea glances over, expecting this remark to be met with a retort along the lines of 'There isn't enough soap in this hotel to manage that,' or some such. But he's silent. Bea sighs. So much for the morning cuddle. Which is fine, she tells herself, since she's not a fan of cuddling anyway, at any time of day.

Bea slides out of bed and shuffles towards the bathroom. She loves hotel bathrooms. This one has two marble sinks and the massive bathtub has golden taps and sits upon claws. As Bea watches the water tumbling from the golden taps like miniature waterfalls she wonders how it must be to live like this. To be steeped in luxury, never worrying how you're going to pay bills or mortgages or all that middle-aged shit Dr Finch witters on about whenever they aren't having sex. At least her *mamá* never—

¡Mierda!

Bea leaps up to twist off the taps. She'd completely forgotten Cleo and their lunch date on Trinity Street. *¡Mierda!* Bea abandons the golden-clawed bathtub and twin marble sinks, nearly slipping and hitting her head on the glimmering floor as she hurtles out of the bathroom and into the bedroom to begin scrambling for far-flung clothes.

'I've got to dash,' Bea calls to Vali. 'I'm meeting *Mamá* for lunch.' She pulls on her jeans. 'And no, you can't come.' Bea scrabbles under the bed to retrieve her shirt. 'And not because of you. It's – I'll explain later – meet me at the buttery tonight?'

Still, Vali says nothing. The man could sleep through an earthquake. Bea pulls on her shoes. Where's her bra?

'I mean, last night was amazing, don't get me wrong.' Bea scans the room. 'And, God knows . . .' She checks the tangled sheets, dives under the bed, nips back into the bathroom. 'Well, maybe we could do it again, but we'd need to . . . Where's my bloody bra?' Bea's about to give it up for good, when she realizes there's one place she's not searched. In three steps she's standing over him.

'Okay, Romeo, get up,' Bea commands. 'I need my bra back. And I'm guessing you've got it somewhere concealed about your person.'

Vali doesn't move.

'Come on, you lazy bugger. Just sit up, I'll do the rest.'

When Vali still doesn't move, doesn't react, Bea reaches down to shake him. She snaps back her hand. *¡Mierda!*

'Val?' Bea's fingertips carry the clammy cold of Vali's skin. 'Is this a game?'

She waits. No response. Surely, even someone as dark and damaged as Vali wouldn't pull a prank like this?

'Please. Please, Val, please tell me this is some sick, twisted game.'

But it's not. And she knows it. When Bea kneels beside him, she's certain. Vali isn't moving. He isn't breathing. He isn't alive. He's d . . . She can't bring herself to use the word.

Bea stands again. What can she do now? Call a doctor? Too late. An ambulance? Ditto. A coroner, an undertaker, the police?

Bea steps back, suddenly wanting to be anywhere else but there.

¡Mierda!

She buries her face in her palms. She wants to cry, to scream, to sob. But she can't. She's got to hold it together. She mustn't break down now or she'll be in serious trouble. Because somehow, Bea knows that she's responsible for this. Her *mamá* is right. She is *evil.* And she's got to get out of here, without calling anyone. Now. Thank God she'd used a fake name to book the room. But, the bra?

Bea squeezes her eyes shut.

¡Mierda! ¡Mierda! ¡Mierda!

When she opens them again, a sudden sweep of good luck, the beating wings of her guardian angel, directs Bea to Vali's exposed foot and the dark red bra strap hanging from his big toe. A bizarrely comic touch in an otherwise tragic situation and, despite herself, Bea smiles.

It takes longer than it should to extract the bra since, at first, she tries to do it without touching Vali's foot. Bea still feels the chill on her fingertips from his shoulder and she's loath to feel it again. But, after much fumbling, Bea surrenders to the fact that she'll have to touch the body. She holds her breath, bites her lip, picks up his cold dead foot with one hand, her bra with the other, and pulls. Bea's gaze fixes on Vali's hairy toes and, for some reason, this brings tears to her eyes. It takes an extra minute of reluctant manoeuvring, before the bra snaps off and Bea stumbles backwards, clutching it to her chest.

She's about to run but finds herself stepping forward to the headboard, to say goodbye. He isn't *so* very ugly, Bea thinks. There's something lovely about him, almost handsome. Bea bends down to wish Vali a safe journey into the afterlife. She wants to say something, something suitably poignant and profound, but can think of nothing. Instead, she takes her left hand and places it lightly against his heart.

'Goodbye, Val.'

As her warm hand meets his cold skin, a snap of electricity shoots through Bea so she's thrown back from the bed and against the wall. Pain flashes up her back and slowly fades. She lets out a low, long groan. When she looks down Bea sees a scar burned across her left hand: thin, red and snaking from her forefinger to her wrist. *What the hell?* She traces it, lightly, with her thumb. Strangely, although it's hot to the touch, it doesn't hurt. For a moment, she's lost in the shock of the mark and in awe of the astonishing, unexpected power that created it. For a moment, Vali is forgotten.

Bea closes her eyes and presses her face into her scarred palm. A snapshot of memory flashes in the darkness, and then another. She's sitting astride Vali as he grins in pre-orgasmic bliss, moaning as she presses her hands to his chest. The beat of his heart quickens, harder and faster, harder and faster. She tightens her grip and he gasps. She's holding his life force and she wants to play with it. What's the harm in that? Bea squeezes and releases, Vali gasps and moans. He's enjoying it as much as she. She doesn't notice, not instantly, when her hand feels hot and wet and heavy, as if she's holding his beating heart in her hands. And all at once she's surging with more power than she ever imagined possible. It courses through her like electricity.

Bea screams. The pulsing stops. The gasping stops.

She opens her eyes to see the shape of Vali still prostrate under the bedsheet, his belly tugging the cotton tight, two hairy toes still exposed. Shock and awe, regret and loss crash together, ripping through what she thought was real and true, tearing it all to shreds. Bea sits amid the destruction, still desperate to pull it back together again, and begins to cry. Quietly at first, tears slip down her cheeks; then, suddenly overcome by a capsizing gust of grief, Bea is seized by great racking sobs that shudder through her, again and again and again.

1.33 p.m. – Goldie

When I arrive at the hotel, two ambulances are stationed outside. My first thought is of Leo. Could something have happened to him? Surely not. That's ridiculous. Leo is invincible. One of the guests must have choked on their overpriced English breakfast, or an overweight, over-privileged, over-the-hill toff has been struck down by a heart attack – it happened once at the Fitz during my tenure.

I take the steps two by two and stumble into the foyer. Paramedics surround a gurney that's being pushed past me. On it is a body – I can't see the face since everything is covered by a white sheet, one of the hotel sheets, a shroud. He, since the body looks too long and bulky to be a she, must have died in his sleep. I must have been right about the heart attack. As I walk on I think of Ma, of finding her dead and cold in her bed.

Then I see the girl beside him: short, slight, with nut-brown hair and skin. She's beautiful, in a striking way that's normally seen only on stage or screen, not in real life. I wonder if that's where I've seen her before, on television. Is she some sort of celebrity? She must be, because I'm sure I know her, I just can't remember her name. Oddly, though, she doesn't feel like a stranger. I feel drawn to her. I want to say something, although I imagine that famous people don't take kindly to being bothered by chambermaids. But it's not for that reason that I don't stop her; it's that she looks so shaken, so scared. And then I see why: she loves the man under the white sheet and she's lost him.

11.57 p.m. – Bea

At some point, after she'd pulled herself from the floor, Bea must have called the ambulance for it came, sirens wailing and lights flashing, intruding on her silence with Vali. Paramedics trying and failing to resuscitate him. The hospital. The police. The questions, respectful but unrelenting. The images, awful and insistent. And the memory of it all isn't a merciful blur. It's stark and sharp, every moment – the sheet pulled over Vali's face, the harping voices over his quiet, the strangers leading her away – seared on Bea's mind as vividly as the scar on her hand. And every thought gone from her head except the insistent refrain: *What have I done, What have I done, What have I done?*

20th October – 12 days . . .

9.45 a.m. – Liyana

The train will arrive at Cambridge station in forty-five minutes. *Forty-five minutes.* Liyana is sitting on a wobbly seat, contemplating whether to move to another, when her phone rings.

Her aunt. Liyana picks up. 'Hey, *Nɔḍi*. How's things?'

'Where the hell are you?'

'Good morning to you too,' Liyana says, fighting the urge to hang up, lest their conversation – shaping up to be an ugly one – be broadcast in stereo to the gentleman sitting beside her.

'Good morning?' her aunt squeals. 'Good morning? It might be if you were here as you promised.'

Liyana coughs. Twice. 'I'm' – she drops her voice to a hoarse, nasal whisper – 'I've meant to call, but' – another cough – 'I've been feeling too . . . weak to pick up the phone.'

Silence. Liyana feels vibrations of suspicion hum across the airwaves.

'You didn't sound remotely ill,' Aunt Nya says, 'until five seconds ago.'

'But I am. So, so ill . . .' Liyana explodes into another coughing fit.

Her train companions shift self-consciously, distancing themselves from both the spray of germs and any whiff of racism. It's then that the train announcer decides to inform everyone that they'll soon be pulling into Finsbury Park.

'Are you on a *train*?'

'Of course not,' Liyana says, attempting a tenuous tone between near-death and vehement denial. 'No, no. Kumiko left the radio on' – Liyana hacks up another cough – 'I'm, er, too weak to get up and switch it off.'

'Oh, really?' her aunt snaps. 'Well, you tell that to Mazmo, who's sitting at the kitchen table right now, expecting you to join us for breakfast.'

Liyana curses to herself. 'Shit, I'm sorry, *Nɔḍi*, I totally forgot. And I . . . Kumiko and I decided to take a quick spontaneous trip to Cambridge.'

'Cambridge?' Her aunt's incredulous. 'What on earth for?'

'To, um, see King's College.'

'King's College?'

'Well, Kumiko's never seen it so—'

'All right, all right,' her aunt says with a weary sigh. 'Enough excuses. Just call Mazmo and apologize, will you?'

'Yeah, of course,' Liyana says. 'As soon as I'm back.'

'Now.'

Liyana sighs. 'Okay, sure. I'll call him right now.'

'Good,' Aunt Nya says and hangs up.

11.16 a.m. – Liyana

Liyana stands outside the entrance to the Fitzwilliam Hotel, practising her lines. Miniature trees flank the flight of stone steps. Grand oak doors, with golden lion heads hanging in their centres, remain closed. Above Liyana's head, a deep green velvet awning with *The Fitzwilliam Hotel* emblazoned in elaborate gold lettering flaps in the breeze.

Each time she reaches the end of the first sentence the words are wiped clean again. She'd been practising on the train, mouthing them to perfection until the gentleman beside her had shifted surreptitiously to the other side of the carriage. And now she can't remember anything after that single line.

Finally, Liyana takes a deep breath and summons the spirit of BlackBird. Be brave, be bold. She strides up the stone steps and through the heavy oak doors. In the glittering foyer, Liyana ruffles her feathers, tucks in her wings and marches towards the front desk.

Standing behind the front desk is a striking woman, with shining blonde hair and a bright red pout, humming to herself. It takes a moment for Liyana to recognize the tune. The Beatles. *Blackbird*. And, all at once, it returns to her. This was the song her mother used to sing.

Liyana stands for a few moments, singing the lyrics silently to herself, thinking of her mother. She exhales. It will be okay. It will all be okay.

'Good morning,' the woman chirrups, as Liyana steps into her sightline. 'Welcome to the Fitzwilliam Hotel.'

Liyana hesitates.

'How may I help you?'

'I, um, I'm looking for . . .' Liyana struggles with her script, 'my sister. She works here.'

The woman – Cassie, according to her lapel – regards Liyana with a sceptical eye. 'And what's your sister's name?'

'I, um, well, we've not seen each other for a long time and . . .'

Cassie waits for Liyana to complete her sentence. Liyana attempts a confident smile. What happened to brave and bold? Where has her courage gone? Suspicion starts to tweak Cassie's smile. 'So, what's your sister's name?'

'Right, yes, I . . .'

Cassie's fingers hover over a computer keyboard. 'What's your name?'

Lie, lie, lie. 'Um – Ana, Liyana.'

She starts to tap. 'Li-ya-na what?'

'Oh, yes, sorry, I – Chiweshe.'

'I'm afraid you must be mistaken,' Cassie says, after consulting the computer. 'We don't have any members of staff by the name of Chi-we-she.'

'Ah, okay, but she . . .' Liyana trails off until, finally, inspiration strikes – 'She doesn't have my surname. We're half-sisters. Different mother, different name . . . She's very pretty, blonde curls, blue eyes . . .'

At this description, recognition lights the receptionist's eyes and Liyana knows she's found the right place.

'And yet you don't even know her first name?' Cassie's smile thins, lips tighten. She has a parched look, Liyana thinks, as if she needs a long drink of water. 'Which tells me that I shouldn't be giving you her details, but I should be inviting you to leave.'

'No.' Liyana frowns. She wonders if – no, she doesn't wonder – she knows that if she were white and her sister black, this conversation would be developing very differently. 'Please,' she says, hating herself for begging. 'Please, it's just – we've never met.'

Cassie narrows her eyes. 'You've never met? Then why are you so sure she works here?' She shifts in the direction of the telephone. 'Have you been follow—?'

'No!' Liyana interrupts. 'No, of course not. I, I . . . I saw her in my . . .'

Cassie reaches for the phone. 'I'm sorry, Ms Chi-we-she, but either you're going to leave right now, or I'm going to call the police.'

Liyana shakes her head, eyes filling with tears, and backs away from the desk. She pushes open the ancient oak doors, her sight so blurred by now that she trips and falls down the stone steps.

20th October – 12 days . . .

5.15 p.m. – Liyana

Having spent the afternoon wandering hopelessly around town, past St Catherine's College, then King's and Gonville & Caius, feeling that the latticed windows were watching her, glittering, winking, jeering that she won't find her sister in this city if she looks for a thousand years, Liyana now climbed the staircase of Great St Mary's medieval tower, puffing and heaving up the 123 steps before stumbling out into the slanting rain, the weather having shifted from sunshine to cloud while she was trudging up the stairs. Which made it worth the trip, for the city was resplendent in the rain.

Below her, Cambridge seemed to rise out of the water like Atlantis: eddying streets shimmering like rivers, rippling flags snagged like seaweed on the tops of towers, gleaming turrets and filigree spires, burnished gargoyles and glistening wrought-iron gates, lustrous lawns spreading like algae on the seabed. Liyana imagined her sister as a mermaid flitting unseen between the submerged buildings, and stood on the tower hoping to catch a glimpse of her, until she was thoroughly soaked through.

After exhausting every effort, Liyana returned to the streets to slump onto a bench overlooking the pillared entrance of the Fitzwilliam Museum, just past the hotel. An hour later, when Liyana's trying to decide whether to go straight home to London or find somewhere to eat first, she sees Cassie walking towards her. Liyana stands, ready to scuttle off in the opposite direction in case the police are following behind. But, seeing Cassie's expression, she stays herself.

'I'm glad you didn't get far,' Cassie says. 'It's too cold out to be searching the streets.'

Liyana sits.

'I'm sorry,' Cassie says, 'about before. I didn't know who you were. You might have been some sort of stalker.'

'So, why don't you think I am now?'

'My boss was ranting about Goldie earlier – long blonde hair, big blue eyes . . . Beautiful, right?'

Liyana nods, knowing, though she can't explain how, that this Goldie is her sister. 'Right.'

'So, I know she's in trouble. She left two weeks ago without a word. None of us know what happened and I thought that maybe you could . . .' Cassie gives Liyana an appraising look. 'But, I don't, how come you're . . .'

'Black?'

'Well, yeah,' Cassie says, uneasy. 'I mean, I don't mean to be— Before, I wasn't being . . .'

Yes, you were, Liyana thinks. But she needs to keep this girl on her side until she gets the all-important address.

'It's all right.' Liyana gives Cassie a wry smile. 'Different mother, different colour.'

'Oh, right. Well, anyway, I don't know what happened, why she left so suddenly, but . . . I was thinking about you and I've got a feeling maybe you'll be able to help her.'

Liyana frowns. 'You do?'

'Sometimes I get these feelings . . .' She shrugs. 'Intuition, I suppose.'

Liyana smiles. 'Me too.'

'Well, that's great.' Cassie rummages in her handbag, picking out a piece of folded paper and handing it to Liyana. 'Her address. She gave my boss a fake one, he's furious. I don't know why she gave it to me, since she never invited me over anytime, but' – Cassie gives Liyana the once-over again – 'I guess maybe now I do. Anyway . . . send her my love when you see her. Tell her we all miss her, especially Jake. I know she can't visit, but tell her to take care, okay?'

Liyana nods.

20th October – 12 days . . .

8.35 p.m. – Liyana & Goldie

If Liyana procrastinated outside the Fitzwilliam Hotel, it's nothing compared with how long she waits outside Goldie's flat, after gaining access to the building by sneaking in behind another visitor. Now she paces the corridor, up and down, up and down, occasionally pressing her ear to Goldie's door. It's only when Liyana realizes how late it's getting that she stops pacing.

Imagining how BlackBird might address the situation – by kicking down the door with steel-capped boots – Liyana gives a tentative knock. When Goldie opens the door it's with the chain on.

'What do you want?'

'I, I . . .' Liyana extends her hand. 'I'm Liyana Miriro Chiweshe. But, um, call me Ana. I—'

'I didn't ask for your birth certificate,' Goldie snaps. 'I asked why you're here.'

Liyana swallows. 'I'm, um, well . . . Cassie, the receptionist at the Fitzwilliam Hotel – you know? – she gave me your address. She told me to send her love. She told me to tell you to take care. She says she misses you, Jake too.'

A guilty look passes over Goldie's face. 'How do you know Cassie?'

Liyana wishes she had a better story than the truth, but she hasn't. 'I met her today. I told her . . . I told her I was your sister.'

The chain slides across the lock and the door opens an inch. Goldie pokes her nose out. Liyana's spirits lift. Then, catching the glint of the large kitchen knife in Goldie's hands, fall again.

'I don't have a sister. Besides,' Goldie says, a raised eyebrow pointedly taking in the colour of Liyana's skin and the bounce of her hair, 'you look nothing like me.'

And yet, despite Goldie's words, Liyana sees reflected in those blue eyes her own flash of recognition, her own tug of memory, a reminder of something lost and long ago. Her sister knows her, though she doesn't know how.

'Please, give me a chance to explain. If you don't believe me, you can kick me out and I'll never bother you again, I promise. Please.'

Goldie scrutinizes Liyana more deeply. Then, perhaps considering that she's the one wielding an enormous kitchen knife, opens the door.

9.59 p.m. – Goldie & Liyana

'How did you find me?'

Liyana looks confused. 'I went to the hotel, Cassie—'

I shake my head. 'No, I mean, how did you know to look for me?'

'Oh, right. Okay, yeah . . .' Liyana stalls. 'Well, um, first I . . . Well, I sort of heard your voice in my head. Of course, I didn't know it was you at the time.'

'What did I say?'

Liyana smiles. 'That you were going to kill Cassie.'

I smile. 'That sounds about right.'

'And you asked your grandma what to do. Then you called her a constipated hamster and—'

'A what?' I frown. 'And I don't have a grandma.'

Liyana mirrors my frown. 'I did think it was strange. Do you know anyone called Ezekiel?'

'No.'

'Then it must have been someone else, I guess.' Liyana looks thoughtful. 'Anyway, I dreamed about you, in the hotel and . . .'

'You dreamed about me?' I say, though, strangely, I'm not shocked.

Liyana relaxes. 'Do you think I'm delusional?'

'I don't know.' I shrug. 'You might be. But I know you're not lying.'

'Thanks,' Liyana says, as if she's entirely used to people thinking her delusional. 'Anyway, I had that strange sense of knowing, that you have in dreams, right? When nothing needs explaining, you just believe it. And, in the dream, I knew you were my sister. I still knew it when I woke up, which was the weird bit, I guess . . .'

'This whole thing is weird,' I say.

'Yeah, I suppose it is,' Liyana concedes. She glances about the flat, then back to me. 'So, why do you believe me?'

'I don't know. I'm pretty sure we've never met, but I feel like I know you.'

Liyana nods. 'Me too.'

Just then, Teddy's snores float across the living room.

Liyana starts. 'What's that?'

'It's okay, it's my brother.'

'Where?'

I nod towards the blue silk shoji screen concealing his bed in the corner of the room. 'He sleeps there. He's . . .' Suddenly I want to show my possible sister my sleeping brother. I stand. 'Come and see his pictures.'

I cross the floor, beckoning Liyana to follow. I pull one of the screen panels aside to reveal Teddy and all the pictures – his gorgeous haute couture designs – stuck to the walls around his bed.

She stares, clearly struck by Teddy's undeniable splendidness. I feel an unbidden and deep rush of affection for them both.

'They're . . . incredible,' she whispers. 'But – how old is he?'

'Nine,' I say, not without pride. 'Nearly ten.'

'And he draws better than I do,' Liyana says. 'How depressing.'

'You draw?'

'Only comic books. And . . . well, I only do them to amuse myself. I was going to the . . .' She leans forward to a drawing of a 1950s tea dress. Teddy shifts in his sleep, mumbling. I step back, so Liyana must do the same, and pull the shoji screen shut. I cross the carpet, avoiding that spot, and return to the sofa. Liyana follows, stepping on that spot, and sits next to me.

'So, you live alone, just you and your brother?'

I nod. 'Ma died when I was fourteen.'

She frowns. Even with her brow furrowed, my God but she's beautiful. I try to think how I'd describe her, in my notebook. Her skin is so smooth and dark, like . . . the sheen on a blackbird's wing. Her bright, black eyes like . . . But no, right now she seems to me unparalleled in nature. I feel a sudden longing to shed my anaemic pallor and unremarkable features to look like her.

'How old are you?' she says.

'Seventeen,' I say. 'Eighteen in two weeks.'

'Yeah? Me too, on Halloween.'

Now I'm surprised. 'That's my birthday too.'

'Oh,' Liyana says. 'How weird.'

'This whole thing is pretty fucking weird,' I say. 'Don't you think?'

'Yeah.' She grins. 'But it's pretty fucking amazing too.'

10.39 p.m. – Goldie

It's madness. Absolute madness. And yet, I'm doing it. Liyana has fallen asleep on the sofa and I am sitting on the carpet, cross-legged with a rose at my feet. A rose I impulsively stole from a stall in the Market Square yesterday afternoon.

I stare at the rose, trying to summon something – I have

no idea what – within me. Okay, so I'm trying to move the damn thing.

After ten minutes of intense focus, of trying to summon up some sort of magical force, of trying to recreate my recurring dreams, I've achieved absolutely nothing. The rose remains a rose and hasn't shifted even a fraction.

Shit, shit, shit.

I throw up my hands, like Teddy does when he's frustrated with an illustration that isn't working. Which is fitting, since only a kid would think she could make her dreams manifest. What'll I try next – leaping from the top of our block of flats to see if I can fly?

Stupid, stupid, stupid.

I glare at the rose then snatch it up. I pluck at each petal one by one, cursing with each velvet rip. Then I stand, walk over to the kitchen and drop the whole mess into the bin.

Something else I won't be telling Liyana when she wakes up.

11.11 p.m. – Goldie

I lean back against the sofa, tucking a blanket around my legs, planning to sleep, when Liyana wakes. She stirs and yawns.

I turn to face her. 'Sorry I woke you.'

Liyana looks at me, slightly startled. 'I – I was dreaming about you.'

I smile. 'You were? What was I doing?'

Liyana frowns. 'We were together in a forest, except it was different, I can't explain . . . enchanted, perhaps. You were standing in front of a tree and making vines of ivy uncurl from the trunk and reach towards the branches—'

'I was? Really?'

Liyana nods. 'And I was suspending drops of rain in mid-air, making them float back up towards the clouds.'

'That's a great dream. I wish I had d—'

'Yeah,' Liyana interrupts. 'But the thing is, I don't think . . .'

'What?'

She shrugs. 'I don't think it was just a dream. I think it happened. I think it's a memory.'

'Really?' Now I frown. 'But how – if it was, then I'd remember it too, don't you think?'

But Liyana is already shaking her head. 'No. Well, not necessarily, I mean. It wasn't recent. We were young, only kids, so – I can hardly remember anything from when I was a child, can you?'

Nothing I'll be telling you about, I think. 'No. Not much.'

'Me neither,' Liyana says. 'But it was so real, I, I . . .'

I'm about to tell her about my own dreams, about the flower. I hesitate. She reaches for my hand and, as our fingers touch, I meet Liyana's gaze and I believe, suddenly and inexplicably, that she's right. It's the reason I recognized her when she knocked on my door. And I know then, though I can't explain how, that we've met not only once but many times before.

11.28 p.m. – Leo

Alone in his room at St John's, Leo tries to focus on something, anything other than thoughts of Goldie. Unsurprisingly, his Law books aren't compelling enough to perform the trick. More frustratingly, even the desire to train has left him tonight. And, given how his feelings for her are weakening his heart, he'll have to strengthen himself to compensate – so that, when the time comes, even if he doesn't have the will to kill her, muscle memory will take over and do it for him.

Leo paces. He should go out for a run. Lift weights. Sneak down to the gym. But, no matter how heavy his methods of persuasion, how inventive his personal insults or how elaborate his curses, still Leo can't propel himself out of his room. The truth is, though he's too stubbornly furious to admit it, the only place he wants to be right now is in bed with Goldie and the only thing he wants to be doing is whatever she wants to do.

But the reality, the tragedy, is that if he won't fight Goldie, another soldier will. So she needs to know. She needs to go to Everwhere before the moon next reaches its first quarter. She needs to train, practise, hone her skills until she's strong, as strong as the best soldier. After that, he can only hope that Goldie chooses to go dark. Because she can't beat her father, no matter how powerful she is. She'll never kill him. It's impossible. Sisters before have tried and all have failed.

Leo glances at his phone, on the desk atop his Law books. He could call her. He could ask what she's up to, invite himself over. He stops pacing, steps over and picks up his phone. He finds her number, contemplates it.

'Fuck.'

He puts the phone down again. Then stacks the books on top of it. And resumes pacing.

11.59 p.m. – Scarlet

When she steps into the kitchen, Scarlet is met with a sight that – after a single moment of immovable shock – tips her instantly into tears. The ceiling. The world has turned too fast, tilting everything on its axis, capsizing the little café and bringing the ceiling crashing down to the floor.

Wet-cheeked, Scarlet stares up at the space where, only two days ago, a crack was snaking across the ceiling.

Now it has split open, leaving a great gaping hole in its wake.

A little less than a decade ago

Everwhere

You think of Everwhere. You wonder if you'll ever go back. You want to but, for now at least, longing is trumped by fear.

You try to forget, but every time you wander past a particularly ornate gate, you wonder if – so long as you arrived on the correct night, at the correct time – it might just take you back to Everwhere. You carry on past these gates, knowing you won't return on that particular night, at that precise time. You're too scared of what happened last time and whether it might happen again. Still, the question of what might happen if you did lingers long after the gate has gone.

Goldie

For nearly a week I didn't go to Everwhere. Instead, I stayed up late watching Teddy – I'd named him after my lost bear – sleep. He was fun to watch. He made silly scrunched-up faces as if he was having strange dreams. He kicked his legs and flailed his arms, as if trying to escape his cot. Sometimes he opened his eyes, darker blue in colour, but in shape mirrors to my own, and I was reminded again that he was mine. Brother, mine. It was only a shame that his tiny hands were always tight shut, since I wanted to hold them. I wanted all his fingers to wrap around one of mine. Sometimes I wriggled my littlest finger between the commas of his clenched fingers until he grasped hold as if he'd never let me go. I hoped, one day, he would do the same on purpose.

It shocked me, every day, how deeply I felt for Teddy. More than I'd ever felt for anyone, even Ma. I loved my sisters, even Bea, but it wasn't the same. Perhaps because he was a baby. I wanted to protect him. Sometimes, when Ma and my bastard stepfather were shouting, firing words at each other over the top of Teddy's bed, I wanted to scoop him up in my arms and run. I wondered if I could take him to Everwhere. I didn't think so. It seemed to be a place only for girls, given what I'd seen. But, perhaps. Bea would know, naturally, though I wouldn't give her the satisfaction of asking. She loved to tease us, her ignorant sisters. She drew great delight from dropping buttered breadcrumbs into conversations and waiting for us to bite. The others always fell for her bait, but I'd learned better. She still hadn't told us who 'he' was.

So, since I probably couldn't take Teddy with me, I whispered stories to him instead, telling him all the secrets I knew about my special place. I didn't know if he heard me or not. Still, I thought the words soothed him, wrapped around his little body like the swaddling Ma sometimes used to still his flailing limbs and help him sleep. I even braved my stepfather during these nights, feeling his gaze on my back while I crouched over the cot. I didn't care. He could do what he liked. He could leave his mark on me, the stench of his sweat, the sourness of his breath, the slick wet of his tongue . . . But I wasn't there anymore to feel it.

I wondered: If I couldn't take Teddy to Everwhere, could I bring my sisters to Cambridge? I hadn't yet asked where they lived; it might be anywhere in the world. So perhaps it was impossible, but perhaps not. I'd like to know them better in this world, though Bea annoyed me and Scarlet slightly scared me, but Liyana seemed sweet. It'd be good to have real sisters, real friends. Ma might feel too ashamed to let me bring them to the flat for tea, but I could sneak Teddy out for a walk in the pram while he napped and meet them in the park. I made a mental note to mention this idea the next time I returned. Though I was still in no rush to go.

Scarlet

'Let's do something fun,' Scarlet said.

Liyana looked up. 'What?'

'Let's play a trick on Bea.'

'Why?'

Scarlet shrugged. 'It'll be fun.'

'All right,' Liyana said. 'As long as it doesn't make her upset. I don't like it when she's upset.'

'Don't worry,' Scarlet said. 'It'll make her laugh.'

If it took Scarlet a while to convince Liyana of this, it took longer to convince her of the necessity of climbing a tree to execute the trick. Scarlet went first.

'You have to be high up if you want to call the rain.' Scarlet coaxed her sister up to the second branch. 'Hurry.'

Liyana refused to climb any higher. 'I think this branch is about to snap.'

'All right, all right.' Scarlet rolled her eyes. 'So, close your eyes and bring the rain to the glade, but a downpour, not a drizzle.'

'How do I do that?'

'I haven't a clue. How did you make that massive wave in the river last week?'

'I don't know.' Liyana gripped the branch. 'It just happened.'

'Well, once you work it out, let me know.' Scarlet started to scramble down from the tree. 'Then we can have some fun.'

'Why?' Liyana said, wishing she could follow. 'What are you going to do?'

Scarlet jumped onto the mossy ground. 'Hot rain,' she said with a grin. 'That's what *we're* going to do.'

Liyana

Liyana adored Everwhere, for the possibilities, the companionship, the grandeur, but what she adored most of all was the weather. The damp mists, the cold fog, the leaves falling like rain. London was a fitting place for a pluviophile, but it couldn't compare with Everwhere. In London one must at least expect the odd ray of sunshine, however rare, but here the weather was always predictable, a constant unchanging drizzle.

As well as the climate, Liyana appreciated the time of night. She'd always slept straight through the night even as a baby, a fact deeply appreciated by her mother. So Liyana had never known the true magic of the moon in her element, during the early morning hours between three and four o'clock. Now Liyana could spend an entire night watching the moon, soaking up her strength, until she imagined that she too could shine brighter than the stars, could pull the seas from the shores, could control the shape and substance of people's dreams.

After her failure last night to drench Bea with hot rain – a failure that had brought great relief – Liyana decided to test herself, to see if the wave had been an anomaly or if she really could control water. Now she stood on a riverbank watching the water flowing beneath her feet, her own shifting silver shadow cast across the stream, her silhouette broken only by the current and the falling leaves.

As Liyana watched the eddies and swirls, she imagined that the brook was being stirred by an invisible spoon, by some great water god enjoying his particular cup of tea.

And as she watched, all at once she knew. She *was* like the moon: she could sway and shape the water, as easily as if she were stirring her own cup of tea.

Liyana smiled and her glowing silhouette stilled, the stream now calm and clear enough to hold not only her shadow but her reflection, as sharp as if she were looking into a mirror. She studied the water for a while, keeping herself straight and unmoving. Then she frowned, simply to see the effect. As soon as the lines drew across her forehead, the stream started to stir. Liyana deepened her frown and the currents began to churn, tiny waves crashing onto the banks, as if a river-storm were coming.

Liyana dropped her frown and grinned. The water stilled and the storm ebbed. She wasn't the one sister without skills after all. And if she could control water, then what else could she do?

Bea

The first time her *mamá* was committed, Bea was eight years old. At first, she hadn't minded, she'd enjoyed staying with her *abuela*, who took pride in indulging her only granddaughter's every whim. And, after their first visit to St Dymphna's, Bea had secretly prayed (when she knelt with her *abuela* at their bedside) that Cleo would extend her stay by a few extra years.

They'd caught the number 6 bus, disembarking at the church and walking a while until they reached the gates of the 'hotel' where her *mamá* was resting. Then Bea sat on the pavement and refused to budge.

'*Vamos, niña,*' her *abuela* insisted, tugging Bea forward. '*Tenemos que irnos, tu mamá está esperando.*'

But Bea planted her feet and shook her head. She didn't care if her *mamá* was waiting. Even outside she could already feel the melancholy heavy in the air, thick as the Everwhere fog. She wasn't going in.

'*Por favor, mi niña. Tu mamá te extraña.*'

But Bea stood firm, shaking her head. '*No, Abuela. No voy a ir nunca.*'

No amount of cajoling, begging or bribery would compel Bea over the threshold. So, finally, her *abuela* picked Bea up and carried her, rigid and spitting, all the way to Cleo's room. When Bea met her *mamá*'s eye, the fog had closed in. She'd been scared of her *mamá* many times before, but never scared for her. Bea had a slight sense of déjà vu then, recalling the time she'd been devastated by the sight of a silverback gorilla at the London Zoo, whose big wet eyes were filled with the same defeated sadness as her *mamá*'s now.

'*¿Mamá?*' Bea stepped forward, lifting her little hand to Cleo's pale cheek. '*¿Que pasa?*'

Her *mamá* didn't reply, didn't say anything for the duration of the visit. When Bea and her *abuela* left, Cleo didn't say goodbye. This didn't matter to Bea, nor the scrutiny of the nurses, the glassy eyed watch of the other patients or the screams echoing along the corridors. But the look in her *mamá*'s eyes lingered long after everything else had gone.

Leo

'Are you scared to be a soldier?' Christopher asked.

'No,' Leo said. 'Are you?'

'Sometimes,' Christopher said. 'I think you'll be better at it than me.'

Leo, since he didn't disagree, said nothing. He didn't want to say that not only was he not scared, he was looking forward to it. He liked the idea of hunting, of fighting. A place he could vent his anger without getting punished. The thought of the killing disturbed him, so he didn't think too much about that. But it was thrilling, this existence of another world. Other boys might talk excitedly into the night about Middle Earth, but that was make-believe. This was real. This was a great and glorious secret that only he and Christopher knew.

21st October – 11 days . . .

3.33 a.m. – Leo

Leo stands on the cobbled pavement in front of King's College and contemplates the chapel, its ancient stonework bleached by a waning moon that seems to lie cradled between the filigree turrets, as if being rocked to sleep. How Leo wishes he could sleep, if only to shut out this world for a little while.

He steps over to the low, cold stone wall and sits. He thinks of Goldie, then finds himself thinking of his first love, his brother, his best friend. Leo had been right. The night he'd finally killed the Grimm girl who'd murdered Christopher, he'd known it.

That night Leo had crept out of the flat, while his parents slept in their respective rooms, to seek out the closest gate. Actually, not quite the closest; when he was home from school Leo didn't use the nearest entrance to Everwhere but the most illustrious. He hurried past the plain gates of the Royal Hospital Chelsea, walking an extra fifteen minutes to the infinitely more remarkable gates of Cremorne Gardens. Leo had loved these gates – featuring four golden lion heads and flanked by three-dimensional pillars inlaid with sculpted roses and topped with ornate lamps – ever since he'd first found them while wandering the streets one night. The gates were always locked, but the heavy chain padlock gave way when Leo pushed at precisely the right moment.

That night she was the first Grimm girl he saw when he stepped through. She fought a good fight, singeing his eyebrows with a well-aimed fiery breath and fracturing his ankle, and would certainly have won against any other soldier. She was exceptional – she'd survived the Choosing after all – and far older than him. But Leo had a singular advantage: he was fearless. He didn't care if he lived or died. He wanted only vengeance.

It wasn't until her final breath etched the tiny crescent moon on his shoulder blade that Leo realized who she'd been. For her breath carried the scent of his friend, as if she'd swallowed his sweat and blood, instead of extinguishing his spirit, and had done so only an hour before, instead of two years ago. Leo had cried out as the mists engulfed the Grimm girl's own spirit and the ground soaked up her soul. He screamed to stop it, to seize hold of them both a moment longer. But the scent of Christopher had evaporated with her and with it any satisfaction of vengeance fulfilled. And Leo was left once more bereft, longing for his beloved brother as acutely as he had the night he'd died.

He feels it still.

Pushing Christopher and Goldie from his thoughts, Leo stands and, with one look back at the exquisite edifice of King's College Chapel, walks away. By the time he's reached the end of King's Parade, they've returned.

7.59 a.m. – Liyana

As the Cambridge commuter train hurtles onwards towards King's Cross, all Liyana can think of is Goldie. Her half-sister. Her white sister. Mazmo, the Slade, even Kumiko are forgotten in the light of her. The shock of finally meeting this sister has even eclipsed the extraordinary events that led Liyana to Goldie in the first place. However, while the immediate past has faded into the background, the more distant past is starting to sharpen. Something once engulfed by mists and fog is beginning to come into view.

Absently, Liyana places her hand on the window, watching the fields flick past, sensing something she can't yet see. She wonders: Is it possible that she's already met her sister somewhere before?

As her thoughts drift, Liyana starts to daydream of a place, a game, a skill she once had, a power to manipulate the elements. The train rocks her and Liyana closes her eyes, her thoughts floating free . . . When the train jolts to a halt in Royston, Liyana opens her eyes, pulls her sketchbook out of her bag and begins to draw her half-sister a story.

9.01 a.m. – Bea

It looks like a heart attack, the male paramedic had said. Highly unusual in one so young, the female paramedic had said. He must have had an underlying heart condition. How soon they'd started talking about him in the past tense. But then, what did they care? They'd never known him in the present tense.

Bea isn't relieved that she's not suspected of murder. She wishes she was. She wants to suffer interrogation, prosecution, the full punishment of the law. She wants to suffer, ought to be punished.

When the police arrived, asking only gentle, tentative questions, Bea had been on the verge of turning herself in. So many times she'd almost shouted: *I did it! You fucking fools! It was me!* But what would she say after that? How could she explain stopping a man's heart? That'd lead to plenty of awkwardness and probably land her in the loony bin – and she'd prefer anything to that, even the death penalty. A shame, she thinks, that it's been abolished, because those enforced Sunday afternoon visits to St Dymphna's have left Bea with an abiding determination to never again set foot inside such an institution.

12.08 p.m. – Scarlet

'Please, I can't wait three weeks . . . No, I mean, it's my livelihood, I need you to come today . . . Okay, tomorrow – next week? At the very latest . . .' Scarlet waits, while the unknown woman on the phone, in an unknown office far away, tells her that this is impossible. 'I know, I know. But, I – please. Please—'

When the refrain of refusal doesn't shift, Scarlet starts to sob, for the second time in as many days.

'You never called.' Walt reaches the counter. 'I hoped you would.'

'Sorry,' Scarlet says, discreetly brushing cement dust out of her hair and slightly embarrassed at being caught wearing dungarees and tattered trainers, even though she isn't especially interested in impressing him. 'I just – it's been, things haven't been easy around here lately, I—'

Walt holds up his hand. 'It's okay. You don't need to explain. It's – I know we didn't exactly have a frisson, like you and that ridiculously handsome bloke. But I thought we had . . . something.'

'You and your frissons.' Scarlet steps over to the coffee machine. 'I'm not selling the café and I'm not seeing him again – look, do you fancy a coffee? We could have our date now. I could do with a break.'

Walt brightens. 'Absolutely. And yes, you are looking a little . . . dishevelled – in an incredibly attractive way, of course.'

Scarlet feels tears pricking her eyes again. 'The kitchen ceiling caved in last night. I've spent all morning cleaning it up. Grandma's still in bed, thank God, or I don't know—'

'Oh, shit, that's awful,' Walt says, rolling up his sleeves.

'Look, forget the coffee, let me help. We'll have it cleaned up in no time.'

'Really?' Scarlet's shoulders drop. She should decline – he's done her enough favours – but she's too exhausted, too overwhelmed. 'Are you sure?'

'Are you kidding?' Walt says, already rolling up his sleeves – though his own shirt looks far too pristine for the job. 'I can't imagine a better date than this.'

Scarlet gives him a grateful smile. 'We can dine on cinnamon buns afterwards.'

'Perfect.' Walt extends his hand across the counter. 'You've got yourself a deal.'

As she shakes his hand, Scarlet glances down. Not a single spark. Shame.

7.29 p.m. – Liyana

'Is everything all right?'

'Yes.'

Liyana stands beside Kumiko at the crossing on Chantry Street, waiting for the light to turn green. She reaches for her girlfriend's hand but Kumiko pretends not to notice. For solace, Liyana's thoughts go to Goldie and Cambridge. She'd always imagined London to be the busiest city in England, but hadn't reckoned on the thousands of bikes in Cambridge, those eddying streets like rivers conveying so many cyclists darting like minnows in every direction. At least, she thinks, cars are easier to see when crossing the road.

'Are you sure?'

'I'm fine,' Kumiko says.

'I don't believe you. You don't seem fine.'

Liyana wants to say that she knows Kumiko isn't fine but furious – otherwise she'd have enquired after her sister. Instead she's playing a passive-aggressive game and pretending she's forgotten. Which means Liyana will be damned if she'll be the one to bring it up first. A light rain begins to fall and Liyana takes comfort from it. Her girlfriend may not want to talk or touch her right now, but at least the rain always will.

'Well, I am. So, you can believe me. Or not. It's up to you.'

Liyana's about to ask again, but resists. It'll only annoy Kumiko, to suggest that she's lying. And Liyana doesn't want to dig an even deeper hole with the Mazmo debacle, about which Kumiko has made her disapproval quite plain. So, for now Liyana must let everything slide, even lies.

'Fancy seeing a film?' Liyana tries.

'Where?'

'The Everyman's showing a double-bill retrospective tonight,' Liyana says. '*Moby Dick* and *In the Heart of the Sea*.'

Kumiko shrugs. A few weeks ago, Liyana wouldn't have tolerated shrugs. But that was before.

'The pub?' Liyana persists.

This time, Kumiko doesn't shrug. Instead she crosses the road without waiting for the light to change. A car honks its horn, but Kumiko walks on. Liyana hesitates, then hurries after her.

'I've not said I'll marry him, you know,' Liyana calls out. 'And I've got a trial shift at Tesco tomorrow.' It's not true, strictly speaking, since she'd only had an email offering her one; she'd been putting off accepting it.

'I give you a day,' Kumiko says, quickening her pace. 'No, you know what? I'll be astonished if you last an hour. You'll be in that rich boy's bed before the week is out.'

'Koko! How can you say that?'

'Because you've been spoiled all your life, Ana.' Kumiko stops and turns back to Liyana. 'And if you're given the choice between having to earn something and being given it for free, I know full well which option you'll take.'

11.59 p.m. – Goldie

I've invited Leo into my bed again. I didn't want to be alone tonight. The sofa feels strangely empty without my sister here. Anyway, I want to be with him. I always want to be with him. As if I have an ache in my chest that abates only when we're together.

'Thank you.' I kiss him, again.

'For what?'

'For being here. For rushing over as soon as I called.'

'Of course.' Leo shrugs. 'I'll always come when you call.'

I smile, but his expression is serious.

'What's wrong?' I ask. When he doesn't answer, I nudge him.

'I'm sorry, I'm just . . . it doesn't matter.' Leo lets out a sigh, a long breath that sits between us. He seems about to say something, then shrugs again. 'It's nothing.'

I look at him, thinking of those scars he hasn't let me see since last time. I try not to think of them, to focus only on Leo, to stay in the uncomplicated, unsullied peace of being with him. I open my mouth, about to change the subject, to tell him all about Liyana, when he starts to speak again.

'I need to tell you something,' Leo says. 'About who you are.'

22nd October – 10 days . . .

1.01 a.m. – Goldie

I study his face.

'Stop,' he says, turning away.

'Sorry,' I say. 'I'm just wondering if there are any more enchanted worlds to which you have secret access. Narnia, perhaps? Or Wonderland? I've always wanted to go to Wonderland.'

I'm smiling, but Leo's still serious.

'So, if this place is real, why can't you take me there?'

'I told you, I can only go on the night when the moon is at its first quarter,' Leo says, an edge of exasperation to his voice. 'And I'll take you then. But we shouldn't wait so long, you need to go yourself first, without me, so you can—'

'I know,' I interrupt, not wanting to hear the whole weird story again. I love Leo and I don't want to confront the fact that he might be a fantasist. I think again of his scars. I wonder again if he's a member of a satanic cult. I pray he isn't.

Though it would be even worse if he was telling the truth. And some of the things Leo said, the way he described Everwhere, tug at denied memories and dismissed dreams. But if I followed those threads, then I'd have to allow the possibility of dangerous things: that I am the daughter of a demon, that on my eighteenth birthday I'll have to fight a soldier to the death, then make a choice between good and evil. And a fantastical land is one thing – perhaps no more improbable than life on other planets – but a fate like that, quite another.

11.11 a.m. – Liyana

Liyana sits on her bed, drawing. Her fingers hurt. The shift at Tesco was only five hours – half of what she'd be expected to do in a day if she takes the job. She's trying not to think about what Kumiko said, but she can't. Is she so spoiled? Is it true that she always takes the easy route, that she'd rather be given something than earn it? No, that's not fair. She crafts her illustrations until they're perfect; she swam until she passed out – one doesn't become an Olympic hopeful without working damn hard for it. Harder than most people ever do. But then . . . she loved swimming more than anything in the world and she loves drawing almost as much. The question is: Would she be willing to work a sixty-hour week of night shifts at Tesco?

Temporarily ignoring that awkward argument, Liyana focuses on shaping BlackBird's current exploits to reflect her own, wondering if her heroine might find a long-lost sister she never knew she had. If so, which bird-woman would she be? A white girl with blue eyes and blonde hair. Liyana scans her internal list of yellow birds, but finds none with suitable superhero potential. A chaffinch? No. Goldfinch? No. But what about the blue eyes – a peacock, perhaps?

Liyana chews the end of her pen. She'd surely do night shifts in Tesco to put herself through art school, wouldn't she? Standing, Liyana crosses the bedroom to her desk and picks up the Tarot cards sitting under the lamp. Unwrapping them from their silk cloth and shuffling as she walks, Liyana returns to her seat on the edge of her bed and deals them out onto the duvet.

'What should I do next?'

First is the Eight of Swords: a fairy, dazzlingly dressed, is blindfolded and bound by thorned brambles snaking up from the soil, twisting around the swords: four yellow, four green.

Entrapment, limitations, waiting to be rescued. Next, the Four of Pentacles: a skinny girl sits in the branches of a thorny, winter tree, clutching her pentacles to her chest. A forlorn cat-like creature hangs on beneath with one slipping paw. *Ownership, protection of possessions, materialistic.* Then, the Two of Swords: an Elizabethan woman crosses her swords, averting her gaze from a mirror behind her back. Birds fill the sky while one nests in her hair. *Compromised judgement, fear, hiding from the truth.* Followed by the Ten of Wands: a boy is bent-backed by the ten sticks roped to his body and the ten boulders he lifts at his feet. He stares sadly at a wilted plant while a parched dog howls beside him. *Overwhelmed, exhausted, pressurized.*

'Yeah.' Liyana sighs. 'Tell me about it.'

She deals the fifth card and scowls down at it. The damned Devil again: that green-skinned, red-eyed horned Satan and his Mardi Gras bride, flashing a stocking-leg, sit atop a locked treasure chest on a mosaic floor. Spiders hang above, weaving webs.

Liyana picks up the card from the bed, squinting at it in the darkened room. The woman is chained to The Devil's hoof, but she's also caressing his cheek and the look on her face isn't despairing but flirtatious. Had she never noticed that before? The Devil has captured his bride, but she's been complicit in her capture. *Greed, temptation, selfishness, entrapment, addiction.*

Liyana stares down at the cards. They seem to stare back up at her. She waits for them to shift, to tell a different tale, to give her a different answer.

They don't budge.

8.09 p.m. – Bea

'What the hell did you do to yourself?' Her *mamá* sits forward, leaning across the table, seizing hold of her daughter's hand.

Bea twists out of the grip. 'Nothing.'

Once a month her *mamá* visits, taking her out to lunch at The Ivy. It's their tradition. Rather, it's Cleo's tradition. Designed, Bea thinks, to keep her under a watchful eye.

'That's not nothing. What did you do?'

What did I do? ¿Y ahora, que hice? *What the fuck did I do?* Every thought other than this has left Bea's head since that frightful night. Three days later, she's still stumbling about in a daze, unable to focus on anything else. She can't read a fucking book, can't hold a two-line conversation, can't close her eyes without seeing Vali's body, without feeling his still-beating heart in her palm before she . . . What the hell *had* she done? Stopped his heart.

'I was washing up. I picked up a knife at the wrong end.'

Her *mamá* cranes for a closer look. Bea tucks her hand into her lap, clenching it into a fist.

'You know I'm all in favour of lying, *niña*,' Cleo says. 'Just don't try it with me.'

Bea skewers a roast potato with her fork but doesn't lift it to her mouth. She nods.

'*Vale*, you'll tell me in time.' Her *mamá* swallows a sliver of bloody steak. 'Was it the reason you rudely postponed our lunch?'

Bea sighs. She has spent three days trying to rationalize, to explain (in the infinite maze of the Internet one could surely find an explanation for anything, no matter how other-worldly weird it might be), to exonerate herself. But she's failed. After all, this was a man. A *man*. How was it possible to stop the heart of a not-insubstantial man? How the hell had she done it?

She looks up to see her *mamá* smiling.

'I've a sneaking feeling that, when you finally tell me what happened, I'm going to be rather proud of you.'

Bea takes a bite of the potato, though she can't taste it. 'How's Little Cat?'

'*Está bien,*' Cleo says, allowing the non-sequitur. 'Misses you, stalks the corridor outside your bedroom protesting your absence.'

'I miss him too,' Bea says, thinking what a relief it'd be right now to bury her face in his soft, purring belly. Cleo had bought Little Cat for Bea after her final release from St Dymphna's, a furry bribe to entice her wary daughter away from the fifth foster-mother, tempting her to visit more often than the court-mandated once a month. And it'd worked. Bea wants to cuddle her cat now, to forget Val, if only for a moment.

'Why don't you visit us next weekend?' Cleo takes another bite of bloody meat. 'Looks like you need a break.'

'In London?'

'*Sí, claro.* Can you think of anywhere better?'

Pushing the rest of the roast potato around her plate, Bea makes a non-committal noise. Under usual circumstances she'd do anything to avoid returning home unless absolutely necessary. But now all she wants to do is curl into her childhood bed and cry into Little Cat's paws. No, that's a lie. What she really wants is to curl into Vali, to bury her face in his fat, furry stomach.

Bea has often thought, while delving into the depths of philosophical questions, that it must be the very worst thing, the cruellest form of mental torture, to not know oneself, to think you're one thing only to suddenly find out that you're quite another. And now this is her state. She's like a brainwashed CIA agent who one day discovers she's committed mass murder because she's been subconsciously programmed as a killing machine by the government. Except that Bea wasn't brainwashed; she's woken one day to find that she's evil when she has always believed she was just a bit of a bitch. How deeply she regrets, now, being so cruel to Val. If only she could have stayed her tongue. If only she'd been kinder, gentler with his heart.

'Well, what do you think?'

Bea looks up. 'Sorry, what?'

Her *mamá* narrows her eyes. 'I was saying you should come and stay next weekend.'

Bea hesitates. She doesn't want to be stuck in *Mamá*'s tiny Kensington flat. She wants to stay, wants to be closer to Val – assuming, as she does, that he's still residing in the Addenbrooke's Hospital morgue.

'We'll celebrate your birthday.' Her *mamá* smiles. 'I'll take you to the Ritz for tea. Like we did when you were little.'

Once, Bea thinks. *That happened once.*

'Come on,' Cleo says. '*¿Y por qué no?*'

Her *mamá* won't stop asking, she knows. And Bea no longer has the energy to fight.

'All right,' she says. 'Why not?'

11.33 p.m. – Goldie & Liyana

'I've written you a story,' Liyana says.

'You have?' I say, trying not to sound too excited.

We call each other often, several times a day. But I've still not mentioned Leo. I suppose I'm savouring him like a sweet I'm not yet ready to share. I've never been very good at sharing.

'Do you want to hear it?'

'Of course.'

'I've drawn pictures too. I'm making you the star of your own graphic novel.'

'Really? That's amazing, Ana. Thank you.' I wonder if anyone has ever given me anything so generous before. Teddy gives me a fair few of his drawings, but never an entire story.

'I'll show you the comic strip when I visit,' Liyana says. 'But I'll read you the story now.'

'Great.' I sit back on the sofa. 'I'm listening.' I close my eyes. 'A bedtime story. Maybe it'll send me back to sleep.'

Liyana laughs. 'It won't be much of a story if it can't keep you awake.'

'It will,' I say. 'You won't hear me snoring, I promise.'

'Glad to hear it,' Liyana says. 'All right then: "Once Upon a Time there was a little girl as good as she was pretty. She had big blue eyes, long golden hair and a smile so lovely that it brought joy to everyone she met. The girl reared baby birds fallen from their nests, rescued worms that'd veered onto paths, enticed wilting flowers back into bloom . . ."'

When Liyana finishes the story and falls silent, I find I can't speak. I should say something, should thank her again but I'm so shocked that my sister could know my life and my heart so exactly that I'm lost for words.

11.59 p.m. – Scarlet

That night, Scarlet dreams of a fire and a flood. It's a flood that started a month ago with a leak unseen and spread by stealth. A flood that destroys the only home she's ever known. It's a fire from a decade ago. A fire stoked by feelings, by fear and fury. The feelings build until sparks snap at the tips of her fingers. One spark falls onto the rug on which eight-year-old Scarlet is standing. She watches it glow, white hot. She watches as it burns itself a tiny hole, singeing the wool, then is extinguished.

Another spark lands on the sofa cushion. This time it eats into the cotton, beginning to burn more brightly. Suddenly, it flares, a flame that's quickly engulfing the cushion, the sofa, the curtains, licking up the walls to the ceiling.

Scarlet wakes with the scream in her throat and sparks

on her fingertips. She started it. The fire, the fire that burned down their house, the fire that killed her mother. *She* started it. How can she not have known this? How can she have forgotten something so seminal? As her screams fall into silence, as her heart slows and the sparks cease, Scarlet understands. Her mind wasn't backfiring like her grandmother's, it was an act of protection, of defence. And she's grateful for one thing: that although she has at last remembered this dreadful thing, her grandma has, if she ever knew the truth, now forgotten it.

Less than a decade ago

Everwhere

Memories of Everwhere mix with the random everyday images thrown up in your dreams, tainting them with a silver moonlit edge and a pale sepia sheen. Sometimes you find yourself awake just past three a.m., especially on nights when the moon is at its first quarter. Sometimes you can't get back to sleep, the question of whether you'll ever return keeping you awake until morning. For a while, you become nocturnal.

Bea

'In a few years we won't remember each other anymore,' Bea said, suddenly and apropos of nothing.

We were sitting in the glade half-heartedly playing games: Scarlet was setting light to twigs before blowing them out, Liyana juggled three dense balls of fog, Bea floated leaves above open palms, and I coaxed tight-curled shoots of ivy from the earth. Bea sat slightly apart, breaking the circle, watching us surreptitiously through her leaves. It was our third night in a row in Everwhere and we were all more exhausted than we'd admit. But I did love it when we were together like this, and our affection for one another always seemed stronger during our silences.

'What?' Liyana looked up, dropping her balls of fog, which evaporated into the mists as they fell to the ground. 'Why wouldn't we remember? Anyway, I thought we agreed that, when we're eighteen, we'll do what our father wants so we can—'

'Speak for yourself.' Scarlet's flaming twig flared. 'I'm going to fight him.'

Liyana ignored this terrifying notion. 'But, until he – I'm not going to stop coming here, are you?'

'We'll all stop coming.' Bea smiled that smile she had when revealing an unexpected and unpleasant secret. She let the leaves waft to the ground.

'I won't,' Scarlet said. 'I'll come here every night for the rest of my life.'

Bea's smile deepened. 'Only till you're thirteen. Then you won't be able to anymore.'

The flames on Scarlet's twig spat fire and sparks. 'That's rubbish,' she said, sweeping the stick in a half-circle. We all pulled back from the flames, even Bea. 'Why won't we be able to come back?'

Bea shrugged. 'Because that's the way it is. *Mamá* told me how it works. When we're young we can come here, but by the time we're teenagers we'll be – our thoughts will be too tied to that world, our feelings too attached to the people there, we'll forget—'

'No.' Scarlet stood. 'I don't believe you. You're lying.'

Bea shook her head. And for some reason, perhaps because I could see that now she was as distressed at imparting this twist of information as Scarlet was receiving it, I knew she was telling the truth.

'We'll stop dreaming so often. We'll stop believing in anything else, except what we can see, what we can touch on Earth. We'll start to think Everwhere was just a childish dream.'

'No,' Liyana pleaded. 'That's not true.'

Bea said nothing and in her silence my sisters finally saw she wasn't teasing, wasn't saying something to shock or disturb us. Otherwise she'd goad and gloat, but Bea's smile had gone as she realized she valued this place, and her sisters, as much as we all did.

In that moment I saw Bea's beating heart, the one she pretended she didn't have, the one she tried to make us believe was impenetrable, but was actually no different from our own exposed and tender eight-year-old hearts. In the next moment, Bea reclaimed her sly smile and seemed to be sucking on her next sentence like sweets she wouldn't share, not until we begged. No surprises for guessing who did.

'What?' Liyana asked. 'What is it?'

Bea licked her lips – an especially delicious sweet. 'We will come back,' she said, stretching the gaps between each word for dramatic effect. 'When we turn eighteen.'

'Eighteen?' We all echoed this word, even me.

'But why? Why so long?' Liyana said, as if further begging could get Bea to change the facts, to reduce the wait.

'That's ridiculous,' Scarlet snapped. 'That's forever.'

Bea was silent. We all were.

'Are you sure?' Scarlet broke the silence, a note of desperation in her voice I'd not heard before. 'Are you sure it's eighteen?'

This was so far from being tomorrow, or next week, that it seemed an eternity.

'I don't know,' Bea admitted, this now seeming the most painful admission of all. 'It's a coming-of-age thing.'

'A what?' Liyana said.

'It's . . .' Bea trailed off, unwilling to reveal the limits of her omniscience. '*Mamá* explained, I can't exactly remember right now. Anyway, that's not the point—'

'Then what *is* the point?' Scarlet spat, clearly still grasping at the dwindling possibility that Bea was lying.

'The point is that we'll see each other again.'

'But how do you know? You said' – Liyana was accusing – 'you said this place was infinite. So how will we find each other again after five years? It was only luck we found each other in the first place.'

'No, it wasn't.' Bea laughed, delighted to have regained her superior position. 'Did you really think that?' She looked to Scarlet and me. 'Did you all think so too?'

Not one of us – Scarlet, Ana or I – either confirmed or denied it. But Bea could tell.

'Oh, that's hilarious,' she said, still giggling. 'I can't believe you all thought that. How utterly—'

'Stop it.' Scarlet waved her fire-stick for emphasis. 'Just explain.'

Bea sat up a little straighter. 'I bet I can guess your birthdays.'

'All of us?' Liyana asked.

Bea nodded.

'Go on then,' Scarlet said.

Bea gave a slight sniff. 'Halloween.'

I glanced at my sisters to see them staring at her open-mouthed, just as I was.

Bea waited like an actor taking her third bow, expecting another round of applause. But we were too shocked even for interrogation.

'We were born on the same day,' she explained, as if we were babies like Teddy. 'At the same hour, the same minute.'

Liyana frowned. 'Are you sure?'

'Even I don't know the exact minute I was born,' Scarlet said. 'So, how can you?'

Bea shrugged. 'It's true. Ask your *mamás*, if you don't believe me. That's why we found each other. There are hundreds of Sisters Grimm here right now, maybe thousands—'

'Sisters Grimm?' I echoed, struck by the words. It sounded so concrete, so real. An inescapable fate.

'Yeah,' Bea said, ignoring my interruption. 'But we're drawn to the ones born the same time as us. That's why we met now and that's how we'll find each other again.'

We stared at her, still sceptical. Bea folded her arms, sat back and regarded us with a triumphant grin. She had outdone herself.

Goldie

Bea might know a lot, but she didn't know everything. True, I was born on Halloween, but that wasn't the whole truth. I was born on the bridge across two days – my feet emerging a moment before midnight on the thirty-first of October and my head a moment after, just as the clock ticked into November. Two diametrical days: All Hallows' Eve and All Saints' Day. The first day shaped by darkness and demons, the second by light and saints.

However, Halloween was when we celebrated – if a small gift and single cupcake could be called celebrating – since that was the date the midwife officially recorded, being forced by convention to pick.

Secretly, I observed my birthday on both days. I sang to myself both mornings and gave myself extra treats in the afternoons: more pudding at lunchtime, then purloining two chocolate bars from Mrs Patel's on the way home. Each evening, I munched my contraband, ignored my homework and wondered, once I started reading the Bible and the Greek myths, if my birthdays meant that I was a half demon, half saint.

Leo

'What do you want to be when you grow up?' Christopher asked.

'I thought we were going to be soldiers.'

Christopher laughed. 'Only once a month. Anyway, you won't get paid for that. You'll have to be something else too.'

'Oh.'

'So, what will you be?'

'Dunno,' Leo said, since he'd not given it a moment's thought. They lay on the forbidden grass of the Headmaster's garden, an after-midnight summer ritual. 'Do you?'

Christopher nodded. 'Prime Minister.'

Leo laughed, until he realized that his friend wasn't laughing with him. 'Seriously?'

'Sure.' Christopher shrugged. 'Why not?'

As the moon slid behind the clouds, Leo cast a covert glance at his friend. In the darkness, he felt a surge of feeling he couldn't understand or explain: admiration, adoration, gratitude . . . In that moment, if someone had asked, Leo would've said he was happier than he'd ever been. He'd found a friend who believed in Everwhere (their great and glorious secret) and also that anything on Earth was possible too. And, in his presence, Leo believed that too.

23rd October – 9 days . . .

9.28 a.m. – Goldie

'There's something else I need to tell you,' Leo says, after we've been walking for a while, turning down streets at random, emerging onto the banks of the river behind Trinity College.

'O-kay.' I wonder if this something is good or bad. I'm not sure I can handle much more of the latter. The fact of Everwhere or, hopefully, the fantasy of it, sits between us like an elephant made of mists and moonlight.

'So, what is it?' I ask, since Leo's fallen silent. 'Tell me. You're making me nervous.'

'I'm sorry,' he says, 'It's just hard for me to . . .'

He sits on a bench by the river. I sit beside him.

Suddenly, something awful occurs to me. 'Is it that you don't . . . you don't . . .'

'What?'

I shake my head, unable to get the words out.

Leo takes my hand. 'What is it?'

'I don't know,' I mumble. 'Is it that you don't' – I drop the words into my lap – 'love me any more.'

'No, no,' Leo laughs. 'I love you, of course I love you. I can't remember a time I didn't love you, even despite myself.' He reaches up to wipe his finger under my eyes. 'Don't cry – why are you crying?'

'I – I d-didn't . . .' I shake my head. 'I – I'm fine.'

'It's not that,' Leo says, brushing his hand along my cheek. 'I mean, it's a lot of things.'

I smile, flushed with relief. If he's not leaving me then I

don't care. He can tell me what he likes. I'm getting used to it now. Another world beyond a gate. Levitating leaves. Sisters. Mists and fog and moonlight. Bring it on.

Leo takes a deep breath. 'I . . . I'm not entirely normal.'

I laugh. 'No kidding.'

'Hey,' he says. 'That's hardly— nor are you.'

I know I'm not, I could say, except I'm not quite ready yet to admit this out loud. Instead, I give him a wry smile. 'So you say.' I think of the dreams, of the flowers, of Liyana. I want to talk about it and I don't. 'So we're both abnormal. But we weren't talking about me, you were going to tell me about you.'

I see Leo steel himself. 'I'm, well, not entirely . . . human.'

'Oh, God,' I say, dearly hoping he's not about to tell me he's a vampire. I'm starting to suspect that Everwhere might be real, and I know that I'm able to do inexplicable things. But a delusional persona is a step too far. *Please don't let the man I love be a lunatic.*

Leo exhales. 'Well, technically, I am, or at least, I was a . . . star.'

I frown. As revelations go, this is an improvement on vampire. 'A star? As in the ones who shine on stage or hang in the sky?'

He glances down at the ground. 'The sky.'

'You're serious?'

He nods. 'I know I sound crazy and I know you won't be able to believe me, not yet. But I . . . In a few nights we'll go to Everwhere and then I'll be able to show you.'

I look at him. I don't believe what he's saying. But, strangely, I see that he does. My joy, my relief, evaporates. Leo loves me, yes. But he's also, quite clearly, delusional.

'Okay.' I take a deep breath. 'Right, well, I'll take that under consideration,' I say. 'So, is that everything? Any more revelations? If so, please tell me now – it's like ripping off a plaster, best done all in one go.'

I catch Leo's eye just before he glances away.

'No, that's all,' he says, then gives me a weak smile. 'I promise.'

And that's when I'm suddenly certain that he's been telling the truth – at least *his* truth – about all this, because right now I know that he's lying.

8.39 p.m. – Scarlet

Scarlet has stumbled through the day, blackening crumpets and scalding coffee, giving customers too much change or too little, asking questions then instantly forgetting the answers. She's functioned, but she's been crumbling, her thoughts always returning to the fire. The shock of this belated memory has even replaced her fears over the flood. It's exhausting, working around the damage, cleaning the dust and debris that collect during the day, but when, at last, she's tucked her grandmother in, Scarlet doesn't want to go to bed herself. She wants to sleep, but doesn't want to dream.

So, she returns to the kitchen, flicks on the kettle and roots about in the biscuit tins for a midnight feast. The café kitchen always provides comfort, even in its current state – so long as she doesn't look up. It's warm and womb-like, filled with sweet smells, even if nothing's baking, as if the walls have soaked up the scent of every cinnamon bun, every cake baked over the past fifty years.

Tearing a bite out of a cinnamon bun, Scarlet tidies the counter while waiting for the water to boil. A clutch of letters slides out from behind a chopping board where she'd stuffed it earlier. Today's post. She shuffles through the bills. She opens a letter from the insurance company informing her – though they'd already done so by email – that the surveyor will arrive to assess the property on the twenty-fourth of October at 10.30 a.m. Tomorrow. Scarlet's still thinking how she'll keep her grandmother safely upstairs during this visit, when she sees a handwritten letter, her name and address in inky script swirling across the envelope.

Reaching for a bread knife, she slices it open and pulls out a single page. It is not a letter, there is no 'dear', no 'sincerely', only a title. Scarlet scans the sentences.

It's a story.

Red Riding Hood

Once upon a time there was a girl who always dressed in red. Every day, no matter the weather, she wore a blood-red cloak her mother had made. In summer she'd sweat, but she didn't care. She often sweated in winter too since she was always hot, as if fire flowed through her veins instead of blood.

Little Red Riding Hood, as the townsfolk called her, was a timid girl. But when she wore her cloak, she felt brave. When she wore it to school, the other children didn't tease her. When she wore it to the bakers, she was offered the best price for bread. When she wore it to bed it kept nightmares at bay.

One day Red's grandmother fell ill. Red's mother made a pot of chicken soup and asked Red to take it to her grandmother's cottage in the woods. Now, Red feared the woods since it was the home of a terrible wolf who'd eaten many a stray child and a few huntsmen too. But Red's mother, who feared nothing, assured her daughter that if she stayed on the path, she'd be safe.

The woods were full of shadows and strange sounds. Red held the soup, and clutched the folds of her cloak until, at last, she had her grandmother's cottage in sight. She started to run towards it, splashing the soup and accidentally straying from the path.

'Where are you going, little girl?'

Red turned to see the wolf. She stared – at his fangs, white in the moonlight; at his dripping tongue – transfixed. The wolf leapt. Red ran. Mercifully, she escaped, but her cloak was torn to shreds.

Red's mother insisted that she visit her grandmother again the following day.

'No,' Red said. 'I can't go through the woods without my cloak.'

'You'll go at dawn, when the wolf will be sleeping,' her mother promised. 'And when you come home your grandmother will light you a torch. All wolves fear fire. He won't come near you.'

And so Red went at dawn, carrying a fresh bowl of soup. And, sure enough, the path was clear and the wolf nowhere to be seen. Red reached her grandmother's cottage safely and they spent a pleasant day together. But when dusk fell, Red begged her grandmother to let her pass the night in the cottage.

'No,' her grandmother said. 'If you hide you will be hiding for the rest of your life. You're stronger than you think. You don't need a cloak to protect you.'

Full of fear and doubt, Red went into the woods brandishing the torch, taking comfort from the heat of the flames and finding her way by their light.

When the wolf appeared, Red froze.

'Where are you going, little girl?' he said, baring his teeth and licking his lips.

Before Red could speak, the wolf pounced. This time Red remembered her grandmother's words and stood firm, wielding the flaming torch and letting out a terrible scream.

The wolf leapt back, tail between his legs. Red screamed again, baring her own teeth, releasing all her rage in another bloodcurdling howl. Seeing the wolf about to flee, Red threw the torch. It fell to the grass at the wolf's paws; a spark caught his fur and set him instantly alight.

The wolf howled as he burned. Red warmed her hands on the fire.

She was never scared to go into the woods again.

Scarlet reads the story twice. And then, as she begins it a third time, realizes that she's read it before. Or heard it. Years ago. She only wishes she knew who'd written it. She wishes too that she was even half as brave as its heroine.

11.24 p.m. – Liyana

'I'm sorry,' Kumiko says.

Liyana, lying on her stomach on the bed, looks up from her drawing of BlackBird about to meet a long-lost Peacock sister she'd never known. 'For what?'

Kumiko, lying on her back, sits up.

At the look on her girlfriend's face, Liyana feels a flash of panic. 'What is it?'

Under the duvet, Kumiko shifts slightly, almost imperceptibly inching away, then pulls her knees up to her chest.

'What?'

Kumiko traces the embroidered lilies splashed across the duvet with her fingertip.

'Koko, please. Tell me.'

Kumiko presses her chin to her knees so a curtain of silky black hair slips over her face, shutting Liyana out. 'I can't do this anymore.'

'Do what?'

'Be with you, but not be with you.'

'Wait.' Liyana puts down her pen. 'I don't—'

'Look, I understand what you're doing with this Mazimoto bloke, with this ridiculous arranged marriage nonsense. I get it, I know it's the easiest way for you to get what you want, but—'

'Hold on,' Liyana says. 'That's not fair. And, you know, he's not as bad as I thought. Maybe if you met him, maybe we—'

Kumiko throws the duvet aside, anger flaring. 'And why the hell would I want to do that? You're a fool, Ana, if you think you can marry him and still have me.'

'But, you said . . .'

Kumiko slides to the edge of the bed. 'I said that because I thought you'd come to your senses and, when you did, you'd pick me.'

'But I *do* pick you.' Liyana's voice pitches. 'Of course I pick you. I love you. I don't – I barely even like him, I'm just doing it for my aunt—'

'You say that, but who I think you're really doing it for is you.'

'No, I—' Liyana reaches to Kumiko, who pulls away. 'Please, don't go.'

'You're a coward, Ana.' Kumiko stands and walks across the room. 'You're taking the easy way out. And, frankly, I can't be with someone I don't respect.'

'Wait, Koko,' Liyana says. 'Please, don't leave.'

Kumiko turns. 'You took the Tesco job, did you? You told that posh boy you won't marry him?'

'I did a trial shift,' Liyana objects. 'I, I'm supposed to call the manager this week to—'

'And the posh boy?'

'Well, um, I' – Liyana falters as Kumiko glowers at her – 'but n-no. No, not yet. But I, I . . .' Liyana bites her lip. 'I . . .'

'No,' Kumiko says, slipping her T-shirt over her head. 'I didn't think so.'

23rd October – 9 days . . .

11.59 p.m. – Bea

'Are you ready, *niña*?'

'Yes,' Bea says, realizing in the wake of her *mamá*'s silence that this is the first time she's spoken with such certainty, without a trace of doubt.

'*Bueno*,' Cleo says. 'Because it's nearly here.'

'I know. Nine days. It's fine.'

'Don't get complacent. Your sisters are far stronger than mine. And you'll be outnumbered three to one.'

Bea waits. 'I might not have to do anything else. Not if they choose the dark.'

'Yes,' her mother admits. 'But you should ready yourself, *niña*, in case.'

Bea says nothing.

'In a fight,' Cleo continues, 'I don't think you'll have too much trouble with Liyana. But Scarlet and Goldie are a different matter.'

'True, she was the most . . .' Bea draws up from her memories. 'Scarlet was the strongest, Goldie was by far the fiercest and Ana was . . . nice, struggling to free herself from her *mamá*'s grasp.'

'But then rather uncorked by her death,' Cleo says. 'It knocked the fury and the fight right out of her.'

'How do you know that?'

Cleo ignores the question. 'Just because my death wouldn't take the spring out of your step, *niña*, doesn't mean other daughters are quite so cold.'

Bea thinks again of those Sunday afternoon visits, of the birthdays and Christmases spent with strangers after her *abuela* died. 'You've hardly been a paragon of maternal devotion, *Mamá*.'

Cleo ignores this remark too. 'Isisa Chiweshe was a nauseating example of motherhood. Those tiger *mamás* living their ambitions through their daughters. It's pathetic.'

Bea frowns. 'How did you know Ana's *mamá*?'

'I didn't, not personally,' Cleo says with a shrug. 'I watched her, heard her thoughts, felt her heart, no more than that.'

'*¿Cómo?*'

'When you stand in the shadows you can see into the light,' Cleo says. 'But when you stand in the light you can't see what's hiding in the dark.'

'*¿Que?*' Bea opens her eyes. '*Mamá?*'

But she's alone. Dreaming? Surely not – the conversation was as vivid as if her *mamá* were sitting on the bed right beside her. Words and sentences return. A plan. What is it? Scarlet. Goldie. Ana. Who are they?

24th October – 8 days . . .

6.33 a.m. – Goldie

I'm shaking when I wake, adrenaline in my blood, a scream on the air. I shut my mouth and pray I didn't wake Teddy. I realize as I settle that my screams weren't fuelled by fear, but courage.

The tendrils of the dream unwind . . . I wasn't a victim, but a warrior. I was Joan of Arc, Artemisia, Boudicca. I was going into battle with breasts bare, spear held aloft. Although I'd stood not on a battlefield but in a forest – one unlike any forest I'd ever seen before. For a start, all the trees were white. And their leaves blew in the winds but also scattered from the sky. Rain fell too and the air was so heavy with fog that the trees were barely visible in the moonlight.

Everwhere.

I wasn't alone. I stood in a glade with three girls: Ana and our two sisters. I knew their names then, though I can't recall them now. I spoke with them in the dream. We stood in a clearing looking up at the leaves falling with the rain. We were meeting after a long time apart. We love this place, we've always loved it. It is our home. But something was wrong.

I reached for my sisters' hands, when into the glade walked a man. He looked at us and smiled. Who was he? Why were we there?

Then I remembered. He was our father. And we were there to fight him.

I bury my face in Leo's bare chest and he, ever awake, wraps an arm around me. I don't speak – I don't want to open a discussion of fantastical worlds – I just breathe him in. I feel his solidity, his surety, and use it to calm my heart. Until I feel less like a clutch of leaves being whipped up by the wind, and more like the ancient and immovable rock of Leo. I think of his claim to be a fallen star. Energetically, it describes him perfectly. He certainly feels as permanent and timeless and ethereal as a thing that's been in the cosmos for a million years. And that dream . . .

I can't help but wonder if, given everything else, that's quite so impossible after all. Is it conceivable he's been telling the truth? The dream felt so real, as real as this man beside me now. Despite my doubts, I feel the seed of hope being sown in my thoughts – desperate and insistent as a weed.

'I had a nightmare,' I whisper, not minding that he can't hear me. I wish I could sleep with him every night of my life. In which case, I'll have to introduce him to Teddy. I take a deep breath. My dream-father was terrifying. I wish I could unsee his face. Yet, even as I shiver at the recollection, I feel comforted now, as if nothing too bad could happen with Leo here. The simple fact of his existence in the world seems to afford protection. He has a great solidity about him, a sort of ancient strength, as if he's been shaped from stone and steel.

I glance up at the kitchen clock and nudge him. 'You've got to go, Teddy will be up soon.'

From under the covers, Leo groans.

'Sorry,' I hiss. 'But he's a hideously early riser.'

'Can't I stay?' Leo mumbles, reaching around my waist and holding me tight. 'Please.'

'I wish you could, but it'd scare the daylights out of Ted if he woke up to find a stranger in his sister's bed.'

'All right.' Leo releases me with a sigh. 'I suppose we wouldn't want that. So, when will I be allowed to . . . ?'

'What?'

'Nothing,' he says, slipping out from under the duvet, reaching for his jumper. 'Sometimes I think we have forever, that's all.'

I feel a sudden shot of panic. 'But we do, don't we? I mean, why wouldn't we?'

Leo is silent, pulling his jumper over his head. 'No one has forever.'

I can't argue with that, but still it seems that he's saying less than he's suggesting. I want to ask him, press him, but I sense he'd either evade or push back and I don't want to risk waking Teddy.

'Well, I suppose you're right. But I hope we have longer than most.'

6.43 a.m. – Bea

After Vali's death, sleep had been an escape. But now Bea doesn't want to sleep, not with her dreams and the sense of foreboding left in their wake. She wants to be elsewhere. She wants to be gliding through the sky, drifting on updraughts of thermal air. But she can't go to Dr Finch, not now. Not today. So, Bea shuns the bed to sit on the bathroom floor, chin pressed to her knees. Now she picks up a razor blade and carefully draws it across her inner thigh.

Bea bites her teeth together, but the stinging pain still fills her eyes.

'Don't cry,' she hisses. 'Don't you fucking cry.'

Bea watches the trickle of blood slide slowly down her leg. She thinks of flying again and hopes that's what death will be like – that she'll be nothing but breath and air. When the blood pools at her ankle, Bea begins again.

10.33 a.m. – Scarlet

The surveyor sent by the insurance company is perfectly polite, if curt – dismissing Scarlet's offer of tea and cinnamon buns before she's even finished her sentence. He's exceedingly thorough too, investigating every remnant of the ceiling that has crashed to the floor – as instructed, she's been keeping the rubble in a bin by the back gate – along with every inch of the gaping hole it has left behind.

While he's upstairs, scouring the bathroom with a magnifying glass, or so Scarlet imagines, she paces the kitchen floor and prays.

10.13 p.m. – Goldie

When I dream again it's not of Ma or Leo, but of Liyana. Ana. My sister. We are flying, above trees, among the stars. We're connected and we aren't. We're together and we're separate. We share the same thoughts, breath, heartbeat, soul. The stars imprint their shadows upon us, marking our skin with an impression of the night sky.

Where are we? We've been here. A long, long time ago.

Eventually, we tire and begin to float down through the trees to settle on the ground. In a glade, we see two young women looking up at us. I'm sure I know them. I try to make out their faces but I can't.

Then I wake.

As the tendrils of sleep and memory – this time I'm certain it was both – slip away, I think that Leo is telling the truth after all. A weed of faith pushes up through the soil. I want to call Leo, interrogate him. I reach for my phone, scrolling to his number. My finger hovers. An earthquake rumbles beneath me, the tectonic plates shifting and tearing apart, the cracks opening up. But I'm still clutching on, postponing the moment of falling until I can't anymore. So, instead of calling Leo, I call my sister.

10.59 p.m. – Goldie & Liyana

Liyana sighs.

'What?'

'I don't know. I've just been feeling weird lately.'

'How?' The weed of faith sprouts a fresh leaf. I'm not the only one.

'I don't – I keep having this feeling that something's going to happen,' Liyana says. 'Like a premonition.'

'Something bad?'

'I don't know. Yeah, I think so.'

'I've been having strange dreams,' I admit. 'Only, they feel more like memories than dreams.'

'About what?'

'About being in a place, another world sort of place. With you and two other girls. And the really weird bit is that I've been to this place many times before and the girls, they're our—'

'—Sisters.'

In my surprise, I lose my grip on the phone. It slips out of my hand and falls behind the sofa. I scramble to get it back. 'Hey, Ana – sorry, are you still there?'

'Yeah, you all right?'

I nod, forgetting she can't see me. 'Yeah, yeah. But how did you know – about the sisters?'

'Maybe we're having the same sort of dreams,' Liyana says. 'But mine are more like, I don't know . . . visions. Did you see anything that could help us find them?'

'No. Because we're not here, we're somewhere else.' I pause, feeling myself about to fall into the abyss. Though perhaps I'm no longer falling but jumping. 'I don't know, I – I think they live here.'

'In Cambridge?'

I nod, forgetting again. 'The redhead works in a café on King's Parade – I even asked her for a job a few weeks ago, but I'd not seen her before that . . . And I saw the other once in the hotel, but I've not seen her again.'

'So, why don't you go back to the café? If you know where she is, you could find her. You could tell her tomorrow.'

The thought of it makes me want to hide under the sofa, to scramble back up to solid, steady ground. 'And what would I say? That . . . what? "I saw you in my dreams"?'

'It's what I said to you.'

'True. And I stuck a kitchen knife in your face.'

'Yeah. Good point.'

We both laugh then, a little too loud and a little too long, perhaps because we want to forget our fears and pretend, if only for a moment, that we're simply two ordinary sisters chatting on the phone at night about silly, inconsequential things.

11.43 p.m. – Liyana

'What's wrong, *vinye*?'

'Nothing,' Liyana says. *Except a longing to be gliding along the bottom of the swimming pool right now.*

Her aunt nods at the television. 'You're not watching it.'

Liyana shrugs. 'I know it by heart.'

'Bloody hell, Ana.' Her aunt sighs. 'If that's a comment on the state of the youth of today, then we are in a sorry state.'

'What?'

'When I was young we learned Du Bois and Ama Ata Aidoo by heart,' Nya says. 'Not *Wonder Woman*.'

'This is a modern classic, *Nɔḍi,*' Liyana says, without looking up. 'It's the greatest female empowerment film ever made.'

'Oh, come on. *Thelma & Louise* is arguably the greatest—'

'Superheroes,' Liyana interrupts, glad to be arguing about something utterly meaningless for once. 'All we had before that was Catwoman and Elektra, but they weren't a patch on this.'

Aunt Nya sighs and Liyana falls back into her thoughts, of Kumiko, Mazmo, Goldie, dreams of her sisters, and the stories her Tarot cards have been telling. Onscreen, as Wonder Woman hurls a tank at Ares, her nemesis and half-brother, Liyana tries to ignore her own feeling of foreboding rising like an ocean wave.

25th October –
7 days . . .

12.33 p.m. – Goldie

'Hey!'

I turn to see Leo waving across the hotel foyer.

'Your hair,' he says, even before reaching me.

My hand goes up to my shorn locks. I'd forgotten what I'd done.

'Do you like it?'

'Of course.' Leo smiles. 'I'd like it no matter what – if you were bald as a coot, I'd still think you the prettiest girl in the world.'

I frown. 'It's not that short.'

'Long, short, I don't care.' Leo says.

I tug at a stray curl, feeling self-conscious. I wait for Leo to ask why I cut it.

'Do you fancy lunch?' he says. 'And don't worry, I know it can't be here. Operation Scandalous Love Affair Between Management and Staff is still classified to NXF Level Five. You've nothing to worry about there. George, the world's most incompetent night porter, may have caught sight of something on Sunday, but I stuck pins under his fingernails until he promised not to squeal.'

'I'm not being silly about this,' I say. 'At the Fitz everyone knew everyone's business, what Cassie did for Garrick to—'

'You don't need to worry about that.' Leo's smiling. 'No one's going to think you're trying to sleep your way—'

'I just don't want everyone to hate me.'

'You've got to let that go,' he says, all of a sudden

serious. 'You'll never be strong enough to fight if you give a shit about stuff like that.'

'Stop it,' I hiss. Last night I found a ledge with Liyana – a narrow one, but a ledge nevertheless – and now he's trying to shove me over the side. 'Stop banging on about all that – you sound like a lunatic.'

Leo draws a breath, as if he's holding back, as if he wants to say more but knows he shouldn't. 'You're right. I'm sorry. Look, let me take you to lunch. How about The Ivy? You can order every drink on the menu – what d'you say?'

'I'd love to. But I can't, I've already got plans.'

Leo frowns. 'You've got a date?'

'Yeah, that's right. I've got a hot date with George the Porter. I've got a thing for bald men with beards. We'd make a good match now, don't you think?'

I smile. Leo doesn't.

'She's just a . . . friend, all right? I'm meeting a friend at Fitzbillies.'

'Right. I wasn't, it doesn't . . .' Leo shakes his head. 'Anyway, it's fine, I've got a load of paperwork to catch up on anyway – I've still got the report on that dead guy in room forty-seven to write – and I really should be studying too, so it's all good.'

I know he's lying, but I let it go. I nod and he glances about, checking no one's there to see us, then gives me a quick kiss on the cheek and turns to walk away. I watch him go and wonder why I'm still keeping Ana a secret from Leo and Leo a secret from Ana. Perhaps I'm simply being selfish, not wanting to share either of them yet. Or perhaps it's something deeper, something darker. I don't know.

3.33 p.m. – Liyana & Goldie

'Bloody hell,' Liyana squeals as soon as she sees me, barrelling into Fitzbillies and crash-landing at my table. 'What the hell did you do to your hair?'

I feel my cheeks flush. Unlike Leo, my sister clearly cares that I've cut off most of my hair. 'I thought—'

'But why?' Liyana interrupts. 'Why would you?'

I glance down at my Chelsea bun, poking it with my fork.

'Oh, no,' Liyana says. 'Wait, you didn't?'

I nod, still not meeting her eye.

'Because of the story.' Liyana laughs. 'You cut off your hair because of my story!'

'Are you going to sit?' I say, wishing she'd drop it. 'I got you a Chelsea bun.'

Liyana sits, still grinning. 'I still can't believe you did it.' She tears into the bun with her fingers, ignoring the fork. 'Hey, this is delicious.'

'Yeah,' I say. 'And only about three thousand calories a piece.'

Liyana chews. 'And worth every one. Can we go to the Fitzwilliam Museum?'

'Of course.' I curl my hands around my teacup. 'It's just down the road. I took my brother to a Vermeer exhibition once, but I've not been back since. I suppose I should've, since I worked at the hotel across the street.'

'Why didn't you?' Liyana asks, as if she can't imagine a reason to justify such neglect of art.

I shrug. 'Long shifts, never had the time.' It's a half-lie, but I'm not about to tell my posh sister that I felt too embarrassed, like I didn't fit in.

'We could go to the Quentin Blake exhibition now,' Liyana says, catching herself staring at my short hair and returning to devouring the Chelsea bun. 'I loved his illustrations as a kid. I had to read Roald Dahl in secret, though; *Dadá* – Mummy – banned all his books.'

'Why?'

'She thought they encouraged rebellion against parental authority.'

'Ma told me they were too scary.' I smile. 'I think she didn't want me getting ideas, in case I made a bid for freedom in a giant peach.'

'Over-protective?'

I nod. 'Massively. I spent my childhood planning my escape. But, when she died . . . I still . . .'

Liyana's dark eyes don't change but still I feel the shift, the sudden weight of her sadness as if it were my own.

'Yeah,' she says. 'Me too.'

'I suppose having the nest ripped away too soon means we'll always long for it more.' I take a gulp of tea. 'Did you bring my comic?'

'It's not finished,' Liyana says, reaching under the table to rummage in her bag. She hands me two folders. 'That's yours and another – a few illustrations from a graphic novel I've been working on for a couple of years and a fairy tale – with yours, I'm thinking I might create a series.'

'Fantastic.' Setting down my cup as far from the folders as possible, I open the one that isn't mine. As Liyana scrapes the last of the syrup off her plate I gaze at the first page, at an image so striking I stare at it for a long time: a falling woman transforming into a bird that shrieks above a dark forest fading into the distance. Tentatively, I turn the pages to see image upon image: pen-and-ink drawings more visually masterful and emotionally arresting than anything I've ever seen before. 'These are, they're . . .' I trail off, failing to find adequate words. 'They're . . . Wow.'

Liyana licks her fingers. 'Thanks. And they're not even yours.' She nods at the other folder. I open it with reverence, flicking slowly through the pages to see a woman with my face and a peacock's wings. 'It's absolutely . . . stupendous,' I say, wishing I had more elegant, descriptive phrases to hand, but in the face of such beauty I'm inarticulate. 'You drew it all yourself?'

'I've been doing it for years.' Liyana shrugs. 'It's no big deal.'

'It is. It's massively amazing. You should be doing this professionally, you should publish them.'

A flicker of disappointment passes over her face. I want to ask why, but don't. Liyana closes the folders, so the brilliant images are eclipsed and the table is dull and ordinary once more. I gaze at her hands, imagining her long, strong fingers gripping a pen with such poise and purpose. If only I could write half as well as she can draw . . .

'I've got a boyfriend,' I blurt out. I hadn't been intending to tell her yet, but suddenly I need to give her something. If not a comic book, then a secret. I press my fingers to my bare neck.

'Oh?'

'He's called Leo. He's . . .' I'm annoyed by my inability to adequately describe him. 'He's, um, pretty fucking spectacular.'

Liyana smiles. 'I'd like to meet him.'

'Yeah, that'd be . . .'

'I've got a girlfriend.' Liyana plucks at the edge of the fairy tale folder, creasing the paper. 'She's . . . she's pretty fucking spectacular too, but . . .'

'But?'

Liyana doesn't meet my eye. 'It's . . . complicated right now.'

'Ah. I'm sorry to—'

Liyana stands. 'Let's go to the Fitzwilliam.'

I don't want to go yet. I want to stay and read my story,

to gaze at my pictures until I can see them with my eyes closed. Reluctantly, I stand, lifting the folders and pressing them to my chest. But my hold isn't tight enough and the pages slip from their bindings, fluttering free across the floor. The door opens and a sudden gust carries them under tables and chairs.

'Shit!'

I scramble about on the floor of Fitzbillies to save the precious pictures before they're crushed beneath muddy shoes or sloshed with coffee. I'd lie down and be trampled upon sooner than allow damage to the best gift I've ever been given.

3.54 p.m. – Bea

Moments later, Bea steps into Fitzbillies. She isn't sure why she's there since it's not a café she usually frequents. She always went to Indigo with Vali. But, walking along Trumpington Street, she feels a sudden desire for one of their iconic Chelsea buns.

It's only when she's ordered, paid and sat at a table by the window that she sees it. Bending down, Bea reaches under the table and picks up a piece of paper. Emblazoned across it is a black-and-white illustration of a woman flying through a dark sky, transforming into a bird. Bea stares at the bird, at its screeching mouth, sharp talons and enormous black wings opening as it rises over a nocturnal landscape of rivers and valleys, over the tops of towering trees, soaring through a midnight sky as if reaching for the moon. A blackbird.

Studying the picture, Bea thinks of how she feels gliding above the Earth in a plane: fearless, invincible, free. She's so absorbed in the picture, so captivated, that she doesn't see the waitress set down the plate. The illustration is so other-worldly, yet so real. Who could have drawn such a thing? Bea looks for a name, a signature, but finds only T.L.M.C. scribbled in the bottom right-hand corner. She traces the lines of the wings, the intricately penned feathers. Bea is so mesmerized that she doesn't feel the tears on her cheeks.

4.14 p.m. – Scarlet

On her way to the newsagent, Scarlet pauses at the palatial wall of St Catherine's College. Every autumn the thousand leaves clothing the bricks turn every shade of red, amber and yellow. When caught by a gust of wind, they flicker: a thousand flames licking the wall like an insatiable fire. During the months of September and October, even into November, Scarlet pays a visit to the wall at least once a day. It's her pilgrimage – one that takes, from the No. 33 Café, all of three minutes to make. Usually, the sight offers her spiritual succour. Today, it's the altar at which she must bow her head and atone for her sins.

Her dream rises. The spark. The fire. Her mother's screams. This last she still can't remember, though it must have happened. And all at her hand. *Murderer.* Before she cries again, Scarlet hurries on.

Passing Fitzbillies, she slows. In the window sits a girl gazing at a picture. Scarlet stops. Pretending to be contemplating the trays of warm, sticky Chelsea buns, she gazes at the girl, who's silently crying.

Scarlet is struck by the strongest sense of déjà vu. She's met this girl before, she's certain. But it's more than that – a feeling she doesn't have words for. She knows this stranger intimately as she might a sister, if she had one. But how can someone be a stranger and a sister all at once? Although, Scarlet thinks, her relationship with her grandma is like that nowadays.

Esme!

She's got to get back. She's left her grandmother alone for too long now. She only popped out for a pint of milk to make blueberry drop scones. With one last glance at the girl, and forgetting the milk, Scarlet runs all the way back to the café.

5.05 p.m. – Leo

In the Faculty of Law building Leo sits in Seminar Room B16, trying to concentrate on whatever Dr Hussein is wittering on about, something to do with the Law of Tort. But it's no use. Leo can't think why he even bothered turning up in the first place. He's been missing so many of his lectures lately – handing in miserable essays to supervisions he's often late for – that he'll surely get summoned by his Director of Studies soon. But if he's sent down it's of no importance. It's likely he'll be dead in a week anyway, so what the hell does it matter?

All Leo cares about now is keeping Goldie alive. Instead of applying his mind to the complexities of tort law, he needs to be solving the problem of convincing Goldie that he's not insane, while at the same time not terrifying her into a nervous breakdown. He needs to find a balance between convincing and careful.

'. . . so, if one uses the case of Beckett vs Hargreaves as an example of this, one must consider . . .'

Leo slams his textbook shut, stands, snatches up his bag and strides out of Seminar Room B16. Thirty startled students turn to watch him go.

6.01 p.m. – Goldie

When I get home that night I decide to try again, this time with a daisy I picked in the park instead of a stolen rose. I tell myself I won't be humiliated by ridiculous hopes, but my spirits are buoyed from seeing my sister and reading the beginnings of my very own graphic novel. Seeing myself as a superhero has given me the fanciful, but not altogether improbable notion that I might have certain supernatural powers after all.

As I set the daisy on the kitchen counter, glancing at my juniper tree, a memory rises, just out of reach: *Juniper bare and bereft of leaves, my hands closing like an oven, a faded heartbeat twitching back to life* . . . I feel a surge of anticipation, promise, nerve . . . I place my hands flat on either side of the flower and focus on it. This time I'm wondering how it feels to be this flower – the breath of the breeze on its petals, the warmth of the sun on its leaves. I imagine Leo is beside me, Ana too. Then I think of Ma. And, all at once, I feel that this was something she could do: small magic tricks, though perhaps she didn't know it.

As they cheer me on, the thought of lifting something, especially something as insubstantial as a daisy, doesn't seem quite so fantastical. No more so than atoms or electricity or radio waves. After all, I think, is telekinesis or telepathy any more extraordinary than email or instant messaging? I bring my forefingers and thumbs together so that the daisy sits in the space between. I stare at the little flower.

Nothing. I close my eyes.

Rise.

I peek. Nothing.

'Rise.'

I peek again. Nothing. I open my eyes.

'Rise!'

And it does. Just a fraction. A twitch in the air. A hair's breadth off the counter. I'm certain. Almost.

8.38 p.m. – Bea

DR JONATHON FINCH
LOGIC AND LANGUAGE

Bea barely glances at the plaque, twisting the handle and pushing so hard that the door slams back into the bookcase against the wall. Striding into the room, she drops her bag, stripping off her coat and clothes as she crosses the floor – until she's only wearing her skirt, riding high on her thighs.

Dr Finch, pen still in hand, stares at her. 'What the hell are you doing?'

Saying nothing, Bea lifts herself onto his desk, displacing student essays that drift to the floor like the leaves of Everwhere.

'No, wait—'

'Leave them.' Bea slides into his lap, wriggling her skirt up her thighs.

'I don't understand,' Dr Finch says, fumbling with his zip. 'Last time, you said it wouldn't happen—'

Bea pulls back. 'You want me to go?'

'No,' he says, freeing himself. 'No, no, no.'

'Right,' Bea says. 'So, shut the fuck up.'

Dr Finch frowns, opening his mouth to speak but letting out a long sigh as Bea shifts her hips and slides on to him.

'Oh, good God . . .'

'I told you. Shut up.' Bea pushes him deeper as he moans louder. She pulls back her hand and, just as he closes his eyes, slaps him hard.

Dr Finch's eyes snap open. 'What the fuck did you—?'

Bea slaps him again.

'Stop!'

She pulls back her hand a third time. 'Make me.'

Dr Finch seizes hold of Bea's wrist, then locks his

fingers around both her hands and holds her tight. Bea arches her back, twists her hips and pulls herself free.

'Wait.' Dr Finch lets her go. 'Please, don't—'

Bea turns, pressing her body, her breasts, her face into his desk.

'Oh, God.' He grasps her buttocks with both hands and slides into her again. 'Oh, good God.'

'Slap me,' Bea whispers. 'Slap me back.'

'What? No.'

'Do it,' she snaps. He hesitates. 'Do it, you spineless—'

The slap stings her skin and clouds her sight. She bites her lip, leeching the blood. 'Again.'

'Are you—?'

'Again! *Otra vez*.' Bea bites down harder and tastes blood on her tongue. 'Again!' Pain shoots up her spine.

'Oh God, oh God, oh . . .'

'Again.'

But he shudders and stops, dropping his cheek to her shoulder blade, hot quick breaths on her skin. Bea twists away, pushing him off, sliding her body back around the desk.

'Wait,' he says. 'Where are you going? Don't you want—?'

'No.' She steps away from him, pulling her skirt back into place, bending down to pick up her discarded jumper from the rug. 'This isn't happening again.'

'Oh, come on,' Dr Finch says, his flaccid penis still hanging through his trousers. 'You can't tell me that wasn't fucking fantastic sex.'

'Zip yourself up.'

He glances down. 'Bugger that. Give me ten minutes. I'll do better next time.'

Ignoring him, Bea crosses the room. Already she feels the dribble of sperm sliding down her thigh. She needs a shower. Now. She needs to wash every trace of him away. She pulls on her coat, her boots; snatches up her bag.

'Wait.'

Bea looks up to his hand pressing against the door. She frowns at him – how had he crossed the room so silently, so quickly? 'Move.'

He smiles. 'You can't fuck me like that then tell me it'll never happen again.'

Bea grabs his wrist. She's half his size but, right now, her fury makes her twice as strong. She thinks of Vali – will there ever be a time she doesn't think of him? If she could do that to an innocent man, a man she loved, imagine what she could do to one she doesn't even like.

'I can do whatever I want,' Bea snaps. 'Now, get the hell out of my way.'

Less than a decade ago

Goldie

He did it. I knew he would. My bastard stepfather flushed Juniper down the toilet. At least, he tried. *Moron*. He could have hacked her up, even burned her. But the idiot thought drowning would be the most effective method of extinction. I suppose I should be grateful for his stupidity. He was jealous, jealous that he couldn't do anything creative. Couldn't cook, couldn't draw, couldn't tend to a tree. He never created, only destroyed. Just as he was destroying me, little by little, every night. I felt his hands on me, inside me, even when he wasn't within touching distance. I felt his gaze on me even when he wasn't there.

I found Juniper one morning, plucked from her ceramic pot, roots stripped of soil, branches stripped of leaves, drowned. I plunged my hand into the water and pulled out my little tree. I held her, dripping, in my hands and my tears only made her more wet. I'd never held a dead thing before. Not even an insect. It was strange, not to feel the pulse of life in her, just the shock between the warm rhythm of my veins and the cold stillness of hers. I locked the bathroom door and sat on the edge of the bath. I held her for a long time.

As I held her my hands grew warmer. I closed them over her, like an oven. I don't know how long I sat there, but after a while I started to feel a shift, a jolt. As if the faint thump-thump of her faded heartbeat was twitching back to life. I frowned at this impossible thing. But then, after my experiences in Everwhere, my parameters of possible had fallen off the edge of the earth.

I opened my cupped hands to peer down at my tree. She didn't look different, still bare and bereft of leaves and, it seemed, life. But she felt different, as if she were gasping for breath after breaking through ocean waves.

She was reaching for life and I reached back. I touched every branch, every root; I whispered to her, breathing fresh carbon dioxide into her air. To make her strong again. Eventually, I got up to search for a new pot in which to plant my little tree. I found an old margarine tub under the sink being used to catch a drip. I took Juniper to the park at the end of the road, dug up handfuls of soil and replanted her.

Three days later my tree's first new leaf started to sprout, a bud of bright, insistent green.

Two days after that, the kitchen flooded. Ma had a fit.

Liyana

Lately, Liyana had been arguing with her mother. They'd started fighting over the littlest things. Liyana said she was old enough to walk to school alone; Isisa said not until she turned thirteen. Liyana wanted to ditch ballet and take up kick-boxing, her mother declined to pay for the classes. Liyana refused to hold her mother's hand when they crossed the road, so Isisa seized her wrist instead, clutching so tight that Liyana's skin was mottled for hours afterwards. Last week, Liyana had demanded a lock on her bedroom door; Isisa insisted that the only lockable door would be the bathroom.

One night, sick of enduring the torture of hair-straightening any longer, Liyana shut herself in the bathroom and cut her hair with the kitchen scissors, chopping off every controlled curl until they lay on the tiles like decapitated snakes. For a moment Liyana thought of those myths she'd learned in school – of Medusa and Samson – and was shot through with regret. Had she just cut off the source of her power? But, when Liyana caught sight of herself in the mirror, she dismissed the thought. Her hair was short, shorn to the scalp in places, with frizzy tufts sticking up like a drunkenly mown lawn. Her mother would certainly kill her but, for once, Liyana didn't care. It looked completely and utterly splendid.

For good measure, Liyana found the bottle of *Dr Miracle's No-Lye Relaxer* in the cabinet and tipped it down the sink, grinning as the stinging white gloop glugged down the plughole. She would pay for this, but it would be worth every smack.

Bea

'Kick-ass hair,' Bea said. 'I bet your *mamá* had a stroke.'

Liyana walked into the glade, self-consciously tweaking the uneven tufts of her hair.

'*Mamá* would've slapped me so hard,' Bea said, grinning as if this were a fate devoutly to be wished for. 'She'd have set fire to the fucking house.' We all looked shocked and she laughed, the sound disturbing the air like a crow. 'You're all so sensitive, I'm going to have to toughen you up' – she paused, looking to each of us in turn – 'before it's too late.'

Her words drifted into the air, parting the fog, waiting to catch our attention. I wanted to ask what she meant, but waited for one of my sisters to ask instead. I knew I wouldn't have to wait long.

'Before what's too late?' Liyana asked, snapping the bait like a fish.

But Bea just smiled her enigmatic smile.

Scarlet slid down from her tree branch. 'Let's do something fun,' she said. 'We can do anything we want here. Why waste our time chatting, or letting her' – she nodded at Bea – 'tease us with silly riddles?'

'I like chatting,' Liyana said. 'It's nice to get to know each other. None of us have sisters in the real world so—'

'This *is* the real world,' Scarlet informed Liyana, then turned back to Bea. 'Now, stop being so annoying and tell us what you're talking about.'

'The choice.' Bea sighed, as if under duress, as if she hadn't been the one to bring up the topic in the first place. 'If you don't choose dark you'll need to be strong to survive.'

'Survive what?' Liyana snapped at the bait again.

'If you don't choose in his favour then he'll send his soldiers to kill you, or he'll do it himself. Depends how special you are,' Bea said. 'So, you'll have to hone your skills, practise, practise until you stand a fighting chance of survival.'

She sounded like she was quoting someone, probably her ma.

'You never said it was a life-or-death choice,' I said.

'I thought it was obvious,' Bea said. 'You didn't expect him to let you live, did you? Just like that. He wants to father an army to support him, not a force to oppose him.'

'I suppose your mother—'

'What if we decided to kill *him*,' Scarlet interrupted. 'Then what—?'

Liyana was wide-eyed. 'We can't do that!'

'It's self-defence, they can't send you to prison for that,' Scarlet said. 'Anyway, we didn't ask to be born like this, did we? It's not our fault, it's his.'

I wanted to echo my sister, but I wasn't quite so brave. Liyana stared at her, incredulous. Bea rolled her eyes.

'You're not that special,' she said, going into arrogant

adult mode again. 'None of us are. He's mightier than any of us will ever be, can ever be. He's like . . . an ancient oak tree and we're . . . seedlings – you wouldn't stand a chance, no matter how strong you got.'

'Why does your mummy tell you everything,' Liyana said, 'and ours tell us nothing?'

Bea sighed, assuming the stance of a schoolteacher. 'I told you. It's because they don't know. They aren't pure Grimms, are they? If they go to Everwhere in their dreams, they won't think it was real.'

'My mother knows something,' Scarlet said, almost to herself. 'She looks at me sometimes, like she's suspicious or scared.'

'She's probably got a bit of Grimm blood then,' Bea said. 'Enough to go through the gates anyway.'

'I don't think Mummy knows anything,' Liyana said.

A few weeks ago I'd have said Ma knew nothing either, but I was starting to wonder. It'd make sense then, why she holds me so tight.

'What if, when it's time to choose, we hide somewhere and don't come back here?' Liyana twisted the spikes of her shorn hair. 'Then we won't have to be in an army or die or try to kill anyone either.'

Silence dropped over the glade, as if all sound had been smothered by a dense and sudden fog. This suggestion of never returning was so shocking, so untenable that no one sanctified it with a response. Death, surely, was better than desertion.

'You can't run away,' Bea said, at last. 'You'll keep coming back, even if only in your dreams, even if you don't want to.'

'Why?' Liyana and Scarlet asked in unison.

'The need to return has been inside us since we were conceived,' Bea said, pausing to recall her ma's words. 'It's a product of the bright-white wishing and black-edged desire. We're like those fish . . . the salmon that always return to the place they were born.'

'So, how will *you* survive the Choosing?' Scarlet asked. 'If you won't be strong enough to defeat him.'

A look passed across Bea's face that I couldn't quite decipher. When she spoke every trace of teasing was gone.

'You don't have to defeat him,' she said, 'if you're going to go dark.'

26th October –
6 days . . .

3.33 a.m. – Goldie & Liyana

'She still loves you,' I say, cradling the phone between my ear and shoulder, whispering so Teddy won't hear. At last, Liyana's told me everything: her mother, the Tarot, Kumiko, the Slade, Aunt Nya, Mazmo, Tesco – at least I think it's everything.

'I'm not sure,' Liyana says.

'I am.' And I am. Even though I've never met Kumiko, I'm still certain. 'Love doesn't suddenly stop, Ana,' I say, as if I'm the sudden expert on the subject. 'You need to win her back.'

I hear Liyana sigh.

'I think she's right about your aunt though.' I'm more tentative now. I want to say something about Mazmo and art school, about having to work hard for things and not being ashamed to do shitty jobs, but I'm not sure how to put it without causing offence. So I stick to the safer subject. 'You can't give up everything for her.'

'I know,' Liyana whispers. 'I know, it's just so hard. She's been, she's done . . . She's . . .'

'She'll be okay,' I say. 'She doesn't need you to save her.'

I hear Liyana sigh again. 'Perhaps.'

'And as for Kumiko, you have to . . . Don't give up.'

'What do you mean?'

'I don't know.' I try to think of an example. 'Show her what she means to you. Walk naked through Trafalgar Square, climb up Big Ben—'

Liyana laughs. 'I can't do that.'

'Do you love her?'

'Of course.'

'If you love her, you'll do anything.'

Liyana's silent.

'Ana . . .' I hesitate.

'Yeah?'

'For what it's worth, I think Kumiko might be right about Mazmo too.'

Liyana's so quiet that I start to wonder if she might have hung up on me.

'But . . .' I try to find a less painful subject. 'I, um, would you – would you give me a Tarot reading?'

Still, Liyana says nothing and I wonder if I've said the wrong thing, again.

'Ana?'

'Sorry,' she says. 'I . . . But yeah, I guess so.'

'Are you sure?'

'Sure,' she says. 'I don't mind, I've just never done it for anyone else before. I don't know if it'll work.'

'If you could try, that'd be amazing,' I say. 'I've – there are things I'm sensing, but I've got no proof.'

'But the cards won't give you that,' Liyana says. 'My readings are more like stories, telling you what's happening and what might happen . . . But, honestly, lately I've not been able to make much sense of them myself.'

Not wanting to pressure her, I say nothing.

'Hold on,' Liyana says. 'I'll get the cards.'

I wait until she picks up the phone again.

'You still there?'

'Yeah.'

'Right, I'll put you on speaker while I shuffle and deal.'

While she cuts the cards, Liyana focuses on Goldie, asking the Tarot to tell a story about her sister. She shuffles longer than usual, trying to impress the cards with Goldie's energy instead of her own, before laying them down. The Ten of Swords: a blue-haired girl faints beneath the points of ten hovering swords, oblivious to the circling butterflies or the glittering stars above. *An ending, entering into darkness.* The Tower: a growling stone beast guards the crumbling tower, flames roaring from the windows, licking the sky. Blown by a ferocious grey wind, vultures soar above the people tumbling to their deaths. *Loss, sudden change, devastation.* The Nine of Swords: a howling phantom haunts a terrified woman who vainly wields six swords in defence. The three remaining blades pierce her dress, pinning her to the ground. *Fear, doubt, psychic dreams.* The Seven of Swords: a yellow-cloaked man courted by snakes points four swords at an unseen assailant who brandishes the other three. *Betrayal, deceit, mistrust.* The Three of Pentacles: three triumphant witches gather in a lush garden casting shape-shifting enchantments while red-eyed rabbits play at their feet. *Teamwork, unity, sisterhood.*

Liyana doesn't need to wait for the story to emerge to know that, with the exception of the final card, this particular spread doesn't bode well.

'So?' I nudge her. 'What do you see?'

'Nothing, it's not . . .' Liyana coughs. 'I did something wrong. I need to do it again.'

I don't need to see her face to know that she's lying.

4.00 p.m. – Liyana

'You're cooking?' Liyana steps into the kitchen.

'Yes,' Aunt Nya says. 'Is that so surprising?'

'Well . . .'

'You underestimate me. I cooked for the fifth husband all the time.'

Liyana raises an eyebrow.

'Okay, not *all* the time,' her aunt amends, setting down cutlery. 'Perhaps it was a more exclusive event. But, as with all things, it's quality not quantity.'

Liyana decides not to press the matter. 'So, who's the lucky recipient this time?'

'I've invited Mazmo to dinner.' Nya tweaks the forks so they perfectly parallel the knives. 'Will you get the wine glasses?'

Liyana pulls out a chair and sits.

'What are you doing?'

Liyana fiddles with a weighty silver fork. 'He's not coming.'

'Of course he's coming.' Nya opens a cupboard, removing three wine glasses. 'I invited him.'

'I can't do it.'

'Speak up!' her aunt snaps. 'I didn't pay thirty thousand a year for a St Paul's education to have you muttering. Enunciate. Project.'

Liyana looks up. 'I . . . I can't do it, *Nɔḍi*. I'm sorry, I can't marry Mazmo.'

'What are you talking about?' Nya holds the glasses aloft. Liyana imagines them dropping, smashing on the stone floor. 'I only invited him yesterday.'

Liyana swallows. 'I called him this morning, then I called the Tesco Metro on the green and took the night job stacking shelves. I know it'll take me a while to save for the Slade and I know we'll have to move but . . .'

With a deep sigh, Nya leans against the kitchen counter.

'I'm sorry, I wanted to do this – for you, for me too – but I . . . I can't.'

Her aunt stares at the wine glasses.

'But it's okay.' Liyana sits forward. 'Look, it might turn out to be a good thing, *Nɔḍi*. Kumiko said some things, about being spoiled and always taking the easy route, and now I realize that she was—'

'Stop right there.' Nya sets the glasses on the table. 'You've got no idea how hard my life has been. Absolutely none. So don't you dare judge me for how I've—'

'Wait,' Liyana protests, 'I wasn't, I didn't—'

'No,' her aunt snaps. 'You wait. You've been raised wanting for nothing. I gave your mother everything she needed to give you all that and more. And, after she died, I gave you even more. You've never had to compromise, you've never had to do things that twist up your soul in order to survive – so don't tell me about being spoiled.'

Nyasha stops, knocks a wine glass off the table. It shatters on the stone floor. Then she turns and walks out of the kitchen. Liyana slumps back in her chair.

She's burying her face in her hands when the white wine in the bottle begins to turn red.

Liyana is pulling herself up from the table when the doorbell rings. Her first thought is of Mazmo, since he hadn't received the news terminating their acquaintance with particular enthusiasm, so she hesitates. When it rings again, Liyana masters her reluctance and goes to answer it. Better now than later.

'Hello?' Liyana regards the two men – one short and fat, the other taller and fatter – standing on the steps below. Jehovah's Witnesses, is her second thought. 'How can I—?'

The taller man holds a letter up, then retracts it before she can read it. She's never encountered such aggressive missionaries of God and wonders—

'This is a warrant of execution.' The short one speaks

in a monotone. 'It says we're authorized to enter your property and seize all non-rented goods for the purpose of sale in order to pursue and settle your debts.'

'What?' Liyana stares at them. 'What? I don't—'

'Step aside, young lady,' the tall fat one says. 'We prefer a peaceful entry to an enforced one.'

'But we won't hesitate to employ the latter if we must,' the short fat one says.

The tall one steps up so he's standing level with Liyana, looking down at her. She stumbles back into the hallway as he pushes past her, quickly followed by his colleague. They've stomped into the kitchen before Liyana's caught up.

She stares at the men – already unplugging the espresso machine – feeling as if the water is rising too quickly, the waves crashing down.

'Stop that!' Nya stands in the doorway, poised and immovable. 'This instant!'

The men turn to face her. The tall man doesn't move, nor does he put down the red chrome Magimix. The short man steps over to Nya.

'The lady of the house, I presume?'

'You have no right to be here.' Nya's voice freezes the waters in which Liyana feels herself drowning. 'Get out, immediately.'

'Oh, but we have every right, lady,' the short man sneers. 'You were sent a Notice of Enforcement seven days ago. You didn't appeal it. So now we're—'

'You're not allowed to enter my premises without permission,' Nya snaps. 'You will leave. Now.'

'You're not wrong there, lady. But your daughter let us in, of her own free will, enabling us to carry out our duties to the fullest reaches of the law.' He nods back at the tall, fat man, who recommences his removal of the Magimix.

Nya glances at Liyana. 'Did you let them in?'

Liyana nods.

'Jesus, Ana! Why would you do that? Now they can do whatever the hell they want, whenever—'

'I didn't,' Liyana mumbles. 'I didn't . . .'

'You've got seventy-two hours to vacate the premises.' The short fat man smirks. 'An extra seventy-two if you appeal it. Either way, you'd better be out by Friday.'

Liyana spins round to face her aunt. 'That's not right, is it? They can't do that – this house is still ours. We own it, we . . .'

Nya says nothing, but her look of pure sorrow and guilt is answer enough.

10.37 p.m. – Scarlet

To its credit, the insurance company doesn't make her wait for the news. The email had arrived that morning. It'd taken Scarlet an hour to find the courage to open it. Its various sentences were the funereal soundtrack to her day. '*I write in relation to your claim made for the ceiling repairs to the No. 33 Café. I am afraid that, following the report of our surveyor . . .*' She shouldn't have read on after that second sentence, but she'd had to twist the knife, to cut out the last growth of hope. '*Given that you didn't maintain the building in accordance with the landlord's instructions we are unable to meet the costs of the repair. I would draw your attention to clause 12.3 in your insurance policy . . .*'

Now Scarlet sits at her grandma's favourite table by the bay window, staring into a half-empty cup of cold coffee. The café is silent. Esme is asleep upstairs. But Scarlet must tell her. She can't keep it a secret forever. They'll have to move – where to and how she'll pay the rent, Scarlet has no idea. First, she'll have to call Eli, to grovel and ask if his offer still stands. Minus £15,000 or so for ceiling repairs. And what will they be left with after that?

The moon shines through the glass, casting a sliver of light onto the little pool of coffee. Scarlet stares at it, caught by a memory of moonlight on the surface of a lake.

Scarlet frowns, trying to hold on to it. She'd seen a girl manipulating water once, creating waves that splashed on a riverbank, causing whirlpools with a clockwise turn of her index fingers. But who was the girl?

Scarlet rests an open palm atop her coffee cup, eclipsing the reflection of the moon. As her hand heats up, she tries to remember more. Then she picks up the cup and takes a sip.

11.48 p.m. – Bea

Bea wakes suddenly and fully. Sitting in the chair beside her desk is a man. Lit by the light of her lamp, he is very tall, very thin and very old.

Strangely, she's not scared. 'Who are you?'

He smiles. 'Oh, my love. Don't tell me you don't recognize your own father.'

Bea stares. It seems as if he's been sitting in that chair for a thousand years.

'I know it's been a while, but I don't think I've aged that much.' He touches a wrinkled hand to a wrinkled cheek. 'Have I?'

Bea sits up in bed. He is the man from her dream.

'But it wasn't a dream. Surely you've realized that by now.'

Dazed, Bea nods.

'It's a great joy to see you again, Beauty. I've missed you.'

Her father waits, perhaps expecting Bea to echo the sentiment. She does not. He studies her. Bea shifts under his gaze. If she'd thought her *mamá* was a falcon, then her father is a ten-headed vulture.

'You were a pretty little girl,' he says. 'But you've become a truly beautiful woman. Like mother, like daughter. Though I suppose I should be allowed to take some of the credit. Half, by rights – perhaps more.'

'How did you get into my room?'

He smiles again. It's a smile that makes her shiver.

'Where have you been for the last eighteen years?'

'That's unfair,' her father says. 'I've visited you from time to time. I know you're starting to remember.'

Bea says nothing.

'Don't worry.' He nods thoughtfully. 'I expected you'd have conflicted feelings upon seeing me again. I hope, in time, we can resolve them.'

'So, you're planning on sticking around then?' Bea sits up straighter. 'You've decided to stay?'

'Well, my love. You've been showing such great promise lately. After the events of last week, I thought it high time we had a talk.'

Bea stares at him, speechless. Vali's ghost has returned to her after all.

'Yes, I was very impressed.' He leans back in her chair, resting his elbows on its wooden arms, steepling his fingers. 'So many of my daughters are a disappointment, but you . . . Your mother has done well with you.'

At the mention of her *mamá,* Bea scowls. Her father smiles.

'And you thought she was deranged – like so many other poor misunderstood souls who simply see what others do not.' He raises a single eyebrow and his eyes seem to glow like a cat's in the half-light. 'I'm delighted that you're also taking after me.'

Bea blinks. 'I don't know what you think you know but—'

'Oh, I know what you've been up to,' he says. 'I've always known. You simply hadn't shown signs of anything particularly worthwhile, until recently.'

'You've *always* known? But how is that—?'

'Possible?' He looks disappointed. 'I know you've been wilfully ignoring your mother, but after what you did to that lovesick pup I'd have thought you'd have expanded your understanding of what's possible. And in case you're concerned, the coroner will rule death by natural causes – heart attack.'

Bea tries to ignore her shaking hands, the increasing thump of her . . . heart. 'I don't know how – but you've got no idea what happened. I'm not even—'

Her father laughs. 'Oh, Bea, I know *everything* about you. I know your favourite breakfast cereal was Coco Pops until you turned five when you began favouring Cornflakes. I know you lost your virginity at fourteen to Kevin Fitzpatrick. A poor choice, I think you'll agree.'

Bea stares at him, open-mouthed. His grin is like the slash of a knife.

'I know that you cheated on your Maths GCSE, simply to see if you could pull it off. I know that you once let Lottie Granger take the blame for that very naughty thing you—'

'Stop!'

Her father tuts. 'Spoilsport. I felt a splash of parental pride at what you did to poor little Lottie. Indeed, I'd hoped . . . Sadly, you made me wait another decade before you fulfilled that potential. But then, you always have been a bit of a tease, haven't you?' His cat-eyes flash. 'Probably why that poor fat pup was drawn to you. Why you were so drawn to him, though, I couldn't quite understand. Still, I suppose there's no accounting for taste.'

'What the hell do you want?'

'You haven't worked that out yet?' Her father smiles, the knife cuts deeper. 'I'm surprised, clever girl like you—'

'What have you been doing all these years? Where have you been?' Bea snaps. 'I bet you've got a wife, other children—'

'Of a fashion. I certainly have a great many daughters.'

'How many?'

'Well, I've never taken a precise count, to be true, but somewhere in the region of four to five . . . thousand, I would guess.'

Bea narrows her eyes. 'Don't be—'

'You're wondering how that's possible?'

'No, I'm thinking you're a shit liar – *mentiroso de mierda* – and a lunatic to boot – just like *Mamá*.'

'No you're not, you've seen too much to think that.' Her father tuts. 'The bad news is that, sadly, most of my daughters are dead. The good news is you'll be meeting three of your surviving sisters very soon.'

Bea thinks of the dream, her *mamá* talking about her sisters. She thinks of the blackbird illustration she found in Fitzbillies. The recognition. The rising memories.

'But we'll get to that,' her father is saying. 'First let's talk about how I'm going to take you under my wing, teach you everything—'

'I don't have a father,' Bea interrupts. 'I don't have one, don't want one, never needed one. *Mamá* is quite enough of a handful. Now, piss off and leave me alone like you did before.'

His laughter slices under her fingernails. 'You can deny it, my dear, you can fight it all you like, but in a few days . . . Well, you just wait and see.'

And, with that, he vanishes.

For a long time, Bea stares at the chair where her father had sat, at the imprint he's left on the air. It's hours before her thoughts and breath begin to slow and calm – though, she thinks, perhaps they never will – and then she starts to shake.

11.56 p.m. – Leo

Leo strides along King's Parade. Tonight, he doesn't even bother glancing up into the lit windows, no longer cares who might be there. The light spilling onto the pavements still reminds Leo of cracked egg yolks, but the thought doesn't slow him, he simply steps through the light and back into the dark.

If he's going to convince Goldie, Leo needs to do something dramatic. Careful and considered aren't working. And, with only five days to go, he can't afford to waste any more time. He knows the one thing he could say that will make her believe. But, if he does that, he'll lose her. Which means he must choose between keeping her love or saving her life.

A decade ago

Everwhere

You don't go back. Months pass. Years. Gradually, the memory of Everwhere fades. When you think about it, if you think about it at all, you berate yourself for ever believing it was real. It couldn't have been. You were foolish to ever imagine otherwise. It must have been nothing but a dream.

A terrific, terrifying, incredible dream.

Goldie

I didn't want to forget and I didn't want to die. I wasn't sure which I feared more. To forget Everwhere would be like forgetting the most essential part of myself: my spirit, my soul. But what could I do?

There was something else. Ever since Bea gave us an end date, a deadline for this life, this experience, it had made me think about things differently. I no longer wanted to compromise, to endure, to suffer through anything I didn't have to. The sharpest thorn in my sole was my stepfather. And it was up to me to stop him, since Ma was clueless and Teddy couldn't help.

I kept thinking on something else Bea had said. About life and death, about the fight for survival. I might not have Scarlet's strength, but I was much stronger than I'd ever believed and far more than anyone suspected. And even if none of us was tough enough to kill our father, I was beginning to think that my stepfather wouldn't be so very difficult to dispatch. I didn't know how I'd do it, didn't yet know if I would, but I was beginning to enjoy thinking that I might, and it was exciting to imagine that I could.

Liyana

Liyana checked the cards, night after night, every time hoping to prove Bea mistaken, hoping that she'd never have to leave Everwhere, never have to give up the place and people she loved so much. But the readings were always the same. The cards differed, but the story they told did not. The Tower. The Five of Cups. The Ten of Swords. The Nine of Wands . . . A story of loss, mourning, longing, suffering and sorrow. She would lose Everwhere, her sisters and herself.

After mourning this for a while, Liyana decided to thwart the cards. They would not predict her fate. She would run. On the night before her thirteenth birthday she would go to Everwhere and not come back. That would defeat the fact of forgetting. After all, how could she become too tied to this world if she left it, and how could she forget the place where she lived?

Liyana would leave a letter. She wouldn't try to explain the truth. Instead she'd say she was running away to Paris or Manhattan. At least then her mother would only fear for her safety and not her sanity too. Liyana didn't know exactly what she'd write. Still, she had several years to think about it. So the plan was set. Liyana would dedicate the first thirteen years of her life to Isisa Chiweshe. Then she would leave and live the rest of her life as she pleased.

Scarlet

Scarlet too had a plan to cheat Bea's prophecy. She would write herself a letter, to be opened the day of her thirteenth birthday, telling herself all about the Place, the Forgetting and the Choice. She would explain everything to the teenage Scarlet and then she'd be able to return whenever she wanted.

Naturally, Scarlet realized the initial flaw in the plan. Her thirteen-year-old self would dismiss the writings of her eight-year-old self as childish fantasy. After all, if she told any ordinary adult about Everwhere now they'd think she was making it all up. So she decided to take a photograph. Not of the place, since she didn't know if that was even possible – could she walk through a gate with her grandma's Polaroid camera? Surely not. It'd be impossible to capture a dream, to fix it in time and space, even a real one.

Instead, Scarlet would take a picture of the sparks that spat from her fingertips on Earth whenever she was angry. It only happened sometimes, but it was enough. All she had to do was wait.

When Scarlet at last had the photograph – a juggling act she hadn't anticipated – she sealed it in the envelope along with the letter and locked it in the top drawer of her desk. She had inscribed upon it, in elaborate but clear script, the words: *to be opened on my 13th birthday*.

Bea

Although she'd pretended to her sisters that she didn't care, she did, perhaps most of all. Bea couldn't bear the thought of not returning to Everwhere, of not seeing her sisters again for half a decade. She supposed she could visit them on Earth, but it wouldn't be the same. Nothing would. And since she didn't share their naivety, since she knew she couldn't get back, Bea tried to resign herself to spending five lonely years with only her *mamá* and *abuela* for company.

27th October – 5 days . . .

8.58 a.m. – Bea

To her shame, Bea took the first train to London that morning, though she hadn't been due to visit for another four days. Still, as much as she hates her *mamá*, the experience of seeing her father again in the flesh was so unsettling that even Cleo as a source of comfort is preferable to being alone. Still, she won't say anything about Vali, no matter how rigorous the interrogation.

'I can't understand why you're upset.' Cleo takes two slices of bread from the toaster. 'You should be happy. Now that you're nearly eighteen, he's come back for you.'

'Well, he's not having me. He lost that chance years ago.'

'*Por amor al . . . demonio.*' Her *mamá* sighs. 'You've always been like this.'

'Like what?'

'Whenever you felt rejected you pretended you didn't care.' Her *mamá* butters the toast. 'You were good at it too – you'd soon convince yourself that you weren't full of hurt but full of hatred.'

Bea ignores this remark, pressing her fingertips into the table.

'Jam or Marmite?'

'What kind of jam?'

'Raspberry.'

'Marmite.'

'*Buen.*' Her *mamá* nods. 'Don't let Little Cat lick your fingers, Marmite makes him sick.'

'It never used to.'

'He's getting old.'

Bea imagines her cat decaying under the apple tree in their garden. She imagines Vali in the morgue.

Cleo stops spreading Marmite. '*¿Que pasa, niña?*'

'Nothing.'

'Then why are you home so soon? Last time I saw you, you weren't exactly keen to come.'

'I fancied a break.'

'Liar.'

'All right then, I broke up with my boyfriend. Okay?' Bea steadies her voice. She'll be strong; she will not let her *mamá* see a single crack. 'And I just wanted to take a few days—'

'How many times must I tell you?' Cleo sets the two plates of toast on the table. '*No me digas mentiras*. Don't. Lie. To. Me.'

'I'm not. It's the truth.'

Her *mamá* pulls out the chair beside her daughter and sits.

Bea waits.

'Your father told me what you did.' Cleo takes a bite of toast. 'I'm impressed.'

Bea stares at her *mamá*, then picks up her own plate of toast and hurls it at the wall. It smashes, scattering shards of bone china across the linoleum floor. The silence is sharp, expectant. As if malevolent kitchen sprites were watching and wondering what will happen next. Bea sits back in her chair.

'Now who's the crazy one?' Cleo mutters.

A few minutes later, Little Cat pads into the kitchen and starts licking at a slice of the Marmite toast on the floor.

9.38 a.m. – Liyana

Liyana and her aunt stand on opposite sides of the kitchen table. In the no-man's-land between them piles of boxes are stacked, like a child's fort. Full, sealed and labelled. Empty, open and blank. Liyana wraps glasses in bubble wrap, though she'd rather smash them to the stone floor and run. Except that she has nowhere to go. Kumiko wouldn't take her in and Goldie has no space.

Nya twists torn strips of newspaper around knives and forks – the ones remaining after the bailiffs' abduction of the silverware.

Liyana wants to ask her aunt where they're going next. But she won't. She wonders if they'll stay in London. She can't imagine her aunt deigning to live anywhere else. But if they do the house will have to be far out, beyond the suburbs, at the end of the line, to be affordable. And even then, how will they afford it? Even if she stacks shelves all day and night and never sleeps, her wages still won't stretch to the cheapest of London rents. She wonders if Nya has been applying for jobs too.

Nya sneezes. Liyana says nothing. Silence pushes between them like a sulking child.

10.52 p.m. – Scarlet

Ezekiel is tied to a thick wooden stake atop a funeral pyre.

'Come down,' Scarlet calls. 'What the hell are you doing up there?'

'Do it!' he shouts. 'You know you want to!'

'No, no, I won't!'

'I want to feel your power, I want to burn!'

'Stop.' But even as she speaks, Scarlet feels the familiar itch at her fingertips. Her skin is hot and starting to spark.

When Scarlet looks up again it's no longer Ezekiel tied to the stake but Walt. She feels a flare of disappointment. As wood, Walt won't burn well. He's too soft for kindling. Ezekiel, now he'll ignite fast and flame far enough to cause a forest fire.

'Scarlet! Scarlet!'

She wakes like a child, springing from asleep to awake in a single bound. She scrambles out of bed and runs, slipping twice in the hallway, to her grandmother's bedroom. Esme is sitting up in bed, crying.

'Wait, Grandma, it's okay.' Scarlet slips into bed beside her. 'It's all right, I'm here.'

'I ran, I couldn't catch her.' Esme gasps. 'I – I let her go.'

'It's okay, Grandma.' Scarlet presses Esme's hand between hers, holding tight until her grandmother's breathing begins to slow. 'It's okay.'

'He took her.' Esme pulls her hand away, wiping her eyes. 'The Devil took my baby girl.'

'It's only a nightmare, Grandma. You don't have a baby, you have me and I'm not going anywhere.'

'Ruby shouldn't have left us,' Esme moans. 'She shouldn't have gone.'

'She didn't leave us,' Scarlet whispers, the memory of the fire she'd caused aching like a bruise that won't fade. 'She died in the fire.' Under normal circumstances, Scarlet would be at pains not to say such words aloud, not to remember and not to remind Esme of her daughter's death. But, in this moment, it seems like the better thing to do.

Her grandmother sits up, startled. 'Fire? Where?'

'No, no, there's no fire now.' Scarlet takes her grandma's hand again. 'It was years ago, the fire that burned down our house, that kill—'

Esme shakes her head and Scarlet can already see that, mercifully, the fog is rolling in. 'No fire.' Her voice shakes. 'No fire.'

'That's right, there's no fire. We're safe,' Scarlet lies. 'We're okay.'

'No fire,' Esme says again. 'She ran – she ran away . . .'

'No, Grandma. She died.'

'No.' Esme shakes her head, her voice rising. 'She's not dead. Ruby isn't dead.'

'You're right, Grandma, she isn't.' Scarlet lifts the blankets. 'She's fine. Come on, let's go back to sleep, okay? Everything will be better in the morning.'

Her grandmother looks confused. 'I don't understand.'

'It's okay, don't worry.' Scarlet tucks her in. 'You had a nightmare.'

'But, I – I . . .'

'Shush, Grandma. Go back to sleep.'

Her grandmother shuts her eyes, moaning softly.

'That's it, that's right, go back to sleep now, go back to sleep.' Scarlet strokes her grandmother's shoulders, until moaning drifts into breath and breath drifts into snores.

11.17 p.m. – Goldie

'The other day . . . you asked about my scars.' Leo sits up, fiddling with the edge of the sheet. We're in room 36, doing things we shouldn't be doing. We haven't talked about Everwhere yet today, and I'm grateful.

'I want – I need to tell you now.'

I nod, alert, though I've learned my lesson. This time, I won't push. Leo looks at me as if he's trying to commit every inch of me to memory. It's a little unnerving.

'I'm a soldier,' Leo says finally. 'The scars are . . . kills.'

I stare at him, wondering if he has at last lost his grip on reality. First a star, now a soldier. And how can he have – there are so many, hundreds and hundreds of scars. It's not possible for someone, a single man, to have done so much.

I try to slow my breath, try to calm myself. 'Kills?'

Leo nods. 'I told you, didn't I? I told you not to say it didn't matter, not to promise that you wouldn't care. You can't, can you? You can't say a thing like that. Not now.'

I'm silent. He was right. Though only if I believe him. 'But tell me . . . explain what happened. I – I just want to . . . understand.'

'You can't.'

'Try me.'

He sighs. 'What would you say if I told you I'd killed insurgents in Iraq? Terrorists.'

'No, that's not possible. You can't, you . . . you're not old enough to—'

Leo shakes his head. 'I'm older than I look.'

'But you're a student. You're studying—'

'Now,' Leo says. 'But not always. And, anyway, the two things aren't mutually exclusive.'

I look at him. 'So, did you . . . ? *Did* you kill terrorists?'

'Well . . . that was the way I saw them, at the time.'

'How many?'

He waits, not meeting my eye. 'Two . . . hundred and eighty . . . one.'

I'm silent. What can I say? There is nothing to say.

'And that isn't the worst of it,' he says.

What could be worse than that? I don't say it but Leo must see it in my eyes. He pulls away, sliding off the bed.

'Wait,' I say. 'Wait. I'm sorry, I—'

'You've got nothing to be sorry for,' he says. 'I don't deserve it.'

I'm silent. Is it possible that he did this? Or is it another fantasy? I'm not sure which I am hoping for more: that he's demonic or delusional.

'I – I . . .' I don't know what to say but know I need to say something.

Leo is buttoning up his shirt, pulling on his trousers. 'Don't say things you might not mean, simply because you feel . . . I've got to go. I've got work—'

'No!' He's leaving me. I've said the wrong thing, I've

done the wrong thing and now he's leaving and he won't come back. I slide out of bed. 'Don't – you can't just tell me something like that and go, it's not fair. Please.'

'I know.' His voice drops. 'I'm sorry. But you need some time to process it, before I, before I . . .'

How can I process the killing of 281 people? But, before I can say anything at all, before I can find my own clothes, the door is banging shut and he's gone.

'Wait!' I run after him. I'm half-naked still but I don't care. I know if I let him go he'll never come back, I'll never have another chance. And even though I'm not certain I want one, I can't let him go, not yet.

'Please,' I say, reaching him. 'Please don't go, not like this.'

Leo doesn't stop.

'Look, you don't have to explain. Give it time. Let's wait, let's see . . .'

Leo turns back to me. 'I'm not a soldier. I didn't kill for any alleged just cause. I did it because I must – it's my function, it's what I was made to do – and in order to survive: each kill gives me life—'

'What?' I'm incredulous. 'How? That makes no sense—'

He cuts me off in turn. 'But . . . most of all I killed to avenge the death of my dearest friend.'

I stare at him, unable to speak.

Finally, Leo fills the silence. 'It's worse than that,' he says.

'What?' I whisper. 'What could be worse than that?'

'What I did to your mother,' Leo says, barely audible now. 'And what I might have done to you.'

28th October – 4 days . . .

12.05 a.m. – Bea

Bea sits on the bathroom floor, the razor untouched beside her. She studies the drawing, the striking blackbird-woman by T.L.M.C. The longer she looks at it, the more she feels that she knows who drew it and, what's more, that it was drawn for her or, perhaps, inspired by her.

T.L.M.C?

All at once it comes to her: the L is Liyana. The dream. The name her *mamá* mentioned. And yet she cannot recall Liyana's face. But she was so close – in Fitzbillies – which means she might live in Cambridge. For nearly a month they have shared the same city. Her own sister. Bea feels a sudden flash of rage at the unfairness of *Mamá* owning more of her memories than she does.

Bea grips the page tighter, since perhaps she might pick something up through osmosis. Her sister. And the thought of this girl she can't quite yet remember, but whose presence she can increasingly sense, makes Bea feel less alone. A balm on the raw wound of Vali's death. Her sister.

Ana.

1.13 a.m. – Goldie

Goldie dreams. She dreams she's in a garden with Leo, sitting together on the grass. But it's not grass, it's moss. And the moss is pale as freshly fallen snow. And it's not a garden but a glade enclosed by white-leaved willow trees. And they're not sitting together but apart. She should, Goldie thinks, be happy. But she's not, she's sad. No, more than that, she's enraged. And so completely, so deeply, that it's as if she's sucking anger out of the air, drawing it up from the soil, like a parched plant ingesting every molecule of fury.

From these nutrients, flowers bloom in her open palms. White roses.

Goldie holds a rose out to Leo and he, smiling with relief, takes it. As he presses the flower to his lips its thorns begin to grow, thickening and lengthening. Still smiling, he doesn't notice, not until a thorn is wrapping itself around his neck. As it tightens, Leo doesn't move, doesn't struggle, doesn't fight. He simply looks at Goldie, his eyes full of sorrow and regret. She makes no move to stop it. She simply watches as her rose slowly chokes out his life. Until he's a pile of dust atop the moss.

She watches and feels nothing at all.

1.59 a.m. – Leo

The way Leo feels, it's perhaps fortunate that he can't get into Everwhere for a few days yet. If he could, he'd instigate a massacre rivalling what came after Christopher's death – four or five kills on the night of every first-quarter moon, for five years, nearly three hundred . . . The figure horrifies him now, especially after seeing the look in Goldie's eyes when he finally told her the truth. She'd thought him a monster. Which he is. Still, this doesn't temper his fury; indeed it only sharpens it. He wants to obliterate everything, everyone. Most of all himself. He has lost her. And by his own hand. Which feels, if that were possible, worse than if she had died by her father's.

He was a fool. If he could, he'd end his own life now. Sadly, for that he must go to Everwhere. The star in him is indestructible, at least on Earth. If he doesn't kill, his light and life will eventually fade and gutter out, but if he wants an instant death it's no use. Leo cannot die by mortal methods or means; he can be killed only by a Grimm girl or by his father, his captain.

Still, he doesn't have to wait long. If Goldie won't kill him when she enters Everwhere again – and given the way she must be feeling right now, she'll probably relish the opportunity – then Wilhelm will. And Leo won't put up a fight, won't give a fuck, won't rage against the dying of the light. Death doesn't scare him. He only wishes it were coming sooner.

2.23 a.m. – Liyana

Kumiko's favourite café, tucked away in a back street in Camden, opens only at night. Liyana hopes it'll be empty. She hopes Kumiko will forgive her. She hopes, by the end of the night, that she'll be held tight in her girlfriend's arms. Because she desperately needs some solace and comfort right now.

Following Goldie's advice Liyana has prepared a grand gesture, involving poetry, glitter and a modicum of nudity. Unfortunately, even at this hour, the café is still crowded. Liyana crosses the chequered vinyl – Beatles records and Bowie and the Stones all pressed into the floor like a Walk of Fame – until she reaches Kumiko's table in the corner of the café, squashed up against the wall.

'Hey, Koko.'

Kumiko looks up from her book.

For one awful moment, Liyana thinks she's going to ignore her.

Kumiko slowly pushes aside her curtain of midnight hair. 'Hello, Ana.'

Liyana shifts from foot to foot, trying to postpone the

yet more deeply dreadful moment of beginning. She's been practising the dance moves to accompany the poem, although the whole performance is still woefully inadequate. At least that will serve to up the humiliation factor.

'Why are you here?'

'To see you.'

'And how did you know I was here?'

'Because you're a creature of habit.' Liyana ignores the brightening spotlight of attention in which she stands, as other customers start to sense that something's happening. 'Once a week you come to read *The Hobbit* and see if you can make a single cup of coffee last till morning.'

Kumiko smiles – a twitch at the corner of her lips.

'I'm here to make a fool of myself,' Liyana says. 'Because I'm a fool.'

'You are. And an idiot.'

Liyana nods. 'An idiot. An imbecile. A—'

'—dunderhead. A dimwit. A numbskull.'

'All that and worse.'

'Well, I'm glad we at least agree on that.' Kumiko's smile deepens. 'And what are you going to do about it?'

'Try again to deserve your heart. If you'll give me the chance.'

Kumiko closes *The Hobbit*. 'Go on.'

'I'm never seeing Mazmo again. I've taken the shelf-stacking job at Tesco. The bailiffs have taken everything we own and we're moving to an estate in Hackney.' Liyana feels herself starting to sweat under the ever-brightening spotlight of attention. She drops her voice. 'And I've written you a poem. A dire poem. It hardly even rhymes, but it's—'

'You took the Tesco job?' Kumiko raises an eyebrow. 'Really? How is it?'

'Hideous, I hate it. But the point is you were right. I was massively spoiled and now I'm trying to—'

'Speak up.' Kumiko sits forward. 'I can't hear you.'

Liyana gives her a wry smile. 'You're enjoying this, aren't you?'

'Yeah, just a bit.'

3.33 a.m. – Bea

In her childhood bedroom, Bea dreams childhood dreams. Tonight, she tracks prey. She begins with birds, stalking them like a silent, stealthy cat. At first, she's excited to catch ravens while they preen or wrench worms from the soil. But she soon tires of this; the explosion of feathers among fallen leaves is too easy. Piercing the heart of a bird in flight with a single hawthorn spike is much more pleasing. Until, after the first few dozen kills, she tires of that too.

A gratifying side effect of each kill is that young Bea absorbs the life force of each bird so she can rise into the air, hovering above the moss and stone, above the blankets of fallen leaves. Every death fuels her flight. A single kill brings her eye-to-trunk with a silver birch; three in a row lifts her over an ancient oak; six carries her a few hundred metres through the air; twelve brings her within reach of the stars.

In her dream, Bea wonders why her father isn't there. But, even as she asks herself the question, the answer comes. He won't lessen her learning by holding her hand. His absence enables her to feel the full impact of her actions, to absorb every flush of pride, every ounce of honour. He lets her run free. He won't permit his presence to leach anything from her and, for that, Bea is grateful. It is something her *mamá* has never been generous enough to do.

With every hour that passes, Bea's strength swells so her sense of herself shifts further from her earthly self. She is different in Everwhere. Not only can she achieve what she previously imagined impossible, but she also feels lighter. The loneliness has ebbed, perhaps because this place is so full of her father, his presence imbuing every tree, every river, every leaf. His whisper threads through the shadows, making threats that further sharpen her focus and hone her skills.

When she wakes, Bea can't remember a single image but is left with an echo of the feelings evoked: courage, certainty, self-possession. She has ripped off her feminine casing. She's free to be fierce, to rage, to act exactly as she wants.

8.33 a.m. – Scarlet

When she unlocks the café door, Scarlet steps over the envelopes on the mat without stopping to pick them up. But, catching sight of a letter addressed by hand, she bends down – thinking of the anonymous storyteller, wondering, hoping, that it might be another story. She could certainly do with the uplift to her spirits.

26th Oct

Scarlet,

Hark at me, sending you an actual bona fide love letter – impressive, eh? Bet you didn't think I had it in me. Yeah, well, neither did I. First time I've written one, in fact. Letter that is, love or otherwise. I've sent a few love texts in my time – though strictly speaking, they were more about sex now I think about it . . . Anyway, I digress. Sorry I haven't called etc since we set fire to that hotel bedspread. How the hell did that happen? I was a little distracted at the time. It wasn't cheap – they charged my card – but worth every penny. Look at that, digressing again. Did you think I'd done a runner, had my wicked way with you then buggered off back to the Big Smoke? I haven't. I'm in London, but only because – since you welched on our deal – my boss called me back. I'll be here a few weeks before I can get away again. Visit me? I promise I'll make it very much worth your while . . .

Eli x

Scarlet reads the letter twice. Anger, desire and fear swirl in her body until her hands are hot and her fingertips sparking. One spark ignites the letter.

'Shit!' Scarlet drops the paper as it burns. 'Shit, shit, shit.'

She stamps it out, looking down at the scattering of ashes across the floorboards. It's an omen. She must call him. Now. She can't put it off any longer.

11.49 p.m. – Goldie & Liyana

I never thought that love and hate could be so fiercely entwined. I certainly never imagined that I could hate Leo like this. Or I thought it would only be if I didn't love him anymore. By rights I shouldn't love him now, I should erase all emotion, rip it out, flush my heart of every soft feeling. But I can't. No matter how I try to will myself free, I'm still tied to him as tight as I ever was.

Perhaps it'll simply take time for hate to set in and burn out love. I hope it doesn't take too long. I can't bear this alchemy of love and hate eroding me, as if my heart were spitting acid into my blood. All I want is to escape myself. And, since I don't drink or take drugs – now would be a good time to start – my only option is unconsciousness. Except that I can't fucking sleep. So, I call Liyana.

She picks up on the second ring.

'I'm sorry,' I say. 'I know you're at work, I just . . .'

'It's fine,' Liyana interrupts, sounding a little breathless. 'I don't start for ten minutes. What's wrong? Why are you crying?'

'I, I . . . I . . .'

'It's okay. It's all right. No rush, I'm here, I'll wait, I'm not going anywhere.'

And my sister waits, simply listening, holding the phone as she might hold me if she were here. Knowing this uncorks me. Having her there I feel safe enough to let myself sink into despair because she won't let me drown.

My cries are long and keening, my breaths shallow and sharp, my pain pulled up from the depths of the earth. My cries are distended fingers of sound, trying to snatch back what they cannot reach.

Eventually, I start to calm, to float up to the surface. With each new breath my sobs subside.

'I'm here,' Liyana says. 'I'm still here.'

I nod, though I know she can't see. I can't move my dry tongue yet, can't find any words I want to say.

'Is it Leo?' she asks, tentative. 'Did he do something?'

I nod again. 'H-he . . . he k-killed my ma.'

'But . . .' Liyana's voice is soft. 'But, I thought she died four years ago.'

'She did,' I say, deeply grateful that my sister didn't detonate. Right now, I need Liyana to be my life raft.

'I don't understand,' Liyana says, still unruffled. 'Isn't he our age? Wouldn't he have been a kid back then?'

'Yes. But' – I take a deep breath – 'and this is going to sound deluded, but . . . he's not, he's only, not exactly or entirely . . . human.'

'Oh.'

'Do you think I'm deluded?'

'No.'

I'm torn between relief and surprise. 'Why not?'

'I don't know. Lately I'm starting to wonder if I am, if we are . . . At least, I'm seeing things, knowing things, doing things that I can't explain. Not rationally, anyway.'

'Yeah,' I say. 'Me too.'

Somehow, admitting this aloud and having her say it too lightens the weight of my sorrow a little.

'I mean,' Liyana says. 'The way we met. How can you explain that?'

'Yes. And he'd been telling me about this place. It sounds – the dreams I've been having . . . It's the same place, Ana. And, how would he know?'

Liyana waits, saying nothing.

'I never told him, I never told him any of the details. But I, I'm thinking all kinds of things, like maybe he drugged me, or hypnotized me, or—'

'But if he was trying to trick you, or seduce you, or something, why would he tell you about . . . what he did?'

'I know,' I say. 'Exactly. He knew it'd make me— he knew I'd hate him for it. He knew I couldn't love him anymore, not after that.'

Liyana's silent for a moment. When she speaks, I know what she's going to say before she says it.

'But you do love him, don't you? You don't want to, but you do.'

29th October – 3 days . . .

12.01 a.m. – Goldie & Liyana

We fall into silence again. Since, what is there to say? My sister is wise enough to know she doesn't have the words, that there aren't words. She understands that all she can do is be there and, for now, that is enough.

'I've been thinking about your dreams,' Liyana says at last. 'About our other sisters. I think we should try to find them.'

I say nothing.

'I mean, you even know where one of them works,' she persists. 'If we don't . . . Anyway, I'm sure the two of us together can convince her. Don't you think?'

'I suppose so.'

I know she's right. And I want to find them too. But, right now, I barely have energy to breathe, let alone face another confrontation.

4.01 a.m. – Bea

'Where are you, Val? Where the hell did you go?'

Bea wipes her eyes, then slaps herself sharply across the cheek. The sting of the strike gives her a moment's relief, but it's not enough. It's only when the physical pain is deep and raw enough to eclipse the emotional that Bea can breathe again. She picks at a scab on her thigh, wincing as she draws it from her skin, the flesh beneath fresh and pink.

'I'm scared, Val.' She closes her eyes, imagining he's

beside her. 'I'm so fucking angry all the time. I don't know what I might . . .'

To calm herself, Bea thinks of Dr Finch, of their last encounter. She thinks of his skinny body beneath her, his chest almost concave as he panted. But then the memory of Vali's plump naked body rises. Her baby owl. Bea pushes it down. She brings herself back to Dr Finch's weak-featured face, scruffy hair and stubble. All affectation. *What a prick.* She'd never found him remotely attractive. At first the sex, after gaining admission to the Royal Aeronautical Society, had been a desire to know him more deeply – every idea, every spark of inspiration in his supposedly magnificent mind. Until it'd soon become clear that he was more of a cuckoo than a hawk and driven by only one desire. Unlike her dear Vali. Who was, in all things, a lovelier human being than any she'd ever met. Her eyes fill again.

'Help me, Val,' Bea begs. 'Please, I can't bear it anymore.'

5.04 a.m. – Scarlet

Scarlet dreams. Shifting, jolting, quivering, sliding in and out of sleep, clutching snippets of images when she wakes. It's a dream she has often, of a place she knows but has never been. A place of forests and rivers, stones and moss, hazy with mists and fog. It might be the Lake District, except that everything is white, as if dusted with snow. Only it isn't snowing. Instead leaves are falling, always falling, not from the trees but from the sky. And it's never day, only night, lit by the light of an unwavering moon.

There Scarlet is a child again, strolling along a path, hopping from stone to stone, thinking that perhaps she'll set light to some leaves tonight, or some sticks, or . . . Then she isn't alone anymore. Scarlet stands very still, peering into the shadows. A girl steps out of the darkness and into the moonlight.

'Hey, Sis,' Bea says with a smile.

Scarlet wakes.

Who was that girl? How does she know her? Even as she's thinking, the girl's face is dissolving and Scarlet is slipping into sleep again.

Now she sits in a clearing with her legs crossed, picking daisies from the mossy ground. Except that the flowers don't grow here, they grew in her mother's garden, and she picked them before the fire. Scarlet sets each daisy in her palm, then incinerates it. Pursing her lips, she blows ash into the air, before beginning again. They shouldn't be here, these flowers. They don't belong. And it's her job to eradicate them.

All at once, Scarlet senses she's being watched.

Her mother sits at the edge of the clearing, perched on a large white stone. She is here. But she is never here, not in this place.

'Hello.'

Her mother says nothing, as distant in the dream as she was in life. Then, in an unprecedented move, she stands and walks slowly over to Scarlet, her feet bare, like Scarlet's own, on the moss and stone. She stops, reaches down and plucks a daisy from the earth. Taking the stalk between finger and thumb, she places it in Scarlet's open hand.

'Take care of it. I couldn't, but you can.'

Then, in those strange slipping shifts that so often happen in dreams, Scarlet is running, stepping over the stones, leaping over fallen tree trunks, legs stretched and then lifting into the air. Then she's standing in the lower branches of a tree, looking up for a foothold, intent on clambering all the way to the top. Scarlet doesn't know why but the urge is insistent. Then she's at the top of the tree, looking down.

Someone below is shouting, telling her to jump, telling her to fly.

'Oh-kay,' Scarlet shouts back. How did she get there? She'd wanted only to run; everything afterwards was like being plucked from the ground and set atop the tree by the hand of God. Perhaps she'll fall and smash on the ground like the Christmas fairy she broke a decade ago. She can still see the fragments of her china face scattered across the floorboards. But no, she won't die.

Scarlet reaches out her arms like wings and jumps.

Scarlet wakes but doesn't open her eyes. She presses her head into the pillow, trying to hold on to the tendrils of the dream. But the mists and fog are evaporating, rolling back out of her reach. Sighing, she brushes her hair out of her eyes. Her finger snags on something caught in a curl and she pulls it out.

A white twig.

Twenty minutes later, finally dragging herself out of bed, Scarlet steps onto the carpet and sees that the soles of her feet are smeared with mud.

11.59 p.m. – Bea

'Welcome back. I've been waiting for you.'

Bea looks up to see the man with the golden eyes swoop down through the mists like her book-eagles, parting the fog with a single sweep of his outstretched arms. Her father.

Bea steps back, feeling his voice slice thin strips from her skin, pricking the scars on her thighs. She presses her hands to her sides.

'Oh, you're not still upset?' Wilhelm Grimm reaches out his hand. 'I thought I'd explained myself. I thought you understood.'

Bea looks at him, torn between the desire to seize hold of him and the desire to run.

He wiggles his fingertips. 'Bygones?'

Bea doesn't speak, doesn't move.

'Oh, sweetheart, don't hold a grudge.' He smiles. 'You're my best girl, don't you know that? I'm so very proud of you.'

Bea hesitates. She wants to resist him, wants to hate him. She refuses to succumb to feeling what she's been fighting all her life: a longing to be loved by him.

'Oh, come on,' he says. 'You can't tell me you feel at home in that other world.' His hand hangs in the air, waiting. 'Tell me you feel seen there. Tell me you have someone who knows you as you truly are, who's glimpsed inside your heart and accepted you just as you are.' He pauses. 'If you have that, go back and enjoy it, for I've nothing more than that to offer you here.'

Bea meets her father's eyes, then reaches for his hand.

They walk together awhile, hand in hand, along the moss-stone paths, the white leaves falling on and all around them, until they come to a valley where the trees part.

'I've brought you a gift,' he says, letting go of her hand. 'To welcome you home.'

'Oh? What—'

Her father holds a finger to his lips; his voice drops to a whisper. 'Just wait. He's on his way.'

Bea holds her breath, scanning the valley. Has her father brought her a man? If so, for what purpose? It seems a strange gift from father to daughter. But he's no conventional father. She sees the stream that runs through the valley, its waters shimmering as the moon shines out from behind the clouds, the eddy and swirl of the currents flicking up droplets like tiny silver fish. As she watches the water, he appears.

A stag, his antlers bone-white in the moonlight, crests above the hill, parting the fog like curtains of smoke, and lopes down to the river and bends to drink.

'He's . . . magnificent,' Bea whispers. 'I've never seen . . . I never knew they were so . . . beautiful.' This word seems inadequate to describe him, but it's the only one she has. 'Majestic' followed soon after, but it too falls short and doesn't seem worth further breaking the silence to say.

The stag's ears twitch when Bea speaks and he raises his head from the river, looking straight at her, large brown eyes unblinking. As Bea observes him, she feels the distance between them fall away, as if she's standing beside him, her hand pressed to his flank, the muscle firm beneath the smooth, thick coat. The sensation is so vivid that she can feel the heat of his skin under her palm, the deep, soft fur of his mane at the edge of her fingertips. She wants to reach up, to have him nuzzle her with his dark, wet snout. She wants to bury her face in his mane and breathe him in.

'Thank you,' Bea says. 'I love—'

Her father shakes his head. 'He's not for you to love,' he says. 'He's for you to kill.'

Bea looks up, eyes wide with shock. 'What? No – why? I can't—'

'You eat steak,' her father interrupts.

'Yes,' Bea admits. 'But . . .'

'And what did you get for it? Apart from extra iron in your blood and a succulent taste on your tongue. When you kill him you'll get his life force: his strength, his stamina, his stature, his dominance and power.'

Bea shakes her head. 'No, I can't. It wouldn't be, it wouldn't—'

'You want to feel what it's like, don't you?' her father continues. 'You want to gallop through these forests, to have his huge heart beating in your chest, his wild blood rushing through your veins, his hooves pounding the ground in your feet.'

Despite herself, Bea nods.

'So do it.'

'How?' Bea asks, hearing her own voice as if she were eavesdropping on someone else. 'But how can I?'

'Oh, my dear, what a ridiculous question.' He laughs. 'Such a thing is child's play. When you were younger I even had to step in, curb your zeal, stop you from slaughtering my entire herd.'

'I can't remember,' Bea says. 'I can't . . .'

'You had great skill, great dexterity. You favoured the spears of the hawthorn tree as your weapon of choice.'

'I did?' Bea says, startled, even as she feels the desire to do it now. She's thinking that she couldn't identify this tree at ten paces when her gaze falls upon its lethal spikes. About to ask how it's possible to extract the thorns and turn them into arrows, Bea remembers. She knows what to do.

Focusing on a single branch, Bea strips it of every thorn, with a twitch of her fingers, as if her fingernails were knives. The thorns hover in the air before Bea brings together forefinger and thumb, shifting the twelve thorns into a line and pressing them together. The thorns fuse, tip to tip, into an arrow.

As she lets the arrow fly, as she watches it pierce the stag's heart, as she feels the thud of his body falling to the ground, the tremors echoing under the soles of her feet, Bea feels the force of his life seeping from his veins and into her own.

In the echo of his death, Bea finds that she doesn't feel fear, only relief. The killing of this stag has finally turned her into who she truly is: a killer, a hunter, a soldier.

30th October –
2 days . . .

3.03 a.m. – Leo

Since he cannot yet die, and since he can think of nothing else but trying to save Goldie's life, Leo is trying to shape her dreams. He could find her, track her down, speak face to face. But since she hasn't been turning up to work since he told her, clearly seeing him is the last thing Goldie wants. Instead, he'll visit her dreams. She won't like him much for that either, but what choice does he have?

Goldie can reach Everwhere simply by dreaming, while Leo must wait for an open gate, must walk through at an exact time and date. But he knows that it's possible for a soldier – if he's imprinted himself upon a Grimm girl's spirit – to travel on the coat-tails of her dreams, just as their mothers can. Just as their mothers can. If he's imprinted himself on her, which he has. Many times. Leo shakes his head, unable to think of those moments without a surge of longing and loss leaching all his strength and leaving him weak.

He isn't well practised at such things, has never needed to be, and doesn't have much time. So Leo applies himself to that and nothing else. He's found a forest, has walked for miles to find the right place: a tree stump enveloped by ivy and cushioned with moss. A seat that evokes Everwhere, so he can call on its power, can harness it to his and hope for a fucking miracle.

He sits there now, fingers twitching in the moonlight, trying to shape Goldie's dreams. It takes enormous effort and a great deal of time for Leo to master even the basics of what he's trying to do. He sits without shifting for hours. Until, at last, he has pulled the possibility close enough to entwine it around his fingertips. He can reach her, he can join her. But there is one more glitch. For his conjuring to work, she must first fall asleep.

3.33 a.m. – Goldie

I'm here.

I'm back.

I look up at the falling white leaves, at the night sky with its millions of stars – far more and far brighter than any I've ever seen – and its sliver of moon. A canopy of dark branches above, gigantic towering trees, moss and stones at my feet—

Then I see him. And I know, somehow, that I'm not simply dreaming; his appearance is no uncontrollable summoning from my unconscious. He has willed it, has conjured himself here. How this is possible, I have no idea – astral projection? – but given everything that's been happening lately, I no longer have such a limited notion of what's possible.

'What the hell are you doing here?' I hiss.

I feel so fragile, like a shattered glass tentatively glued, still sticky, still soft. At the sight of him, I might shatter all over again.

He doesn't step forward. He keeps his distance, as if he thinks I'll either attack or run if he comes any closer.

'I'm sorry, I had to come.'

'Why?' I shift from foot to foot, desperate to leave, desperate to stay. I won't scream. I won't cry. I will maintain a modicum of dignity and composure, as I promised myself I would if I ever saw Leo again.

'Because you'll be back here in a few nights,' he says,

'when you turn eighteen, and I need to tell you, I need to show you—'

'—how to defend myself from a soldier sent to kill me,' I say. 'From you. Yes, I remember.'

I begin walking. I've no idea where I'm going but I don't care, suddenly I can't bear to be standing in front of him. I can't bear to catch his gaze, to meet his eyes so full of remorse.

'But you know it's true, don't you?' Leo hurries after me, stepping over the slick stones as if they weren't even there. 'You can't deny it anymore' – I turn to see him throwing his arms up to the sky – 'now that we're here.'

I stop walking so suddenly that we almost collide.

'Yes, we're here,' I say, trying hard not to cry. 'So, what are you going to do now? Kiss me? Kill me?'

I step forward, defiant. 'Go on, I won't put up a fight.'

Leo doesn't move.

'Go on,' I say again, pushing him hard now, my hands slapping the centre of his chest. Not expecting it, he stumbles back. 'Show me, show me what you did to Ma, what you planned to do to me.'

Leo drops his head. It's better, now that I can't see his eyes, with their every shade of green an echo of all the leaves I've ever held.

'Did you ever love me,' I whisper, 'or was it all a trick?' Tears slip down my cheeks. 'Fuck! No, I've cried enough. You don't deserve it, you don't . . .' But then I can't speak, can't breathe; I can only cry.

Leo steps forward, pulling me to him, holding me tight against his chest. I hear his rapid breaths and I realize he's crying too.

'I love you,' he says, his mouth pressed into my fresh-cut hair I feel his breath on my bare neck. 'I was a total shit, yes. And I'm sorry. But I loved you, even when I didn't know it, I loved you.'

I pull away from him. 'A *shit*? That doesn't even begin to—'

'I know,' he says. 'I know.'

'Then w-why did you do it?'

'I don't know,' Leo says, dragging the backs of his hands across his cheeks. 'I don't— I've been doing it since I was a kid, I didn't . . .'

'You've got no reason,' I say, stepping back. The fog is rolling in. 'You're not even going to tell me you were following orders? In this stupid fucking war of yours . . . Or you're one of those soldiers who kills for fun. You're a psychopath.'

Leo frowns, as if I'm speaking a language he can't comprehend. 'Following orders is no excuse.' He pulls his hand through his hair, dislodging settled white leaves that drop onto his shoulders. 'But, I – I had to kill to live.'

'What?' I slip on a wet stone, stumbling. 'You didn't— why?'

'All part of his infinite plan.' Leo shrugs, as if death were nothing at all. 'As stars fallen to Earth, part human, part celestial. Once we turn thirteen we start to fade.'

'I don't understand.'

'Our light begins to go out,' he says. 'And it's only fuelled by the extinguishing of another soul – the stronger the spirit, the brighter the light. I still take food and water, but it's not enough to live.'

A rain starts to fall with the leaves.

'Wait,' I say. 'You were going to . . . extinguish me. Are you— does that mean, if you don't, then you'll die?'

Leo shrugs and pulls his hand through his wet hair again, and I'm reminded of the first time I saw him, looking as if he'd been uprooted, transported from another place. And now I know from which place. He never quite looked as if he belonged in Cambridge. But here he looks as if he belongs absolutely. And now he's going to uproot himself.

'But, but . . .' My heart is beating too fast and I can't catch my breath. 'In two days, I don't . . .'

'Don't worry,' Leo says. 'It's fine. It's far less than I deserve. It'll be quick, I'm afraid I won't suffer as much as I deser—'

'It's not fine,' I snap. 'Don't be so fucking stupid. It's not – it's not . . .'

I don't see him move but Leo is beside me again, touching his fingers tentatively to my face. 'Don't cry, please, don't.' He brushes my wet cheeks, wiping away my tears. 'I'm not worth it. I'm a savage, a sadist, you should hate me, you should . . .'

'I do,' I say, wanting to sink into him, wanting to pull away. 'I do. I hate you.' I swallow. 'I hate you for what you've done and, most of all, I hate that I love you.'

'I'm sorry,' Leo whispers. 'I'm sorry, I'm sorry, I'm . . .'

He says it, over and over and over again.

3.33 a.m. – Bea

Tonight Bea returns to Everwhere, travelling on the tides of her dreams, waking once she gets there, as she had as a young girl. When she opens her eyes all the pieces of the puzzle – the half-memories, the images, the echoes – snap suddenly into place.

So now Bea has it: certain and irrefutable proof, the truth of who she was and who she is. Paradoxically, she's both shocked and unsurprised, since it has been building for days, weeks. Or, indeed, years and lifetimes if her *mamá* is to be believed. Vali was right after all, to believe in fate. Bea is dark. She doesn't have a choice. Be it fate or destiny, what it's not is a decision.

If only it were, she'd be free to make a different one.

30th October – 2 days . . .

9.17 a.m. – Scarlet

'Get up, Grandma. It's a beautiful day. Let's go for a walk.'

Sitting in bed, Esme pulls the blankets up to her chin.

'It's sunny,' Scarlet persists. 'The sun is actually shining. Come on, we can't let that go to waste. Grandma?'

But Esme shakes her head, refusing to meet her granddaughter's eye.

Scarlet refuses to admit that her grandmother is getting worse. She decides it's a blip, a slight downslide before she'll perk up again. Of course, she knows this isn't how the disease works. She can feel Esme retreating further and further into herself, so it seems sometimes as if she's already halfway into the next world. Sometimes it's as if her grandmother is travelling to this place and isn't sure she wants to come back. Sometimes, when Scarlet walks into a room, her grandma will look at her as if she wishes Scarlet wouldn't come any closer, wishes she'd leave again, so that Esme won't have to return to Earth.

'Okay, Grandma, I'll go by myself.' Scarlet keeps her voice light, bright. 'I'll stop at the market, I'll bring yellow tulips to cheer you up.' She leans in to kiss her grandmother on the cheek, but Esme turns away.

When Scarlet reaches the doorway, she stops. She's a coward. She'd vowed that today she'd tell her grandmother the dreadful news. So, what's she going to do? Wait until the removal van arrives? Scarlet turns back, walking slowly to Esme's bedside, as if she were walking to the gallows.

'I – I need to tell you something, Grandma.' She crouches beside the bed. 'I, we . . .'

The seconds stretch and swell, time elongates and thins, until Scarlet is taut as a copper wire about to snap.

'I'm sorry, Grandma, we can't live here, we have to move, we can't afford to keep the café anymore. We . . . I tried to save it but I, I couldn't.'

Every word on a single breath.

Scarlet inhales. Her grandmother is looking at her as if she's seeing something else entirely. Scarlet waits for her to scream, to slap her, to sob. When she does none of these, Scarlet wonders if she'll have to repeat herself until she's sure that Esme has heard. And then a tear slips from the side of her grandmother's eye and slides down her cheek. And Scarlet feels as if a surgeon were sticking his fingers into the ventricles of her heart and slowly cleaving her apart.

She will have to replay this moment over and over. Every hour of every day. When the café closes. When the packing starts. When they leave, when they're living in a strange new place. Scarlet will have to explain. She will relive her guilt and shame, again and again, until the time when finally her grandma remembers nothing at all.

10.52 p.m. – Liyana

Liyana takes a deep breath and sinks slowly under. She opens her eyes to the filmy expanse of water above. It's her first night in the new flat – Clapton Way, Hackney – and in the dismal little bathtub. Squirming and shifting, she tries to fully immerse herself. But in this cramped plastic piece of shit, Liyana can only fully submerge while assuming the foetal position.

Her shift starts in an hour. Midnight until ten. She can't stand another night at Tesco. But she will. Liyana pictures her aunt slumped on the sofa, ignoring the call of the boxes to be unpacked, watching repeats of *EastEnders*. Since they moved into the flat, Nya hasn't stirred. Stuffing herself with Waitrose cheese crackers (charitably left behind by the bailiffs) and inhaling cheap Chardonnay, Nya has ensconced herself in a bell jar of denial, the glass too thick for Liyana's voice to penetrate, no matter how loud she shouts.

Liyana rises. Water droplets cling to her hair and skin, unwilling to let her go. She uncurls her legs. Shitty tiny bath. Shitty Tesco. Shitty life. The dissonant shrieks of Tiffany Butcher seep through the flimsy walls. Liyana feels a sudden wave of fury gathering force. If Aunt Nya hadn't been so bloody selfish and irresponsible, Liyana wouldn't be in this fucking mess right now. She'd be sitting in a bathtub that didn't cramp her muscles, she'd still be living in her family home, she'd be studying Fine Art at the Slade. She'd have Kumiko – who still hasn't fully forgiven her – in her bed.

The furious wave subsides, drawing back, only to swell again, undulating along the bottom of the bathtub as Liyana imagines snatching her aunt's wine glass and smashing it to the floor. Water laps at the islands of her knees as Liyana's hand draws sharply across her aunt's cheek, a slap so hard it elicits a scream, finally snapping Nya out of her catatonic state. Waves splash over the sides as Liyana imagines seizing her aunt by her cornrows, dragging her through the hallway then plunging her face into the water. Nya flails but Liyana holds firm, pushing down until, at last, her aunt stops fighting and her body goes slack.

Fuck.

Liyana snaps out of her reverie. The bathwater is bubbling, suddenly so hot it's starting to boil. She scrambles out, slipping like a seal onto the wet floor, pulling herself up, shivering, staring in horrified wonder at curls of steam lifting from the surface of the water.

11.59 p.m. – Goldie

It was a while before I wanted to kill my stepfather. But, after I had the thought, I knew it was only a matter of time. A matter of how. A matter of when.

I discovered he was allergic to nuts by accident. He never told me. I think he saw it as some sort of weakness, a vulnerability, a chink in the armour. It was Ma who let it slip, because of Teddy. I'd come home from school munching a Snickers and offered it to him. She came screaming out of the kitchen, pushing me away, stuffing her fingers into Teddy's mouth. He started to scream from the shock. Then I was screaming too. When we'd all calmed she explained why I must never bring nuts into the flat again. 'Promise me,' she said. 'Not ever.' And I did, immediately. I was terrified of hurting Teddy. 'Your stepfather,' Ma added, as an afterthought. 'He has it too.'

The idea didn't occur to me straight away, I'm ashamed to say. It was so simple. And it was. I only had to be patient, enduring his near-nightly visits, until the evening Ma finally went out, abandoning her family for a few pints with her friends, entrusting me with getting my stepfather's tea and putting Teddy to bed.

I was meticulous in my planning. As meticulous as a ten-year-old, albeit a gifted one, could be. On the way home from school I stopped at the newsagents and bought a packet of salted peanuts and a Snickers. I crumbled the peanuts into the curry Ma had made for tea, adding dried chilli powder to disguise the taste. I watched him eat, every bite. I was calm. I felt no remorse, no regret. If it wouldn't have betrayed me to force his face into the bowl, I would have done that.

Afterwards, I scrubbed the plates, the sink, everything half a dozen times. He was slumped over on the carpet, having fallen from his chair – sitting on that spot I never touch, now wet with piss. The TV was still on. Tottenham beating Arsenal 3–1. I stuffed the empty peanut packet in my underwear – to be discarded in a bin on the way to school the next morning – and bit off an inch of the Snickers, leaving the rest beside him. I caught sight of Teddy's wooden rattle, which had rolled under the sofa, and felt a sudden urge to smash it into my stepfather's face. I wanted to bludgeon every inch of his lazy body, to beat him beyond recognition. Of course, I couldn't. And even if I had, I wouldn't have been able to mark him even half as deeply as he'd marked me.

So I clenched my hands into fists, digging my nails into my palms until the rage ebbed and I started to cry. Then I called Ma. She never understood what'd happened. She kept asking why he'd eat something he was allergic to. It made no sense. The police agreed but, though they interviewed me, they never seemed to suspect me. Ma had a solid alibi. So that was that. And when Ma died, four years later, the question died with her.

31st October – 1 day . . .

3.13 a.m. – Bea

Bea sits on the bathroom floor in a puddle of her own blood. She's discovered that the opening of old wounds is far more painful than the opening of new ones. So now she draws the razor along the raw red flesh of cuts made only a few days ago. Pain shoots up her spine, tears roll down her cheeks, as the cuts open again.

With every day that's passed since Vali's death, her rage has only been rising. Which accounts for the dreams of black feathers and slaughtered stags. It is rage she must expel which means inflicting it on herself, lest she embark on a killing rampage across London. She even fears for her *mamá* sleeping in the next room, since the desire to inflict harm often swells so suddenly, so forcefully, that it's all Bea can do not to act upon it. The scream builds in her chest like a dreadful wave of nausea but, though her body is desperate to expel it, she manages to swallow it down.

As she draws a finger through the blood on the linoleum floor, Bea understands where this will lead. It's inevitable. She cannot contain this fury forever. It will escape. So it's only right that she turn it on herself, detonating the bomb under controlled conditions before it explodes in the vicinity of innocents. And they are all innocent, excepting her.

Exactly how she'll do it, Bea isn't sure. Ropes are too unreliable, guns too quick, pills too painless. She'll probably stick with razors. She has an affinity for them now and they'll produce the right amount of pain. Timing is the only question. It's simply too morbid to do it the night she turns eighteen. And too cruel to her *mamá,* something Bea feels guilty—

You'll do nothing of the sort. Now get up off that floor and come to me.

Bea turns. But she's alone in the bathroom and the door's still locked.

Get up. Get up. Get up!

And so she does.

3.33 a.m. – Goldie

Last night, Leo begged me to return to him again. My eyes close and I prise them open. I'm exhausted. All I want to do is sleep. But I know where sleep will take me, and I'm scared to see him again. My eyes close. I force them open. I don't want to see him and I do want to see him and, eventually, I know that I will.

Then I am walking along a stone path through an avenue of trees. Then Leo is standing in front of me. I don't stop. He falls into step beside me.

'I don't expect forgiveness, and I'm not asking for it,' he says, as if he's already been carrying on a conversation without me. 'I don't even want it. What I did was unforgivable. Still, I hope you know . . .'

I stop walking.

'You know . . .' His green eyes cloud with tears. 'That I did, that I do, that I will . . .'

I look at him. I look at him for a long time without saying anything. Then I nod. After all, how can it be any other way? He is in my heart.

'So, will you let me teach you?' He's tentative. 'Will you let me help you learn how to fight?'

I nod again. And I try not to think that, if he doesn't kill soon, he'll die.

3.33 a.m. – Esme

Esme feels herself slipping, as if her bed has become a boat waiting to bear her away on a journey from which she will never return. She's not scared. She only wishes her granddaughter were sitting beside her now, so she could hold Scarlet's hand as she goes.

Her granddaughter's name sits on Esme's lips, if only she could summon the energy to say it, to shout it. Still, Scarlet must be here, for the last thing Esme feels is her granddaughter's hand. The last thing she sees is her daughter's face. Ruby is speaking, but Esme can't hear. The words take shape in Ruby's eyes: words of gratitude, apology, prayer.

Esme's lips move, though no sound escapes. Still, it doesn't matter. In this space between life and death, mother and daughter are connected again. Here, in the unknowable, all is known. All is understood. And forgiven.

6.29 a.m. – Scarlet

'Scarlet! Scarlet!'

Scarlet wakes, sitting before she's even opened her eyes. Esme's calling. Scarlet is stumbling halfway down the hallway when she realizes – it wasn't her grandmother, it was her. She was calling her own name.

Scarlet falls silent, stopping outside the door. She doesn't want to go into her grandmother's room. Not tonight. She wants to sleep, wants to dream, wants to pretend her way into another world. The one with the rivers and trees, the unwavering moon and perpetually falling leaves.

But something has shifted.

There is a stiller stillness, a quieter quiet. There is absence, loss.

Scarlet doesn't need to step into her grandmother's

room to know she's no longer there, doesn't need to walk to her bedside to see she's not breathing, doesn't need to touch her cheek to know it will be cold.

Still, Scarlet creeps forward, treading on the carpet as if Esme will feel every step. She stands beside her grandmother's bed, watches her inert chest, brushes a fingertip along her cheek. Then places a kiss on her grandmother's lips. She sits holding Esme's hand, sinking into memories – dancing in the kitchen and setting fire to toast. At the edges of memories wait decisions, necessities, the question of what she must do next.

No doubt doctors believe it's impossible to die of a broken heart. But when they give Scarlet the official report, she'll know better. Her grandmother, already skirting the edge of the next world, was pushed over the precipice by shock and grief. So Scarlet must face the impossible fact that she killed the two women who had raised her, loved her and kept her safe.

Scarlet looks out of the bedroom window, to the lightening sky. Outside, the sunrise is like a dying fire and the remaining stars flicker like greying embers in the grate.

11.15 a.m. – Goldie & Liyana

'Are you all right?' I ask.

'Yeah, I'm fine,' Liyana says.

I wait, since I know she's not – I can feel anxiety coming off her in waves, crashing to the shore at my feet.

'It's just . . . There's a lot of . . . Kumiko's still not properly forgiven me, my aunt's having a nervous breakdown, we've been kicked out of our house . . .'

'Shit.' I wait, and when she says no more, I don't ask. I know my sister well enough now not to push her. I wonder what she'd say if I told her about Leo.

Liyana follows me along Trumpington Street towards King's Parade. Passing St Catherine's College and the wall of red leaves, I quicken my pace and Liyana hurries to keep up.

'We're nearly there.'

Liyana grins at me. 'I still can't believe you cut off your hair because of my story.'

'Shut up,' I say, stroking my bare neck.

When I see the sign for the No. 33 Café, I slow. All at once I'm not sure. What will I say to the red-haired girl? That I dreamed of her and think she's my sister? When Liyana did the same with me, I held her at knifepoint. And this girl works in a café. She has access to plenty of sharp knives.

'Here.' I slow to a stop.

We both look up at the *Closed* sign on the door.

'Oh,' I say, not wanting to admit my relief. 'It's a shame but we could . . .'

'Don't be such a defeatist,' Liyana says.

'Hey, you're not the one who—'

'Look!' Liyana bends to pick something up from the pavement then stands again, holding a black feather. She smiles. 'It's a sign.'

'I know,' I say, surprised since my sister hasn't shown any signs of stupidity so far. 'It says "closed".'

'No.' Liyana nods at the feather. 'Not that, this. *This* is a sign.'

I look at her, not certain how to respond. 'The feather?'

'It's . . . never mind.' Liyana drops the feather. It floats to the pavement. 'Let's knock. What can she say?'

'A lot,' I say. 'Let's come back another day when she's open.'

'I can't, I've not got another day off for two weeks.' Liyana peers through the glass door. 'Look, there she is.'

Our red-headed sister sits at a table with a man. He's not

handsome, not a man you'd notice if you didn't know him. But he holds her hand with such tenderness, as if trying to contain her sorrow. For she looks like a fire has burned through her, destroying every emotion but grief.

'Oh!' Liyana says, not noticing – but perhaps I see the girl's sorrow only because I'm full of it too. 'I've seen her before.'

'You have?' I say. 'Where? Asleep or awake?'

'I'm not sure.' Liyana bites her lip. 'I'm not having dreams like you. At least, I don't think – but I'm remembering things . . .'

We watch as our sister drops her head and the man reaches out to cup her cheek in his hand. The gesture is tender, tentative, and I feel my eyes fill.

'Let's go,' I say. 'Let's come back another day.'

Liyana slips her arm around my waist and gives me a quick, tight squeeze. We turn together and walk away.

1st November

Revelation

I start to shut the door before I've even fully opened it.

'Wait, please,' Leo begs. He stops short of wedging his foot between the door and the frame, but his desperation hits me with such force that I catch the door before it slams shut.

I shake my head. It's one thing to see him in my dreams, quite another to see him now. It's too real, too sharp, too soon. I'm not ready. I need more time.

'We don't have more time.'

I'm no longer surprised that he hears my thoughts.

'Please.' His voice claws through the gap. 'It's tonight. You're going to Everwhere tonight. And I still need to teach you—'

'You've taught me.'

'A few things. There's so much more. You don't even remember how to control your element yet, let alone . . .' I feel his anxiety rise, thickening the air. I let the door open an inch and I'm gratified to see how devastated he still looks.

He gives me a cautious smile. 'Happy birthday.'

'Hardly,' I say, finding that I still want to hurt him. Love and hate entwined.

Leo nods. 'I under— Look, you don't have to come with me now. I can meet you there tonight, but if we go now we'll have more time. I can show you . . .'

I glance down at my bare feet, stubbing the toes of my left foot into the door jamb.

'Please,' Leo begs. 'Please.'

It's not the begging that does it. It's realizing that I've never heard Leo sound so scared. I think of my brother in London, post-Macbeth, sleeping soundly (or having nightmares) with his friends. If Leo's been telling the truth, I might never see him again. I've written him a letter. I hope he'll never read it.

'I only wish he was here tonight so I could kiss him goodbye.'

Gateway

'I don't understand. Where are we going?'

'You wouldn't believe me if I tried to explain,' Leo says. 'And I know it's asking a lot, after everything, but please, trust me.'

I follow. Not because I trust him, but because I trust myself. My senses are sharpening daily, giving me confidence in the instructions of my instincts. Leo walks quickly along the moonlit pavements so I have to dash every few seconds to keep pace.

The filigree pinnacles of King's College rise up beside me as I scurry past. I glance at the carved turrets of Great St Mary's Church, the stumpy chimney stacks of the Senate House, the squat towers of Gonville & Caius . . . It seems that everything is shifting, as if the curtain of daylight has been drawn back to reveal the dark, and now, lit by moonlight, the truth of the world is revealed. Not as I've always seen it but as I once believed it to be. I imagine elegant stone spires elongating into the fine-spun branches of birch trees, chiselled turrets transforming into the trunks of ash trees, the sawn-off chimney stacks into witch hazel, the thick towers into adolescent oaks . . .

Leo starts to slow along Trinity Street, then stops outside

St John's College. Everwhere fades as I admire the vast red brick pillars enclosing the wooden gates, culminating in turrets so venerable, so imposing that they might be concealing knights in chain mail ready to tip pots of hot tar on our heads. A stone sculpture of an unknown saint or king stands above the college crest painted in gold. I take a step back.

Leo meets my eye; for a moment, I forget who he is and what he's done.

'Am I about to be initiated into an antiquated college cult?' I say, needing to bring a little light to the dark. 'I won't do any weird rituals – I draw the line at chicken blood.'

Leo gives me a half-hearted smile. Taking a key from his pocket, he unlocks a small door cut into the grand wooden gates. He holds it open. I hesitate.

'Come on. It's nearly time.'

I step through, thinking that perhaps I should have told someone where I was going, what I was doing. But who? And what would I have said? Leo hurries across the court, sticking to the stone paths. I glance up at the rows of darkened windows carved into the ancient walls edging the lawns. I wonder if anyone is up this late. I follow Leo into a stone corridor, our footsteps echoing like those of a child scampering after a single-minded parent. We cross another courtyard before Leo comes to a sharp stop outside a walled garden. On the gate is a sign: *The Master's Garden*.

'I don't think we're allowed in there,' I say. 'Even at half past three in the morning.'

'Lucky then that we're not going there,' Leo says.

I say nothing.

'At three thirty-three a.m., the moon will slip from behind the clouds to illuminate the gate. Then we'll open it and walk through, not into the Master's Garden, but into your world—'

'Look,' I interrupt. It's all too much, too soon. 'I think

perhaps – I don't think I should be out so late. I should be getting back . . .'

Leo reaches towards me as I'm inching off the stone path, my heels hitting the grass verge. 'Wait, Goldie, don't be— Don't you trust me?'

I nod, then think again of Ma. 'It's just that . . .'

'What? You think I'm bringing you here to . . . You really think I'd be able to . . .' He can't finish the sentence, but I hear the final words as if he'd spoken them aloud.

'No, but it's— With Teddy I can't afford to take chances.'

Leo looks stricken. 'Shit, Goldie. How could – how can you think that of me? I know what I've done, but after everything we've—'

'Can you blame me?' Anger flares in my chest. 'You killed my mother. You were intending to kill me. You've changed your mind now, but still . . .'

As I speak tears fill Leo's eyes and slip down his cheeks. And I'm struck by the fact that I've never seen him like this before. Hate recedes and as love rises, ribbons of desire begin to unfurl within me, unbidden, as they did the first time we met.

Leo takes a hesitant step towards me, as if I'm a skittish deer he's trying to feed. 'You know – you know I would never, never . . .'

I nod. 'I know.' And I do.

Leo steps forward again. This time I let his hand touch mine and I slip my fingers into his.

'I wish I hadn't left this too late. I wish I'd brought you here the night of the first-quarter moon just after I met you, then at least you'd stand a fighting chance of . . .'

I'm about to fill in his words, to point out that when we first met his aim had been to exterminate me. But I know that he's thinking the same thing, that he's hating himself, so I don't.

'Right.' I step forward so we're standing side by side in front of the gate. 'I'm here. Just tell me what to do.'

'It won't be a moment.'

And sure enough, the moon slides out from behind the clouds and the iron gate is illuminated, each midnight curlicue shimmering with a silver hue. Leo reaches up with his free hand to push the gate open and, together, we step through.

Arrival

Leo's right, it's most definitely not the master's private garden. It's not St John's. It's not this world at all. It's the place from my dreams. It takes a few minutes for my eyes to adjust to the dense fog that hangs in the air, a few minutes until I can make out the shapes of towering trees and fallen trunks, until I focus enough to hear the rush of a river nearby, of water running over rocks.

'Why is everything so pale?' I whisper, as if someone might be eavesdropping. 'It's . . . it's like stepping inside a black-and-white photograph.' I reach up to brush a fallen leaf from my hair and see blanched leaves falling above and all around me, like rain. 'Or a very strange snow globe.'

Still holding Leo's hand, I walk on. We step from stone to stone, sometimes sinking into basins of moss, everything sprinkled with a dusting of dried white leaves. They gather in drifts, shoring up the edges of the fallen trunks and the long-fingered roots of the trees. They float along the streams, swirling in the currents of the water. I feel the earth hum under my feet, the stretch and pull of unseen growth deep beneath. When I step into pools of moonlight, it feels warm on my skin.

I feel something I can't quite place, can't quite remember. And then it returns: the feeling of coming home.

Bea

Bea walks quickly along the streets of South Kensington. She has no idea where she's going, nor does she care. She only wants to be as far from her *mamá*'s flat as possible. She hasn't heard her father's voice again since stepping out into the cold night air, but she doesn't care about that either. She will go where she damn well pleases. And, right now, all she wants to do is keep walking.

On Cromwell Road she slows. Bea's always been drawn to the Natural History Museum and, as it comes into view, she remembers the school trips, seeing the diplodocus skeleton for the first time, being struck by its massive power.

Now she stops at the entrance, her hand resting on the thick brass lock of the gateway barring her from the museum steps. She gazes at the towers flanking the vast doors, the dozens and dozens of great stained-glass windows, the turrets reaching towards the stars.

As a wash of moonlight falls over the gate, in the silver glow the memory of that place returns, suddenly and completely, as vivid and real as every pane of glass and brick that built her favourite museum. Bea glances up at the moon, then pushes open the gate and walks through, stepping from a street in South Kensington and into Everwhere.

Liyana

Liyana is woken by music, the strumming chords of a guitar. She wrinkles her nose and rubs her eyes before peering into the darkened room. Annoyed to be awake at – she glances at her phone – not yet three o'clock in the morning, Liyana shuts her eyes again and burrows her head under the pillows. But even when she presses the pillows down hard, Liyana can still hear the music.

'What the hell?' She flings back the duvet and slides out of bed. Crossing the carpet she yanks aside the curtains, unlocks the latch, and sticks her head out of the window. Wincing at the rush of cold night air, Liyana peers out onto the street below. Standing in a yellow pool of artificial light, a man strums a guitar. Liyana squints at him.

'Mazmo?'

'Hey, Ana!' He waves up with great enthusiasm, as if his arrival under her window in the middle of the night were a perfectly respectable or, indeed, anticipated rendezvous. 'Happy birthday!'

'What the hell are you doing?' Liyana hisses. 'Are you drunk?'

Mazmo laughs. 'I'm being romantic! I'm serenading you, like that bloke, what's he called? Cyrano de something, or . . . Romeo.'

'That's not romantic.' Liyana raises an eyebrow. 'It's massively inappropriate, given that I'm certainly not Roxane or Juliet.'

'Oh, I wouldn't say you're so far removed from two of the most beautiful women of all time.'

'Mazmo,' Liyana warns. 'I told you we're not—'

'I know, I know, but can't you let me play a little make-believe?' Mazmo sets down his guitar. 'It's fun.'

Liyana yawns. 'It'd be a lot more fun at a decent hour. At, I don't know, any time before midnight or after dawn.'

Mazmo grins. 'Come on.' He beckons her down. 'I've got a surprise for you.'

'Can't it wait till morning?' Liyana asks. 'It's freezing.'

'So put on a dressing gown and slippers. It'll be worth every toe lost to frostbite, I promise.'

Liyana rolls her eyes. Mazmo Owethu Muzenda-Kasteni is one of the more persistent suitors she's ever encountered, but he's harmless enough and, now that Liyana is slightly more awake, she's curious.

'Give me five minutes,' she says, pulling the window shut.

Scarlet

Scarlet is locking the café door when, through the glass, she sees the woman. She hasn't opened today, has barely left her bed since returning from the morgue – except when Walt paid a brief surprise visit. Scarlet squints at the woman, lingering in the shadows cast by King's College across the street. She holds a cigarette between her lips, exhaling long puffs of smoke. Scarlet stares as the woman throws down her cigarette, steps out of the shadows and walks across the street. As she steps under a streetlamp Scarlet sees that the woman has cropped her hair and dyed the red to black, but her wood-brown eyes are surely the same, as is the way she walks: ready to pierce anything daring to come between her and her destination.

The recognition is instant, but the confusion takes longer to clear. How can this woman who was once her mother be striding across the street? Her mother is dead.

Scarlet isn't certain how Ruby Thorne enters the café, since she doesn't recall unlocking and opening the door, but she is still so dazed, so disorientated, that it might have happened in the usual fashion. All Scarlet knows is that her not-dead mother is now standing within touching distance, although still feeling as untouchable, as unreachable as she ever did.

'You're . . . alive,' Scarlet says at last, when it becomes clear that her once-mother won't be the first to speak. 'But you're—'

Her dead-mother nods. 'I'm sorry.'

'That's not . . . I don't understand. How are you here? I don't, I don't . . .'

'I can't make excuses,' Ruby says. 'I know what I did was unforgivable. I—'

'You. Died.' Scarlet sounds out the words. 'You died in a fire that burned down our home, a fire that I . . .'

'Perhaps you should sit down.' Ruby nods towards a table surrounded by chairs.

Scarlet does not. 'How . . . What . . . ?'

The woman takes a deep breath. 'I need a cigarette. Do you mind if I smoke in here?'

Scarlet stares at her. 'It's illegal.'

'Oh, yes.' Ruby Thorne sighs. 'I've been away too long, I keep forgetting. But I don't think anyone will notice, do you? Not at this time of night.'

Scarlet narrows her eyes, the shock starting to thin a little. 'Tell me why you're here. Tell me why you're not dead.'

Her resurrected-mother takes a packet of cigarettes out of her pocket and fiddles with the plastic wrap. 'We . . . Your grandma thought it would be better for you not to know. She thought it would be less traumatizing – that death was better than desertion.'

'What?' Scarlet stumbles into a chair and sits. 'But— No, that's not— No.'

Ruby Thorne nods.

'Grandma knew?' Sparks fire from Scarlet's fingertips. 'No. You're lying. She wouldn't, she . . .'

And then Scarlet remembers her grandmother's dream. Esme knew.

'She thought it would be better—'

'You keep telling me what she thought,' Scarlet snaps. 'And I can forgive *her*. What's so cruel is your timing – why the fuck are you telling me this now?'

'Because I had to—'

'Why didn't you just stay dead?' Scarlet's hands burn by her sides. 'After all this time, it would've been better.'

Ruby is silent.

'But, I still don't . . . Why now? I'm guessing you know about Grandma – so why taint my memory of her. Are you really so cruel?'

Ruby sighs. 'I'm sorry for the timing, truly, but I couldn't come before and I couldn't wait any longer—'

'Why?' Scarlet interrupts. 'You've come to say what? That you've been watching us all these years and you didn't want to turn up at Grandma's funeral – you thought that'd be in poor taste?'

'Look, I know you're furious, you have every right to be. And you can scream at me all you want, as you should. But right now, I need you to listen.'

'Thanks for your permission, "Mum",' Scarlet snaps. 'But I don't exactly need it, you know. I—'

'Your father,' Ruby interrupts. 'You need to know . . . He tried to kill me once; I escaped.' She meets her daughter's eye. 'I didn't realize then that you were in even more danger than I was.'

Scarlet glares at the woman who used to be her mother. For a moment, shock trumps fury, and she must know. 'What the hell are you talking about?'

'Your father is . . .' The fear in Ruby's voice cools even the fire at Scarlet's fingertips. 'He's extremely dangerous.'

'So you say. And why should I believe you? Surely you've now proved yourself to be the most deceitful, most deceptive' – Scarlet's hands begin to heat again – 'most untrustworthy bitch who ever—'

'Did you read my letter?'

'What letter?'

'The story. Red Riding Hood,' Ruby says. 'I read it to

you when you were a little girl. I hoped it'd help you remember happier—'

'No,' Scarlet says, not wanting to believe it, not wanting to credit Ruby Thorne with something so touching. 'You didn't, I don't believe you.'

'I hoped you'd know it was me.'

'I didn't, I don't.'

'I read it every night for years.'

Scarlet shakes her head. Blue sparks fire from her fingertips.

'I thought, if you remembered you trusted me once, that it'd help you now.'

'Help me?' Scarlet snaps. 'You mean help you.'

Ruby meets her daughter's scowl and holds her gaze. Scarlet looks into the only eyes in the world that exactly reflect her own. And then she remembers: curling into her mother's arms, listening to the words she knew so well, lulled to sleep by the same story again and again.

'You need to come with me.'

'Why?' A moment ago, Scarlet would have told her to go to hell. Now she'll at least allow an explanation.

'Because if you don't, your father will try to seduce you. And if you resist him, he'll kill you.'

Scarlet frowns. 'If he's that dangerous, then I'll go to the police—'

'You can't,' Ruby says. 'It's not here he'll get you. It's in Everwhere.'

'Everwhere?' Scarlet looks at her mother as if she's lost her last tenuous grip on reality. 'What the fuck are you talking about?'

'I know you hate me, Scarlet. And you should. But I'm only asking that you at least let me help you, let me take you to this place, let me show you what you can do, so you stand a chance of surviving your father. Please.'

It is this last word that does it. Her mother has never begged.

'All right,' Scarlet concedes. 'You can show me, then you can leave.'

Goldie

'You should be wearing your shoes,' Leo says. 'You don't know when you might need to run.'

We're walking alongside a river. I've taken off my shoes and am carrying them, so I can feel the wet moss on the soles of my feet. I'd like to step into the stream, to feel the current rushing between my toes, but I suspect Leo wouldn't allow it.

'Where are we going?' I ask. 'I'll put them on when we get there.'

'To a place where you can practise your skills,' Leo says. 'So when you fight you stand a chance of—'

'Survival,' I say.

Leo says nothing.

'But I don't have any skills.' I'm worried by his raised expectations. He clearly has misguided notions as to my potential and I'm reluctant to disappoint him. I brush my fingers along a tree trunk, peeling off a long strip of bark. I crumble it with one hand as I walk, watching the woody flakes fall and settle on the stones beneath my feet.

I know Leo keeps warning me of what's to come, telling me to be on my guard, trying to scare me into alertness. But it's difficult to believe him because I don't feel fearful here. Indeed, with every step I feel stronger and safer than I've ever felt before.

Bea

'Dr Finch?' Bea frowns when she sees him, lingering in the shadows. She has the feeling he's been here awhile, watching her absorbed by the infinitely falling leaves and towering willow trees reaching for the moon. 'What the fuck are you doing here?'

'Why shouldn't I be here?' He steps forward onto the moss. 'I've as much right as you.'

Bea shrugs and starts walking. 'I wouldn't have credited you with any Grimm blood in your veins. You're not much of a man, let alone . . .'

But she still can't entirely remember the rules, the physical laws governing this place. She doesn't know who's allowed and able to be here and who is not. All she remembers now is that she's here to meet her sisters, for which she is curious and keen, and her father, for which she is not.

'Wait.' Dr Finch hurries to catch up.

'Shouldn't you be at home with your wife?' Bea asks, wishing he was.

'She's asleep,' he says. 'She's not missing me.'

'Yeah, well, nor was I. So why don't you take a different path?' Bea nods in the direction of a river that winds away from them.

Dr Finch says nothing, but continues walking beside her. And, because he's silent, she allows him to stay. The moon disappears behind clouds. A dense, dark thing swoops down between them, before soaring up again into the pitch-black sky.

A blackbird. Bea thinks of the illustration she found in Fitzbillies. A memory tugs at her.

'A bat,' Dr Finch says.

Bea ignores him.

The memory rises.

I could fly. Once upon a time I could fly.

The moon breaks away from a bank of clouds, illuminating the path. Bea picks up her pace, walking faster and faster until she breaks into a run, legs lifting over the stones in great, swift strides. As she runs, Bea lets out shrieks of delight carried on the fog that rolls back to Dr Finch who walks in her wake.

Scarlet

'Where the hell are we?' Scarlet stands on a patch of moss, refusing to move. 'How— I don't understand . . . How did we get here?'

'You've been here before.'

'I have?'

'And you've been dreaming about it.'

This isn't a question. Scarlet gives a single reluctant nod.

'You came here as a child,' Ruby says. 'And you've been readying yourself to return.'

'I – I . . .' Scarlet wants to defy her mother, deny it all, except she can't.

'It's a place for you to realize your strengths, to hone your skills,' Ruby says, 'to become dominant enough that you might actually stand a chance of winning the fight.'

'What fight?' Scarlet frowns. 'And I don't have any—'

'Stop that,' Ruby snaps. 'Enough. Modesty, self-doubt, those things might get you approval at home, but here they'll get you killed.'

'I'm not being modest.' Scarlet shakes a white leaf free from her head. 'I simply don't know what you're talking about.'

'Oh, please.' Ruby rolls her eyes. 'Don't tell me you haven't noticed anything strange, anything—'

'What?'

'That look – you just thought of something, didn't you? I know that look.'

'No, you don't.' Scarlet curls her warming fingers into fists.

'I do. I'm your mother, I—'

Scarlet gives a wry laugh. 'Are you? I hadn't noticed.'

Ruby sighs. 'Scarlet, I'm sorry, but we don't have time for this. What I did was awful. I abandoned you. You hate me. I know, I deserve it. But now I'm risking my life to try and save yours. And if you don't at least stop punishing me long enough to let me help, then we'll both be dead before—'

'All right, all right.' Sparks of frustration fire from Scarlet's fingertips. 'I've got no idea what you're talking about, but I'll pretend I don't hate you, just for tonight. Okay?'

Truthfully, hate is already softening into dislike, not that Scarlet will admit it. She's still far from ready to let her mother off the hook. Love weighs less than fury – silver against lead on the chemical scale – but they might yet balance. One day.

'Thank you. Now, come on.' Ruby walks along the stone path, stepping over the snaking ivy, sinking into the moss. She stops and turns. 'Come on.'

Scarlet takes a tentative step. She snatches a leaf out of the air, watching its edges singe and curl in her palm before scrunching it to dust. 'What is it with all these bloody leaves? Where the hell are they falling from?'

'I don't know,' Ruby admits. 'I've never found anyone who knew.'

'I don't have you to thank for my sparkling mind then? I suppose my father is the one with the brains.'

Ruby stops so sharply that Scarlet almost falls against her. When she turns, the fear in her eyes again cools the fire at Scarlet's fingertips.

'Watch what you say about him.'

'Why?' Scarlet frowns. 'He can't hear me.'

'That's what you think?' Ruby says, incredulous now. 'He doesn't need to be here, he only has to think of you to hear your thoughts. I stand some chance of concealment, but you – he created you. So long as you're alive, you'll never escape him.'

Liyana

'I'm impressed, Maz,' Liyana says, a little breathless. 'I am.'

Mazmo, having ditched his guitar at the gate, gives a courtly bow with a flourish of his outstretched hand. 'I aim to please, my lady.'

'I don't know how the hell you did it, or even what you've done.' Liyana spins in circles, her face upturned to the stars. 'But it's . . . I've never seen stars so bright, and everything as white as if it's covered in snow – honestly, I didn't think you had it in you.'

Grinning, Mazmo steps towards Liyana with an open hand. With a shrug, she rests her hand in his. 'You're so beautiful, Ana. You make me forget every woman, man, being I've ever—'

'Maz, don't,' Liyana warns. 'This is all . . . astonishing, but it doesn't change anything. You know how I feel about . . .'

'I know, I know.' Mazmo plucks a leaf from the air, twirling it between finger and thumb. 'But you can't blame a boy for trying, now, can you?'

Liyana sighs. 'I don't understand men. I'd never— You don't mind seducing a woman by a process of wearing down her defences until – what? – she finally gives in and marries you?'

'Something like that.'

'But why would you want anyone who's not wild about you?'

Mazmo shrugs. 'It doesn't much matter how they feel in the beginning, it's how they feel at the end that counts. Anyway—'

'And there you go, the patriarchy summed up in a single sentence. God, if I had only a drop of your confidence.'

'Unfair. It's more animalistic than that. It's about the thrill of the chase.'

Liyana sighs. 'Courtship isn't a foxhunt.' She drops his hand and walks on alone, feeling a sudden longing for Kumiko. If only Liyana could bring her here. It'd be the grandest of grand gestures. Although she's a little fuzzy on the particulars of how they actually arrived, so she must make sure Mazmo explains everything before they leave. 'Where exactly— Are we still in London? Is this place like Winter Wonderland? It all feels so real, but— Oh!'

'Sorry, did I startle you?'

'N-no, I didn't realize you were so close behind, that's all . . .' Liyana distances herself again. 'But perhaps we should be going. It's late. I've never been out all night before. If my aunt—'

'Liar.'

Liyana frowns.

'Don't tell me you've never been out all night before. I bet some weekends you don't even go to bed.' Mazmo grins. 'Not to sleep, anyway.'

Liyana meets his eye, about to deny it. But the way he's looking at her now – as if he's a mackerel and she's a minnow – is so disquieting that she doesn't want to disagree, doesn't want to rile him. She feels the strength of him beside her. What did he call her once – athletic? Even so, she's no match.

'Well, I suppose . . .' Liyana turns to walk back the way they'd come. At least, she thinks it is, but can't be sure. All at once every towering tree looks exactly like every other, their trunks enveloped in tendrils of ivy, their pale leaves blown by a cross-hatch breeze. And the stones seem to have re-scattered themselves so that the path forks when it hadn't forked before, and the confetti of leaves is falling faster, threatening to blanket everything in white in a matter of minutes, rendering the land unnavigable. 'Maybe I have, I can't remember.'

'We're not leaving yet,' Mazmo says, his voice smooth as water over rocks. 'Not until I've shown you something. You can't leave without seeing it, since it's the reason I brought you here.'

Liyana stiffens as he takes hold of her hand again. 'What is it?'

'It's a surprise.' He tugs her forward so sharply that she stumbles, slipping on a stone. 'Come on. We'll have to walk awhile but it'll be worth the wait, I promise.'

Liyana blinks as raindrops settle on her lashes – when did it start raining? Between one second and the next a thick fog has rolled in, and Liyana realizes that she has no choice but to go with Mazmo now because, if she ran, which way would she go?

Goldie

'So, what is it you think I can do?' I'm scrambling up a fallen tree trunk, realizing too late that, since it's wider than I am tall, it won't be as easy as I'd anticipated. I reach out to Leo. 'A little help over here . . .'

He steps forward and clumsily hoists me up, his shoulder pushing under my thigh. Once I'm seated, straddling the trunk, Leo pulls himself up in a swift, elegant lift.

'So . . .' I dig a finger into the bark. 'When are you going to tell me?'

'Tell you what?'

'How you were planning to kill me.'

'What?' Leo's startled.

I shrug. 'Shouldn't I know, if I'm hoping to defend myself? I'll be better prepared if I know what's coming.'

'It's hard to say.' Leo burrows his fingernail into the tree trunk. 'Each soldier has his own preferences. Some play with their prey before . . .'

'Do – did you?'

Leo shakes his head. 'No. I was quick. Most soldiers are extremely strong and have the element of surprise to their advantage – since most sisters don't know what's coming. But—'

'Well, at least I have that in my favour.'

'More than that,' Leo says. 'You'll have the ultimate advantage tonight. Each soldier has his target. You were mine. So whichever soldier you fight, he won't know what's coming.'

'What?'

Leo peels off a long strip of bark. 'We need a little time to prepare, but after that you should be fine. Your sisters, on the other hand, it'll be much harder for—'

'Wait. What?' I stare at him. 'You never said anything about my sisters.'

Leo frowns. 'I thought you realized. I'm sorry, I didn't . . .'

I think of Liyana. Why didn't I take Leo seriously before, why didn't I warn her?

Leo reaches out, takes my hand. 'I'm sure she'll be fine. She's strong.'

'How do you know? You never met her.'

'She's a Sister Grimm,' Leo says, as if this says it all.

I take a deep breath. 'And what will he do to you? When he realizes what you've done.'

'I'm not certain.' Leo tries to smile. 'I don't think a soldier's ever disobeyed a direct order before.'

'He'll punish you,' I suggest, allowing myself to hope this might be the extent of it.

'Yes,' Leo concedes. 'He probably will.'

'But . . . he won't . . . ?'

'I'll take care of myself,' he says.

'But what if . . .' I still can't bring myself to say it.

'Well,' Leo says, attempting a smile. 'Given your abilities to give life, I'm sure you could resurrect me, even if he did.'

I stare at him, horrified. 'Don't even joke about that. Don't—'

'I'm not joking,' Leo interrupts. 'I'd imagine that with the combination of your powers and the potency of Aether here, you'd be able to do anything.'

I scowl at him. I won't ask about Aether. I don't want to know.

Leo gives me an apologetic smile. 'Don't worry . . . I'll take care of myself,' Leo says again. 'You need to prepare yourself for the kill.'

I look at Leo but, my instincts overwhelmed, I don't know if he's lying. Does he know what his father will do? I think of this soldier. I don't want to fight him; I certainly don't want to kill him. No matter what Leo claims about the necessity of it.

'If you don't,' Leo says, reading my thoughts again, 'you'll stand no chance of survival. Your father will kill you tonight. No question.'

'Yes, but—'

'I'm sorry, but we don't have time to discuss the merits and morals of all this.' Leo snaps a piece of bark. 'This is an eternal war and you've been conscripted into it. Any soldier here will kill you, given half a chance. If it makes you stronger, know that it's self-defence.'

I think of my stepfather.

'All right.' I sit up straighter. 'So, what is it you think I can do?'

Bea

'Wait,' Dr Finch calls. 'You're too fast – wait!'

But Bea doesn't wait, she can't, her legs have their own life and they refuse to slow. And she's glad to leave him behind, doesn't care she's being rude, doesn't care for anything other than running as fast as she possibly can.

Bea can't remember the last time she ran like this. Occasionally she's dashed for a train in the Underground, darting between closing doors, breathless. But with wobbling body parts, cramping muscles and aching lungs, it's not a nice feeling. In Everwhere, it's different. It is magnificent.

Bea runs faster than she's ever run, hurtling through the mists, feet darting over moss and stone so swiftly they seem to never touch the ground. She's light as a feather, a single swift arrow of muscle and breath. She is air, and the force of her body powerful as a hurricane. Bea grins into the wind, hair whipping back, heart pounding, lungs pumping. She runs on and on.

Far away, a whisper on distant winds, she hears him still calling.

Bea picks up such speed that she's no longer taking great steps over the stones, she's sailing over fallen tree trunks, legs stretched out in a perfect balletic leap. With another, Bea lifts into the air. She rises higher, higher still, above rivers and rocks, through falling leaves, beyond the thinnest branches of the tallest trees, soaring up into the moonlight.

Now that she's flying she remembers it all.

Scarlet

'If all that is true,' Scarlet says, 'then I don't see what I'm supposed to be able to do in self-defence. I might as well surrender right now.' And, in the wake of losing her grandma, Scarlet doesn't particularly care for life much right now. She sits with her resurrected-mother in a glade, a circle of stones pressed into the mossy ground. Scarlet sits on one side of the circle, Ruby on the other.

'Don't be ridiculous,' Ruby snaps. 'You'll do nothing of the sort. You're far stronger than you think, and you've not even tested yourself yet, so how would you know? I always told you never to give up, not ever—'

'I'm sorry.' Scarlet tears a vine of ivy from a nearby branch. 'Forgive me if I can't recall your pearls of mothering wisdom.'

Ruby ignores the barb. 'You have fire at your fingertips, yes? On Earth, you can't make much more than sparks. But here you can set light to fields, you can burn through entire forests, you can—'

Scarlet frowns. 'How do you know that?'

Ruby shrugs. 'What do you think I've been doing for the past ten years?'

'Oh, I don't know, joining circuses, robbing banks – whatever you fancied, I imagine, being finally unencumbered by a daughter you never wanted.'

Ruby is silent. When she speaks her voice is a whisper. 'I did. I wanted you more than anything else in the world.'

'You had a fucking funny way of showing it.'

'I sold my soul to get you. The consequences were more than I expected.'

Scarlet frowns but says nothing.

'For the last ten years, I've been hiding from your father and doing my research.'

'I don't—'

'For goodness' sake.' Ruby meets her daughter's gaze and holds it. 'There is a soldier stalking you here, right now. If he finds you, he will kill you. So, please, will you just give it a try?'

Scarlet is about to protest again but, at the furious

determination on her mother's face, closes her mouth and clenches her teeth. She's aware that it always sparks when her emotions are heightened. Scarlet looks at Ruby, focuses on channelling all her feelings of hatred and anger into the palms of her hands.

At first, Scarlet feels nothing.

Then her hands start to heat as if she were holding two burning hot coals. As she stares down a sudden flare of electricity arcs from the centre of each palm, cutting through the fog, the two uniting into a single bolt. For several moments, as Scarlet stares open-mouthed, it curls and sparks like an electric eel. Then, all at once, it dives, piercing the trunk of an ancient oak, splitting it down the middle. The almighty crash of the sliced tree as it falls sends shockwaves that tremor through the ground at their feet.

For a second the falling leaves are suspended, immobile, in the air. Scarlet stares at her mother, who stares at Scarlet, speechless.

The soldier watching from behind a willow tree takes a step back.

Liyana

'I know how much you love water,' Mazmo says, coming to a sudden stop.

Liyana stumbles, stubbing her toe on a stone. 'I don't remember telling you that,' she says, reaching down to rub her toe.

'The first time we met, at the swimming pool. Remember? Anyway, I've brought you to this place because it has the most beautiful lakes I've ever seen.' He smiles – Liyana can't see this through the thick fog but hears it leak into his voice. 'The most beautiful lake I've ever seen for the most beautiful girl I've ever met. That's fitting, isn't it?'

Liyana says nothing.

'Don't be like that.' He squeezes her hand. 'It's no fun if you sulk.'

'I – I'm only thinking that it's, um, a shame I won't be able to see it in this fog,' Liyana says. 'Maybe we should come back another night?'

'And waste that walk? No, the weather's always changing here. We'll wait. It won't be long.'

'All right,' Liyana says, since it's clear from Mazmo's tone that she doesn't have much choice in the matter. She only hopes it won't be long. She wants to go home. She wants to be back in bed. She wishes she'd never left. What had she been thinking, following a virtual stranger to somewhere unknown?

Then, sure enough, the fog begins to lift.

'See, I told you so,' Mazmo says. And now she can see his smile.

They are standing on the bank of a lake. The water is still as glass, the moon casting a slice of silver across it like the seam of a dress. Willow trees line the banks, their long leafy branches swaying in the breeze. The white leaves are still falling, though none fall on the lake – the water remains untouched, unrippled, unbroken.

Liyana exhales. 'My God, it's so—'

'See?' Mazmo grins, excited as a schoolboy. 'Didn't I tell you it would be worth the wait?'

Liyana nods, unable to shape the messy enormity of her feelings into comprehensive words. 'It's so, so, so . . .'

And suddenly, she remembers. She has been here before, when she was a child. It's real, special, secret. Only certain people are able to . . .

'It's Everwhere.'

Still grinning, Mazmo nudges her. 'That's right. You got it.'

'Thank you.' Liyana kisses his cheek, suddenly overwhelmed with gratitude. 'I'm sorry I didn't – thank you.' Images flicker at the edges of memory, but she's looking at them deep underwater, shifting and blurred. Voices call to her, but they're too muffled for Liyana to make out the words.

'You know,' Mazmo whispers, 'there's no one about. We could go swimming.'

'But I don't have my— Oh.' Liyana nudges him back. 'You cheeky bugger.'

Yet, as unwise as it might be to disrobe in present circumstances, she wants to. She wants to feel the cool water on her bare skin, wants to submerge herself, wants to hear nothing but the thrum of the lake, its heartbeat in her ears. She wants to see nothing but water all around, from the end of her nose to the edge of the earth.

'Well . . .' Liyana hesitates. 'I don't—'

She never says the next word, for, in the next moment, she's falling. She's slipped on the wet riverbank and is falling into the water. Her chest hits the water first, the impact a sharp slap to her ribs, then she's under, holding her breath, opening her eyes, pushing back against the sucking force of the water, as if her arms were bird's wings in flight. She must have sunk deeper than she thought, since air and breath aren't coming yet. But it's okay, it won't be a moment, the lake wasn't so deep. Liyana's lungs begin to sting, sore with the wait for air. She needs to open her mouth, needs air to rush in right now. It's then Liyana realizes she hasn't fallen into the water. She's being pushed under.

Goldie

I'm not doing this, I think, even as I am. *I can't, it's impossible.*

I'm still sitting astride the fallen trunk, facing Leo who's coaxing me on as a long tendril of ivy uncurls from the branch of a nearby tree and stretches into the air. I flick my index finger and the ivy begins to sway back and forth like an enchanted snake.

Leo applauds. 'See? I told you it'd be easy here, didn't I?'

I shrug, though admittedly I'm relieved. 'But I still don't see how this – it's a nice parlour trick. But how will it stop a soldier from killing me?'

'That's just intention,' Leo says, as if that is the simplest thing in the world. 'Once you know you can do it, then it's only a matter of directing it.'

'What do you mean?'

'Well, you can make the ivy dance,' Leo says, a flicker of light returning to his green eyes. 'Or you can wrap it around my neck and choke the life out of me.'

'Oh.'

'You see?'

I nod. I wish we weren't here. I wish we were still in the hotel, days ago. Before I knew anything, when I could still stroke the soft skin of his scars and wonder.

'So, do you want to try it?' Leo says, as if suggesting I string a daisy chain.

My fingers go limp. 'You want me to try and choke you?' The enchanted ivy falls to the ground.

Leo looks at me, as if I've not quite understood the purpose of this place. 'Goldie.' His voice drops. 'You do realize that Everwhere is teeming with soldiers tonight. It's not only for you and your sisters that they've come – every month on the first-quarter moon . . .'

I glance at his hands resting on the trunk. I want to reach out and ask Leo to hold me.

'Think of Teddy,' he says. 'If you don't do this, you won't stand a chance against your father.'

I have no choice, I realize. This is my fate. I cannot escape it. So I nod and, with great effort, draw myself up.

'All right then,' I say lightly, as if I too am only talking about making a daisy chain. 'Let's give it a shot.'

Bea

Bea is the wind through the trees, she's the light of the moon, the breath of the birds. She imagines her sisters walking on the rocks and moss far below. Up in the heavens the white leaves don't fall, which leads her to wonder exactly where they come from.

Is Dr Finch still calling her name? Well, he can wait. She might return. She might not. For now, Bea is lighter than air, swifter than moonlight, stronger than any superhero. She thinks again of the blackbird illustration that could have been drawn for her. It strikes Bea how ordinary flying feels. How natural, how normal. When was the last time she felt this way? When was the last time she flew?

I was going to fly away, Bea thinks, as she soars over the highest tips of the tallest trees. *I was going to fly to Everwhere and never return to Earth.* The thought slows her down so she's gliding, drifting on warm currents of air. Bea thinks of Vali, of what she took from him, of how he'll never experience this. Sorrow and guilt flush her lungs with her next breath and sit heavy in her chest.

Slowly, Bea sinks from the heavens to float below the tops of the trees. Soon she's so close to the ground that her feet graze the bleached stones. She tries to shake the thoughts from her head, to dislodge the feelings from her heart. She points her nose to the moon, kicks her legs as if trying to restart a playground swing, urging herself up.

Fingers wrap around her booted ankle. Bea glances down to see Dr Finch below reaching up, pulling her down.

'Let go!' She kicks him off. She wants to be airborne again, untethered, unshackled, unbound. She wants to be flying; she wants to be free. Dr Finch catches hold of her ankle again. 'What the fuck are you doing?'

'I want to show you something.' His grip tightens. 'You can mess about later.'

I'm not messing about, Bea thinks. *The rest of my life, that was messing about. This is the only thing I want to be real, the only thing I want to be true.*

'Let go! Let me go!'

He tugs her down. 'Come on.'

'Piss off!' She thinks again of Vali, of how she must be careful, must control herself lest she hurts someone else. 'Okay, okay.'

Bea alights onto the mossy ground.

Dr Finch takes her hand. 'Let me show you something beautiful.'

But what could be more beautiful than flying?

'All right then.' Bea tells herself to be kinder, more grateful, more gracious. 'But let's be quick.'

And they begin to walk side by side along the path again.

Liyana

So, this is how I'm going to die: at the hands of Mazmo Owethu Muzenda-Kasteni. Everything returns in the flood of water into her lungs – her sisters, the soldiers, the eternal fight. She remembers it all. But too late.

Death is a shocking thought, a sobering thought. It isn't how Liyana imagined she'd die and she certainly didn't think it would be so soon. As Liyana thrashes in the water, she thinks of Aunt Nya, of Kumiko, of her sisters. Arms flailing, eyes stinging, lungs exploding, she thinks her goodbyes.

A memory snaps into focus.

Liyana stands on a riverbank watching the water. She casts a shifting silver shadow, broken only by the current, by the falling leaves. She watches the brook's eddies and swirls, as if it were being stirred by the hand of some water god. Another leaf falls. Now she knows what she can do with water. She can sway and shape it. Like a water god, she can command it. *This* is what she can do.

Suddenly, Liyana stops flailing. She is perfectly still. She closes her eyes. She opens her mouth, drinking in fresh water as if she's parched, as if she has not drunk a drop for days. When she exhales, releasing fat bubbles that rise and pop to the surface, Liyana opens her eyes.

At her fingertips, the water begins to churn.

Bea

'So,' Bea says, as she follows Dr Finch into the clearing, 'what's the surprise?'

'You're the most impatient girl I've ever met.' He steps onto a high square-shaped stone. 'Don't rush me, you'll ruin everything. Come here.'

Bea steps forward. She doesn't want to and, in that moment, has the sudden feeling she should run again, so fast that he'll never catch her, not in this world or the next. But he's right, she is impatient, and that's the least of it. So Bea lets Dr Finch slip his hands around her waist, lets him pull her close, until there's not a shimmer of moonlight between them. She hopes this isn't his idea of a romantic seduction.

'Look, I don't mean to be rude but—'

Dr Finch leans in. 'It won't take a moment,' he whispers. 'It'll be over before you know it. If you don't fight, it won't hurt.'

'Wait, what the fuck?' She tries to pull back but his hold on her is tight. And then she remembers. 'You're a soldier.'

Dr Finch smiles. 'I am.'

His grip tightens, trapping Bea's breath in her lungs.

She shakes her head, frantic. 'N-no . . .' She kicks at him, twisting away.

'Don't fight it.' His voice is gentle, tender. 'It'll be painless, I promise . . .'

Bea grits her teeth as a wind of fury blows through her.

She. Will. Slaughter. Him.

The storm begins to build, rage pulses in her veins as she turns the full force – then Bea thinks of Vali, of what she took from him, of what she deserves to have taken from her. Suddenly, the storm dies. The fury fades. She doesn't deserve to kill, she deserves to die. And she doesn't need the razor blades, this will do. It's better, more fitting. It's not right that she should take her own life. She murdered Vali and now this soldier will murder her. Just as it should be. She won't fight, she won't fly. Justice will be served. Val will have his revenge.

'No,' Bea says, her voice already floating away. 'I want it to hurt.'

Dr Finch frowns down at her. He's too gentle and it's too late. Her head is heavy. She doesn't want him to be the last thing she sees. She closes her eyes and remembers Vali as he'd been, laughing, eating, loving. She sees the view of Everwhere from just beneath the moon.

It is a soft fall, a drop into sleep.

And her soldier is true to his word: she feels no pain.

Scarlet

I wrote myself a letter, Scarlet thinks, as she watches the split tree burn. The wood cracks, spitting out fiery sparks that scorch holes in the moss. *When I was little, I wrote myself a letter about this place.*

'I've been here before,' she whispers. 'I've been here many times before.'

Her mother stands beside her, watching the flames. 'I know.'

'How do you know?' And what happened to— *It burned in the fire.*

'I told you, I've been doing my research. There are more girls like you out there than you think.' She smiles. 'Well, perhaps not quite like you.'

'No, that can't be . . .' Mesmerized by the flames, Scarlet forgets her mother, forgets herself. She has something else to do, she's sure, but she doesn't care. She wants to watch the fire till it burns out, till it's only embers and ash.

'Scarlet, we've got to go. I don't . . .'

Her mother is talking, but she can't hear the words. As Scarlet stares the flames seem to be shaping themselves into an image, a blazing image of four girls sitting in a glade. One is making plants grow, one is juggling balls of fog, one is levitating leaves and one – she is setting fire to sticks. Her sisters.

'. . . we're not safe here,' Ruby is saying. 'We've got to—'

A twig snaps and both women turn. A man steps out from behind the tree. He smiles and lifts his hand in a half-wave.

'Oh, it's okay.' Scarlet exhales. 'It's not— He's Walt, my . . . electrician.'

Her mother stares at him. 'No. He's not, he's—'

Walt's nod cuts her off. 'A soldier. That's right, my dear. *Your* soldier. Though, I'm afraid, not in the chivalrous sense.'

Scarlet stares, speechless.

'You thought I spent so long on that dishwasher because I fancied you?' His features seem suddenly sharper, no longer soft and indistinct. The spluttering flame has flared into an inferno. 'I will say, though, it was delightful getting to know you – as pleasurable as preparing a meal before you taste it. You must agree?'

Scarlet opens her mouth. Before she can answer, Walt is behind her, his hands at her throat. She gasps for breath, for words, for sense. But he is too fast, too strong and she can do nothing to stop him.

Ruby screams. 'Scarlet! Scarlet, kill him!'

Where is her fire? Why are her hands so cold?

'I'm afraid she's not got the strength to toast a marshmallow right now.' Walt smirks. 'Let alone me.'

For one eternal second Ruby is rooted to the spot, watching her daughter's eyes wide with fear as she twists and thrashes and kicks. Then she lunges for Scarlet. But Walt steps back, gliding away as if the ground were ice instead of moss and stone and Ruby falls at his feet, cracking her wrist against a rock. Pain tears up Ruby's arm as she looks up to see her daughter's face begin to pale.

'This'll teach you' – Walt presses his mouth to Scarlet's ear – 'that angels can be demons in disguise.'

And vice-versa, Scarlet thinks as she starts to fade. Her mother, Ezekiel, neither as she'd imagined them to be. She fights him, flailing in his grip. But Walt holds tight.

Then, Scarlet is still.

Slowly, Walt slides her to the ground. Her limp hands flop out, arms spread wide as Walt sets her head down gently, a pool of red curls on a patch of white moss. He gazes at her, stroking a thumb along her cheek.

'Death is such a beautiful moment, I don't know why you all fight it so hard.' He looks at Ruby. 'You celebrate birth and mourn death. It's all backwards. One of the many reasons your world is so—'

In response, Ruby screams. A scream of helpless agony and frantic longing, of fury and despair, of blood and ice.

Walt smiles, as if the sound is sweet to him. For Ruby, it knits the air, stitching every space between mother and daughter, connecting them by invisible threads, so all at once she's at Scarlet's side.

But Scarlet is still, silent, stone.

Walt looks on as Ruby brings her hands together. Warmth becomes heat as she lays them on her daughter's chest. To bring comfort on a cold day, to heal a graze, to cure a cancer that's crept in. With everything she has, Ruby wills life into Scarlet. But her daughter doesn't move. Not a millimetre, not a molecule.

'Whatever you're trying to do,' Walt says. 'I don't think it's working.'

She looks at him. 'Will you take me instead?'

Walt laughs. 'And what use would you be to me? I can live for half a year on her light – yours will give me no more than a month.' He shrugs. 'But I'll take you both, why not?'

'Fine,' Ruby says, since she no longer wants to live.

In a split second, Walt has shifted to her side, hands at her throat. As the breath starts to leave her body, Ruby surrenders. It is a relief not to fight for life anymore, not to run, not to— and then Ruby sees it, or thinks she does: the slightest twitch of Scarlet's finger, a spark flickering and spluttering, trying to ignite. Her mother focuses, summoning all the breath, all the life she has left, into her daughter.

Scarlet is still.

Ruby closes her eyes.

Walt grins.

Then, all at once, a sudden spike of lightning flares from Scarlet's immobile hand, arcing into the air, curving back to Walt; a flash of fire straight into the centre of his chest.

And he's gone. Incinerated, as if she'd detonated a bomb in his heart. Leaving only a pile of ashes on the white moss and a vivid scar on Scarlet's hand, snaking from the tip of her little finger to her thumb.

Ruby sinks to her knees, fresh breath flooding her lungs, her body curling like a comma over her prone daughter. Ruby puts her palm to Scarlet's cheek, the heat from her hand warming her daughter's skin.

Scarlet's eyelids flicker.

'Oh, thank God,' Ruby whispers. 'Thank God.'

Goldie

'It's too soon. I'm not ready.'

'You are.' Leo pushes his palms against the trunk and, in a single swift movement, he springs from sitting to standing. 'You have to be. Anyway, the more you kill, the stronger you'll become. Then you might stand a chance against him.'

'What? But—'

Then he's a few metres from me, feet on moss and stone.

'Can't we stay here?'

Leo touches the burning red mark on his neck – the imprint from my ivy rope. I feel the bareness of my own exposed neck. 'We've done all we can. Now you need to go out and hunt.'

I smile. 'You're saying that like you won't be coming with me.'

'I won't.' Leo takes a deep breath. 'This is something you have to do alone.'

'What?' I sit up straight. 'No. Why?'

'Becau—'

'No, no, no.' I scramble down from the trunk. 'No, you can't leave me here, I can't, I don't know how . . .'

'You can. You do. And you will.' Leo takes my hands. 'Trust me.'

He gives me a quick kiss, then steps back.

'No, please,' I beg, as he lets go. 'Please, don't . . .'

A thick fog starts to roll in, rising in the glade like smoke.

'I can't stay,' he says. 'Another soldier won't come near you while I'm here.'

'But I need longer.' I grab for Leo, clutching his fingertips. 'I need to practise, to perfect my—'

'You don't have time, and you don't need it,' Leo says. 'You're far stronger than you think.'

'No. No, I'm not . . .'

'Don't worry, I'll meet you later. Afterwards. When you've found your sisters.'

'Wait.' I need to touch him again, I need to feel his warmth, his strength. 'Wait!'

But he's already halfway across the glade.

'I don't know where to find them.'

'You do,' Leo says. 'You'll find them in the same place you always did.'

'Will you—?' My words are swallowed by the fog.

'Of course. We'll face him together. With five, we stand a chance.'

I nod, wanting to believe him even though I can tell he doesn't even believe it himself.

'It'll only be a moment.'

'Wait.' I reach for him again.

But Leo is gone.

Liyana

Liyana knows the precise moment Mazmo sees the gathering wave, for she feels his hands – still gripping the back of her skull, fingers twisted into her hair – freeze. Summoning all her strength, Liyana pushes back, lifting her head from the water, knocking Mazmo into the lake.

He's quick to right himself, to stand, but Liyana's faster.

He might be a mackerel, but she's a shark. With one swift tug, she drags him under. The churning currents gather force, swirling beneath, tying liquid ropes to Mazmo's feet, tethering him to the riverbed. Now he flails with wild arms and terrified wails. The waves crash down over him. Again and again and again.

Liyana looks on, the violent water soft on her skin, a wet balm that brings as much comfort as rain. When Mazmo finally begins to tire, when his limbs go limp and his eyes close, Liyana pulls herself reluctantly from the lake.

She stands, sodden, on the bank, watching the waves ebb until the lake is almost still – strangely untouched by falling leaves – except for the twitching body sending out fitful ripples across the water.

Liyana narrows her eyes. On the surface tiny bubbles begin to break, as if a pan of broth were being brought to a simmer on a hob. With a flick of her fingers, she turns up the heat. The skin of the lake begins to blister, as bigger bubbles rise and pop. The water starts to boil.

Mazmo's cries fork like lightning through the air.

At last, the fog rolls once more over the water – a shroud that brings a pleasing silence.

In the quiet, the leaves start to fall again, sending fresh ripples across the stagnant lake.

Liyana smiles. She'll wait for the water to cool a little before she returns for a swim.

Goldie

I curse Leo for leaving me. I curse him and I call for him. I wait a long time before I know that he's not coming back. Not yet, not until I've done what I need to do. And I know he's right, though I wish he wasn't, though I wish I had longer to practise, to postpone. But I don't.

Still, I'll wait for the fog to roll back. I'll stay pressed against the fallen trunk until I can see again, at least well enough to walk on. Leo hasn't told me how to track a soldier, so I know he trusts me to follow my instincts. And though the fog will render me invisible, it'd also render me blind.

As soon as it lifts, I leave the glade – staying here I feel too much like a lame rabbit cowering in an undefended burrow.

As I walk my spirits start to lift. I have purpose, aim. Though I try not to think too much on the object or outcome. If I could evade my mission, I would. If I could escape, I would. If I could run home to hide in my bed, I'd do it in a heartbeat. Though I know that Leo is right. Still, I wouldn't be doing this if I had a choice. But I don't, so I go on.

As I walk deeper into the woods I begin to watch, scanning my surroundings more closely, stepping more carefully, avoiding the thwack of branches, the snap of twigs. I try to move through the fog so I'll leave no mark on the air. I flex my fingers, summoning my strength, readying myself.

I can do this, I think. I've killed before, I can kill again. And this man – this soldier – deserves it. He's a killer, a killer of my sisters. At the crack of a twig, I freeze. I'm still for several minutes before I dare to move, slowly, on.

I hear Leo's voice. *Remember – you're the hunter. Not the hunted.*

And that's all it takes to make the shift. I'm stillness and stealth now, silencing my mind, thinking of nothing except seeking my target.

I see him beside a willow tree, biting his thumbnail as if he's considering a choice, as if he's not sure what he'll do next. I know I have only a second or two before he sees – or senses – me.

You are predator or prey. You will kill or be killed.

I focus on the vines of ivy wrapping around the willow tree and snaking along the ground at his feet. I focus on my fingers. I focus on how I made the ivy twist around Leo's neck like a boa constrictor. I pretend that's all I'm doing now.

Slowly, the veins of the ivy leaves begin to swell and pulse, as if flowing with my own blood. With two twitches of my index fingers the plants on the ground pull free from the soil, slithering up the soldier's feet, encircling his ankles, tying him to the earth. He's so startled that he nearly falls, but steadies himself in time.

When he sees me, when our eyes meet, I see that he's so uncommonly beautiful that I'm startled in turn. He looks at me with such longing, such sorrow. My hands drop to my sides. Without my command, the vines of ivy fall slack and begin to unwind. Suddenly, the soldier lunges for me – there's delight in his eyes now, desire.

I fall back, hitting stone instead of moss, scrambling up as he pulls me down again. I kick out at him but he's strong, far stronger than I, locking me against his chest with a single arm. I squirm in his grip, but the more I wrestle the harder he squeezes and I feel my lungs tightening, my strength seeping into the air with each diminishing breath. My head is so heavy my neck bends with the weight of it. My eyes close. Everything, once white, is dark.

Inside me a light flickers: a trace of love, a flame about to go out. I think of Leo, of Teddy and Liyana. I draw on that final light, pulling on its heat, its power. I curl my fingers into flimsy fists; I call on the ivy beneath my feet. But I don't have strength enough. Then the light snuffs out and all is black.

In the darkness I am drifting, sinking into the ground and floating into the sky. My soul is returning to the earth, my spirit to the sky.

Then the darkness is scarred by a flash of red, like a spurt of arterial blood. When it vanishes, I see neither black nor red but nothing at all.

Breath returns like an electric shock, surging through my chest, reigniting my heart. My eyes snap open to see the soldier, writhing on the ground as ivy sheathes him in tight-leafed bandages, spreading so fast that, in a moment, he's mummified – only one terrified, startlingly blue eye blinking out at me – and then he is swallowed up into the soil. Gone.

Bea

Don't you dare. No daughter of mine is dying like this.

Bea hears her father's voice on the horizon, a faint echo through a dense fog. She ignores him. The echo sharpens, his words scratching the air, searing her skin, burning her flesh into a scream.

No, she thinks, *let me go.*

Silence falls. Darkness. And Bea is floating again.

Where is your honour? Where is your spirit, your dignity?

Her father reaches inside her, his fingers in her veins, injecting his own poison: a refined dilution of pure rage.

Bea opens her eyes.

She looks at the soldier, her glare unbending. In his shock, Dr Finch loosens his grip and Bea breaks free.

Kill him. It is your duty, your destiny. Kill him.

As the poison pulses through her veins she feels such strength, such power as she's never felt before. It beats with her heart, igniting anger that swells into a circling tornado of uncontainable fury, dragging her into its vortex. She battles against its pull, fighting to tear herself free.

Surrender to it. You'll be invulnerable. You'll never feel pain again.

Finally, Bea succumbs. It's a relief to stop struggling, to allow the rage to swallow her whole.

She straightens. Dr Finch steps back. The falling leaves suspend in the air. The mists dissipate and the fog rolls back. Bea raises both hands and the largest stone in the clearing lifts into the air, hovering between the leaves. With a flick of her fingers, Bea brings it down on his shoulder, piercing skin, shattering bone. He collapses, one arm clutching the other. His screams would crack the stone, had it been glass.

Bea smiles as she steps over to the squalling man. She places her booted foot over his non-existent heart, kicks down hard and crushes his chest. Then she takes hold of his feet and begins to rise into the air, higher and higher, until she's grazing the tops of the trees. Then she drops him.

When Bea alights again on moss and stone, she steps over the dead soldier's broken body and walks out of the glade to find her sisters. Her father has fallen quiet, but he's loud inside her. And she knows that, if she drew a razor blade across her thigh now her blood would no longer be red but inky black.

The suspended leaves start to fall.

Scarlet

'I wish you'd run.'

'No.' Scarlet is still thinking of Walt and how wrong she'd been. 'I can't.'

'Why not?' Her mother hesitates. 'Your grandma . . . she doesn't need you any more.'

'I'm not abandoning her now,' Scarlet says. She sits beside her mother on a blanket of white moss and stone, only inches from a little pile of ashes. 'I . . . I can't. Not till I've laid her to rest.'

'I wish I had the strength or skills to fight your father. But I'll come with you. I might be a momentary—'

Scarlet strokes her neck, wincing slightly. She looks at her mother as if seeing her for the first time, again. 'You've been running from him for nearly ten years, and now you'll just let him kill you?'

'I'd be a distraction; it might give you an early advantage.' Ruby plucks a leaf of ivy from its vine winding beneath her feet. 'It's the least I can do.'

'No,' Scarlet says, her voice fierce as fire and immovable as stone.

'I want—' her mother begins, but Scarlet shakes her head.

They sit in silence for a while.

'Are you sure you'll be—?'

Scarlet nods. 'I'll be fine.'

'Then look, I . . .' With the aid of a nearby rock, Ruby pulls herself up from the ground to stand. It's an effort, Scarlet sees. 'I should go.'

And even though Scarlet had said that she could go, she finds that she'd hoped her mother would choose to stay, despite the futility of it all. But the sacrificial and the selfish had fought within her mother and, ultimately, the latter had won. As it always had.

'I mean, if you won't come with me. If I can't, if you don't want me to . . .'

'It's okay,' Scarlet says. 'Go.'

Ruby reaches out, places a hand on her daughter's shoulder – heat flushes Scarlet's arm – then she turns and walks away.

Liyana

Liyana stands at the edge of the lake, face turned to the moon, allowing the water to evaporate. She has proved her strength, has killed her soldier; now she needs to go, to find her sisters, to face her father. Liyana glances down at the droplets still clinging to the backs of her hands. In the moonlight her black skin has the blue sheen of a raven's wing. Liyana thinks of BlackBird. No longer her idol but her equal, her counterpart.

It was her sister, Liyana realizes now. It was Bea she based BlackBird on, the sister she always aspired to be. As fierce and furious, as full of confidence and contempt, as brilliant and brave. A slow smile spreads across Liyana's face. She aspires no longer. She has arrived. She is stronger now, more spectacular, than she has ever dreamed she could be.

When she fought back, when she pulled Mazmo under, that was the moment Liyana reclaimed herself. She is no BlackBird, no raven either. She is greater even than her sister. She is a shark, a predator unparalleled.

She is ready for anything.

With a final shake of her head, flinging fresh droplets in every direction, Liyana turns to stride away from the lake. She isn't lost anymore. She knows exactly which way to go.

Goldie

I close my eyes. *Where are you?*

I'm coming.

I'm walking along a path, not knowing which direction to take but continuing anyway. I have no idea how I'll find Leo or my sisters, but I have no doubt I will. Still, I can't wait until then to talk to him. So I meet him in my mind – I'm not remotely surprised that I can, not here.

He'll try to kill you, won't he?

Leo is silent.

He'll want to kill you, I persist. *Because you didn't kill me.*

It wasn't a choice.

If not for my brother, I wouldn't have let you make it. I walk on. *I'll fight him.*

So will I.

I pick a falling leaf from the air and hold on to it. *I love you.*

He says nothing in return. He doesn't need to.

Bea

'I thought – I came to meet my sisters.'

'That can wait. First, we need to talk.'

'But my sisters,' Bea persists. 'Did they survive?'

Wilhelm's yellow eyes flash, gleeful. 'Goldie did, naturally. It'd take much more than a soldier to vanquish her.' He's unable to suppress the pride in his voice. 'When I think of all the havoc she could wreak if she wants to . . . Scarlet and Ana both surprised me, rather spectacularly. They both got a taste for killing, so it's certainly possible they'll favour the dark.' A smile breaks onto her father's face, a smile that Bea wishes would shine upon her. 'But Goldie – by the devil, but she's glorious!'

'And if they don't?' Bea interrupts his eulogizing. The relief she'd felt hearing they lived has already evaporated. 'Then what?'

Her father falls silent and, for a moment, a dread breeze shivers through Bea. But then she sees he's not about to scold her insolence, he's contemplating the loss of his favourite daughter. He seems to summon the words with great reluctance. 'Then it'll be time for you to step in and do what your mother did.'

Bea sees the sorrow that clouds his eyes. It pierces her, then is gone. Before it can seize hold, Bea suppresses her own love, her own sorrow – years of overriding her emotions, it's easy. 'And what do I do before that? What do I say when I see them?'

'Lay the groundwork.' He fixes her with golden eyes.

'Say whatever you like to sway them, to seduce them into the dark.'

Bea nods, her heart lifting. Goldie may be the strongest, the most special. But *she* is the one her father trusts with his secrets. And that, perhaps, trumps her rival. Making Bea his favourite, by a whisper.

Reunion

I walk a path of stones scattered with leaves. I clamber over rocks and fallen trunks. Sometimes the clouds glide across the moon and the path slips away for a while, with no sign of which direction to take, but it doesn't matter. I have no doubt which way to go.

Then, I'm no longer alone. I step into a clearing where ivy twists up the trunks of four gigantic willow trees and weaves across the ground, knitting itself into a carpet of white-veined leaves. I've been here before. A long time ago.

Then I see my three sisters.

As I step towards them I think of Teddy and his *Macbeth. When shall we three meet again?* I hear no clap of thunder, see no strike of lightning, but I feel it coming. The world is about to break apart. *When the hurlyburly's done, / When the battle's lost and won* . . . Who of us will live, I think, and who will die? I cut the thought like a weed.

My sisters look spectacular. Mists swirl around them, as if their presence is agitating the air. They stand straight as spears and look thrice as sharp – their tongues forked, their fingers talons, their hair snakes – as if they've slain six soldiers before breakfast without a second thought. Their veins pulse with hate and their skins shimmer in the moonlight as if they radiate light. They're as fierce as they are tender, as furious as they are calm, as evil as they are good. Just as I am. '*Fair is foul, and foul is fair; / Hover through the fog and—*'

'Goldie!' Liyana shouts, gleeful. 'You made it!'

My sister. My sisters. I step forward to meet them.

Sisters

We're sitting in our glade once more. In a circle, as we'd done a decade ago. I'm slightly surprised by how happy I feel to be with my sisters again. I hadn't realized how much I'd missed them. I feel that I've come home, to a home unlike any I ever had on Earth. With them I'm able, at last, to be exactly as I am.

Soon, we've fallen back into old rhythms. Scarlet is setting light to twigs, Liyana juggles three dense balls of fog, and I am coaxing tight-curled shoots from the earth. Bea watches us, smiling. And, as usual, she is enlightening us with all the vital information of which we might be ignorant. Ever the fount of knowledge, ever the know-it-all.

Scarlet sighs and the flame on her stick flares. She could, if her account of killing her soldier is anything to go by, set fire to a whole forest right now, just as Liyana could turn a lake into a tsunami and I could uproot every tree in Everwhere. Bea is the only one who hasn't divulged any details of her own battle, hardly a surprise.

'S-o.' Bea elongates the word. 'Tonight we choose.'

'Right.' Liyana nods. 'What's everyone thinking?'

She isn't, I note, assuming the decision is a foregone conclusion, that we'll naturally favour the light. Of us all, Liyana has changed the most. As a child she was so timid, wanting to be liked by everyone, always eager to please, trying to keep the peace. Now she's reckless, fearless, as if she doesn't give a damn about anything at all.

Silence falls over the glade, like the static before a storm. I shift, my skin irritated by the prickle of the air.

'Well . . .' Liyana prompts.

'You say it like we're choosing what to have for dinner,' Scarlet says. 'Not between good and evil, for the rest of our lives.'

'And life and death,' Bea reminds us. 'If we don't choose in favour of our father, we won't live to tell about it.'

'So you keep saying, but we're far stronger than we were.' Liyana slices a finger through a ball of fog and rain-tears fall like juice from an orange. 'I say we fight him.'

'Oh, you have no idea.' Bea lets out a wry laugh. 'No idea at all.'

'Don't be so defeatist.' Liyana stands. 'We're like, I don't know, the Four Horsemen of the Apocalypse. If we combined forces, I bet we'd be powerful enough to kill him.'

'Kill?' Bea's tone is torn between mockery and praise. 'I remember when you couldn't even say that word.'

'You seem to remember more than any of us.' Liyana eyes her. 'But you're the most secretive too.'

'I don't see we have another option,' I say. 'If we don't try, he'll kill us anyway – so what do we have to lose?'

I think of Leo and how he'll have no choice but to fight for his life. I'd have a challenging time explaining Leo and who he really is, so I'm hoping he'll arrive any moment and explain himself. He's taking a degree at Cambridge, after all; he has more of a way with words than I do. Hardly surprising that Bea's studying there too. She'd shoehorned that fact into the conversation pretty quick. But even though she still irritates me, I know I'd defend her to the death. She's my sister, my blood, my spirit. Dare I say, even more so than my brother. I adore Teddy far more than Bea, but it's . . . different. I can't explain how, but it is.

'We have another option,' Bea says. 'We can go dark.'

Her words hang in the air, like the white leaves, except they don't fall.

'Oh, come on.' She stands to face Liyana, who glares at her. 'Don't tell me you're not tempted. Aren't you fed up with being so . . . weak, so pathetic, so—'

'Speak for yourself.' Scarlet expels sparks from her fingertips that singe the moss at Bea's feet.

'Careful, Sis.' Bea steps back. 'Killing a soldier is one thing, it gives you a taste for the dark. But killing your sister . . . Now, that'll send you right over the edge.'

Leo, where are you? I wait but hear nothing in return.

'I don't think going dark is the answer,' I say. 'I mean, we don't even know the consequences.'

'Oh, please, what do we need to know?' Bea starts to pace across the glade, like a general corralling troops. 'On Earth we're virtually powerless. Plus we're underestimated at every turn, undervalued, treated like sex objects, paid less, regarded as second fiddle by virtually—'

'That may be true,' I interrupt. 'But it's hardly reason enough to turn evil.'

Bea raises an eyebrow. 'Don't you want to know what it's like to live your life without fear?' She gives a little shrug. 'The only way you'll ever be that powerful is if you go dark.'

We're silent. I don't know what Ana and Scarlet are thinking, but I think of Leo's words: *kill or be killed, predator or prey*. I think of Garrick, of my stepfather. I think of that soldier's hands slowly taking the life from me. I can't deny that it'd be a glorious thing, never to be scared again.

'You'll be impenetrable in every way. And not just physically.' Bea looks to Scarlet. 'All that pain you feel, the grief – you won't feel any of it anymore.'

I think of Leo, of Teddy. 'What about love? Will we still feel that?'

Bea hesitates, almost imperceptibly. 'Yes. You will.'

Again, I think of Leo. I wonder if, if I went to my father's side, I'd be able to make a bargain for Leo's life.

'How long do we have till he comes?' Scarlet asks, again deferring to our resident expert. 'Shouldn't he be here soon?'

She sounds calm but I can see that my sister is far more scared than she seems. Just like the rest of us, with the exception of Bea, who has quite clearly made her choice. I wonder if we'll still know her afterwards – that is, if we survive. I wonder if our lives would be the same, on Earth at least, if we became dark. I realize how little I know about any of this, and I wish, even as I sense it's too late now, that I hadn't been too proud to ask. I notice then that Ana didn't respond to Bea's proposal. Indeed, she hasn't spoken since.

'I have a feeling' – Bea stops pacing – 'that he'll be here any moment now.'

Our father

'The four victorious.'

His voice is a rumble of thunder above the trees. Then he appears, stepping out of the mists and fog and into the glade. A chill wind picks up, churning the falling leaves. As he sets foot on the ivy and moss a tremor rumbles through the soil, shaking the ground beneath our feet.

I feel my sisters beside me. I feel their hearts begin to beat faster, I feel my own. Our father is ancient and immovable as a redwood, at his core a force of unparalleled ferocity. I can see that there is nothing he wouldn't do.

'Congratulations, my dears.' Our father surveys us, his golden eyes glinting in the moonlight. He's tall, thin, with white hair and a face so wrinkled he might be ten thousand years old. He steps towards us, his hands outstretched.

When we make no move towards him, he stops in the middle of the glade and brings his hands together.

'So my four favourite daughters have finally come of age. I feel as if I've been waiting two centuries for this moment.' He raises both hands. 'Welcome home, my girls.'

Dozens of shoots emerge from the soil, rapidly thickening and lengthening, fresh branches reaching out, growing leaves and blooms, until the rose bushes are sinking under the weight of hundreds of blood-red flowers that look almost black. He has turned our glade into his garden.

'A little gift.' He smiles at us each in turn.

We are a tense row – even Bea – standing as straight and stiff as if we're balancing on a high wire and a single slip from anyone would mean the death of us all.

'I must admit, I thought you might not all survive the initiation. Too few do. I'm afraid my daughters often disappoint me in their . . . willingness to surrender.' He brushes a fallen leaf from his lapel. 'But, moving on. How are you each feeling now?'

We stare at him, silent, still.

'Oh, come now.' He grins, the falcon eyeing the clutch of mice in its claws. 'Don't pretend to be passive females – you're so much better than that. You've got darkness in you now, and you should be grateful for it.' He brings his hands together and another chill wind blows through the glade. 'Look at your miserable little lives – they don't even begin to reflect how magnificent you truly are. And I'm offering you an escape from drudgery, from the dullness of being second-class citizens. I'm offering you greatness and glory – *carpe diem*!'

I want to look to my sisters but I can't, I can't pull my eyes from him. As if I'm watching the premonition of my own death made manifest. I'm seeing how my heart will be ripped from my chest and I can't look away.

'Look, my dears.' Wilhelm Grimm steps forward. 'I want the chance to be a good father to you now. And isn't it what every father wants, to see his daughter flourish to her full potential?' He stops. 'But I won't force it upon you. Ultimately the decision is yours.'

I think of the soldier I killed, I think of my stepfather.

'Oh, Goldie.' My father smiles, as if I'd spoken my thoughts aloud. 'I'm afraid the murder of that mortal hardly counts. And the extermination of soldiers is immaterial. You'll have to do better than that.'

I stare at him, saying nothing. What can I say to the one who sets the rules?

'So.' He starts to pace – a far more chilling general than Bea had been. 'Given that you all have delicious amounts of death and darkness pulsing through your veins right now, I'm thinking you're ready to embrace' – he brings his finger and thumb together, leaving a sliver of moonlight between them – 'a soupçon of evil . . . What do you say?'

I sneak a glance at my sisters. But they aren't looking at me, they're still fixed on him, terrified. Except for Bea, who's gazing at our father as if he's an angel, a prophet, the love of her damnable life.

'Oh, please.' He stops pacing to sigh. 'Don't pretend to be so puritanical. You're almost there. You only need to take the last teeny, tiny step. I know you got a taste for it, didn't you, dear Ana?'

I snap my head round to Liyana, who's silent now, all bravado evaporated. I too am wilting in the presence of my father. I press my feet into the moss, wondering how Ana might react. She doesn't move.

'Oh, come now, don't be such spoilsports. Give me a chance to be a father, after so long. I'll be the papa bear, you be my cubs, and I'll show you how much fun you can have in the dark!'

He waits for one of us to speak. None of us does.

'I must say, I'm disappointed by your manners.' He scowls at us, deepening the furrows etched into his face. 'Didn't your mothers teach you anything?'

Where the hell is Leo?

I feel Scarlet twitch beside me. Instinctively, I reach for her hand, then instantly let go – her skin is so hot it's like sticking my fingers into fire. I bite my lip to keep from crying out.

'Well then,' our father continues, 'I see I'll have to educate you myself. We've clearly got a lot to catch up on.'

Liyana looks up, meeting his eye. 'I'll learn nothing from you.'

I stare at my sister in shock. Scarlet and Bea stare at her too, incredulous.

'On the contrary, my little Ana,' Wilhelm says, 'judging by how gleefully you boiled your soldier alive, I'd say you've already learned quite a lot.' He grins again, his mouth like a furnace, his tongue turned to flames. 'And how about you, Red? I did so enjoy watching you incinerate that hapless boy – but not as much as you enjoyed doing it, I'd wager.'

Scarlet says nothing.

'What?' He waits. 'Wolf got your tongue?'

I wonder if it's possible that Leo's deserted, abandoning me to my fate to save his own life.

'You might be right.' My father catches my eye. 'He should be here by now, shouldn't he?'

I try to shrug but can't. My shoulders are frozen in place, as if I've finally turned into a tree, a soft little sapling. My father, the redwood, towers above me.

'Don't worry.' He smiles. 'Leo will get what's coming to him. Speaking of which, time is ticking on. So if you're not going to join me, then I'm afraid we'll have to part.'

At this, Scarlet takes a step back. She tries to take another but, all at once, she's stuck fast, as if she'd taken root in the soil.

'Your mother was right about one thing, my dear.' Wilhelm's eyes flash. 'If you don't go dark then I'm afraid I'll have to – *quel est le mot juste?* – slaughter you.'

'I . . . If – if I do . . .' My voice is a whisper on the breeze. 'Will you spare Leo?'

'Interesting proposition.' He smiles, as if cheered by a particularly delightful thought. 'Would you kill one of your sisters to save him?'

I don't hesitate. 'Of course not.'

'That's a shame.' He sighs. 'Since you can't get something for nothing. Not on Earth, not in Everwhere.'

'But, I . . .' I want to protest, to bargain, but I've lost words and reason. I feel the shock of my sisters beside me. We might have contemplated evil in the abstract, but it's clear that none of us had truly considered what it might entail.

'It's of no matter anyway.' Wilhelm floats a hand above the rose bushes, brushing their petals. 'I can't spare him. He broke the rules. Without rules there's anarchy. And we can't have that, now, can we?'

I close my eyes and pray.

'Oh, that won't do you a bit of good,' my father snaps. 'Not here. Right, let's get on with it, shall we?' He looks to Bea, who nods. 'But it isn't fair that he misses this spectacle, is it? Since he was supposed to kill you himself. Not quite the same, but it has a sense of poetic justice nonetheless, wouldn't you agree?'

Bea claps once and, in the echo of the sound, Leo appears: standing under an oak tree, shocked and confused. Whatever had kept him away, it wasn't by his own hand.

'All right.' Wilhelm plucks a rose petal. 'Now that we're

all here to witness it, I'll give you one last chance to choose. What'll it be? Dark or light? Life or death?'

We're silent.

'I'm waiting.' Slowly, he begins to rip the rose petal. 'I don't like to be kept waiting.'

I don't glance at my sisters. I wish we'd had the chance to form a plan. Still, I hope that our father's bark is worse than his bite. He reminds me of my stepfather, when he'd escalate his threats – the more extreme he became, the more desperate he felt and the more the balance of power shifted between us.

'Come now, I haven't got forever.' Our father sighs. 'Well, I have. But I'm not wasting it waiting.' He pauses to consider. 'Am I asking too much? Do I need to give you a little incentive?' He looks at me and I feel myself wilting under his gaze, like a flower under a hot lamp. I glance at Leo.

'Good idea!' My father's eyes glint gleefully. 'Let me show you how to bind someone – your first attempt lacked a little finesse.'

Instantly, the hanging branches of the tree lift and curl around Leo's wrists and ankles, wrapping him to the trunk so fast he cannot run, so tight he cannot move. My hands are clammy, my heart racing. I was wrong. There's no balance of power where my father is concerned. He has it all.

'Well then, Bea,' Wilhelm says. 'Would you like to do the honours?'

For a second I'm frozen by confusion, shock. I watch my sister raise her hands.

'Wait!' I shout. 'No, wait! What are you going to do?'

I run towards Leo, focusing on those branches, flicking my fingers, clenching my fists. But nothing happens. His bonds don't slacken, don't loosen even a little.

When I halt, I'm close enough to see the tears in Leo's eyes. Bea hesitates, then steps forward. She lifts her hands above her head again and I hear an almighty ripping, as if the ancient oak were being torn asunder. Instead, hundreds of thorns are ripped from hundreds of roses. They rise into the air, gathering like a swarm of bees. I lift my hands and they start to fall. Bea brings her hands together and they rise again. We stand apart, fighting for control of the thorns. I think I see a flash of regret in her eyes, but it's obliterated by the intensity of her determination. Now we're soldiers on opposing sides. But she's stronger, more practised than I. And her focus is undivided.

The thorns turn, aiming at Leo: a hundred arrows pointing at his heart.

'No!' I run through the rose bushes, over the stones, the moss. I run as the thorns fly. I throw myself in front of him, a moment after every inch of Leo is pierced. Too late. He is impaled on the tree, crucified.

As I fall to the ground, praying he might survive the attack – he's hardly human after all, he's a soldier, a star – the man I love is blown apart, exploding as if a firework had detonated in the centre of his chest, scattering his dust to the four corners of the glade.

He is gone. Quicker than a heartbeat, quicker than a breath.

A great crack of lightning splits through the dark sky as I scream, striking the trunk of the oak tree, flaying its bark, leaving a glimmering white scar that twists from roots to crown.

Battle

I'm screaming as I hurtle towards my sister. I am all scream, propelled by the force of the sound. I collide with Bea so fast, so hard, that she falls, smacking the back of her skull against stone. I wince at the crack, even as I hope it kills her. I stumble, but Bea is already pulling herself up. I curl my fingers, tugging at the ivy so it twists its tendrils around her ankles and wrists, pulling her down again, fixing her to the ground.

I catch sight of a rock and reach for it, but Bea barely flinches.

'Who do you think I am, a piffling little soldier?' Contempt twists her face. 'Your snivelling boyfriend? Your ropes can't trap me.' She breaks free, snapping each thick bond with a single flick of her wrist. Awe and rage surge through me.

'Look out!'

The pain is a searing shock as I fall. In the distance, I hear my father's applause. I scrape the ground, my fingers encircling something: an antler? I wrap my fist around the spear of bone piercing my scalp. Blood drips into my eyes. My sight begins to blur, as if the fog were rolling in, the darkness returning. I press my hand to my temple, the pain ebbing, warmth spreading slowly through my skin. I feel the leaves falling and settling on my body. I think of Ma, how she used to pull a blanket over me when I napped.

The leaves. Ma. I sense something but can't quite see it.

Somewhere, I hear Bea shouting. One of my sisters is fighting for me, holding her back. I have a chance. I have a little time. I drift in and out of consciousness, of light and dark. The pain ebbs and flows but the warmth spreads. Gradually, just as I heal my plants, I am healing myself.

I hear my sisters' screams. The realization is immediate.

These leaves: the spirit of every sister, every mother that he and his soldiers have killed is in these leaves. They *are* the leaves. Their power is palpable: a bolt of lightning, a hundred thousand volts. If only I could harness it.

I pull myself up, slipping twice, legs shaking as I stand.

A stag's antler lies at my feet, the tip sticky with my blood. I blink to see Scarlet holding Bea back with scorching flames sparking from her fingertips. Liyana stands between us.

'Oh, that's hardly playing fair now, is it?' our father tuts. 'Ganging up on your sister like that.'

He doesn't do anything that I can see, but Scarlet is yanked back, thrown through the air, landing in a drift of white leaves at the base of a willow tree. A branch snaps out to whack Scarlet's knuckles. Bea smirks as Scarlet yelps and, in that split second of distraction, I draw a hefty rock from the soil and lift it above Bea's head. She sees the stone as it falls and shifts just in time, so it strikes only her shoulder, smacking her to the ground.

In a moment, I'm standing above her, the rock returned to my hands, holding it over her head. Bea looks up at me. I look down at her. I will smash this rock into her skull again and again and again.

No.

I'm pure scream, pure hate, pure dark. I—

No!

My veins are ink, my fingers spider's legs on the pale stone. Vines of ivy undulate beneath my feet. The leaves fall but do not touch me. The fog rolls in through the moonlit night, but I can see as clearly as if it's a summer's day.

I grip the rock.

No, don't lose your light, not for me.

Unbidden, the ivy twines around Bea's hands and feet, tethering her to the ground. A preparation for crucifixion. She tries to twist and thrash but she cannot move. She fixes me with a look of pure disgust.

I'm about to let the rock fall, when I see that beneath the disgust is despair. And then I feel it, coming off my sister in waves. She speaks, but I can't hear. I hear nothing except blood pounding in my ears, power coursing through my veins.

But Leo's voice rushes through me too. *Don't do it.*

I draw the stone back, ready to bring it down as hard as I can. I take a deep breath. In the distance, I hear my father's cry.

'Oh, yes! To the victor go the spoils!'

I stay myself.

'Come now,' he snaps. 'What are you waiting for?'

I look down at my false sister. She looks up at me. I hear the echo of her words: *Killing a soldier gives you a taste for the dark. But killing your sister . . . Now that'll send you right over the edge.* Neither of us shifts. Our father's impatience crackles through the glade. Rain starts to spill from the sky.

'What's it to be, Goldie?' he shouts. 'Light or dark? Death or life? Fragility or power? Your sister or me. It's time to make your choice.'

Showdown

I hesitate. I remember that spark of regret in Bea's eye, before the kill. I want her to suffer, I want her to die, I want to be the one who— But does she deserve it? It's my father who demands my rage. It's he who turned and tainted us all. I stay my hand.

'Come on! Chop, chop!' His voice is a whip that cracks across my knuckles. 'Make up your fucking mind!'

The rock is wrenched from my grip. It lifts into the air, hovers for a second, then falls. I see shock in Bea's eyes as it drops, fear too and relief. Then her face is gone.

I whip round to see my father, golden eyes flashing, grinning like a naughty schoolboy caught with his hand in the biscuit tin.

'Oops.'

'What did you do?' I scream. 'You wanted me to kill her – why did you do that?'

He shrugs, as if he'd done nothing more than swat a fly. 'She'd served her purpose. I had no more use for her.'

I step away from Bea's body. 'Her purpose?'

My father sighs. 'It's you I want, Goldie. It's you I've wanted all along. From the beginning, from the moment you were born – the darkness in you . . . By the devil but it's magnificent.' He plucks the petal of a rose, rubbing it between finger and thumb. 'Bea had darkness, certainly, but her motivation was off – she only wanted to please me.' He shrugs. 'Daddy issues. But you . . .'

My father looks at me as if I'm the only girl in the world – either on Earth or in Everwhere. Only Leo has ever looked at me this way. It's intoxicating. It's all I've ever wanted, to be loved like this.

My father steps towards me. I look up at him, lifting my palm to his face. He covers my hand with his own and he holds me. My small hand rests in his and I gaze into his golden eyes, so soft, so safe.

'Imagine what we could do, you and me.' His voice is a whisper, his smile kind, his eyes full of love. 'Imagine, an eternity together . . .'

I nod. My father leans down to kiss my cheek. I close my eyes.

No – this is not love.

I shake Leo off. I don't want to hear him now. My father wraps his arms around me. I sigh into his chest. My first love. Without him, I wouldn't even be . . .

'Daughters like you come along once in a century,' he whispers. 'I've been waiting all your life for you to join me. You have such power, such potential' – he holds me tighter – 'I got giddy thinking of all the destruction we could inflict together, the devastation, the despair . . .' He tips his head down to kiss my lips. 'So, would you like to do the honours, or shall I?'

I pull back to look up at him. 'Do what?'

A flash of annoyance creases his face. 'Why, kill your sisters, of course.'

The shock of his words pins me. I can't let go, can't step away. The air is dense, pressing down, trapping my breath, fogging my thoughts.

'I'm happy to do it.' He gives a slight shrug. 'But I thought you might like them to be your first—'

I shake my head.

'Come now, don't be so quick to dismiss me.' His smile spreads slowly, as if anticipating the massacre. 'You might even enjoy it. And, afterwards' – desire fills his golden eyes – 'we can . . . celebrate.'

'No,' I say, finding my voice. I pull away, step back. 'I won't.'

'Oh, Goldie.' His voice is soft with disappointment, sorrow. 'Don't you want an eternity together?'

Slowly, I shake my head.

'You're so strong.' He sighs. 'Why do you have to be so weak?'

I stare at him, meeting the disgust in his golden eyes.

Leaves settle on my shoulders as I step towards my sisters. Splinters of lightning cleave the air and pierce the soil, shattering stones, scorching blankets of moss, igniting ivy, sending fiery streaks across my path as I walk.

But, I think, what if my strength has nothing to do with the dark? I am hate and love, dark and light. I am powerful beyond measure. *I can command armies. I can topple nations.* Flames scorch my feet, but I feel no pain. Rain spills down in great sheets now, but I'm dry. My inky veins pulse with accelerating strength. I am fiercer than every crack of thunder in the sky.

I turn from my two sisters to fix my gaze on my father. I snap together my finger and thumb.

The sound of the willow tree, its roots rending from the

soil, its trunk crashing to the ground, is tremendous. I feel the shockwaves shudder through my body, through the earth, through my sisters. I feel their shock and his. But even caught by surprise, he's still too quick, sidestepping the falling tree before it's even halfway to the ground.

'Oh, Goldie.' He's standing in front of me. The fog rolls back. The rain lifts. The leaves suspend in the air.

'I thought you were special.' Wilhelm says, 'I thought you were . . . I allowed hope to cloud my . . .' He sighs. 'Intuition requires impartiality. Another lesson learned. And now . . .'

The fire ignites in his eyes. He lifts his right hand.

I freeze.

I see the giant bolt of lightning flare from his hand, bridging the gap between us, shooting straight for my heart. But it's stopped by a flare of electricity firing from the opposite direction. I turn to see Scarlet focusing all her strength to hold her father back.

It's not enough. I look up at the leaves falling again. Their power is intensifying, vibrating the air. If only I knew how to harness it.

'Oh, please, not that again.' Wilhelm flicks his wrist, sending Scarlet crashing against the fallen willow tree. 'I applaud your efforts, my dears. But I'm afraid' – he steps forward – 'if you're not going dark then you're going to die. Sister to sister.'

A fork of lightning strikes from the sky, cracking into the centre of Bea's dead body, and she is extinguished. Just as Leo was.

Ashes to ashes, dust to dust.

We watch as Bea's soul sinks into the ground, as her spirit lifts into the air, soaring high into the black and silver sky.

We aren't strong enough. I was wrong, Leo was wrong. I feel my strength start to ebb; I tug at its threads. Am I not the fighter I believed myself to be? I ball my fingers into fists and every stone in the clearing lifts into the air, suspended for a second before a hundred rocks fly at my father. But he's too fast, a streak through the air, catching each and every one, crumbling them all to dust. I stare at him, deflated, defeated. But he's looking at Liyana.

'Alright then, Ana. Show me what you can do. Make me proud.' He pushes out his chest. 'Go on, I'll give you the first shot for free.'

Even before his words are out, Liyana is reaching into the air, seeming to beseech the sky. Huge clouds gather above our heads, emptying cascades of rain so suddenly that tremendous pools of water flood the glade. Cupping her hands, Liyana scoops up the lakes, channelling them into a great wall of water. She pulls back her arms, fists clenched, then pushes forward as if to punch the wall – the water rushes, building into a tsunami that crashes over our father, dragging him under, holding him down, filling his lungs so he's choking. I watch him, pinned to the ground under a flood, drowning.

At last, Liyana drops her hands and the water subsides, sinking into the soil. Our father lies across moss and stone, open eyes staring up at nothing. We stare at his body, watching for movement, but there's none.

Then: a cough.

Wilhelm Grimm sneezes and stands, brushing raindrops from his cuffs as if he'd just stepped out of a light drizzle. I look on, hope extinguished. What's the point in fighting? He is invulnerable, invincible. I glance at my sisters and see that they are thinking the same. *I'm sorry, Teddy.* A heavy rain starts to fall. I drop to my knees, hands over my eyes, when I hear her.

Bea's voice tumbles through the rain.

Even the strongest sister cannot defeat him alone. You must do it together.

I steady myself, listening.

Channel the leaves, the spirits of all your sisters, your mothers, your aunts. Conduct the power of all the women he's ever killed. Together you have the strength—

'Stop!' My father's command ricochets through the glade, obliterating every other sound. He glares at me, golden eyes flashing and furious again.

I feel my sisters look to me, questioning. They heard her too. But we don't know how. For a moment, I'm paralysed. Then I think: *together*. Each of our powers brought together as one. I recall the first time I saw Leo, the first time I spoke to him in my mind. Now I do the same with my sisters.

Watch me, you'll know what to do.

I take one quick, deep breath to ready myself. I draw on my dreams. I focus every synapse, every cell. I feel strength, power coursing through my body once more. I look up to the falling leaves. I twitch my fingers, I tug at them. I whisper, I call. An invitation, a request, a direction. *Follow me.*

Rise.

Stronger, louder.

Rise, my sisters. Rise!

One by one, the falling leaves of Everwhere still, suspended in the air. Then they begin pulling together until they are circling, in flurries and funnels, siphoned by the quickening rain, every falling drop drawing together tornadoes of leaves, until an aerial tower forms, a whirlpool of bright white.

My father, shocked into stillness, stares up. Within the roar of water I hear a single scream, the pitched scream of a woman in the throes of birth and death, a piercing, primitive, primal scream. Then it's a battle cry, a clarion call. A hundred thousand cracks of thunder, a hundred thousand sisters howling for destruction, annihilation, obliteration . . .

The roar penetrates everything, everyone. It fills me so that I shake with the sound of my sisters and their mothers, my chest a cathedral of screams. And I see that my father is shaking too, shuddering from deep within, as if he's being torn apart, unstitched at the seams.

I turn to Liyana. She is drenched, rivers running from her fingers as she conducts the rain. I see that she is screaming too, though I cannot hear her.

Now.

Liyana springs forward, fuelled by the roar, funnelling the great torrent of water and leaves towards our father. The force is like a sword plunged into a stone. Liyana drags the liquid blade down, splitting the seams, wrenching him open. I join the roar, the battle cry of our sisters, our mothers, all the women he's killed, all the Sisters Grimm. I'm certain I hear Ma's cry among them, and Bea's too.

For a second everything is still, suspended, petrified. Liyana lifts her hands and the whirlpool of rain, the tornado of leaves is twisting through the air, borne on the screams, funnelling down, driving a river of white blood into our father and cleaving him apart.

I turn to Scarlet.

Now!

Scarlet presses her hands together. Sparks ignite. Electricity catches. Flashes of lightning shoot from her fingertips, curling in huge arcs through the air. She sets him alight.

And we all watch him burn.

LEGACY

Inheritance

We each feel the darkness at our fingertips. We feel the twitch. The flares. We've shared it, as all sisters should, so none of us has too much. But then none of us has a little, either. It's there. We don't use it. Well, only on occasion, when necessary. Or when we can't control it. But we are moderate. And nothing terrible happens. At least, it hasn't yet.

Commemoration

After Leo died, I went to Everwhere every night for a year, though I never told my sisters. They were too afraid to go back, thinking they might meet our father's spirit. I was afraid of that too, but I didn't care. I'd brave anything, any depths of darkness, to feel close to Leo again.

I visit still.

Sometimes I'll see a stray soldier skulking in the woods and think for a moment that it's him. Then I'll remember, and my spirits will fall before they've barely had a chance to lift. The remaining soldiers have disbanded, I believe, since I hardly see them anymore.

I go to the glade where he died, where the air is infused with his spirit and the soil with his soul, and sit on the trunk of the fallen oak tree. I hoist myself up by one of the long, thick tendrils of ivy that's encroaching on every inert thing, every tree and shrub and stone. I sit; I close my eyes.

I think about spirits. I remember what Leo said about Aether and I wonder on the possibility of resurrection. I feel his breath on the wind, his touch in the falling leaves, his voice in the rush of the river. I imagine he sits beside me. I talk to him, I ask him to tell me secrets. And sometimes, when the rain falls hard, when the clouds part and the sliver of moon illuminates the silver birch trees, he will.

Communication

Where Bea's soul has seeped into the soil, a single rose grows: blood red, velvet soft. A splash of colour on a white canvas. Her spirit, though, is in the air. She falls with the cascading leaves, floats on the mists and drifts in with the rolling fog. She glides with the winds, flying through the forests, brushing the tips of birds' wings. She soars above it all, among the stars, pure moonlight and air.

Bea watches her sisters. Sometimes she sends them messages: a blackbird feather dropped in Ana's path, an image in Goldie's dreams, a shadow at the edge of Scarlet's eye-line. Now that Bea has access to humanity in its every shade and hue, she marvels at the extraordinary capacity humans have for good and evil, for love and hate, the contradictory nature within them all. It's a source of astonishment, even now.

She still misses Vali, still regrets that night, still thinks of him every day. She wonders where his spirit is and wishes he were here with her. Occasionally, Bea feels a twinge of jealousy that her sisters are together. Not that they are alive but that they have one another. Then Bea shifts from being the air beneath the birds' wings, transforming into a raven to soar above Everwhere, black feathers glistening in the moonlight, swooping under the stars.

Solitary, strong, free.

Future

We visit Everwhere together. We find our remaining sisters under the first-quarter moon. We show them who they are and what they can do. We teach our young apprentices how powerful they can be. We show them that here they are bound by nothing, not even the laws of gravity, only the limits of their own imagination. We watch them ignite sticks and create waves and make tendrils of ivy dance.

We remind them, over and again, of their limitless potential, so they won't forget. For, even though they'll no longer have to fight the devil when they turn eighteen, the potential danger of the stray soldiers remains, and there'll be many battles in their lives that'll require great strength.

We warn them of what's to come in their teenage years, that they will be tethered to Earth, their ankles tied by ropes of doubt and fear. We tell them to write letters, take photographs (stored in fireproof boxes) and, the night before their thirteenth birthdays, we offer to tattoo their wrists. Most get a symbol of their particular power: a flame, a drop of water, a feather, a leaf. Underneath we inscribe these words:

Validior es quam videris, fortior quam sentis,
sapientior quam credis.

You are stronger than you seem, braver than you feel,
wiser than you believe.

We tell them to seek the other Grimms, their sisters scattered throughout the world. There'll be no more born now, so we must find the family we have left. And they do. They spread the word. They talk of hidden magic, of whispers that speak of unknown things, of signs that point in unseen directions to unimagined possibilities.

I hope they'll find you soon, so you won't have to live any longer without realizing who you truly are.

The End

Goldilocks

Once Upon a Time there was a little girl as good as she was pretty. She had big blue eyes, long golden hair and a smile so lovely that it brought joy to everyone she met. The girl reared baby birds fallen from their nests, rescued worms that'd veered onto paths, enticed wilting flowers back into bloom. She gave food to the hungry, shelter to the homeless and her most treasured possessions to the poor.

The girl was so good that she soon became famed throughout the lands. Parents, hoping to redeem their children, told bedtime stories of her deeds, and those lucky enough to meet her swore that she was so saintly her hair glowed golden as a halo.

The girl's father was so proud of his daughter that he gave her the name Goldilocks. Every night he sat Goldilocks on his knee and asked her to tell him of all the good deeds she'd done that day.

'Today I sold my silver necklace,' she said. 'And bought a cow for a farmer who'd just lost his to a sickness.'

'Very good,' her father would say. 'You're a blessing and example to us all.'

Every day Goldilocks alleviated suffering and brought joy. And every night, she fell asleep imagining all the things she might do tomorrow to make the world a little happier than it had been today. And when she saw the smiles on people's faces, and the approval in her father's eyes, she was content.

Yet, as she grew, Goldilocks noticed that she no longer always felt the desire to be good, nor always felt joy when she was. She found that people often asked for more than she wanted to give and, sometimes, she gave away not only her precious possessions but herself as well. Gradually, Goldilocks fell into a deep sadness. Still, she did her best to keep smiling and being kind, since she didn't know what else to do, or how else to be. Then, one day, her baby brother was born.

At first, Goldilocks loved and doted upon him as tenderly as she did every other living thing. But, despite her best efforts, she watched him grow into a boy as wickedly wild as he was handsome. Urso, named for the fact that he liked to roam the village roaring like a bear and scaring dairy maids into spilling their pails of milk, spent his days behaving brutishly.

Shocked as she was by her brother's behaviour, what shocked Goldilocks most of all was that Urso didn't mind when their father shouted or the villagers hurled stones and curses at him. He simply continued on in his wild ways regardless, laughing into the long shadows of their scorn.

Seeing how much fun her brother was having, free from coveting the good opinion of others, Goldilocks started secretly following his example. She stopped simply being good and started being a little bit bad. Sometimes she stole and sometimes she lied and sometimes she wasn't very nice at all. On moonless nights Goldilocks wore Urso's bearskin and they enacted shamanic rituals, evoking their ancestral spirits who emboldened her further still. Goldilocks chopped off her halo of golden curls and stopped rouging her lips and cast off her frilly dresses, so people no longer thought her pretty. She laughed too loudly and spoke too soon and no longer did what she didn't want to do.

'You won't be famed for your goodness anymore,' her father warned. 'People won't love you as they once did.'

Goldilocks discovered that this was true. Villagers who'd previously deified her now shunned her, whispering harsh words behind her back. Saddened by this,

Goldilocks tried to return to her old ways, to always smile and be kind. But she found that she could not. Now that she was free she could not willingly step back into a cage.

So, instead of spending her days seeking loving smiles and approving looks, she sought other satisfactions. She dressed exotically and sang badly and danced wildly. She pleased herself in every way and, for the first time in her life, knew pure happiness and true joy.

One day, discovering she had a talent for growing things, Goldilocks began creating gardens so beautiful that visitors came from all around to see how she charmed reluctant shoots from the soil and coaxed the brightest flowers into bloom. Soon Goldilocks was travelling far and wide to every kingdom, sculpting public gardens into spectacles of unparalleled wonderment. Until, one day, Goldilocks was famed throughout the lands not for goodness but greatness.

And she learned that, while she still laughed too loudly and spoke too soon and did exactly as she wished, some people, most of all Urso, loved her no matter what. As for the rest, Goldie found that she no longer cared.

Acknowledgements

With great thanks to . . .

My peerless agent Ed Wilson, for your insights and your growls. Your superlative feedback transformed this story into something spectacular. Simon Taylor, for the gentle but precise touch of your editing pen, for (almost) loving Jack's Gelato as much as I do, and for seeing the Sisters so clearly. Ten seconds into talking, I knew you were The One. This book is better than I ever imagined possible because of the two of you.

To all at Transworld who took the book into their hearts, I'm beyond delighted that *The Sisters Grimm* found its home with you. Especially Dredheza Maloku, for all the excellent emails and tolerating mine. Beci Kelly, for creating a cover I adore! Tom Hill, for most magnificent publicity skills. Sophie Bruce, for most marvellous marketing talents. Elizabeth Dobson, for her sharp eye and even sharper mind. Vivien Thompson, for her infinite patience and catching everything else we missed!

To Ova and Umut for creating PaperCharm and all the social media buzz – every author deserves you brilliant angels!

Bridget Collins, for being the first to say yes and so beautifully – she says she wasn't being kind, but she was.

Alastair Meikle for putting my words into pictures more magnificent than I could ever have dreamed. You truly are a genius and I thank all the muses that we met again.

Naz, for making a dream come true in creating my very first book-map, and such a splendid one.

Ash, keeper of the flame and writer of the most magical

letters. Anita, for celebrating the ups and making me laugh during the downs. Al, always my first editor, for telling me that I needed to rewrite the final act when I didn't want to. Laurence, for his brilliant feedback, especially on the script. Natasha, for being my first educator in fantasy fiction – for the fairies and the fantastical worlds. Sarah, for all the glorious books and brilliant book-chat – Heffers is my favourite bookshop because of you and Richard. Virginie, for knowing how much it matters. Steve, for offering to teach me all those years ago in the coffee shop and for all the cake since. Alice, for being excited whenever I talked about this book and for being the best gift giver. Ova, for believing before she'd read a single sentence. Bea, for so deftly correcting my Spanish.

Idilia, for being my soul-sister and always echoing my enthusiasm. Jack, for his gelato, his generosity and our movie nights. Dad, for telling us bedtime stories and giving me my earliest education in storytelling. Oscar, for inspiring me with his own beautiful writing and his enormous heart. Raffy, the reason I was writing fairy tales at four a.m., without whom this book would never have come into being. Fatima and Manuel, for being the loudest and most loving cheerleaders. Artur de sá Barreto, the most generous man I've ever met, who led me through the darkness and into the light. Vicky van Praag, for absolutely everything – despite being a writer, I have no words.

And for all the friends and readers who brighten the bookish and non-bookish parts of my life, I can't fit you all on these pages but you're in my heart.

About the Author

Menna van Praag studied English at Oxford, but other than that has lived in Cambridge all her life. Working as a reader for the BBC and as a script editor helped inspire her to tell her own stories and so she began to write novels. Menna adores her husband and two small children and asks them to forgive her for spending so much time immersed in fantasy worlds.